Also in the Never Mind the Botox series:

Alex Fisher is a high-flying lawyer close to making partner and busy planning her perfect wedding to Elliott. But life suddenly becomes complicated when she's faced with a hot junior lawyer on her team and an actress threatening to jeopardise the deal by exposing her dodgy cosmetic surgery. Soon Alex is forced into a series of impossible choices that are all inextricably linked and life will never be the same again.

Stella Webb is a successful but bored cosmetic surgeon whose career is going in a very different direction to that of the A&E doctor she's dating. With credit card bills larger than the latest implants, this deal should be the answer to her prayers, but it seems that not everyone has been playing by the rules. Desperate to leave her working-class roots behind, will she be forced to choose between money and love?

Meredith Romaine is an ice cool senior banker whose competitive world revolves around men and money. This deal will cement her reputation as the office rainmaker and put her in line for a huge bonus. But only if no one finds out about her relationship with a doctor at the American buyers and the completely unethical way she set the deal up. Can she pull it off without her past coming back to haunt her?

The series can be read in any order.

MIXING BUSINESS WITH PLEASURE

Never Mind The Botox

Rachel

PENNY AVIS AND JOANNA BERRY

Matador
9 Priory Business Park
Kibworth Beauchamp
Leicester LE8 0RX, UK
Tel: (+44) 116 279 2299
Fax: (+44) 116 279 2277
Email: books@troubador.co.uk
Web: www.troubador.co.uk/matador

ISBN 978 1848766 624

British Library Cataloguing in Publication Data.
A catalogue record for this book is available from the British Library.

All characters in this publication are fictitious and any resemblance to real persons,
living or dead, is purely coincidental

Typeset in 11pt Aldine 401 by Troubador Publishing Ltd, Leicester, UK
Printed and bound in the UK by TJ International Ltd, Padstow, Cornwall

Matador is an imprint of Troubador Publishing Ltd

For our children, who delight and amaze us every day.

CHAPTER 1

Rachel woke up with her hair sticking to the side of her face. Her head was pounding and her back was aching from dancing in high heels. She felt beneath the duvet – knickers and a t-shirt. That was better than last week, when she'd woken up still fully dressed. She lifted her head and peered at the clock on her bedside table. Nine fifty-five. Christ!

'Harry, wake up! It's nearly ten o'clock.' She poked the shape under the duvet next to her. Nothing moved. 'Harry, come on. Get up!'

Rachel jumped out of bed and then quickly lay back down again as the room started spinning rather too fast. She should have been at work well before nine but Harry's usual 'just one more for the road' trick was having its full effect. There was no way she could go in yet.

Rachel worked in corporate finance at a well established firm of city accountants and they would expect to know where she was. She leant over and picked up the phone.

'Good morning, Payne Stanley,' said a clipped voice.

'Er yes, Pauline Rowe please.' Rachel's voice sounded like a darts commentator. She grabbed the glass of water on her bedside table and took a large gulp.

'Hello, Pauline Rowe speaking.'

Pauline was the staff manager at Payne Stanley. She had a rather full opinion of herself and a figure to match. Things had been a bit frosty with Pauline since Rachel had indulged in a few too many drinks at the Christmas party and told her that she was an interfering busybody with all the interpersonal skills of a wardrobe.

'Hi, Pauline, it's Rachel Altman. You won't believe what's happened. I'm stuck in the communal hall of my flat. When I left this morning, I shut the front door and then realised I'd forgotten my keys. When I went to open the main front door that I share with the upstairs flat, I found it was double-locked. I can't get out of the front door without my keys and I can't get back inside my flat either. So here I am, stuck. What a nightmare! I've rung the landlord, who's on his way over, but he was in North London and is not going to be here for another half an hour or so. So I guess I'm not going to be in until nearly lunchtime.'

'I see,' said Pauline.

From the tone of her voice, Rachel wasn't sure that she did.

'I shall let the partners know. Can you come and see me when you're in?' said Pauline.

Just at that moment Harry's alarm clock went off, beeping loudly.

'What's that noise?' said Pauline.

'Oh, it's my stopwatch,' said Rachel, frantically climbing on top of Harry to hit the snooze button. 'I've got my gym stuff with me as, er, I'm training for a ten-k run in a few weeks.'

Harry let out a few grunting objection noises that Rachel tried to stifle with a pillow.

'Anyway, thanks, Pauline. So sorry for the fuss; one of those really annoying things. I'll let you know once I'm in. Bye now.'

Harry rolled over and opened one eye. 'What was that all about?' he said.

'Work,' said Rachel. 'I gave them one of those fantastic excuses that's so farfetched they just have to believe it, as no one would make something like that up.'

Rachel rolled on top of Harry and kissed his forehead. 'Face it, I'm a genius,' she said.

'Really? Well, you're very good at hiding it,' said Harry, wrapping his arms around her waist.

'I'm starving,' said Rachel, rolling off Harry and gently pushing his arms away, 'and in need of a serious injection of carbs.'

She grabbed the phone again and scrolled through the stored names until she found 'Pizza', which was shortly followed by 'Prostitute' – one of Harry's 'funny' jokes.

'Hi, Marco. Yes, hi, it's Rachel. The usual please. Oh, hold on. Harry, do you want extra pepperoni?'

Harry nodded.

'The usual with extra pepperoni and a large diet

coke, oh and some headache tablets. Cool, thanks, Marco. You're a star. See you in fifteen minutes.'

Rachel got out of bed more slowly this time and headed for the shower. The clean white gleam of the bathroom made her feel slightly sick. Despite the frequent chaos in her life, Rachel hated mess. Her flat was modern and very tidy. She'd once been told that you can tell the state of someone's mind by looking at their underwear drawer. Rachel's was very organised, all sorted by colour and style. She often wondered what the drawer of someone with a terrible state of mind would look like. How bad could it get? Some unholy jumble of bras, tiny briefs and grey pants, probably.

Feeling marginally restored by several cups of tea, slices of pizza and painkillers, Rachel eventually made it into the office at two o'clock. It was Friday and she'd decided to head home for the weekend. She'd used her gym bag instead of her usual pull-along overnighter case so she could keep up the whole ten-k story thing with Pauline. Typical of Harry not to have told her that he didn't need to be up early and that he'd set his alarm for ten a.m. – never mind when she had to be up.

Harry made no secret of the fact that he was totally disinterested in Rachel's job. He was a freelance writer, mainly writing sports stories for newspapers, so worked pretty much when he felt like it. As far as Harry could see, Rachel's office job just seemed to get in the way of their social lives. He seemed to conveniently forget the steady income it brought in each month.

Rachel wandered through the open plan office with

her gym bag strategically placed on her shoulder and went over to Pauline Rowe's desk. Pauline had a pale blue cardigan on the back of her chair and pictures of cats on her desk partition. She was gossiping with the secretary at the next desk.

'Hi Pauline, made it in now. So sorry, was totally my fault for forgetting my keys. Any plans for me for next week yet?'

Pauline looked at her watch and then up at Rachel.

'Yes, Carl Stephens wants to see you. He's got a new piece of work and I've told him that you're free to help. He's in this afternoon if you could go and see him. Ideally before you go to the gym,' she added, looking at Rachel's gym bag.

'Don't worry, I'm going after work,' said Rachel.

'On a Friday?'

Good point, thought Rachel.

'Well, I'm taking this ten-k quite seriously, so I need to get some decent training in.'

Mark Tan, an associate sitting a few desks away, overheard their conversation.

'Hey, Rachel, which ten-k are you doing? I'm training with a few of the other lads in the office for one next month. Maybe you could train with us? We run before work a couple of times a week and then once after, usually on a Wednesday. What do you think?'

'That sounds like a great plan to me,' said Pauline slightly too quickly.

This is getting ridiculous, thought Rachel. Damn Harry and his alarm clock.

'Thanks for the offer, Mark, but I've got my own

routine pretty sorted out now and I don't really want to start messing about with it. Anyway, better go: Carl Stephens wants to see me. See you later, Pauline.'

Pauline didn't look up, so Rachel went to find Carl.

Carl Stephens was a senior partner. Rachel had worked for him a couple of times before and they'd got on pretty well. She knocked on his door.

'Come in. Oh hi, Rachel, sit down. Just finishing an email.'

Rachel looked around his office as he typed: pictures of the kids, a few books, a sporting trophy of some sort – the usual. Quite tidy too, she thought and then quickly had to get rid of the mental image of his underwear drawer. She looked at his side profile as he typed. He wasn't bad looking, had probably been quite a catch when he was a bit younger. Stop! she thought.

Carl finished his email and spun round in his chair to face her.

'Pauline probably told you that I want you to work with me on a new project,' he said. 'You have some time, right?'

'Yes, I finished the report on the pet food business last week and I don't think we'll need to do any more on it for a while. The buyers are away for the next month or so. So I'm pretty free.'

'Great. A good friend of mine from the Beau Street Group rang a couple of days ago. Have you heard of them?'

Rachel shook her head.

'They're a cosmetic surgery group, leaders in their

field apparently. Anyway, they've been approached by some American buyers and they're thinking of selling up. They want us to do a report for the Americans setting out how they make their money, which procedures are most profitable, which doctors are most successful, what sort of clients they have and so on.'

'Sounds really interesting,' said Rachel and meant it.

It was a big improvement on her last few projects. The pet food job had seen her rushing round the country reviewing the performance of grubby factories cooking chunks of meat of indeterminate origin. Before that she'd worked on the sale of an engineering company that made parts for buses. Hardly glamorous. This was much more like it.

'I've agreed with the finance director that we'll get a small team out there from Monday,' Carl continued. 'AJ and Rosa are both free too, I think, so they can go with you. I'll forward you an email that sets out exactly what the report needs to cover.'

'Okay, no problem. I'll get organised this afternoon,' said Rachel.

'This will be an important job for you, Rachel. We're really looking for you to show us that you can handle these key client relationships. You are the face of the firm and that face needs to be a professional one at all times. Do you understand what I'm saying?'

Rachel nodded.

'On time and on the case, that's what I want to see. Plus a great report. Okay?'

'Okay,' said Rachel.

'Okay, good. And I don't want any more emails

from Pauline saying that you've rung in with some ridiculous hangover story.'

Rachel's face fell. Damn that woman!

'So let's make this our last chat about it,' Carl continued. 'The director promotions are in a couple of months, so you'd better make this job count.'

Rachel went back to her desk, dropped her bag and notebook and picked up the phone.

'Shali? Hi, it's Rach. Fancy a coffee?'

Shali Kapoor was one of Rachel's close workmates. They'd trained together at Payne Stanley and had been friends pretty much from day one.

'God, absolutely. If I have to look at this screen for another minute I'm likely to jump out the window,' Shali replied.

'See you across the road in five minutes. Natalie's in too, so I'll see if she wants to join us.'

A few minutes later Rachel was sitting in a steamy coffee shop nursing a large latte. The previous night's partying was starting to catch up with her. She watched Natalie and Shali dart across the road and come banging in through the door.

'What a day!' said Shali, dropping her bag on the floor and slumping into a chair.

'One latte, extra shot, no foam and a decaf cappuccino,' shouted Natalie at the girl behind the counter.

'Who's having decaf?' said Rachel.

'I am,' said Natalie. 'Latest health drive.'

'Well, my health needs a chocolate croissant; get me one while you're up, will you?' said Rachel.

Natalie Smith had joined Payne Stanley a couple of years ago. She was outspoken and funny and Rachel really liked her. She was also dead bright and had often pulled Rachel out of a hole when she'd got behind on her work.

'Big night?' asked Shali.

'It wasn't meant to be,' said Rachel. 'We were just having a few quiet drinks at the pub but they had a band on. They were really good and of course we ended up dancing like idiots until closing time. Then Harry got all carried away and persuaded me to head to Luci's wine bar for a couple more, then we ended up going for a kebab, and before you know it, it's gone two a.m. So I had rather a slow start this morning.'

'Did you get spotted?' Natalie asked.

'Oh, I rang dozy Pauline and gave her some story about being stuck in the communal hall of my flat. I thought she'd totally fallen for it, but instead she emailed all the partners and told them I had a hangover, the miserable old cow,' said Rachel, staring into her coffee.

'Well, I'm having a crap day too,' said Shali. 'I'm working for old Martin Wainwright — what a 'mare,' Shali continued. 'I'm getting the full treatment. Orders barked at me, emails every five minutes but no real help, and I can't face asking him any questions. That breath would kill a buffalo at fifty paces. And he insists on wearing those awful short-sleeved shirts. Hasn't anyone told him he's not an airline pilot? Honestly, he'll be wearing brown shoes next.'

Looking the part, as well as being good at your job,

was a big thing for Shali. She was, as usual, immaculately dressed in a sharp trouser suit and crisp white shirt.

'Anyway, I have exciting news,' said Rachel.

'Ooh, what?' said Natalie and Shali in tandem.

'Carl Stephens has asked me to work on a new project with him, looking at a cosmetic surgery business, no less. Can you believe it − at last I get on a project where the business is really interesting,' said Rachel.

'I quite fancy Carl Stephens,' said Shali.

'You fancy everyone,' said Rachel. 'And besides, he's married.'

'Only window shopping. No harm in that,' said Shali.

'What's the business called?' said Natalie.

'Beau Street Group. Apparently they do every sort of procedure you can think of.'

'Maybe they have celebrity clients,' said Shali.

'God, I hadn't thought of that,' said Rachel. 'How exciting!'

'You'll have to let me know how much they're charging for boob jobs,' said Natalie.

Rachel and Shali both looked at her.

She added quickly, 'This good friend of mine is thinking of having one. She's a TV make-up artist and they're all into that sort of thing.'

'I wonder if they do all those weird things like you see on TV − you know, toe reshaping, injections to stop your armpits sweating, all that sort of thing,' Shali added.

'Maybe they'll even do, well, you know…' Natalie nodding knowingly.

'What?' said Rachel.

'Well, how shall I say it — tightening operations.'

Rachel nearly choked on her latte. 'God Natalie, where did that come from?'

'I saw it on one of those dreadful car crash TV shows that you can't help watching. This woman in her forties wanted the fanny of a teenager, so the surgeon gave her one — sorry, I mean, you know, created her one.'

At this point Rachel and Shali were laughing so much that the girl behind the counter waved at them to keep it down.

'Lucky you, Rach,' said Shali, catching her breath. 'What a great job to be working on. I'm so jealous. You'll have to report back regularly, you know, give us the whole scoop.'

'Well, I'm not sure I can — you know, business ethics, need-to-know basis and all that. After all, I am the ultimate professional.' Rachel flicked her hair as she spoke.

'Since when? And besides, we definitely need to know,' said Shali.

'Look seriously, though, it's highly confidential that the business might even be up for sale, so you guys mustn't talk to anyone else about it, okay? But if I see any celebrities, you'll be the first to know,' said Rachel, tapping her nose.

'No accepting any inappropriate gifts while you're on this job either,' said Shali, laughing. 'We'll have to report you if you start turning up with a smooth forehead.'

By now it was nearly half past three and Rachel hadn't done a stroke of work all day.

'Better get back,' she said. She picked up her gym bag. Natalie and Shali stared at it. 'Don't ask,' she said. 'It's actually got my weekend stuff in. I'm off home after work as my brother's back.'

'How is your handsome brother these days?' said Shali. 'I definitely fancy him.'

Rachel's brother Rowan was a couple of years older than her and he'd always been popular with her friends. He'd be thirty this year.

'Married with a baby. God, do you have an off switch?' said Rachel.

'Not so I've noticed. Anyway, let's go,' said Shali. 'You've got an important project to plan for.'

Yes, thought Rachel, and I need to make it count.

CHAPTER 2

Having briefed her team for Monday and sent a few carefully placed emails, Rachel sneaked out of the office. She was paranoid that she would bump into Pauline any minute and be forced to pretend she was off to the gym. Fortunately she didn't and she was soon getting out of a cab at the station.

'Return to Bath, please.'

The ticket man didn't even look up. 'What day ya coming back?' he said.

'Sunday, early evening.'

'Makes no odds to me what time you travel on a Sunday,' the ticket man said, seemingly annoyed that Rachel had bothered him with such irrelevant information.

Rachel glared at him but he didn't notice. He printed her tickets and passed them under the window.

'Which platform for Bath?' Rachel asked in her politest voice.

''S'on the board,' said the ticket man, nodding his head towards the large screen in the middle of the station.

'Gosh, thanks for your help,' said Rachel.

'No problem,' said the ticket man, oblivious to her sarcasm.

It was going to be a long trip.

On the train, Rachel got herself a large gin and tonic from the buffet car and settled down to read a stack of trashy magazines she'd bought at the station newsagent. As she read, she was struck by the number of articles about cosmetic surgery. Stories about actresses having liposuction were clearly big news. Intrigued, she got out her phone and opened the email from Carl Stephens setting out what work they needed to do on the Beau Street Group.

She started reading the list:

Full details of sales split by procedure.

Price lists by procedure.

A list of key clients.

Oh good, she would have to get details of every type of operation they did and how much each cost. Also, she would have the perfect reason for having a good nose through the client names to see whether she could spot anyone famous. She was really looking forward to this job.

Rowan met her at Bath station.

'Hey, sis', how are you?' Her brother gave her a big hug.

'Great form, thanks,' said Rachel. 'Actually, I'm hungover and knackered, but other than that great.'

'Well, I'm totally knackered, but sadly not hungover,' said Rowan. 'I tell you, this baby thing is hard work. There should be a warning on the side of the box saying "Caution: This product could seriously damage your health".'

Rachel laughed. 'You don't mean that. Naomi is so cute. How old is she now?'

'Nearly seven months – can you believe it?' said Rowan.

They got into Rowan's car and headed out of the station. Rachel's parents' house was a rambling farmhouse in a small village twenty minutes outside of Bath. They'd lived there all Rachel's life and although they'd often talked of buying somewhere smaller, Rachel couldn't imagine them moving.

As usual, Rachel's mum greeted her at the front door like she'd just been released from a ten-year prison sentence – hugging her until she couldn't breathe and then ushering her into the sitting room for a dry sherry.

'Do you have any gin?' Rachel asked.

'Bit early for gin, don't you think?' Rachel's dad replied, despite the fact that it was gone seven p.m.

Rachel's dad was a retired engineer and a pretty straight-laced character who hadn't met Rachel's mum until they were both well into their thirties. Her childhood had been full of ordinary holidays and getting your homework done on time. He also liked the sound of his own voice and regularly told the same very dull stories over and over again. Her mum would try to say, 'I think they've heard this one, dear,' but he would plough on regardless, often snorting with laughter over Fred's golfing disaster or some chaotic Rotary Club meeting. It wouldn't even occur to him that the others listening hadn't found the story funny the first time they'd heard it, let alone the third, fourth or fifth time. He was also obsessed with journeys.

'Was your train on time?' he asked as he poured Rachel a sherry.

'Yes, it was actually. I was quite surprised,' said Rachel.

'You were lucky,' he said. 'That line is very hit-and-miss. I went up to London last week and it was twelve minutes late getting in and nine minutes late getting back. No explanation, nothing. Don't know why they bother with timetables. Those buffet cars are expensive as well. It was a good thing your mother had packed me a couple of sandwiches. I only had to buy a cup of tea and that was bad enough. Daylight robbery, I say.'

Rachel and Rowan caught each other's eye and tried not to laugh.

'Did you write to *The Times* about it?' Rachel forced a straight face as she spoke.

'No, I didn't. Not really one for *The Times*. Think I might write to the train company, though. Mind you, you'll probably find you can only telephone some dreadful call centre, and then they'll charge you a fortune for a phone call that they take ten minutes to answer.'

Rachel decided to change the subject. 'How has your week been, Mum? Any gossip from the shop?'

The local charity shop was her mum's lifeline. She had stayed at home the whole time Rachel and Rowan had been children, dedicating herself to looking after the family. She was naturally a shy person and working mornings in the shop was the one thing that managed to bring her out of herself.

'Well, we've had such a busy week,' Rachel's mum said. 'We were given several large bags of clothes last weekend, really good quality things. We think someone must have died — sad really. Anyway, it took us ages to sort and price them. Then on Wednesday this young girl came in looking for things for a seventies fancy dress party and she was raving about the new clothes. She phoned some of her friends who were going to the same party and before we knew it the shop was packed. We sold more clothes that afternoon than we'd normally sell in two weeks! Plus we got a donation of plants left over from the local school fête and they did really well too. Grace and I were rushed off our feet. Still, all in a good cause.'

Rachel found it hard to believe that her mum knew what being rushed off your feet meant and began to wonder why she'd come home. Why was it that the thought of being home was always much nicer than the reality? It had been the same pattern since university days. She put up with truckloads of banal conversation in return for getting her washing done and a Sunday roast.

Rachel looked around. 'What time are Laura and Naomi arriving?'

'Oh, they're not coming,' said Rowan. 'Naomi is waking up a bit early at the moment, which Laura is trying desperately to sort out. She thought moving her about might set her back a bit. They'll come next time.'

Rachel knew how disappointed her mum would have been when she found out.

Rowan seemed to read her mind. 'It's no reflection

on you, Mum, honestly,' said Rowan. 'It's just the way the timings worked out. Laura normally would have loved to come.'

Rachel's eyes gleamed. Her brother on his own for the weekend. It had been ages!

'Shall we pop to the pub after supper?' Rachel suggested.

'Good idea,' said Rowan, trying to hide the relief in his voice.

After they'd eaten, Rachel and Rowan headed off to the local pub.

'God, what are they like!' said Rachel.

'They mean well,' said Rowan. 'We'll probably be just like them one day.'

'What an awful thought! Do you think we'll see anyone from school at the pub?' Rachel asked, keen to get away from the idea of turning into her mother.

'Probably,' said Rowan. 'Loads of them still live and work round here.'

The local was a traditional style pub with low-beamed ceilings that worked hard to make itself look more olde worlde than it really was – brass plates by the fire, the odd scythe stuck on the wall and a series of big fireplaces. Rachel bought them a bottle of wine and brought it over to the quiet corner of the pub that Rowan had chosen.

'Not the greatest but at least it's cold,' said Rachel. She poured them both a large glass. 'Cheers. How is Laura? Shame she's not here.'

'She's fine,' said Rowan, but Rachel could tell from his voice that she wasn't. 'Actually, we're having a bit of a tough time. The last few months since Naomi was born have been pretty stressful — not like I'd imagined it at all. Laura's been so uptight and I can't seem to get anything right. If Naomi is crying, anything I suggest is bound to be wrong. I know Laura's tired but she won't let me give her a break. She's convinced herself that she's the only one who can look after Naomi properly. This whole waking up early thing is just another example; she's completely neurotic about it.'

'You're a great dad and I'm sure it will blow over,' said Rachel, aware that her ability to give advice in this area was not the best.

Rowan didn't seem to hear her and carried on. 'The other morning, I had to get an early flight to Stockholm and I got up at five a.m. to have a shower. The noise woke Naomi up and Laura went mad, shouting about how selfish I was and that now she would have the whole day with a grumpy baby whose routine was all mixed up. I pointed out to her that the toughest thing she had to do all day was have coffee in Starbucks with all the other mums, whereas I had six hours of meetings with three hours of travelling either side.'

'Helpful,' said Rachel.

'Yeah, not really,' said Rowan. 'It just cost me a large bottle of perfume and two nights in the spare room.'

'Have another glass of wine,' said Rachel, lost for anything else more useful to say.

They sat in silence for a few moments. Then across the bar Rachel spotted someone familiar.

'God, Rowan, look — it's Dawn Hunt. I haven't seen her for ages. Let's go and say hello.'

Dawn and Rachel had been in the same class at school. Before Rowan could answer, Rachel was up and heading across the pub. Dawn was with a group of friends, most of whom Rachel either knew or vaguely recognised.

'Hey, stranger, long time no see! You look well,' said Dawn, getting up and hugging Rachel. She saw Rowan hovering behind. 'And your lovely brother too. We're lucky! Come on, sit down.'

They both sat down and Rowan was quickly engrossed in watching the football on the TV with a couple of the other guys at the table.

'So, how are you, city person? Still loving the big job?' asked Dawn.

'Yes I am, really enjoying it actually, and very busy at the moment, so that keeps me out of trouble. Plus I get to meet lots of interesting people, so I can't complain,' said Rachel.

'I've never really understood what you do,' said Dawn.

'It's not that tricky really,' said Rachel. 'You know when you buy a house and you get a survey done? Well, we do the same thing, just for people buying and selling businesses.'

'How many businesses do you see that need new windows and a damp-proof course?' Dawn was laughing.

'More than you might imagine,' said Rachel. 'Mostly, though, they just need some decent management. Anyway, talking of management, how is the salon doing?'

Dawn had left school to train as a beautician. Once she'd qualified she got a job working at the local beauty salon and had steadily progressed to become the salon manager. She was likable, streetwise and understood what it took to run a small business.

'God, really well actually. You'd be amazed what people will pay for a scrub down with some warm mud. We've also just started this new cleavage facial that I read about it in a Swedish beauty magazine. We give the old pair a bit of a birthday at the same time as a standard facial and then finish off with firming cream and a light coating of fake tan all over. It's so popular that we've had to take on an extra girl on Saturdays.'

Rachel was slowly realising that there was a whole world of beauty treatments and cosmetic surgery that she knew nothing about.

'What's the most unusual thing you do?' Rachel asked, feeling slightly like someone from one of those car crash TV shows that Natalie had talked about. All in the interests of research, she thought weakly.

'It's got to be Hollywood waxing,' said Dawn, 'which actually isn't that unusual any more but it is a bit of a weird concept. All that talc and getting on all fours, just to get rid of every hair God gave you. I really don't get it, but it brings in plenty of regulars, so who cares? If that's what they want, that's what we do.'

'Do you find many of your customers have also had some work done – you know, the odd lift or tuck here and there?'

'Quite a few actually. Loads have had Botox or fillers, even though they're dead expensive. No idea where people get the money to keep doing them every few months. You can always spot those with boob jobs too, especially when you're doing massages.'

Dawn and Rachel sat chatting until the wine and the football were finished.

'We're off to Club Tropicana after closing time,' said Dawn. 'Fancy joining us?'

Club Tropicana was a nearby nightclub so stuck in the eighties even the building had shoulder pads. The seats were arranged around circular tables under plastic palm trees, connected by a series of intertwining bridges leading to a black and white mirrored dance floor. They served two-for-one cocktails, made with watered-down spirits and adorned with huge umbrellas. It had been the scene of so many nights out for Rachel over the years — nights either spent in dark corners, or in tears, or in the ladies' throwing up.

It had been ages since she'd last been dancing — well, apart from last night, but that didn't really count. That had just been a pub band, not a proper nightclub. Rachel had a busy few weeks coming up and she deserved a good night out. She knew that baby-free Rowan would be up for it too.

'Yes, why not,' said Rachel. 'Let's go.'

The next morning Rachel woke up when her mum knocked on her door.

'Tea, darling,' her mum said as she entered the room.

Rachel groaned and rolled away from the light that came streaming in the gap in the open door.

'Gosh, you were late back,' her mum said. 'I'm sure I heard you around three a.m.'

'Not really sure. Thanks for the tea,' said Rachel, praying her mother would then leave.

Instead, she sat on the side of her bed. 'It's so lovely to have you here, darling. I do miss you,' her mum said, stroking her head. She clearly wanted to chat.

With great effort Rachel sat up and picked up her tea. Waves of nausea swept over her.

'It's lovely to be home too, Mum. What time is it?'

'Just after eight. I know how early you normally start at that job of yours, so thought you'd appreciate the lie in.'

You have no idea, thought Rachel, recalling her two o'clock start the previous day.

'Thanks.'

'Did you have a good night?'

Rachel thought for a moment. She could vaguely remember some very dodgy dancing and persuading some lanky builder that she had a boyfriend, but mostly she remembered laughing – Rachel had no idea what about, but that didn't seem to matter.

'Yes, it was a real laugh, thanks. We ended up at Club Tropicana.'

'Oh not that awful place,' said her mum. 'I'm surprised it hasn't closed down by now. Anyway, your father and I thought that we could all have a trip to Hayfield House today. Have a wander round, maybe get a pot of tea and a scone. Then we could pop into the garden centre on the way back. I need to get a few new bedding plants. What do you think?'

Rachel thought that she would rather stick knitting needles in both eyes.

'Er, sounds great. Maybe I could have another hour first? Get my energy up.'

'Yes, of course, dear. I'll wake you again in an hour or so. And don't forget to drink your tea. I'm sure it will make you feel better.'

And with that, she shut the door.

Two hours later Rachel and Rowan were in the back of their parents' car heading for Hayfield House. As they were getting ready, her dad had packed two litres of water and an emergency pork pie 'just in case', even though it was a sunny day and the journey would last no more than half an hour. Rachel had no idea what type of disaster could befall them in which they were likely to be saved by a pork pie, but she knew there was no point asking.

'What did we do in life to deserve this?' Rowan whispered as the car wound its way slowly through country lanes.

'Too little sleep, too many cocktails,' Rachel whispered back. 'And please don't let me be sick, I couldn't bear it,' she added.

In the front of the car, her parents were having an in-depth discussion about the best route to take.

'We should stay off the main road,' said her dad. 'All those Saturday shoppers: we'll be stuck for ages. I suggest we take the B139 and then cut up past the old vicarage and then down to that T-junction. You know, the one with the sign for the lavender shop.'

'Yes, dear, whatever you think,' said her mum. 'We

should avoid the road up to Lanes School as well. Grace said that they've a car boot sale on today and there's bound to be a queue.'

'Ah yes, good point. I'll turn off by the supermarket,' said her dad.

Rachel put her head in her hands in despair.

Rowan looked over and squeezed her leg. 'Nearly there,' he said.

The day was pretty much as bad as Rachel thought it would be: hours of trailing round dusty rooms full of old furniture. Her parents stood and admired the craftsmanship, while she and Rowan pretended they were presenters on *The Antiques Road Show* to relieve the boredom. The only high point was the enormous piece of chocolate cake that she had in the cramped tea shop.

On the way back, as promised, they stopped at the garden centre. Her parents ended up arguing as her dad refused to ask where the daffodil bulbs were, preferring to look for them himself. He was still looking for them fifteen minutes later, by which time Rachel's mum had asked someone, been through the tills and was loading them in the car along with her new bedding plants.

Eventually they got back home and Rachel and Rowan both fell onto the sofa to watch TV. As they sat there watching sad Saturday game shows, Rachel suddenly couldn't wait to get back up to London. After all, she had a big day on Monday to prepare for: first day out at Beau Street and she needed to be ready. On time and on the case, as Carl Stephens had said. She could do that, she thought. No problem.

CHAPTER 3

Rachel got back to her flat on Sunday evening. As she opened the door she was hit by the smell of stale pizza. Harry had left after her on Friday and hadn't bothered to clear up. She stared wearily at the mess. How hard was it to put a few things in the bin? Just as she finished clearing up, Harry rang.

'Hi, how were the Dullards?' he said.

'My parents are not dull,' said Rachel defensively, still cross about the pizza.

'Since when?' said Harry.

'They just like their routines; nothing wrong with that,' said Rachel, not in the mood to have a debate about the dullness or otherwise of her parents.

'No, nothing at all,' said Harry.

'Also, the flat really smelt of pizza when I got back. You could have put it in the bin, you know,' said Rachel.

'Sorry, I went back to sleep and ended up leaving in a bit of rush. Anyway, I was ringing to see if you fancy a drink?'

'No, no tonight. I'm really tired and I've got an early start. Maybe tomorrow,' Rachel said.

'Oh come on, Rach, just a quick one. I haven't seen you all weekend. I promise to get you home on time.'

Rachel hesitated. Harry didn't often admit that he missed her. But she needed a clear head in the morning. 'Sorry, Harry, not tonight. I've got stuff to get organised.'

'Okay, you be a good girl, go and polish your shoes ready for school tomorrow.'

'Don't tease me, Harry. I've got a new project starting and I could do without having a raging hangover on the first day.'

'Alright, I guess I'll survive. Call me tomorrow, though, okay?'

'Yes, I will,' said Rachel and they hung up.

The next morning Rachel woke up early and spent quite a while getting ready. She had a vision of the Beau Street Group being full of immaculate people floating about in white coats and she wanted to make sure she created a good impression.

Their offices weren't far from Harley Street and she was meeting the two other members of her team, AJ and Rosa, in the reception. Rachel got there a few minutes early and as she went into the building, the security guard popped his head out of a small room just inside the front doors.

'Lovely day,' he said, looking out of the large glass pane to the side of the rotating doors. 'Wind was a bit south-westerly earlier, but it's dropped now. Shouldn't be any rain either, so that's good.'

From inside his room Rachel could hear a radio, a

lady's voice reading slowly what sounded rather like the shipping forecasts but it was probably just the news. The security guard was a twinkly sort of guy in his sixties, the sort who'd probably worked there for twenty-five years and would soon be joining the carriage clock generation.

'Now, who are you here for?' He spoke to her as if she was a small child.

'Beau Street Group.'

'Ah yes, let me show you where to go.' He moved over to where there was a map of the building on the wall and stood by it, slightly to one side, facing her. He coughed slightly as if he was about to start a speech. 'Now, you are here,' he said, waving his arm in a theatrical manner towards a large red 'You are here' arrow on the map. 'You need to proceed across the lobby to the reception desk, where you can sign in, here.' He turned his hand and ran the back of his fingers across the map and then tapped his finger on the square box marked 'Reception'.

'What, that reception desk over there?' Rachel asked, pointing to the reception desk that was in full view about twenty feet away.

'Precisely,' said the security guard.

'Thank you very much,' said Rachel, rather bemused as to why they had needed the whole map on the wall presentation thing. 'I'll, er, just walk over there, shall I?'

'Yes, you do that.'

'Thanks,' said Rachel and walked over to a striking but slightly scary looking receptionist.

'Can I help you?' the receptionist said, tossing her

hair slightly as she spoke. Her smile looked slightly lopsided and Rachel suddenly had an overwhelming urge to leap across the desk and peer at her face for signs of surgery. She resisted.

'Yes, thank you. I'm Rachel Altman from Payne Stanley, here to see the finance director, Tom Duffy. He should be expecting me.'

'Take a seat. I'll let him know you're here.'

'I'm just waiting for two colleagues,' said Rachel. 'They should be here in a few minutes. I'm slightly early.'

She sat down and looked around. If the reception was anything to go by, the offices were going to be lovely. The surfaces were adorned with opulent flower arrangements and the decor was deep red with heavily textured wallpaper. The seats in the waiting area were a mix of finely upholstered chairs and soft leather sofas. Small boxes of leaflets advertising various miracle treatments sat on the coffee table, next to a neat pile of beauty magazines. Rachel sat and flicked through one, listening to the quiet hiss of the air conditioning while she waited for the other two to arrive.

AJ arrived first, shortly followed by Rosa. By the time they'd all signed in, Tom Duffy had arrived in reception. He walked over to them and looked at each of them in turn. Rachel could see that he wasn't quite sure which of them was in charge, so she quickly stepped forward and held out her hand.

'Hello, Rachel Altman, very nice to meet you, Tom. Can I introduce my team: Alistair James, but everyone calls him AJ, and this is Rosa Castelli.'

'Hello, welcome to the Beau Street Group,' Tom

said, smiling at them and gesturing towards the small lift behind reception. 'Let's go up, shall we.'

The three of them followed Tom into the lifts, up and into a meeting room.

'Can I get you some coffee?' Tom asked.

'That would be great, thanks,' said Rachel.

After the obligatory tea party, they all eventually sat down.

'I understand that you and Carl Stephens have known each other quite a long time,' said Rachel.

'Yes, probably ten years or more now,' said Tom. 'We've worked together a few times before. How much has Carl told you about this job?'

'He's given us the basic briefing and we've seen the email you sent, but it would be great to hear it from you directly,' said Rachel.

'Well, it goes without saying that this is all totally confidential,' said Tom.

Rachel, AJ and Rosa all nodded earnestly.

'We've been approached by the Equinox Practise, a large US-based cosmetic surgery business who are planning to expand in Europe and are interested in buying us. We weren't looking to sell, but if we can get a good price for the business then we'll definitely consider it. In order to work out how much they might be prepared to pay, Equinox have asked for a load of information – how much we charge for the procedures we do here, what profits we make, what sort of client base we have, that sort of thing.'

'Yes, I saw the list you sent to Carl,' said Rachel, nodding.

'Well, we'd like you guys to prepare that for us and then present it to the Americans when they come over in just over a month's time. It will be much better if it comes from someone independent; avoid them worrying that we might have been selective about what we tell them.'

'Okay, no problem,' said Rachel.

'Good,' said Tom. 'It will be interesting to see how much they might be prepared to pay for us,' he added, staring up at the ceiling as he spoke.

He didn't quite rub his hands but Rachel could tell he was imagining the prospect of a large wad of cash coming his way. She'd seen this before, in other businesses they'd worked with. Management teams had often started out very positive about selling, only to be disappointed by the offer that followed. She hoped that this business was as good as they thought it was. It would make a nice change to be able to deliver good news.

'I'll have the team start bringing you in the information you need. You can work from this office, and I'm just around the corner so just come and find me if you have any questions,' said Tom.

Rachel spent the rest of the day finding her way around, organising their project room and briefing Rosa and AJ.

'Don't forget we need to be professional at all times,' said Rachel. 'This is no different to any other business that makes money out of providing a service.'

'Quite right,' said AJ, laughing. 'No different at all. Apart from the fact that we're not in a factory and there are still pictures of tits everywhere.'

31

'They're hardly the same as girly calendars, AJ,' said Rosa. 'They're just adverts for boob jobs.'

'I think you'll find the expression you're looking for is breast augmentation,' said Rachel. 'And it's what they do, so it's hardly surprising that they're advertising them. We're going to have to get used to talking about this sort of thing and using all the proper expressions as it won't be that long until we're standing up presenting about it.'

'I think it's hilarious,' said AJ. 'I have no idea how I'm going to talk to the doctors about what they do with a straight face.'

'You wait until you have to meet the doctors who do penis enlargements,' said Rachel. 'That will take the smile off your face.'

AJ looked horrified. 'Do they do those here?'

'I expect so,' said Rachel. 'Carl said they did pretty much everything going. Anyway, we'll find out soon enough. We're getting all the sales figures tomorrow.'

When Rachel got home she rang Harry and arranged to meet him for a drink. As she got ready to go out she looked at herself in the mirror. She pulled her brown, shoulder-length hair away from her face and peered at it closely. She had a few lines around her eyes and her mouth that she hadn't really focused on before. Laughter lines, she was pretty sure. That was a good thing, surely? It meant that she was happy and had plenty to laugh about. Rachel hoped this job wasn't going to start making her obsess about what she looked like. She'd never even thought about cosmetic surgery and now she was going to spend a few weeks studying it in detail. Would it make her more likely to want to have it? Or maybe it would put her off for life. Rachel comforted herself with the thought that the latter was the far more likely option. She was bound to come across some horror stories.

Harry was playing on the fruit machine when Rachel arrived at the pub.

'Hi, get me a pint, will you?' he said without looking up. 'Nearly done.'

Rachel went over to the bar and ordered a pint and a gin and tonic. She sat down at a table near the fruit machine and watched Harry as he finished using up his credits. His hair flopped slightly onto his forehead as he peered into the machine, trying to see if the matching shapes were just a couple of nudges away.

He's very good looking, she thought, remembering how totally spellbound she had been when she first met him. Harry had a very direct way of talking, and that included talking about his feelings for Rachel. She'd never met anyone before who had managed to do that while still being totally cool. A couple of weeks after they'd met, Harry had said to her, 'You know, Rach, I think it's the fact that you're so smart as well as pretty that makes me crazy about you.' He'd said it in such a matter-of-fact way that it came across as simply that, a fact. She'd been so surprised and flattered that she'd had no idea what to say in reply. So she'd said nothing. Instead, she'd got up, taken his hand and flagged down a cab to take them back to her flat. What a night that had been. For a long time Rachel hadn't quite been able to believe her luck and kept waiting to find out what the catch with Harry was.

Eventually she worked it out. His directness made him incredibly persuasive and she found it almost impossible to say no to him. As a result, he was constantly leading her astray. When he wanted to go on somewhere and she wanted to go home, he would say to her, 'It's not as much fun if you don't come. I just want you with me, Rachel.' And she knew he meant it.

Harry finished his last spin and came over to join her.

'Good day at school?'

'Yes, really good actually,' Rachel said.

Normally she wouldn't bother to tell Harry much about the details of her day as she knew he wasn't interested. Office jobs were just that, as far as he was concerned. Rachel often wondered how Harry could be so into her at the same time as being so disinterested in something that was such a big part of her life. However, this project was different: she was sure he'd be interested in this one. Yes it was confidential, but this was only Harry. He didn't exactly move in the same circles as cosmetic surgeons.

'I've started a new project: a cosmetic surgery business that's up for sale,' she said, quickly adding, 'I think quite a lot of celebrities might go there.'

'Wow, how cool! What sort of things do they do?' Harry asked.

'Most things, I think. We'll be finding out tomorrow. Certainly plenty of boob jobs, though, judging by the posters they have about the place.'

'Will you get to see the before and after photos?'

'Harry!' Rachel gently punched his arm. 'I know

we get to look at most things but even we don't have good reason to start rifling through medical photos. I might get to find out which celebs have had stuff done, though, as we're going to be having a good look at the client base.'

'Might be a few good stories in that,' said Harry.

'I'm sure the whole place is full of stories. Anyway, I haven't got long to learn all about it as we're going to be presenting to the American buyers in a few weeks. So I'll need to know my Botox from my buttock lifts by then.'

'Buttock lifts? Too weird,' said Harry. 'Why would you bother doing that?'

'Because people don't like having saggy arses, I guess,' said Rachel.

'Well, they should use you as their after model,' Harry said, slipping his arm around Rachel's waist.

'What are you after?' said Rachel.

'You,' said Harry.

Rachel laughed. As usual Harry was pushing all the right buttons.

'How was your day?' Rachel asked.

'Not bad. I spent most of it trying to track down this bloke who's promised me an intro to a golf pro he knows. Apparently he's teaching some great new putting technique and I want to interview him about it. He's already got a few of the top golfers on his books and I want to get to him before it becomes old news. Found the bloke eventually, and I think after a few rounds of golf and a couple of decent lunches, the story's mine.'

'It's a tough life,' said Rachel. 'One sporting event

or long lunch after another. I don't know how you cope.'

'I know, it's taken years of training,' said Harry.

'Years of watching sport and drinking lager more like.'

'Every job has its own type of training. I just happen to be perfectly suited to mine.'

Rachel had to agree with him. Harry was perfectly suited to his job. Mind you, she was pretty good at hers too; well, most of the time anyway.

'I'm starving,' said Harry. 'Let's go and get a curry.'

'Good idea,' said Rachel, suddenly realising how hungry she was.

As they were eating, Harry's phone beeped with a text message.

'It's Paul,' said Harry. 'He's got some spare tickets for the comedy club and wants to know if we want to meet him there?'

'What time do you think it'll finish?'

'Probably around eleven thirty. It should be a laugh. I'll text him back yes.'

'Okay, but I can't be too late — early start in the morning and I need my beauty sleep,' said Rachel.

'Hardly,' said Harry.

The show actually finished well after midnight and by the time Rachel got home it was closer to one a.m. She reluctantly set her alarm for six a.m. and climbed into bed.

CHAPTER 4

Rachel sat in the meeting room at Beau Street convinced that she was sweating curry. The room wasn't that big and it had got quite warm with the three of them working in it. Rachel grabbed two breath-freshening mints from her bag and put them in her mouth, swilling them round to get rid of any hint of last night. The double shot latte that she'd drunk on the way in had kicked in though, and she was raring to go. One of Tom Duffy's team had dropped off a large set of files containing sales and client information that morning and they'd also been given a computer with access to booking records.

'Right, guys, let's get going. We need to work out a way to divide the work up. I've had a look through the files and the sales are split by the top five procedures and then by the rest. They have most of the information set out at the front of the sales records for each month. So Rosa, why don't you take the top five, AJ, you look at the rest, and I'll start work on the client base.'

Rachel read from the files. 'Right, these are the top

five procedures: breast augmentation, liposuction, adominoplasty — that's a tummy tuck, I think — face lifts and nose reshaping.'

'I'd take the lot if I were you,' said AJ, laughing.

'Shut up,' said Rachel, smiling too. 'Now, if you can both go through the files. We need to look at the trends over the last couple of years — which areas are growing fastest, what are the average prices by procedure, et cetera, et cetera.'

As well as the top five, Rachel looked at the very long list of other procedures being offered. It had all the things on it that she'd thought they might do, and some!

'Okay, everyone clear?'

AJ and Rosa both nodded.

Rachel divided up the files and left herself with the one entitled 'Client master file'. The Equinox Practise wanted details of the client base, average age, spend levels, frequency of visits, that sort of thing. Rachel began looking through the records. She should probably start by looking at average ages, but instead she found herself just flicking through the records looking at the client names. But after more than an hour of looking, Rachel hadn't seen one name that she recognised. How disappointing. Still, it was only day two: plenty more time to play celebrity spotting. It would take them a few days to get through this part of the job and then they'd be ready to start meeting the doctors.

After three days of working through the files of information out at the Beau Street Group, Rachel headed back into the office. She started to go through her in-tray, checked a few emails and then rang Shali.

'Hi, guess who's in the office?' said Rachel.

'Rachel! Great, about time. Urgent meeting, Bar Q, lunchtime,' said Shali. 'I have a couple of managers working with me today so I'll bring them too.'

'AJ and Rosa are still out at the client's, so it'll just be me. Is Nat in?'

'Think so. I'll email her. Can you book a table?'

'Yup, will book one for twelve thirty. See you then.'

Nothing like a quick team lunch to recharge the batteries, thought Rachel. Shame she didn't have any juicy celebrity stories yet.

Bar Q was a modern brasserie style restaurant set in a waterfront development about five minutes from Rachel's office. It was also a popular meeting place after work, priding itself on having one of the biggest choices of wine by the glass in London. The others were already there when Rachel arrived, sitting in a large booth with black leather seating. After they'd ordered, the conversation soon turned to Rachel's project.

'So, come on,' said Shali. 'How's it going?'

'Fascinating,' said Rachel. 'I can't tell you anything about the deal, obviously, but it's going to be a real eye-opener. I just can't believe the range of procedures they do…'

'Oh yes, it's a really fast growing market,' piped up one of the managers working for Shali. 'There's almost nothing that you can't get done now,' she continued. 'And you can travel abroad for treatments, which sometimes cost less than half what you'd pay here.

Your business needs to watch out for that, Rachel. The only issue really is if you need lots of follow up consultations. Prague is apparently quite popular. The magazines are full of it.'

She suddenly stopped as if she'd only just realised what she was saying. The others looked at her. She certainly didn't look like a cosmetic surgery expert, or if she was, she should be asking for her money back.

'Yes, I'd heard that about Prague. Thanks, I'll bear it in mind,' said Rachel. Sensing the manager's embarrassment, she quickly changed the subject. 'So what's the news in the office?'

'Ooh, invites to the department's summer party are out,' said Shali. 'Have you got yours?'

'No, not yet,' said Rachel. 'Still going through my in-tray.'

'It's with other halves this year, so Shali is already in a panic about who to bring,' said Natalie.

'I am not!' said Shali. 'Spoilt for choice more like.'

Rachel felt slightly sick. Work events with Harry were a nightmare. He hated them and in the past had nearly always ended up drunk and badly behaved. The director promotions were not that far away and she couldn't afford any more horror stories.

'I'm so glad it's black tie too — gives us a chance to dress up for a change,' said Shali.

Aah! Harry hated getting dressed up even more. The whole thing was going to be a disaster. Rachel briefly wondered if maybe she shouldn't tell Harry and then pretend to work that he was ill on the day. But she soon realised that was far too risky: someone was bound to mention it to him at some point. She'd just have to talk to him and explain how important it was. He would have to get used to the fact that this was part of the programme.

As they walked back to the office, Shali and Rachel dropped back behind the others.

'So what was all that with your "I'm off to Prague" manager?' Rachel asked.

'No idea,' said Shali. 'Sounded like she'd been doing some serious research to me.'

'Maybe just helping a friend,' Rachel suggested generously. 'Just like Natalie with her request the other day for the cost of a boob job, allegedly for her make-up artist friend.'

'God, I'd forgotten about that!' said Shali. 'She doesn't need a boob job – she looks great already, bitch. No need for her to worry about what frock to wear to the summer party. She could wear a duvet cover and still look fab.'

'Unlike Miss Prague, who could definitely do with running up a few air miles,' said Rachel.

They both laughed loudly.

'Shali, I'm so worried about the summer party. Harry hates that sort of thing. You know what he's like,' Rachel said.

'You'll just have to tell him that he needs to behave. All that bar diving and dropping his trousers has to stop. Next time it might be a client function and then what will you do? He'll have to grow up at some point.'

'I know but I don't think that's quite how he sees it somehow,' said Rachel.

'Well, you need to make him see,' said Shali.

After a quiet weekend (Harry was off on a jolly with some uni mates), in which Rachel did little more than lie about, watch TV and eat ungodly amounts of cheese and crackers, Monday morning saw her heading back out to the Beau Street Group. She'd decided to forget about the summer party for a while. There was plenty to keep her mind off it, as information on the business was rolling in thick and fast. She was looking around the room at the piles of files and papers and wondering whether they'd have time to get through it all when she noticed that Rosa was flicking through her notes looking rather puzzled.

'Are you okay?' Rachel asked.

'I'm having a few problems with this analysis,' said Rosa. 'Could you give me a hand?'

'Sure,' said Rachel. She got up and moved round the meeting room table to sit next to Rosa. 'What's up?'

'I'm trying to get the sales breakdown by procedure that we need, but quite a lot of the sales records don't have the procedure details noted on them. It just says "other". At this rate I'll end up with "other" being one of the top procedures, which isn't exactly helpful.'

'Is the information somewhere else?' Rachel asked.

'Not that I've found so far,' said Rosa. 'I've checked the summary patient records and they also just say "other".'

'It's probably just a glitch,' said Rachel. 'I'll go and ask Tom about it.'

Rachel walked down the corridor to Tom's office. Tom's PA was sitting at the desk outside his office.

'Hi, Linda, is he free?' Rachel asked.

'He's heading out in about ten minutes, so you can probably just catch him if you don't need too long,' said Linda.

Rachel knocked on the door, opened it slightly and stuck her head round.

'Hi, Tom, can I bother you for a couple of minutes?'

Tom was sitting behind a large, old-fashioned desk with a green leather top.

'Yes, come in,' he said.

Tom's office was very different in style from the ones at Payne Stanley but Rachel couldn't help noticing the similarities to Carl Stephen's office. Pictures of his family and the obligatory sports trophy sat on his bookshelf. He also had some team photos of what looked like rugby players on the wall. What was it with men and the need to display their sporting prowess at work? Maybe she should bring in her under-sixteen netball team photo and her twenty-five metre swimming certificate and put them on the wall in their project room. Or then again, maybe not, she thought.

'How can I help?' Tom asked.

'I just had a quick question about the sales records,' said Rachel. 'We're trying to get a breakdown of sales by procedures but quite a few of the records just say "other" on them. There are no details of what procedure was actually carried out. Do you know why?'

'I think it's probably from when we moved onto the new computer system. Some of the old records hadn't been coded properly so they got transferred over as "other". You'll probably have to go back to the original invoice to get the details.'

'Oh, okay,' said Rachel. 'Is it alright if we prepare a list of the ones we want and give it to the finance team to dig out for us?'

'They're still working on some of your other information requests, so it might take them some time. They're filed in the accounts office, so if one of your team can do it instead, that would be quicker,' said Tom.

'Alright, we'll do that,' said Rachel. 'Thanks.'

'How's it going otherwise?' Tom asked.

'Yes, not bad,' said Rachel. 'We're working our way through the information you've given us and we can really see how fast you've been growing over the last couple of years. Very profitable business too, so that's all good.'

'Cosmetic surgery is a great business to be in,' Tom replied. 'Most people want us to be reassuringly expensive as that implies quality, and once they've found a doctor they're happy with, they stick with us.'

'Reassuringly expensive,' said Rachel, smiling. 'I like that expression.'

'That's the idea,' said Tom. 'People want to know that they're in the best hands and they understand that low cost means cutting corners. You get what you pay for in this business. Anyway, I need to run, so if you'll excuse me…'

'Of course,' said Rachel. 'We'll get on with pulling out those invoices we need.'

Rachel went back to the project room and explained

the situation to Rosa. She wasn't exactly delighted at the prospect of having to go through filing cabinets of paper invoices to find the details they needed.

'That will take ages!' Rosa protested.

'I know,' said Rachel. 'I'm sorry, but we don't have any choice, and I'll give you a hand. Look, maybe let's leave it for today and resume battle in the morning.'

She could do with leaving a bit earlier than normal. She was seeing Harry later and was going to have to talk to him about the summer party. She wanted to have a bit of time beforehand to think about exactly how to deal with it. She packed up her things and headed down in the lift to the foyer.

The security guard nodded at her as she left. 'Have a good evening,' he said. 'Nice and mild too, perfect for a barbecue.'

'Great, thanks. Goodnight,' said Rachel.

She left the Beau Street office and got on the tube home. As usual it was packed and there were no seats. She watched a man reading a newspaper folded neatly long-ways in one hand. He was hanging on to an overhead strap at the same time and seemed oblivious to the people around him. She wished she could do the same but she had nothing to read except her work notebook, which was hardly escapist literature. Instead, she amused herself by deciding which man in the carriage she would marry if they were the only ones left in the world: a regular game during her commute home. She looked around, examining the men in the carriage: the standard mix of portly businessmen, office workers and tourists. Tonight was easy. It would be the scruffy but acceptable looking student type sitting down the far end of the carriage. If only choosing a partner for life could really be that simple.

When she got home she ran herself a bath. She lay soaking in it for ages, slowly drinking a glass of wine and mulling over the conversation that she needed to have with Harry later. She really wanted him to understand how important it was to her that he didn't show her up at the summer party. She wanted to show the partners that she was level-headed and responsible, and that included her choice of boyfriend.

Harry arrived shortly after eight p.m. and was in a typically chirpy mood. She gave him a glass of wine and they sat in the kitchen chatting.

'Our summer party invites have come through at work,' Rachel said after a while. 'It's with other halves this year. Will you come with me?'

'If I have to,' said Harry.

At least that's a yes, Rachel thought.

'Great, I'd really like you to,' said Rachel. 'It's black tie so we'll have a chance to dress up for a change, which will be fun.' She held her breath slightly.

'Oh, you're joking! That's not my idea of fun. And besides, I don't have a penguin suit,' said Harry.

'That's okay, I can hire one for you. There's a suit hire place just near the office.'

'Fine,' he said, looking sulky.

'Come on, Harry, it's not that bad. I go to loads of your work things.'

'That's because they're fun. Your work parties are boring as hell.'

'That's so not true,' said Rachel. 'You just can't be bothered to make an effort.'

'Rubbish. I talked to loads of people at the last one,' said Harry.

'Only after you'd pretty much drunk your own body weight in red wine and then you mostly insulted them.'

They sat in silence, glaring at each other, for a few moments.

Rachel decided to change tack. 'Look, Harry, I really need the next few months to go well for me. The director promotions are coming up and I could do with staying under the radar. Let's just go and try to have a nice time, shall we? I promise I'll make it up to you.' She put her hand on the inside of Harry's thigh and gave it a gentle squeeze.

'If you say so,' said Harry, pushing her hand away and getting up. He went into the sitting room and turned on the TV.

Rachel stayed in the kitchen. Why were these conversations so hard? And why did they always end up arguing? To most people, getting an invitation to a party was a good thing. Maybe she just had to accept that Harry would never be interested in her work. She knew he was interested in her, and after all, that was what mattered.

CHAPTER 5

Rachel and Rosa spent the next morning preparing a list of invoices that they needed to get out from filing. Once they'd finished they went into the accounts department and set themselves up on a spare desk near a long row of grey filing cabinets. Around them, the finance team were chatting away, making coffee for each other and generally getting on with the jobs of the day.

'It's got a nice atmosphere this place, don't you think?' Rosa said.

'Yes it has. They're a pretty friendly bunch. I wonder if they get an employee discount on treatments,' said Rachel.

'Ooh, I hadn't thought of that,' said Rosa. 'That would be quite a perk! We should see if we can spot people who've had something done. Mind you, I guess if they're as good as they say they are here, we probably won't be able to tell those who've had something done from those who haven't.'

'But don't you think that the office staff here are

generally more attractive than your average accounts team, though?' Rachel asked. 'Where's the standard stock of dowdy women and overweight men in zipped cardigans?'

Rosa looked around. She had to admit that the number of flat stomachs, pouting mouths and feline eye shapes was probably quite a bit higher than in the rest of the population.

'Yup, fair point,' said Rosa. 'You can't blame them, though, can you? I mean, if you work in a cake shop where they give you free cakes, you're bound to eat them at some point.'

Just as Rosa was talking, a tall skinny woman with a smooth, expressionless face walked past their desk. Rachel nodded at Rosa knowingly and sucked in her cheeks. Rosa looked at the woman, who immediately smiled at her and said 'Good morning' in a singsong voice.

'Oh, er, yes, good morning,' said Rosa, rather caught off guard and trying hard not to laugh. 'Rachel!' she said once the woman was out of earshot.

'What? You were the one who wanted to play spot the nose job,' said Rachel, laughing. 'I couldn't let a classic frozen fish face go unnoticed. Anyway, that's quite enough taking the piss out of the client. We should get started.'

'Yes, quite right,' said Rosa.

Rachel read out the first invoice number and Rosa carefully worked her way through the filing cabinets until she found it.

'Does it have the procedure details on?' Rachel asked.

'Yes it does,' said Rosa.

'Great, let's get out the ones we need then, make copies of them and then put them back. Then we can use the copies to build up the sales analysis.'

Rachel helped Rosa for a while and then headed back to the project room to carry on with her own work, looking at the average ages of the client base. She still hadn't spotted a single celebrity name in the information she'd been looking at and was determined to try to find some. She sat down and went back over the analysis she'd been doing over the past few days. The most common age group was coming out at twenty-five to thirty years, which was younger than she'd expected. She'd thought that most people would be having something done to them in their forties. It was probably something to do with the fact that breast augmentation was their most popular procedure. Rachel made a note to chat to Tom about it next time they met.

She moved on to look at average price per procedure, starting with breast augmentation. There wasn't really that much of a range. Most of the patients had been charged somewhere between four and five thousand pounds. But as Rosa had found, quite a few of the sales records just showed 'other' for the procedure type.

It took Rosa two days to find and copy all the invoices they needed.

'That was a rubbish job!' she declared as she came back into the project room clutching a large pile of paper.

'Well done,' said Rachel. 'Right, let's have a recap as

to where we are, shall we? AJ, why don't you talk me through where you've got to?'

'Right,' said AJ. 'I've been looking at the growth rates of procedures outside of the top five. Some of the fastest growing areas include light treatments for things like thread veins and age spots, Botox and fillers, as you might expect, and also um, um…'

AJ stopped talking. He had started to go red.

Rachel and Rosa looked at each other in amusement.

'Also what?' Rachel asked.

'Well, it's er, well, um,' AJ stammered.

'Spit it out, man!' Rachel said. 'You're going to have to present on this soon enough. No point being embarrassed.'

'Alright, one of the other fast growing areas is vaginoplasty,' said AJ eventually.

As he spoke, Rachel and Rosa burst out laughing. He looked cross at first, but soon starting laughing too. They were all still laughing when the door of the project room suddenly opened. It was Tom Duffy. They all stopped immediately.

'What's all the hilarity?' Tom asked.

For a moment none of them said anything as they searched for an answer.

Then Rachel said, 'Oh, er, AJ was just telling us about a funny best man's speech that he heard at a wedding he went to at the weekend.'

AJ looked at Rachel in horror.

'Oh yes, what was that AJ?' Tom asked.

AJ froze, seemingly totally unable to think of a reply.

Rachel stepped in quickly. 'He was telling us about the best man who, as it happens, also has a bit of a drug habit.'

AJ looked even more horrified.

'And he stood up and started his speech by saying, "I had prepared a couple of lines for this speech but I'm afraid I've snorted them both." The young people at the wedding thought it was hilarious but it didn't go down too well with the bride's family!' Rachel said.

Tom laughed loudly. 'Ah yes, very good, very funny. And what nice company you keep, AJ. Anyway, I'd just dropped in to check that you'd got the information you needed from the invoices you had to pull out.'

Rosa patted a large pile of paper. 'Yes thanks,' she said. 'All here.'

'Right good, don't want Equinox to think we can't keep our books properly. Also, we're having an all-party meeting on Monday for the deal advisers, bankers, lawyers, et cetera. You guys need to be there to give us an update on your progress. I'll email you the details. Is that alright?'

'Yes, no problem,' said Rachel.

'Good, I'll see you then.' And he left, shutting the door behind him.

'Why on the earth did you tell him that wedding story?' AJ said. 'He'll think that I'm a right loser now who mixes with a load of druggies!'

'I'm so sorry, it was just the first wedding joke that came to mind. Anyway, you weren't exactly leaping in to help and I could hardly tell him that we were laughing at you saying vaginoplasty.'

As she said it AJ winced and they started laughing all over again.

'Oh dear, we've got to get a grip,' said Rachel, wiping a tear from her eye. 'We really can't start laughing every time we talk about these things. We need to be professional about it.'

'I think we need some practice,' said Rosa.

Yes, we really do, thought Rachel, with an all-party meeting in a few days' time.

The rest of the day flew past as they worked through the rest of the information they had.

'I think we're just about ready to start interviewing the doctors,' Rachel said. 'I still need to go through these papers, but I'll take them home with me tonight and finish them.'

That evening, Harry was in the kitchen in Rachel's flat cooking pasta while she was working at her desk. Rachel had the pile of 'other' invoices that Rosa had pulled out from the filing cabinets and she was going through them, separating out those that were for breast augmentation. She started putting the cost for each one into the analysis of average cost per procedure that she'd prepared earlier. As she did, she began to notice that the cost of each one was much higher than those she'd taken from the normal records. Some were as high as nine thousand pounds. Rachel took out her notebook and checked the list prices for breast augmentation. The highest list price was five and a half grand. Why would they be charging so much above the list price? These were just records that hadn't been coded properly. There would be no reason for them to have different prices to any other records.

Harry peered over her shoulder. 'What are you doing?' he asked. He picked up an invoice. 'Breast augmentation? I assume that's a boob job. Eight thousand seven hundred quid! Wow, that's not cheap!'

'Put that down,' said Rachel. 'And yes, it is expensive, which is a bit odd actually. It's more than it should be.'

'And they paid in cash,' said Harry, putting the invoice down. 'Flash gits.'

Rachel picked the invoice up and looked at it. He was quite right. In the method of payment box it simply said 'cash'. She picked up a few more invoices and looked at them. They were all paid in cash too. How often did people pay for this sort of thing in cash? That didn't seem right. Rachel sighed and leant back in her chair, stretching her neck and back. It was gone nine p.m. and supper was ready. She'd look into it in the morning.

The first thing Rachel did when she got into Beau Street the next day was to look at the other sales records that had the procedures properly noted on them. Not a single one had been paid in cash. Maybe this was another computer glitch caused by the new system. Rachel took a couple of cash paid invoices and headed to the accounts department. Tom had introduced her to most of the team and she was pretty sure which one of them looked after the cash books. She approached a smiley lady in her fifties who was sitting at a desk near the window.

'Hi, Chris,' said Rachel in a friendly tone. 'I've got a couple of invoices here that say they were paid in cash. We've had a few bits of information missing that may be down to when you moved onto the new computer system. I just wanted to check whether these were actually cash payments. Can you have a look for me?'

'Sure,' said Chris. 'What's the invoice number?'

Rachel read out the number and Chris checked the bank records.

'Yes, definitely a cash payment. It was paid in over the counter at our local bank.' Chris checked the next one. 'Yes, that one too.' She glanced at the invoices. 'By the way, they're both the same doctor, if you want to talk to someone about them.'

'How can you tell?' Rachel asked.

'The first three letters of the invoice number are a code for each doctor. These both start with six-zero-two. Shall I look up who that is?'

'Yes please, that would be great, thanks,' said Rachel.

'Six-zero-two is Lloyd Cassidy,' said Chris.

'Okay, thanks. I'll go and talk to him.'

Rachel went back into the office the team were working in. She looked through the list of documents that had all been coded with 'other' as the procedure type. They all started with code six-zero-two.

'Right, time we started meeting the doctors, I think. Where's the list?'

AJ handed it to her.

'I'll speak to Tom's PA and start getting appointments set up. Hopefully we can start later today.'

She picked up the phone and dialled Tom's PA.

'Hi, Linda, it's Rachel Altman. We're ready to start meeting the doctors now. Would you be able to sort out making appointments for us?' There was a pause, then, 'Great, thanks, you can split them between us but could you schedule me to see Lloyd Cassidy? Okay, thanks. See you shortly, bye.'

Rachel turned to AJ and Rosa. 'Linda will drop round appointment times for us in a bit,' she said.

She spent the next hour or so planning a standard agenda for them to follow when they met the doctors and talking AJ and Rosa through what she'd found out from Chris.

'Okay, so this is the plan when we meet each doctor. We need to know what areas they specialise in, what types of clients they have, the level of repeat business they get and what they see as the next big growth area.'

Linda popped in with the list of appointments and Rachel was scheduled to see Lloyd Cassidy at four p.m. that afternoon. Good, she thought. She wanted to get things sorted out as quickly as possible so they could get on with preparing their presentation.

When Rachel arrived outside Lloyd Cassidy's office at exactly four p.m., his assistant's desk was empty, so she went ahead and knocked on his door.

'Come in,' said a low voice.

Lloyd Cassidy was sitting behind his desk looking through some papers as Rachel went in. He was smartly dressed with neatly cut silver hair and a light suntan. His office was a mixture of plush luxury and medical functionality. Oak-panelled cupboards and heavily framed pictures sat alongside a hospital-style bed and a trolley covered in instruments. The surfaces and walls were covered in impressive looking certificates and industry awards.

'Hello, I'm Rachel Altman from Payne Stanley,' said Rachel, holding out her hand.

'Well hello, Rachel Altman,' said Lloyd in slightly flirty way. 'Please do sit down.'

'Thank you. I'm not sure how much Tom has explained to you about what it is we're doing here?'

'He's told us most of it, I think. We've been briefed on the interest from the Equinox Practise and that you guys are here to write a report giving us the all clear, so to speak. Is that about right?' Lloyd asked.

'Well, yes, sort of,' said Rachel. 'As part of producing our report, we're speaking to all the doctors so we can understand a bit better where your work comes from and what sort of thing you're best known for.'

'I'm known for being good at many things,' said Lloyd. 'But I assume you're focusing solely on my medical abilities.' He smiled at her.

Ugh, how smarmy, thought Rachel. She half-smiled back. 'Yes I am. Would you mind telling me a bit about your work?'

'Yes, of course. I'm one of the longest serving doctors here at Beau Street Group. I've been qualified as a plastic surgeon for more than ten years and was a general surgeon before that. Let me give you a copy of my CV.' He opened his desk drawer and took out a printed information sheet. 'This is what I give to my patients. You can keep that copy.'

Rachel looked at the sheet. It had a large picture of

Lloyd in the top left-hand corner that looked more like a photo of an actor than a surgeon. She sensed that Lloyd rather liked giving out his CV.

'I do a lot of facial cosmetic surgery — face lifts and so on — but I also do a number of our other main procedures, such a breast augmentation. I'm particularly well known for my short-scar or mini facelifts, which are very subtle and have much lower levels of scarring than a more traditional facelift.'

Rachel nodded as she wrote her notes. 'Where do your clients mainly come from?'

'A combination really. I've lectured quite extensively around the world, which means that I'm pretty well known in the industry. As a result, I have quite an international client base. Many clients come from word of mouth referrals from satisfied customers and then there's a reasonable level of repeat business.'

'I see,' said Rachel.

'You've probably seen my sales figures,' said Lloyd. 'I'm sure they will look good on one of those pretty charts you people always end up producing.'

Rachel bit her lip. 'Yes, we're just going through those and it's clear that the business has been growing pretty quickly,' she said, not able to bring herself to flatter him directly. 'There is one thing that I wanted to run through with you. It's about some of your sales records — they don't seem to have the procedures noted down on them correctly. Do you know why that might have happened?'

'Ah, we will have to bring in my lovely assistant at this point. She takes care of all my paperwork,' said

Lloyd. He picked up the phone. 'Audrey, would you mind popping in? Thanks.'

A few moments later there was a knock on the door and a tall, blonde woman came into the room. She was dressed in a white coat teamed with a pair of high gold sandals.

'Rachel, this is Audrey Fox. She's my assistant nurse.'

Audrey Fox was probably in her late forties, although Rachel found it a bit difficult to tell. She was very attractive but in a way that somehow spelled trouble. Maybe it was the slightly overdone make-up or the out of place shoes; Rachel couldn't quite put her finger on it.

'Could you just explain to Audrey what it is that you wanted to know about my paperwork?' said Lloyd. 'She's boss of that department. Bedside manner is more my forte than paperwork.'

He put his arm around Audrey's shoulder and gave it a slight squeeze.

Rachel explained the problem again to Audrey.

'Oh, there could be quite a number of reasons,' said Audrey. 'Sometimes the systems are down so we can't look up all the codes. And we had a new secretary for a while and it took her quite some time to get the hang of things. Or sometimes Lloyd gets so busy that we have to work late and we do the paperwork manually.'

'Oh, I see,' said Rachel. 'I also noticed that a number of payments by your clients were made in cash. Is that normal?'

'As I was telling you earlier, we have quite a number

of overseas clients and many of them like to pay in cash,' said Lloyd. 'Plus, you know sometimes people save up, cash under the mattress, all that sort of thing.'

Rachel didn't think that was likely to happen very often, and certainly not as often as the number of cash payments she'd found. But she was hardly the expert here and they both seemed quite certain.

'Right, okay. And would it also be normal for you to charge people well above the list price?'

'Well now,' said Lloyd, puffing his chest out slightly. 'I don't wish to blow my own trumpet but I do often charge my clients a premium. They know of my reputation, you see. I do also tend to get referred some of the more complex cases and they're also more expensive.'

'Okay, thank you both for your help. I just have a few more questions for Lloyd,' said Rachel.

Audrey went back to her desk outside Lloyd's office and Rachel spent another half an hour running through the rest of her questions with Lloyd.

When the meeting finished, Rachel went back to the project room and sat down. She wasn't totally happy with the answers she'd been given, but a bit of sloppy paperwork was hardly a major issue. The business was growing quickly and Lloyd's sales figures were impressive, as he'd been so quick to point out. Even so, she'd better talk it through with Carl.

CHAPTER 6

Rachel was sitting at her desk waiting for Carl Stephens to ring. While she waited, she flicked through her Beau Street file and thought about how to raise her concerns about the missing sales details and cash payments with him. She had no real evidence that it was anything more than a minor issue with record keeping, and for all she knew paying in cash might be really common. Both matters were easily fixable and hardly likely to worry the buyers if the basic business was trading well. But her gut feeling was that there was more to it, yet if she raised it again with Beau Street she would effectively be accusing Lloyd Cassidy and his nurse of lying. On the other hand, Carl was bound to want a thorough job. He was a stickler for detail and she had Payne Stanley's reputation to think of. It would be a disaster if she missed something. Hopefully Carl would help her work out what to do next and without upsetting everyone.

She jumped when her phone rang.

'Rachel Altman. Oh hi, Carl, yes, I'll pop round. See you in a second, thanks.'

She spent the first few minutes of their meeting giving Carl a general update on how the project was going.

'That all sounds like great progress,' he said. 'It's good that they're getting you the information you need so quickly. That will help us to finish on time.'

'There's a meeting on Monday at two p.m. with all the other advisers to go through the deal timetable. I think it would be good if you could be there. I can give them a progress report, so you won't need to prepare, but I think Tom would like it if you came,' said Rachel.

Carl checked his diary. 'Yes, I can just about do that. I need to be away sharpish, though, as I have another meeting at three thirty,' he said.

'Okay, that's good. There are a couple of points that I wanted to just chat through with you now; not problems necessarily, but I'd quite like your advice on how to deal with them,' said Rachel. She went on to explain her concerns to Carl.

'It doesn't sound like anything much to me,' said Carl when she'd finished. 'I've known Tom for many years and he runs a pretty tight ship. The new computer systems probably didn't help; there are always a few teething problems.'

'I just thought that maybe I should look into it a bit further? Widen the sample out a bit maybe and see how common a problem it is?'

'I don't think there's any need,' said Carl. 'Just add a section to the report with recommendations for improvement and note it there. That way we've made it clear that it needs sorting, but I'd definitely categorise it as minor. No need to raise it at the meeting on Monday.'

'Well, if you're sure,' said Rachel, rather hesitant to just dismiss it.

'I am,' said Carl. 'Right, anything else? Are we done?'

'Yes, I guess we are.'

'Great, thanks. Let's have another catch up next week. Sounds like this is going to be a good project for you, Rachel. I know the client is pleased so far.'

How did he know? He must have been speaking to Tom Duffy.

Rachel felt a bit deflated as she went back to her desk. Carl seemed to think she was making a bit of a fuss about nothing. Maybe he was right. She should write it up as a minor recommendation in the report and then forget about it.

She rang Rowan on his mobile. 'Hi, how are you? Fancy lunch sometime this week? I could do with a break from the office,' she said.

Rowan was a property consultant based to the west of London but he often came into the city visiting clients.

'I can do tomorrow, if that's any good for you,' said Rowan. 'My afternoon meetings don't start until three, so we wouldn't need to rush.'

'Perfect, where?'

'I have a meeting at The Brook Hotel in the morning. That's quite near you and they have a good restaurant; why don't we meet there?'

'Sounds ideal. Meet you there at twelve thirty.' The next day Rachel jumped out of a taxi outside The

Brook Hotel at just before twelve fifteen, as the traffic had been quieter than she'd expected. The doorman, dressed in a red and grey uniform, opened the door for her, and as she entered the hotel the cool hush was a welcome change from the hot and noisy road outside. Rachel decided to wait for Rowan on one of the rather inviting looking sofas in reception, instead of sitting on her own in the restaurant. She sat down in the corner on a deeply upholstered tan sofa and ignored all the broadsheet newspapers on the glass coffee table, opting instead to read the fashion pages of a tabloid.

As she sat there a woman walking across reception caught her eye. She seemed familiar. Rachel looked up. It was Audrey Fox, Lloyd Cassidy's assistant nurse at Beau Street. Rachel didn't exactly feel like being sociable, so she hid behind her newspaper, leaving just enough space to watch Audrey sashay into the hotel bar. She was wearing leather trousers and another pair of impractically high sandals. Rachel had to admit she did look pretty good for her age and wondered how much she'd been availing herself of her boss's talents.

Rachel had just resettled herself when, to her horror, she saw Carl Stephens walk into the hotel. What a nightmare! She was meant to be getting away from work and this was turning out to be a roll call for the cast of her current project. Rachel hid again behind her newspaper and peered round the side, only to see Carl Stephens heading into the bar where Audrey Fox was sitting. As she watched in disbelief, she saw Carl walk over to Audrey. They embraced in too friendly a manner for Rachel's liking and then sat down.

Rachel's mind was racing. Surely Carl couldn't be having an affair with her, could he? As far as Rachel knew, he was happily married. Maybe he'd met her through Tom Duffy. The only thing she knew for certain was that neither of them would want to see her. She'd better move into the restaurant.

She got up and started to walk towards the restaurant, trying to look more closely at the couple out of the corner of her eye as she went but without turning her head in case they noticed her. As a result, she wasn't really looking where she was going and walked straight into a large stone pillar. Her forehead hit the pillar with a thump and she fell over backwards onto the floor.

A passing waiter tried to grab her as she fell, dropping his drinks tray with a loud crash as he did so. 'Gosh, are you alright, madam?' asked the waiter as more people rushed over to help and deal with the mess on the floor.

'Yes, perfectly fine, thank you,' said Rachel, getting up and brushing herself down. She then quickly ran round to the other side of the pillar, out of sight of the bar.

The slightly bemused waiter followed her. 'You've got a bit of a red mark on your forehead, madam. I'll get some ice to put on it,' he said.

'No, please don't worry. I'll just head into the restaurant. I'm meeting someone for lunch. So sorry about the mess.'

'Rachel, are you okay?' said a familiar voice.

It was Rowan.

'What on the earth happened here? I heard the crash as I came in. Typical of my sister to be in the middle of the action,' he said, laughing.

'Oh nothing, just had a slight accident. Look, shall we sit down?' said Rachel, hurrying away from the disaster zone.

They sat down and as soon as the waiter arrived Rachel ordered a glass of wine.

'I see you're on for a large one, then,' said Rowan. 'I haven't even looked at the food menu yet.'

'I need a drink and quick,' said Rachel. 'I'm in shock.'

'Well, you did have a bit of a bump by the looks of your head,' said Rowan.

'No, it's not that. You won't believe what I've just seen!' said Rachel.

'What?'

'I've just seen one of the partners at work, whose project I'm currently working on and who's married, meet a woman in the bar. And from the way they greeted each other, it clearly wasn't a business meeting. What's worse, I also know the woman. She works at the business I'm currently looking at. What a mess!' said Rachel.

'Sorry, you lost me. Say that again?'

'I think my boss is having an affair with his client,' said Rachel pointedly.

'Right, got it. That sounds like great gossip to me,' said Rowan. 'Shall I go and have a look for you? See what's happening? I can pretend to go to the toilets. They won't know me from Adam.'

'Yes, alright. Maybe they were just waiting for some

others to join them,' said Rachel, not really thinking that was very likely. 'You can't miss them – the women is blonde and wearing leather trousers.'

Rachel watched Rowan head out of the restaurant. In a few minutes he was back.

'Yup, he's having an affair. They were holding hands and drinking champagne and will be heading upstairs soon, I bet.'

'Oh please don't.' Rachel couldn't bear the thought of it. 'What a disaster.'

'Why do you care?' Rowan asked. 'Surely it's his problem?'

'Unfortunately he's made it my problem. We aren't allowed to have relationships with clients and my current project involves both of them.'

'Do you need to report him or something then?'

'God, I don't know. Probably. It would be easier if I just forgot I saw them.'

'Can you do that?'

'Maybe. I guess holding hands isn't absolute proof that they're an item. They might just be good friends.'

Rowan looked at her.

'Alright, I know, clutching at straws. Anyway, look, I'm sorry. It's not your problem. I'll talk to one of my workmates about it. I haven't even asked you how you are?'

'All the better for seeing my mad sister,' said Rowan. He lifted his glass. 'Let's drink to more trips to country houses and less work dramas, shall we?'

'Definitely the latter,' said Rachel. 'Cheers. How's Laura?'

'Oh, she's on quite good form at the moment. We haven't argued for, ooh, at least a week. That's not bad by current standards. I'm trying to do all the right things, you know: listening intently to the latest "whose baby can do what" stories, being enthusiastic about looking at schools even though Naomi can hardly hold a spoon yet, let alone a pencil. We even went out for dinner last week, although Laura did ring the babysitter three times in two hours.'

'That doesn't sound like her,' said Rachel.

'I know, but it just seems ages since I had a really good night out, you know,' said Rowan.

'Remember all those great nights we had at home last summer and your birthday last year? She was the life and soul of the party. It's just a phase. I'm sure it'll pass as Naomi gets older. You need to adapt too, by the way; make sure you're pulling your weight.'

'Yes, miss, I'll do my best,' said Rowan.

'You do that,' said Rachel, laughing. 'Maybe you should come with me to our work summer party instead of Harry. It should be a great night and at least I can rely on you to behave yourself.'

'Do you want me to?' Rowan asked. 'I will if you want.'

'No, that's okay — just wishful thinking,' sighed Rachel. 'I'd better take Harry. He'd only end up sulking if I didn't, even though he insists he doesn't want to go.'

Rachel tried not to think about Carl being in a hotel room somewhere above her head as she and Rowan ate. They finished lunch late and as a result Rachel drifted through the remainder of the afternoon in a rather pleasant haze.

The following Monday Carl arrived at Beau Street half an hour before the all-party meeting was due to start, by which time Rachel was feeling pretty flustered. It was hardly the time to ask him if he was having an affair with a client. It really worried Rachel that he'd dismissed her concerns that directly involved someone that he was almost certainly sleeping with. She hadn't mentioned Audrey by name, but she'd referred to Lloyd Cassidy's assistant nurse. Carl was bound to know that was her and probably therefore assumed she must be telling the truth. He'd also specifically told her not to mention it at the meeting, making it hard for her to raise it again later on.

'Right, all ready?' Carl asked.

Rachel tried to keep her voice steady. 'Yes, my plan is to run them through the information we've had so far and explain that our preliminary analysis is that the business is showing steady growth in its core business and strong growth in some of the newer procedure types. Also that we, er, haven't identified any major issues to date.'

'That sounds about right. Are we going to make the report deadlines as per the timetable?' Carl asked.

'Yes, just about. It's tight, though, so we'll need the rest of the project to go smoothly.'

'All right, good. Can you talk me through how you plan to put our report together? I want to make sure I'm happy with the structure.'

Rachel spent the next fifteen minutes talking Carl

through their report outline and then they both headed up to the boardroom. Tom was already in the room when they arrived and Carl went over and shook his hand. They stood chatting and laughing while Rachel sat down and placed her papers in a neat pile in front of her. Did Tom know about Audrey? she wondered. If he did then it didn't seem to worry him. After a few moments Carl sat down too and a few people she didn't recognise started to enter the room.

Rachel instinctively got up and held out her hand. 'Hello, Rachel Altman from Payne Stanley corporate finance,' she said to a tall, dark-haired, rather Amazonian looking woman who seemed to be in charge.

The woman shook her hand briskly. 'Good afternoon, Meredith Romaine, Clinton Wahlberg, but I suggest you sit down as we'll do the introductions when everyone's here.'

It was like she was being told to sit down at school.

'Oh, I see, we just…'

But before she had a chance to finish, Meredith had already turned away as Charles Sutton, the chief executive and founder of Beau Street, had come into the room, shortly followed by Tom Duffy.

'Charles, hello,' said Meredith. 'Please do sit here.' She gestured to the chair in the middle of the long table. 'And Tom, why don't you sit next to him.'

Rachel was beginning to worry that there was some sort of invisible table plan for the meeting and that they were bound to have sat in the wrong place. Carl seemed oblivious to the implicit pecking order being established and was leaning back in his chair with his hands behind his head and his papers spread messily about in front of him. He certainly seems relaxed, thought Rachel.

Movement at the door caught her attention. She looked round just in time to see an attractive, smartly dressed woman trip into the room and almost squash a timid-looking bloke from the Clinton Wahlberg team who was sitting at the table. The woman caught herself at the last minute, looked momentarily mortified, and then managed to smooth her expression into a polite, professional look. Behind her in the doorway, her colleague – a tall, dark-haired man – looked like he was trying to suppress a smile. Glossing over her dramatic entrance, Tom introduced the woman as Alex Fisher, one of the lawyers acting for Beau Street, and her companion as Dan Furtado, another lawyer. Rachel nodded politely at them.

Also joining Tom and Charles was a female doctor whom Rachel recognised from the doctors' profiles they'd been given as Stella Webb. She didn't seem to know many people in the room either and Rachel wondered what her role in the deal was. It soon became clear: she introduced herself as the doctor who would be in charge of bringing together the medical side of the two businesses should the deal go ahead.

The meeting kicked off with a rather long and tedious discussion about the timetable. Rachel wasn't paying too close attention until Meredith suddenly put a speakerphone into the middle of the table and announced that the project leader from the Equinox Practise was going to be joining them on the phone. No one had mentioned the other side being at the meeting! She'd be pretty unpopular if she told Equinox that there were no major issues and then came up with a load of problems late in the day. She didn't have much choice, though, without any evidence that there was actually anything wrong.

Before she could think about it any more, she heard Meredith mention her name.

'Thank you for that update, Alex,' she said, nodding at the lawyers. 'Rachel Altman from Payne Stanley is now going to give us an update from their side.'

'Oh, yes, th-thank you,' Rachel stammered.

She looked down at her notes for a few seconds as she gathered her composure. Carl began to look a bit concerned but soon Rachel looked up again and started talking.

'We've been on site now for two weeks and the company has been extremely helpful in getting us the information we requested. I'd say our information request is now about ninety per cent complete, with the last few items expected in the next few days. We're still going through our analysis, but preliminary results show that the business is growing steadily in the core business and there's strong growth in many of the newer procedures, such as the lunchtime facelift, eyebrow transplants and toe tucks.'

The assembled mass of serious faces quickly killed her urge to laugh.

'We haven't identified any material issues to date, but as I said we still have quite a bit of work to do. We expect to be able to report on time, assuming that all goes well from here on.'

The voice on the end of the phone blasted loudly into the room. 'Hey, Rachel was it? It's Ryan Miller here from Equinox. Thanks for that update; that's exactly what we want to hear. We're pretty sure that it's a smart business over there.'

Rachel winced. He was clearly only wanting to hear good news. Let's hope that's what we deliver, she thought.

Meredith closed the meeting. 'The Equinox Practise will be over in the UK in three weeks and they're looking forward to getting final reports from each of you then,' she said. 'Please make sure that you let Alfred…' she gestured at her colleague, '… or I know straight away if you're having any problems meeting the timetable. Thank you all for your time.'

Rachel wasn't sure many people would be calling Meredith and certainly not with bad news: she was far too intimidating. She was pretty sure that it would be Alfred getting those types of calls.

After the meeting, Carl had a taxi waiting.

'Right, got to go. That all seemed to go pretty well and Tom was on good form. Keep up the good work and let's speak soon on next steps, okay?'

'Okay,' said Rachel.

Once Carl had left, Rachel suddenly felt rather worn out and wasn't sure she really had the energy to look into Lloyd Cassidy's records any further. It would be much simpler for the project, and for her promotion prospects as well, if she just ignored what she knew.

She decided she needed a break and rang Shali.

'Hi, how's it going?'

'Not bad actually, for once I'm just about on top of things. You?' Shali asked.

'Oh, you know, not bad — tight deadlines, lots to do, the usual,' said Rachel.

'Any good celebrity spots yet?' Shali asked.

'No, none, not even a sniff. Very disappointing. It seems like just the sort of place they'd go to. Anyway, I'll keep at it.'

'Summer party next week,' said Shali.

'Don't remind me. Harry has just about agreed to come, under protest.'

'I don't have anyone to take yet,' said Shali.

'I thought you said you were spoilt for choice?'

'Not as spoilt as I thought, it would seem. Ooh, I know, do you think your brother might come? I'm sure he'd enjoy a night out with us and he'd make great arm candy.'

'Shali, my brother is not arm candy!'

'Er, what I meant to say is that he'd be great company,' said Shali quickly. 'Anyway, would you ask him? Pretty please.'

'Yes, okay, as it happens he could probably do with a great night out. He's finding the whole new baby thing quite hard work.'

'Ah bless,' said Shali. 'A night out would do him good.'

Rachel hung up and rang Rowan. As she suspected he jumped at the chance. She rang Shali back.

'All sorted,' she said. 'Rowan will come with you to the summer party.'

'You star, thank you. I'm really looking forward to it,' said Shali.

Rachel wished she could say the same thing. At least Rowan would be there now. He could help her keep Harry in check.

CHAPTER 7

A couple of days after the all-party meeting, Rachel headed out of Beau Street in the direction of the suit hire shop. The previous evening Harry had reluctantly allowed her to take his measurements so she could get him a black tie suit for the summer party. He hadn't been exactly helpful as she did it, hardly standing still and continually asking if she'd finished. Her efforts to cheer him up while taking his inside leg measurement had had no effect at all. He'd decided the evening would be rubbish, he was grumpy about it and that was that.

She entered the slightly musty smelling shop and a man with large glasses and a bulbous red nose appeared from the back.

'Can I help you?'

'Yes, I'd like to hire a man's black tie suit, please,' said Rachel.

'We do prefer to fit them ourselves to make sure they're right. Is the gentleman able to pop in?'

'No, I'm afraid he isn't, but I've taken all the measurements I think you'll need.'

Rachel took out the used envelope on which she'd written Harry's measurements. The man looked at the random list of numbers suspiciously.

'Do you know which is which?'

'Oh yes,' said Rachel. 'I started at the top and worked down.'

'Hmm, I see, so this is the chest measurement?'

'Yes, that's right.'

The man looked at the envelope carefully and started going through the rails of jackets. He picked out a jacket and then looked again at the measurements.

'Where did you measure the inside leg from?' he asked.

'Er, from the top of the inside of his leg, where else would I measure it from?' Rachel felt herself starting to go red.

'You're meant to measure it from the crotch of a pair of trousers. If you measured right to the top of his leg, I'll need to take a bit off this measurement otherwise his trousers will be too long. Are you sure that's where you measured from?' The man looked at her impatiently.

Rachel suddenly wasn't exactly sure where she'd measured from. She hadn't been paying that much attention.

'Yes, I think so, pretty much the top of his actual leg.'

'Look, I'll take an inch and a half off this measurement. That should be about right. But do ask the gentleman to check them, and if they're not right, just bring them back.'

'Great, thanks, I will,' said Rachel, glad to get away.

Later that evening when Harry came round, she showed him the suit.

'Looks good, doesn't it? What do you think?'

'It's a black tie suit, what do you expect me to say?'

God, he's so touchy, thought Rachel.

'Would you mind trying it on, just to check I got the measurements right?'

'I'm sure it'll be fine,' said Harry.

'I think you should try it anyway, just to be sure.'

'For God's sake, Rachel, it'll be fine! Just stop going on about it.'

'Fine,' said Rachel and she marched into her bedroom and put the suit away in her wardrobe. 'Will you come here to get ready on Saturday?'

'Guess so.' Harry changed the subject. 'Anything good on TV tonight or shall we go out for a drink?'

Rachel thought they should go out, break the atmosphere a bit. 'Oh let's go out. A pub supper and a few beers sounds like a plan.'

As they ate in the pub, Rachel chatted breezily about nothing in particular. She was careful not to mention work or the summer party again. Harry didn't reply much to begin with but once they'd both had a couple of drinks, the conversation started to flow again, and after several more they were back to laughing and joking as normal. And also as normal, Rachel woke up the next morning late and hungover.

It was just after six a.m. on the morning of the summer party and Rachel hadn't slept well. She looked at the clock for what felt like the hundredth time and tried to go back to sleep. After a few minutes she gave up and got up to make a cup of coffee. She sat at the kitchen table in a pair of oversized pyjamas staring blearily out of the window. There wasn't much to see really, just back walls and a few small patches of grass, but the familiarity of it was quite comforting.

She ran through the day ahead in her mind. Harry was coming over around six thirty to get ready and she was going to spend an easy day doing a bit of shopping and generally pottering about. She had a bit of work to do on the Beau Street report, but that could wait until Sunday evening.

She'd decided to wear a pretty safe black dress and heels, not too short or showing too much flesh. She'd booked a pedicure and blow dry, though, as well groomed was definitely the order of the day. That would take up most of the afternoon. But she was tired, so maybe she could squeeze in a quick nap before lunch to make up for the tossing and turning of the night before. God, men were lucky. Harry would have a five minute shower, run some gel through his hair and that would be it.

She'd really wanted to talk to Harry about how important it was to her that the summer party went smoothly, but she hadn't dare mention it again. They were bound to just end up rowing. Plus she didn't want to make the evening bigger than it was. It was just a party after all. She'd managed to talk to Rowan briefly when she rang to check his ticket had arrived. He'd promised to keep an eye on Harry and that had made her feel slightly better.

Rachel did go back to bed and slept so heavily that she was almost late for her beauty appointments. Her vision of spending a relaxing afternoon being pampered was ruined by the fact that she had to run for ten minutes once she got off the bus and arrived at the salon out of breath and sweating. But after a couple of hours of massage and magazines, she began to feel quite mellow. She had a long bath when she got home, and by the time Harry arrived she was feeling calm and actually starting to look forward to the party.

She opened the door to Harry in her dressing gown, as she was saving putting her dress on until the last minute.

'Just got up?' Harry asked.

'Ha, ha,' said Rachel, mildly irritated by the remark considering how long she'd spent doing her hair and make-up. As Harry walked past her into the living room, a strong smell of alcohol wafted in his wake.

'Where have you been?' Rachel asked.

'Football, great match.'

Harry wandered unsteadily into the kitchen, took two slices of bread out of the bread bin and put them in the toaster. 'God, I'm starving. I only had a pasty for lunch,' he said.

Rachel followed him into the kitchen and popped the bread back up. 'Harry, we're about to go out for dinner!'

Harry popped the slices back down again. 'I'm hungry now. And besides, I need a cheese toastie, not some fillet of fish with a load of rabbit food.'

Rachel hesitated, trying to decide how best to react. She could tell Harry had already had quite a few drinks and the last thing she wanted was a row before they'd even left the house. Plus he should probably eat something.

'Alright,' she said, 'but don't take ages – our taxi will be here in half an hour.'

Rachel was relieved to see Harry wolf down his sandwich and head in the direction of the shower. She'd already left out his black tie suit on the bed. True to form, Harry was out of the shower and getting dressed five minutes later. He walked back into the sitting room and stood in front of her, glaring.

'What?' Rachel asked.

Harry looked down at his feet. His suit trousers were at least an inch too short.

'Oh shit!' said Rachel.

'Yes, oh shit!' Harry replied.

'I told you to try them, you idiot,' said Rachel.

'You're the idiot that measured them,' retorted Harry. 'Honestly, how hard can it be to get right?'

'Well, if you'd stood still for ten seconds rather than dancing around like an eel on speed, I might have had a better chance of getting the measurements right.'

'Well, I'm not going wearing these.'

Rachel felt slightly panicked. What a start to the evening.

'They aren't that short. Let me have a look.' She loosened the fastener on the waistband of the trousers and pulled them down so they sat a bit lower on Harry's waist. 'Look, that's better.'

Harry looked down and seemed marginally placated by the adjustment.

'The taxi will be here soon. Why don't you watch TV while I put my dress on? I'll get you a beer.'

Rachel quickly grabbed a beer out of the fridge and turned on the sports channel before there was any more talk of not going. She jumped into her dress and had just finished getting ready when the doorbell rang. Harry finished his beer and much to Rachel's relief they left. As Harry walked in front of her to the taxi his beer-induced sway seemed to accentuate the shortness of his trousers. Rachel shook her head.

The summer party was being held in a magnificent Georgian hall in the centre of London. Between the columns at the front were burning torches that were flicking gently in the light wind and Rachel could see an enormous sweeping staircase inside. Her heart started pounding slightly. The two doormen who greeted them were dressed in fairly comical outfits that included red socks, knee-length britches with tassels at the bottom, gold jackets and pointed red hats. Seemingly unaware of the fancy-dress-like qualities of their outfits, they greeted Harry and Rachel with very solemn nods and waved them in the direction of the great staircase.

'Christ, this place is posh,' said Harry.

'I think it's beautiful,' said Rachel. 'Look at those paintings on the staircase.'

Large gilt-edged portraits of regal men and women regarded them from the middle of ornate panels as they climbed the staircase.

'It feels like they're all staring at me,' said Harry. 'Freaky load of old, dead people.'

As they reached the top of the stairs there was a

waitress holding a tray of champagne while an efficient-looking lady in a black trouser suit from Rachel's office was discreetly checking invitations. Rachel took a glass of champagne.

'Do you have any beer?' Harry asked the waitress.

Rachel cringed.

The poker-faced waitress didn't. She smiled politely at Harry. 'Certainly, sir. They will have beer at the bar in the Rose Room where you're having your pre-dinner drinks.'

'Thank you,' said Rachel.

She put her arm through Harry's, straightened her back slightly and guided him through into the Rose Room. The room was already full of people chatting and laughing. Harry made a beeline for the bar and ordered a beer. Rachel looked around for people she knew and was relieved to spot Rowan and Shali standing on the far side of the room. Shali had clearly not gone for the safe dress option like Rachel. She was wearing a very short silver puffball dress with a plunging neckline and a pair of sparkly slingback shoes.

'Wow, look at you,' said Rachel to Shali as they kissed each other on both cheeks.

Harry and Rowan shook hands.

'Thanks, you look fab too,' said Shali.

She also hugged Harry and Rachel noticed her momentary glance at his trouser length.

Harry looked at Shali's dress and gave Rowan an approving nod.

Rowan grinned. 'Thanks so much for inviting me,' he said to all of them. 'What a great place!'

'I had a look at the seating plan. We aren't together but both our tables are okay, no total losers,' said Shali.

'Thank God,' said Rachel. 'Do you remember last year? I had that miserable bloke Michael Morray and his wife on my table. They were such hard work. He hardly said a word all night. I hit all my best tennis balls of conversation over the net but none of them got returned. She was a vegan and hated that we were all eating beef. She also clearly thought that it was our fault that her husband worked too hard and she never saw him.'

'If I had a wife like that, I'd never be home either,' said Harry. 'I'd just stay in the office all day eating bacon sandwiches.'

They all laughed and Rachel was pleased that Harry seemed relaxed.

There was then a loud knocking noise.

'Ladies and gentleman, dinner is served,' bellowed a small, rotund man standing in the doorway to the Rose Room.

'Great, I'm starving,' said Rowan. They found their places on the seating plan and went into the Great Hall. Huge chandeliers hung above circular tables decorated with crisp, white tablecloths and strikingly tall red roses. A string quartet was playing soft, lilting music.

'See you after dinner,' Rowan said to Rachel and he squeezed her arm as if to say good luck.

Rachel and Harry found their table, which they were sharing with three other couples. Marcus, Simon and Louise were all from her department and here with their other halves, none of whom she knew. She and

Marcus were the most senior people. Much to Rachel's relief there were no partners on her table.

Rachel could see Rowan and Shali's table from where she was sitting and Rowan was busy walking round shaking hands with the other people on his table. He's so polite, thought Rachel. By contrast, Harry had sat down already and was studying the menu.

'Thank fuck for that! It's lamb,' said Harry to no one in particular.

The others looked slightly shocked.

'Oh, shall we do introductions?' said Rachel quickly. 'This is Harry. He's my, er, partner.' Boyfriend somehow sounded a bit tacky all of a sudden.

'Hi,' said Harry, raising his hand like he was answering a question at school but without actually looking up from the menu.

Marcus followed Rachel. 'Good evening, everyone. I'm Marcus and this is my wife Melissa.'

Rachel paid close attention as they all introduced themselves, repeating their names in an effort to remember them all. Good networking practice. Harry focused, instead, on pouring the wine, his glass first.

To Rachel's relief, dinner was relatively uneventful. Marcus' wife fortunately asked Harry what he did, giving him the opportunity to exaggerate and show off at the same time, two of his favourite pastimes. But he didn't offend anyone and the stories he entertained the table with were just about decent.

After dinner the disco began playing and people started to move about between tables.

'Come on, let's mingle,' said Rachel.

They went and found Shali and Rowan who were chatting at the bar in the Great Hall.

'Rowan, why don't you stay with Harry for a bit while Shali and I do the work rounds,' said Rachel.

'Great plan,' said Harry, turning to order at the bar. 'Large scotch, no ice. Rowan, what are you drinking?'

'Your brother's a good laugh,' said Shali as they walked away.

'Yes, and he's married, don't forget,' said Rachel.

'I know, calm down. I'm just saying he's great company,' said Shali.

'Yes, you're right, he is. Look, catch you in a bit — I'm off to chat to a few people.'

Rachel circulated around the room, making sure she said hello to most of the partners and anyone else she felt was important. Harry had started off drinking at the bar with Rowan, but the last time she'd looked over he was talking to Paul from the post room. Harry had a habit of making new best friends at this sort of event, particularly those who hung out at the bar and liked sport. Paul fitted the bill perfectly. She could see them drinking and laughing and was slightly concerned that things might get a bit out of hand, but at least it left her free to chat.

'Hello, Rachel, are you having fun?'

Rachel turned round. It was Carl Stephens and his wife. Rachel composed herself.

'Hello, Carl, and you must be Sarah, very nice to meet you.' Rachel held her hand out to an attractive but unremarkable woman in a flowery dress with short dark hair that feathered around her face.

'Hello, are you in Carl's team?' Sarah seemed genuinely interested.

'Yes, I am. We're working on a project together at the moment, so he's keeping my nose well and truly to the grindstone.'

Sarah laughed. 'Don't you listen to him. He's a right old softie underneath.'

Carl looked slightly uncomfortable and was about to reply when Rowan walked past them. Rachel grabbed him, pleased to be able to change the subject.

'Carl, can I introduce you to my brother, Rowan. He's here as Shali's guest. Rowan, this is Carl Stephens. He's one of the partners in my office.'

'Ah yes, so he is, pleased to make your acquaintance, Mr Stephens.' Rowan was slurring his words as he spoke. 'Sorry if I seem a bit drunk,' he continued. 'That's because I am. Haven't been out that much lately — you know, new baby and all that. Seems I've turned into a bit of a cheap date in the meantime.'

'How lovely, a new baby. Is it your first?' Sarah asked.

'Yes, well, that I know about anyway!' Rowan laughed and tried to punch Sarah on the arm but missed and stumbled sideways a bit. 'Sorry, think I better carry on my journey to the gents' before I fall over completely. Very nice to meet you. And try not to spend too much time in hotel bars now, will you, Carl, hey?'

Rowan winked clumsily at Carl and wandered away in the direction of the gents'.

Carl looked shocked and Rachel was both mortified and speechless at the same time.

'What did he mean by that?' Sarah asked.

'I have no idea,' answered Carl. 'Rachel, it seems that your brother can't take his drink.'

'I'm so sorry,' said Rachel. 'He's not normally like that at all. I think he's just a bit worn out by his new baby and a bit out of practice as he hasn't been going out much for the last few months. I'll make sure he doesn't have any more.'

'Yes, you do that,' said Carl and spun away to talk to another group of people.

Rachel marched over to Harry at the bar.

'What on earth have you done to Rowan? He can hardly stand up!' Rachel said.

'I haven't done anything. We've just been having a very nice evening, as instructed,' said Harry. 'Rachel, meet Paul. Other than being a Reds fan he's a great bloke. We share the same taste in whisky, which is lucky.'

Harry was obviously now very drunk too.

'Yes, we know each other, thank you.'

Paul nodded at her with his chin resting on his hand. 'Just making sure my head doesn't fall off,' he said.

Paul and Harry both starting laughing.

'Really,' said Rachel.

'And Paul thinks my trousers are rather cool, don't you?'

Harry got off his bar stool and paraded up and down, hitching up his trousers to make them look even shorter. A few people looked round at him.

'Harry, we're going to leave very soon. So just sit

down and stay here while I track down Shali.' She didn't want him wandering around in that state.

Harry sat back down. 'Why would I go anywhere? I'm at my favourite bar, with my favourite mate and my favourite whisky. This is a bloody great night.'

Rachel was fuming. Why was Harry incapable of drinking in moderation? And worse still, he'd got Rowan drunk too. She couldn't believe Rowan had mentioned the whole hotel thing to Carl in front of his wife. It was definitely time to go.

Rachel walked around the Great Hall a couple of times looking for Shali. She couldn't see her. Maybe she was in the ladies'. When she didn't find her there either, she checked the Rose Room. That was empty and being cleared up. Where was she?

Rachel was walking back towards the Great Hall when she heard laughing coming from a corridor just off to the side. She walked over and looked round the corner. Rowan and Shali were coming out of the door of a small anteroom. Shali had her arm round Rowan's waist and was nuzzling his neck as they walked.

They stopped dead as soon as they saw her.

'Where the hell have you two been?' Rachel asked.

She looked at their faces and their dishevelled clothes and suddenly realised what a stupid question that was.

'Oh my God, no, I don't believe it!' Rachel looked at them in shock.

Shali looked at the floor and Rowan stepped hurriedly sideways, dropping Shali's arm from his waist.

Before Rachel could say anything else, two waiters walked down the corridor carrying trays of glasses.

'Can we help you with something?'

'We were just, um, looking for the ladies',' said Rachel.

'They're over there, on the left. This is the way to the kitchens.'

'Oh yes, thanks, sorry,' said Rachel, ushering Rowan and Shali back towards the Great Hall where she grabbed Harry.

'Right, get your coats, we're going outside to flag down a black cab. This evening is turning into a right bloody disaster,' said Rachel, forcing herself to keep her voice down.

The four of them got into the taxi in silence. Harry soon fell asleep, shortly followed by Rowan. Rachel couldn't bring herself to look at Shali, who said nothing until the taxi reached her road.

'Just here on the left thanks,' Shali said to the taxi driver as Rowan woke up. 'Good night everyone.'

Only Rowan replied.

Rachel prodded Harry as they reached his flat. He looked out the window.

'Can't I come to yours? It's still early.' He tried to put his arm round Rachel.

She pushed him away. 'No you can't, and you have no idea what time it is,' said Rachel.

'Yes I have, it's…' Harry peered at his watch, trying to focus enough to see the hands. 'No, you're right, no bloody idea.'

'Harry, go home. Call me tomorrow when you get up.'

Reluctantly Harry got out of the cab.

The taxi dropped off Rachel next.

'I'll call *you* tomorrow,' she said, scowling at Rowan as she got out of the taxi. Rowan nodded sheepishly.

When she got into her flat, she sat down on the sofa and put her head in her hands. Despite the fact that she'd had a few drinks, she felt stone cold sober. What would Carl have made of Rowan's remark about hotel bars? What if he'd seen her when she walked into the pillar in the hotel reception? The crash was so loud that they were bound to have looked round. And then there was Rowan and Shali. How could they? How could Rowan? Rachel couldn't decide which nightmare she was most unhappy about.

She shivered: it was late and she was cold. She crawled slowly into bed and pulled the duvet up over her head in an attempt to block out the images that were dancing through her head.

CHAPTER 8

The next day was Sunday. Rachel decided it might not be best to ring Rowan at home, so she sent him a text message instead: *Call me when you can, R*. She resisted the temptation to add 'Judas' at the end: too melodramatic.

Rowan rang after lunch.

'Hi, it's me.' His voice sounded croaky.

'Hi, can you talk?' Rachel asked.

'Yes, I'm in the park with Naomi. Laura's having a lie down.'

'How are you?' Rachel asked.

'Feeling sick as a dog,' said Rowan. 'You?'

'Not bad, a bit rough round the edges but could be worse.' She couldn't keep up the polite chat for long. 'God, Rowan, I can't believe you and Shali. What were you thinking?'

'Rachel, it's none of your business,' said Rowan.

'What do you mean it's none of my business? It was me who invited you, it was my work party and you were with my friend. How much more of my business could it be?' Rachel was furious.

'I mean that it's my business to sort it out,' said Rowan.

'Oh really, and how exactly do you intend to do that?'

'Look, I really didn't mean for anything to happen. I had too much to drink and just got carried away,' said Rowan, not answering the question.

'That's no bloody excuse! What are you going to do now, leap on someone every time you drink too much?'

'No, of course not.'

'Well, why did you do it then?'

'I don't know. It just sort of happened,' said Rowan.

'These things don't just happen, Rowan — you've got to want them to happen. And what about Laura?' Rachel asked.

'Laura and I haven't been getting on that well lately. She just seems to have, well, you know, lost interest in me. All she cares about is Naomi.' His voice cracked as he spoke.

Rachel paused slightly. He sounded pretty upset. Well, he deserves to be, she thought, and carried on. 'I also can't believe that comment you made to Carl Stephens, and in front of his wife, about not spending too much time in hotel bars. Are you trying to get me sacked?'

'Shit, Rachel, did I? I don't remember that at all. I'm so sorry, what an idiot. Did he figure out that we saw him?'

'I don't know. He looked pretty cross, though. I'll have to see how he is tomorrow, I guess, and just try to bluff my way through it. Thanks for nothing.'

'I am sorry, Rachel, really I am.'

Rachel couldn't bring herself to say it was okay. 'What are you going to do now?'

'I don't know. I think I'd better tell Laura what's happened.'

'Christ, Rowan, don't do that!'

'Why not? You think I should just lie to her?'

'Well, oh I don't know. I just think piling in with a confession straight off the bat might not be the best plan. What if she walks out on you?'

'Don't say that, Rachel. Shit, what a mess.'

'Are you going to see Shali again?'

'Absolutely not! It was a stupid one-off.'

It sounded like he was trying to convince himself.

'Look, don't say anything to Laura. Why don't you try to book yourselves a weekend away somewhere? Spend a bit of time together and try to sort things out. Mum would love to have Naomi,' Rachel suggested.

'I'm not sure that Laura would agree to be away from Naomi for that long.' Rowan didn't sound that enamoured by the idea either.

'Well, you can try. Talk to her, Rowan. Tell her you miss spending time with her. We girls love all that sort of stuff.'

'Alright, I'll try,' said Rowan reluctantly. 'Do you think I should call Shali, and well, you know, apologise or something?'

'No! Don't do that. I'll speak to her tomorrow.'

Rachel was afraid that if they spoke it might spark things off rather than cool things down.

'Don't be cross with her, Rachel. It isn't her fault.'

'Well, I am cross. She should know better and she's meant to be my friend.'

'Rachel, please, this is bad enough without you two falling out. Promise me you won't shout at her.'

'Alright, I won't shout. I can't promise that I won't speak rather loudly, though.'

Rowan sighed. 'Look, I've got to go, Naomi's crying. I really am sorry, Rachel. I feel just awful about last night. And tell Shali that I'm not that sort of bloke, really I'm not.'

'I know,' said Rachel. 'Let's speak in a few days, okay?'

'Okay,' said Rowan and they hung up.

Rachel sat looking at the phone. She was sure Rowan did feel awful but he was right, what a mess. Damn Harry; she was sure he was partly to blame by getting Rowan so drunk in the first place.

Harry came round later that afternoon and collapsed on a chair in the kitchen as she made bacon sandwiches for them both.

'Well, I feel bloody awful,' he said cheerfully. 'Anyway, it was actually not a bad night for one of your work dos. And I think you'll agree that I was pretty well behaved. I didn't fall over or insult anyone and you had plenty of time to go off hobnobbing. I didn't even make a fuss about the fact that you got me a suit that made me look a total arse.'

Harry got up and put his arms around Rachel's waist and kissed the back of her neck as she fried the bacon. 'So how were you thinking of rewarding my good behaviour?' he asked, pushing himself up against her.

Rachel stiffened and then turned round.

Harry stepped backwards slightly.

'Harry, last night was a total disaster.'

'Was it? Why?' Harry looked confused.

'How did Rowan end up getting so drunk?'

Harry grinned. 'He was rubbish at spoof, kept losing and it was a double shot penalty each time.'

'You played drinking games?'

'We had to amuse ourselves somehow while you were off brown-nosing with the big chiefs,' replied Harry.

'I was not brown-nosing, I was circulating; there's a big difference. And anyway, it's important that I catch up with the right people at these things. I don't get that many opportunities as we're all so busy.'

'So you keep telling me,' said Harry. 'Anyway, what's wrong with a few drinking games?'

'Well, Rowan was off his face thanks to you, and as a result he and Shali ended up in some side room and, well, you know…'

She hadn't told Harry about seeing Carl Stephens in the hotel over lunch, so there seemed little point in also mentioning Rowan's unhelpful comments.

'He never did! The old dog. He did say that Shali had been coming on to him a bit during dinner.'

Rachel looked at Harry in surprise. 'Did he? What did he say?'

'Nothing much, just that she was flirting with him and that if he wanted to he could probably get off with her. He asked me what I thought,' said Harry.

'What did you say?'

'I told him he should grab it with both hands, make

hay while the sun shined, so to speak. Sounds like he did just that,' said Harry, laughing.

'You did not!' Rachel was horrified.

'I did — what's wrong with that? He's a big boy. He can make his own decisions.'

'Did you not think about the fact that he's married and has a new baby?'

'That's his lookout. And anyway, that wasn't what he asked me,' said Harry.

'So that's your view of marriage is it — doesn't matter when it comes to a quick shag. If you're offered it on a plate, you take it?' Rachel couldn't hide the warning note in her voice.

'Rachel, this isn't about me, it's about Rowan,' said Harry, shifting uncomfortably.

'I know it is, but you got him drunk and you encouraged him.'

'Oh right, so it's my fault now, is it? I knew you'd end up finding something wrong about last night. Never mind how hard I try, still not right for perfect Rachel,' said Harry, glaring at her.

'Last night was you trying hard, was it? I'd hate to see what you'd be like on a night when you didn't try then. You could hardly stand up by the end of the evening.'

Rachel felt close to tears. Harry took his sandwich and they ate in silence.

'Think maybe I should go after this,' he said after a pause.

'No, don't,' said Rachel. Maybe she was being a bit harsh blaming it all on Harry. 'I'm sorry, you're probably right: it is Rowan's mess to sort out. He said the same thing. It's just all a bit too close to home for my liking,' said Rachel.

'Did anyone else from work see them?' Harry asked.

'No, I don't think so,' said Rachel.

'Well, you see that's okay then. It can be just you and Shali's little secret.'

'And Rowan says he's not going to see her again. I've got to tell her that tomorrow.'

Maybe then it will just blow over, thought Rachel. And maybe with a bit of luck Carl will think Rowan was just a rambling drunk.

'I guess there's not much point worrying about it,' said Rachel.

'Correct,' said Harry. 'Now come here and let me make you feel better.'

Rachel decided she'd better go into the office on Monday morning rather than going straight out to Beau Street. She sent AJ a text saying that she'd see them about lunchtime. That would give her time to talk to Shali and hopefully also check out the lie of the land with Carl. She stood in a long line of people patiently waiting to place over-complex coffee orders with the overworked coffee shop staff. There should be two queues, Rachel thought for the hundredth time: one for those who wanted a tall, decaf latte, extra hot with no foam and hazelnut syrup, and one for those, like her, who just wanted a black coffee.

She got into the lift with Pauline Rowe.

'How's the training for the ten-k going?' Pauline asked, smiling.

'Yes, not bad thanks. Did a bit of training yesterday. Legs aren't too bad today, so I guess that's progress,' said Rachel.

'What time are you aiming for?'

Christ! Rachel had no idea. She could vaguely remember marathon times, some people saying they wanted to run in under four hours or something. That was for twenty-six miles. How many kilometres was that? Rachel quickly tried to do the maths in her head.

'Oh about, er, forty minutes, something like that.'

By the look on Pauline's face, she'd clearly got the maths wrong.

'Gosh that's fast,' said Pauline. 'You must be a very good runner.'

'Well, you know, I try,' said Rachel.

Thankfully the lift doors opened and Rachel quickly walked away to her desk.

She couldn't see Shali anywhere; maybe she was working on another floor. She was probably trying to avoid her. Bad luck, thought Rachel, and rang her.

'We need to talk,' she said. No point beating around the bush.

'I'm working in a meeting room today as I need to be near the team up here. It's just me, so why don't you pop up,' said Shali.

Rachel could tell that Shali was nervous as soon as she opened the door.

'Hi,' said Shali. 'Coffee?'

'No thanks, just had one,' said Rachel.

They looked at each other for a few moments.

'Look, I know you aren't happy about me and

Rowan,' said Shali eventually. 'But I didn't exactly force him, you know.'

'You took advantage of him,' said Rachel.

'I did not! He made his own choice. It's not my fault his marriage isn't working.'

'Shali, he was drunk and feeling lonely and you threw yourself at him,' said Rachel, her voice shaking with anger.

'How do you know? You weren't there. It was him that made the first move!' Shali retorted.

'You could have said no,' said Rachel.

'Why should I? I'm single and he's gorgeous. Nothing wrong with that.'

'What about his wife?' Rachel asked.

'What about her? Maybe she should have paid him a bit more attention and then this might not have happened.'

'Shali, that's a bloody awful thing to say. She's just had a baby!' Rachel was conscious that she was shouting now.

'Shh! There are people in the next room. All I'm saying is that it's not my fault. If you don't like your brother's attitude to marriage, take it up with him, not me,' said Shali, and she sat down and crossed her arms.

'I have. I spoke to him yesterday.'

Shali's face softened. 'How was he?'

'Awful, he feels absolutely terrible. He wanted to call you and apologise but I said I'd talk to you instead.'

'Why would he need to apologise to me?' said Shali. 'I'm telling you, Rach, definitely no apology needed this end.' Shali grinned.

Rachel didn't think that was funny. 'Shali, I don't

want to know. Anyway, he asked me to tell you that it was just a one-off and that he doesn't want to see you again. Sorry to be so blunt.'

'Is that what he said?' Shali asked.

'Pretty much. He's going to try to work things out with Laura.'

'Oh, I see.' Shali stared out of the window. 'I got the impression he really liked me.'

Rachel wasn't sure what to say. 'Well, I'm sure he did, at that moment, but it's all a bit different in the cold light of day.'

Shali didn't say anything.

'Anyway, I think it was a pretty crap thing to do. He's not a free agent, so you need to forget about him and move on, okay?'

'Guess so,' said Shali.

'I mean it, Shali. It's not going anywhere.'

'Fine, fine,' said Shali. 'Is that it? Lecture over?'

'Yes, that's it,' said Rachel.

'Well, I'd better get on then,' said Shali.

'Me too,' said Rachel and left the room.

She headed off in the direction of Carl Stephen's office. He was just walking along the corridor back to his office as she arrived.

'Hi, Carl, how are you?'

'Oh, you know, alright,' he said, smiling at her.

Not too bad a reaction, thought Rachel. She took a deep breath. 'Look, Carl, I'm really sorry about Saturday night and my brother being a bit stumbling drunk. He's really not usually like that. He was just a bit, well, overtired.'

'Oh don't worry about it,' said Carl. 'I remember when we had our first baby, bit of a culture shock.'

'Yes, I think it has been. It all just caught up with him a bit. Did your wife enjoy herself?'

Rachel looked at Carl's face: not a flicker of a reaction.

'Yes she did, thanks. It's always nice for other halves to be able to put faces to the names they hear about so much.'

Rachel was relieved. It didn't seem like Rowan's comments had caused any big problems.

'Good, I'm off to lunch soon — not that far away from Beau Street, actually. Maybe I should pop in afterwards and have a look at the latest version of our report?' Carl asked.

'Oh gosh, I'm not sure we're quite ready for you yet. Maybe in a couple more days. Going anywhere nice?'

'The Brook Hotel. Do you know it?'

Rachel was a bit taken aback by the mention of the hotel. She tried hard not to show it. 'Er, yes, a bit. Quite good I've heard.'

'Yes it is, one of my favourites actually.'

'Oh right,' said Rachel. She had no idea how else to respond.

'Anyway, let me know what time works for you and I'll start having a look through the report,' said Carl.

'Yes, I will,' said Rachel.

Carl went into his office and Rachel went back to her desk. Was he meeting Audrey again? Maybe she should find out.

CHAPTER 9

It was nearly lunchtime by the time Rachel got out to Beau Street. As she arrived, the security guard stuck his head out of his office.

'Morning, Ms Altman. How are you today?'

'Yes, fine thanks. You?'

'Mustn't grumble,' he said. 'Mind you, forecast is for rain later. Make sure you have a brolly with you when you leave.'

What was it with him and the weather? Rachel thought. It was probably just his way of making conversation. She didn't have an umbrella with her but thought it best not to mention it.

'Thank you for letting me know. I'll make sure I do that,' she replied.

AJ and Rosa were in the project room working on a draft of their report.

'Hi, guys. How's it going? Did you enjoy the summer party?' Rachel asked.

'Yes, we had a great time, thanks,' said Rosa. 'Really

good night. The disco was fab. You couldn't get old AJ here off the dance floor.'

'Luckily I was surrounded by people who couldn't dance either, so it wasn't too obvious I was rubbish,' said AJ.

'Yes it was!' said Rosa. 'You were the only one sliding across the dance floor on your knees playing an air guitar.'

'Hey, that's a cool move. Everyone loves a bit of air guitar.'

'I heard there was some gossip too,' said Rosa.

'Really, what?' Rachel asked.

'Well apparently someone overheard one of the bar staff saying that they'd seen a couple from our party sneaking off into one of the side rooms. They were all having a right laugh about it.'

'Who was it?' said AJ.

'I don't know. Everyone's dying to find out,' said Rosa.

'You know, the partners take a really dim view of that sort of thing at work events. After all, they're paying for everything. Hardly professional. I bet they'll want to know who it was,' said AJ.

Rachel sat down. God, Shali would be mortified; she was bound to hear the story. Rachel wasn't going to be the one to tell her and there was no point telling Rowan. She really didn't need to get embroiled in some office scandal but it was a bit hard to avoid when one of the people involved was her brother.

'That's awful,' said Rachel, thinking aloud.

'It's not awful; it serves them right,' said AJ. 'They should pay for a room like everybody else.'

AJ and Rosa both laughed.

Rachel thought she'd better change the subject. 'I saw Carl in the office this morning and he was talking about reviewing the report. When shall I tell him it might be ready?'

'I need at least a few more days,' said AJ.

'Me too,' said Rosa.

'Okay, I'll tell him next week, but we need to crack on. He needs to agree everything before we present to Equinox.'

Rachel felt a bit guilty that she'd spent all morning trying to paper over the cracks from the summer party and not working on her part of the report. 'I had a few things to sort out in the office this morning from one of my other projects, so I'll stay a bit later this evening to catch up,' she said.

The others nodded.

'But I've just got a couple of things to follow up on from my meetings last week, so I'm going for wander to see a few people. Back in a bit,' said Rachel.

She wanted to see if Audrey Fox was in. She walked down towards her desk; it was empty. One of the other nurses was working at a nearby desk.

'Excuse me, is Audrey Fox in, do you know?' Rachel asked.

'She's out for lunch,' replied the nurse.

'Oh, okay. What time is she expected back?'

'I think she's picking up some lab results after lunch, so she said she'd be back in around four o' clock. Can I take a message for you?'

'No, that's okay. I'll pop back later.'

I bet she's with Carl, thought Rachel. Now what should she do? She really had no idea.

Not much was said that afternoon as Rachel, AJ and Rosa worked hard assimilating the information they'd been given and drafting sections of their report.

'My section reads pretty well,' said AJ. 'The business has been doing well, plenty of growth in some of these newer procedures. The doctors I spoke to were all pretty confident that the market for this sort of cosmetic surgery was on the up. You've only got to pick up a newspaper or magazine to see what they mean — it's everywhere.'

Rachel's analysis looked good too. Lloyd Cassidy did stand out as being a bit of a star, but there was nothing wrong with that. The buyers would be delighted to have a doctor whose reputation meant he could charge more than everyone else.

AJ and Rosa started packing up their things shortly after six o' clock. Rachel stayed at her desk working for another hour. She finished writing quite a long section and decided to get a cup of coffee. Most of the offices were empty as she wandered down the corridor. The coffee machine was in the same room as the photocopier, a small room crowded full of boxes and notices reminding people to keep the sink clean. The machine spat out a sludgy looking drink in a brownish-yellow plastic cup. Rachel stood for a few minutes warming her hands on the cup, reading a poster about the charity fun run that Beau Street were having later that month. As she did, she heard voices and a door bang not far away. Who was still here? she wondered.

Rachel walked down the corridor in the opposite direction to where she'd come from, towards the doctors' offices. The offices were separated by glass partitions and she could see a light on in Lloyd Cassidy's office. As she got closer she could hear Lloyd talking to someone.

'She'll be here in a few minutes. I told her to ring my mobile when she's outside, so then you can pop down and get her,' said Lloyd.

'Yes, no problem,' said a smooth voice that Rachel instantly recognised as belonging to Audrey Fox.

Rachel walked quietly into an office not quite opposite Lloyd's. The light in that office was off and she could see quite clearly into Lloyd's. She was pretty sure they wouldn't be able to see her but she stood behind the coat stand just in case. Why am I hiding? she thought. She didn't know why; it just seemed like the right thing to do. After a few moments, she heard a mobile phone ring.

'Lloyd Cassidy.' There was a short pause, then, 'Ah, Francesca darling, well done, you found us. My assistant will be right down to let you in.'

Audrey hurried off in the direction of the lifts. After a few minutes Rachel heard the lift doors open and two female voices talking. She could tell one was Audrey but she also recognised the other voice. Surely it wasn't going to be someone she knew; that would be too weird. As they walked past her and into Lloyd's office Rachel tried to get a good look at the other woman. She was wearing a white trench coat with the collar turned up and sunglasses. Her long, brown hair bobbed from side to side as she walked. Rachel was sure she knew her. Francesca, that's what Lloyd had said. She racked her brains. Who did she know called Francesca? She couldn't think of anyone.

She watched as the three of them sat down in Lloyd's office. Audrey shut the door so she couldn't hear what was being said but she could still see them quite clearly. After a few minutes of the woman talking, Lloyd took off her sunglasses and began examining her face. Rachel watched as he spun her chair round to the side so he could look at her profile, putting her face into full view. Rachel's hand flew to her mouth. Oh my God! It was Francesca Hart, the actress. How could she have been so stupid! No wonder she looked familiar. She was only one of the most photographed women in the world. Wow, not a hint of a celebrity anywhere and now suddenly a serious A-lister!

By the looks of it, she was booking in for a nose job. Lloyd spent a few minutes taking photographs of her face and then Francesca opened her bag and took out a large brown envelope and handed it to Audrey. As Audrey opened it, Rachel could see it was full of cash. Lloyd got up from his desk and took a key out from under a small square vase on his mantelpiece. He used it to unlock one of the large drawers in his pedestal desk and took out a black leather book. The three of them were deep in conversation and there was lots of nodding as Lloyd carefully wrote things down in the black book. That book must be some form of manual record, thought Rachel.

Eventually they finished talking and Lloyd put the

book and the envelope of cash back in the drawer. He locked it and put the key back under the vase. Francesca got up to leave and Lloyd opened the door.

'You're welcome, my dear. It's no trouble at all,' he said.

Audrey disappeared with Francesca, presumably to show the actress out of the building, and then came back. Lloyd and Audrey stood talking for a few minutes. They spoke very quietly and Rachel couldn't hear what they were saying. Then they put their coats on and left.

Rachel sat down on the desk chair in the office she was in. She really wanted to see what was in that black book. But what if she got caught? She had no right to start sneaking around people's offices. She walked up and down the corridor a few times. There was nobody in any of the offices. It would only take her a couple of minutes to have a look at that book.

Before she had time to think about it too hard, she slipped into Lloyd's office. She took the key from under the vase and opened the drawer in his desk. Her hands were shaking as she opened the book. On each page were several columns of neatly written information. The first column contained a name, as did the second column. The next three columns contained details of different procedures, dates and amounts. She turned to the latest entry. It read: 'Francesca Hart, Sarah Riley, rhinoplasty, 25 May, £6,500'.

So they were recording that Francesca Hart was having a nose job in May costing six and a half grand, but who was Sarah Riley? Rachel couldn't make the link. Perhaps it was another client who'd recommended

Lloyd, or maybe it was someone else at Beau Street who was going to help. She would need to check both the client and staff records in the morning.

She quickly ran round to the photocopier and copied a couple of pages of the book so she had a few more entries to check out. Then she put the book back, locked up and scarpered back to their project room. She sat down, caught her breath and then looked at the photocopied pages. Was there anything wrong in keeping this sort of record? She couldn't think immediately that there was, but she was sure that something wasn't right. She packed up and headed to the lift. She pressed the lift button, but nothing happened. She then noticed the card reader at the side of the lift with a notice that said 'Please use out of office hours'. She put her temporary pass against the card reader. It didn't work. Shit!

She decided to try the stairs. There was no card reader on the staircase. As she trotted down the stairs she could hear the rain outside. The security guy had been right: she was going to get soaked. She got to the double doors at the bottom of the staircase where there was a large sign saying 'For emergency use only'. Did that mean the door was alarmed? She'd better not go that way.

She turned round, went up one floor and left the stairwell. There must be another way off the floor. She found another staircase and headed down that one. At the end she got to a single door with a push bar on it. There was no emergency use only sign. She put her hands against the glass and peered out of the door into the rain. The door led into the central office courtyard. Was there a way out from there? She couldn't remember.

She gently opened the door and nothing happened, so she wedged her briefcase in the doorway to stop the door shutting and sprinted round the courtyard looking for a way out. The puddles splashed water over her legs and the rain hurt her face. Where the fuck was the way out of this place! There were no external doors in the courtyard, so she came back inside. This was a nightmare. How hard could it be to get out of a building? She would just have to go out of the emergency doors. To hell with it.

She went back to the main staircase and through the double doors. She pushed the handle and the instant she did so the alarm went off. She felt an overwhelming desire to run but instead she shut the door behind her and walked slowly out into the car park. She was at the back of the building, so she started walking round to the front. She was cold and her hair was beginning to drip. She was just thinking that things couldn't get much worse when she saw the security guard running towards her with a torch. Shit!

'The alarm's gone off!' he shouted.

'Yes, I can hear it,' said Rachel, trying to look calm.

'You're working rather late.'

'Got a deadline to meet. You know how it is,' said Rachel, waiting for him to ask her how she'd got there. He didn't.

'And look at you, you're soaked. I told you that you needed a brolly,' he said.

'Yes you did, and as usual you were absolutely right.'

The security guard beamed. 'Well, truth is, I've always wanted to be a weather man, like one of those ones on the television. I read up on the weather all the time. This job just pays the bills. One day I'm going to get there.'

Rachel suddenly understood all that theatrical waving by the location map when they'd first arrived. He'd been practising! He had no chance of ever becoming a weather man but this didn't seem like the time for giving out career advice.

'I'm sure you will,' said Rachel, squeezing his damp arm.

'Right, better go and see what's set this damn alarm off before the police get here,' he said.

The police! Rachel hadn't thought about that. She'd better get out of there before they arrived. It had clearly not occurred to the security guard that she'd set the alarm off. The police were unlikely to be as stupid.

'Well, good luck sorting out the alarm. See you tomorrow,' said Rachel.

'Good night, Ms Altman,' said the security guard. 'And it should be sunnier tomorrow.'

God, I hope so, thought Rachel.

CHAPTER 10

The next evening, Rachel was sitting down in a wine bar not far from Beau Street with a bottle of wine and two glasses when Rowan arrived.

'You look exhausted,' she said.

'Not sleeping well,' Rowan replied.

'Naomi still waking you up?' Rachel asked.

'Actually, she's sleeping quite a bit better now,' said Rowan. 'I'm just having problems getting off — you know, lots on my mind. Typical, isn't it? Just as Naomi starts sleeping better, something else comes along to stress me out instead.'

Rachel resisted saying that he only had himself to blame. But he'd sounded pretty stressed when he rang, which is why she'd agreed to meet when she should have been working late.

'Has Laura noticed anything?' Rachel asked.

'Only me falling over myself to be nice to her,' said Rowan. 'Sometimes I think she should be able to smell the guilt on me, it feels that obvious. But she just thinks I'm making an effort, which I guess I am.'

'So you haven't told her?'

'No, not yet anyway. I'm going to see how it goes. Hopefully I can get things back on track without having to.'

Rowan didn't look that optimistic.

'I'm sure you can,' Rachel said. 'Did you speak to her about going away?'

'Yes, actually I did. She was surprisingly positive about it. In fact she seemed totally amazed that I'd even suggested it and when I gave her the spiel about wanting to spend more time with her on her own she was totally bowled over.'

'You see, not hard, is it? I should become a relationship counsellor,' said Rachel.

'You might still need to,' said Rowan. 'Long way to go yet. Anyway, the reason I wanted to see you was to ask a favour.'

'Shoot,' said Rachel.

'Well, Laura was fairly happy about leaving Naomi at Mum's but was a bit concerned that, well, sometimes Mum can be a bit dippy. She'd feel a lot happier if you were there as well.'

'Me! I don't know anything about babies. Why would she want me there?'

'She just thinks that you're smart and organised and that you'd be a big help to Mum — you know, check that she sticks with the schedule, pays attention, that sort of thing.'

'She managed to bring both of us up just fine,' said Rachel, suddenly feeling rather protective of her so-called dippy mother.

'Apart from when she left the back gate open and you ended up playing in the road by yourself until one of our neighbours brought you back. You were only four. Or when she forgot to get me from school and went to play bridge with her friends. It took the school three hours to get hold of someone to come and get me,' said Rowan.

'Alright, fair enough,' said Rachel, nodding. 'When were you thinking of going?'

'This weekend. Strike while the iron is, er, hot, so to speak.' Rowan realised he hadn't chosen the best expression.

'I'll need to take some work with me,' said Rachel, thinking of her report deadline.

'I'm sure that would be fine. Mum will be looking after Naomi most of the time.'

That might work quite well, thought Rachel. It would give her a chance to get plenty of work done away from the distraction of Harry.

'Okay, no problem. I'll go.'

'Thanks, Rachel, I'm really grateful,' said Rowan.

'I spoke to Shali, by the way, told her that you didn't want to see her again,' said Rachel.

'I know, she texted me,' said Rowan.

'She didn't! When?'

'The next day,' said Rowan.

'What for? What did she want?' Rachel asked anxiously.

'Oh nothing much, just to say sorry and check how I was.'

'Did you text her back?'

'Of course I did. I'm not that rude. Anyway, it was just pleasantries, nothing more.'

You don't know Shali, thought Rachel. She was furious. Shali needed to back off and leave Rowan alone.

'You're not going to see her again, are you?' Rachel asked.

'No I'm not, stop worrying. It's all about Laura now.'

'Hmm, well make sure you don't. I know what Shali's like; she'd have you twisted round her little finger before you know it.'

'For goodness sake, I'm not that easily led,' said Rowan.

Rachel just raised her eyebrows at him and said nothing.

'Anyway, I'm not seeing her, so let's not talk about it any more. Will you call Mum and square off this weekend with her?'

'Yes, I'll call her tonight.'

'Thanks, sis', you're a life saver.'

Let's hope I'm a marriage saver as well, thought Rachel.

She called her mum later that evening. Her mum was over the moon at the prospect of having both her daughter and granddaughter for the weekend. Rachel also broke the news to Harry, who was much less enthusiastic.

'What, a whole weekend again?'

'Rowan really needs to take Laura away and try to sort things out. They really want me to help Mum, so I said I would. Plus I've got a stack of work to do, so I wouldn't be much fun anyway even if I was here,' said Rachel.

'You and your work, honestly. Is it still that tits and arse job?'

'Cosmetic surgery job, I think you mean, and yes it is. We're reporting soon and there's a lot riding on it. I can't afford to miss the deadline.'

Rachel decided to tell Harry about seeing Francesca Hart. Perhaps if he thought the job was a bit more exciting he'd be less grumpy about her working on it all weekend.

'Look, Harry, you really mustn't say anything but you'll never guess who I saw when I was out there,' said Rachel.

'Who?' said Harry, intrigued.

'Only Francesca Hart. She came in one evening for some sort of private appointment when I was working late.'

'No!' said Harry. 'She's a total babe already. What on the earth is she having done?'

'A nose job, I think. It's not exactly huge now, just a bit prominent. I guess she wants one of those little button noses instead.'

'You should sell that story to the papers,' said Harry. 'It would be worth a fortune.'

Rachel was horrified at the suggestion. 'Don't be an idiot. I can't possibly do that. Not only am I bound by about a thousand ethical rules at work but it would also be illegal.'

'It's not illegal, not if you have evidence to support it.'

Rachel thought fleetingly about the photocopied pages from the black book, but then dismissed them firmly from her mind.

'Harry, we are not having this conversation. I only told you about it as a bit of work gossip. You are not to mention it to anyone, okay?'

'Okay, keep your hair on,' said Harry. 'So what am I supposed to do while you're at home beavering away on your "Celebrity doesn't get a nose job" report?' said Harry.

'Honestly, Harry, I've never known you be short of things to do. Stop being such a drama queen — it's only a weekend. And besides, I'll be back on Sunday afternoon, so we can still go out Sunday evening.'

'Alright, I guess I'll live. So can we go to Jimmy Macks on Sunday then? They've got a band on I really want to see,' said Harry.

Jimmy Macks was a scruffy pub turned club with beer on the floor and disgusting toilets. Rachel hated it. What a rubbish compromise.

'If you like,' she said.

'I like,' said Harry.

You would, thought Rachel.

As she lay in bed later, Rachel was still furious that Shali had been texting Rowan. She wasn't sure why it annoyed her so much. Maybe she was being unfair. She knew she should be equally livid with Rowan, but somehow she just wasn't.

She'd also found out from AJ that the venue had complained to Payne Stanley about 'inappropriate behaviour by certain guests', sending the office into a frenzy of rumours. What if the partners decided to launch an investigation? Would it matter that it was her brother? She didn't know and didn't want to find out. Maybe she should talk to Natalie, see what she thought. She was never short of an opinion.

Rachel got into Beau Street early the next morning so she could get enough work done to meet Natalie later on.

'Good morning, Ms Altman,' said the security guard as she arrived. 'Sun was up just after five a.m. today, not long after you, I think.'

'Good morning, Fred, busy day ahead,' said Rachel.

'You work too hard,' said Fred, shaking his head at her.

'Only as hard as I need to,' said Rachel.

She worked on her report without stopping for five straight hours. She got all her sales analysis finished and most of the expenses analysis too. She'd expected to find looking at the Beau Street cost base quite boring, but in fact had found it fascinating. She'd been shocked at the mark-up on Botox: it cost much less to buy than she'd thought. God, what a swizz. She bet most people had no idea. The salary information had been quite an eye-opener too. The doctors all did very nicely, thank you. And there were the big bills for incontinence pants. What was that all about? Rachel didn't know and didn't want to.

Once she was done, she decided to have a look at some of the names she'd written down from the pages of Lloyd Cassidy's black book. She obviously hadn't said anything to Rosa and AJ about her spying on the

Francesca Hart meeting or breaking into Lloyd's office. Hardly role model behaviour.

'Could I use the computer?' Rachel asked Rosa. They'd been given a computer with access to the accounting records so they could run sample accuracy tests on some of the databases.

'Yes, I'm done for the moment thanks,' replied Rosa.

Rachel started with the Francesca Hart entry. She searched the client database for her name. Nothing. Maybe they hadn't put it on the system yet; it had only been a day. She went to an entry from a month earlier: 'Lisa Albrecht, June Mayfield, breast augmentation, 22 April, £6,850'. She vaguely recognised the first name, so she did a quick internet search. Lisa Albrecht was a children's TV presenter. Rachel searched the client database for her name. Nothing. That was odd; her record should have been on the system by now. She searched again for the name June Mayfield. Bingo! A client record popped up on the screen. She looked at the details. The procedure listed was showing as 'other' and the invoice was shown as paid in cash. The doctor code was six-zero-two, Lloyd Cassidy.

Rachel was confused. What was the connection between June Mayfield and Lisa Albrecht? Why were they together in the black book? She didn't get it.

She checked the employee database for both names. Maybe there was a connection there. Neither came up. She sat back in her chair and stared out the window. What was she missing?

She hurried out into the accounts department

and pulled out the original invoice. It showed that June Mayfield had had breast augmentation on 22 April. What had happened to Lisa Albrecht? And then it was like someone had turned the light on – Rachel suddenly got it. They were the same person! Lisa Albrecht had been booked in under a false name. So that was the deal! Lloyd Cassidy was working for celebrities who would pay over the odds for total anonymity. By booking them in under a false name, there were no records that they'd ever had anything done. And that's why they had to pay in cash. Credit cards or cheques would show their real names. Christ! It was all a bit grubby, as well as totally unethical.

Rachel felt a bit sick. Her gut feeling had been right. There was an issue, a proper big ugly deal issue that she couldn't make go away. Shit, she would have to tell Carl, but if she did she'd have to deal with the Audrey question. Audrey was clearly right in the middle of some dodgy scam, and if Rachel was going to blow the whistle, she had to know for sure whether or not Carl was seeing her first. And what would they tell Equinox? No one was going to be happy. Fuck, fuck! What a nightmare!

Rachel needed some fresh air and decided to walk to meet Natalie. As she paced her way anxiously up and down the busy streets towards the tapas restaurant where they were meeting, she ran through her options. Maybe she should just do nothing. After all, no one else knew what she'd found or seen. If she did nothing then the deal would probably still happen. That would be better for her career. And if she did nothing, she wouldn't have to ask Carl about his relationship with Audrey. That would be better for her career too! Doing nothing was definitely an attractive option.

But it would be going against every ethical standard she'd ever been trained in. She was a professional and that meant she should investigate the matter thoroughly and report her findings, whatever the consequences. That would be the right and proper thing to do. Equinox could find out anyway after buying the business and then try to sue Payne Stanley for negligence or something. That would be a disaster. She should report what she knew.

But what if she did that and it fucked up her career? She had the director promotion panels coming up. Shopping her boss for shagging a dodgy client and killing his big deal at the same time hardly seemed like ideal preparation.

It was a total and utter mess. She decided she needed more time to think.

She was exhausted and starving by the time she met Natalie. 'I need food and soon, otherwise I might fall over,' said Rachel.

They grabbed a table in the corner of the restaurant where they ordered a jug of sangria and enough plates of tapas to feed a small army.

'Tough day?' Natalie asked.

Rachel thought about telling Natalie all about her Beau Street crisis but decided she needed to keep the 'do nothing' option well and truly open and that meant keeping it to herself. At least for now. She did want to talk to Natalie about Rowan and Shali, though, which suddenly seemed almost like light relief.

'Yeah, not the best. We're right up against it with this reporting deadline on Beau Street. I've been working late most nights and I guess it's just catching up with me,' said Rachel.

'Have you heard about the summer party "incident"? Apparently the venue has complained.'

'Yes, I heard; my team told me,' said Rachel.

'The whole place is talking about it, trying to work out who it might have been. Most people reckon it was a couple of the new graduates. Young enough to still have the energy and inexperienced enough not to know better,' said Natalie, laughing.

'Natalie, I need to tell you something and you have to promise not to say a word to anyone. I mean it, not a word,' said Rachel.

'Rachel, you can trust me. We've been friends forever!'

'I know, I know, but just to make it totally clear, this is between you and me only, okay?'

'Okay, not a word to anyone,' said Natalie and sat forward in her chair expectantly.

'I know who the couple are,' said Rachel.

'You do?' Natalie was amazed. 'How?'

'I saw them come out of the side room.'

'Well, come on then. Who was it?'

'Shali and Rowan,' said Rachel.

Natalie's face dropped. 'You're joking?' she asked eventually.

'I wish I was,' said Rachel, rubbing her forehead.

'God, I'm shocked. You could have lined up half the room, in fact nearly all of the room, before I would have got to them.'

'I couldn't believe it either. I was bloody livid,' said Rachel.

'What about his wife and baby, not to mention the whole happily ever after bit?'

'Not that this is any excuse but Rowan hasn't been getting on that well with Laura recently. He thinks that she's not interested in him since the baby arrived. And Harry got Rowan totally off his face playing stupid drinking games, which didn't help.'

'You know there's going to be an investigation,' said Natalie.

'Are you sure?' Rachel asked. 'I heard that wasn't confirmed.' Rachel was still worried by the prospect. It would hardly help her reputation.

'You may be right. I don't think it has been confirmed. That's just the general view I've heard. They could be wrong, though,' said Natalie. 'Honestly, trust Shali – what an idiot she is!'

'Bloody disgrace, more like,' said Rachel, unable to help herself.

'Hmm, well, not exactly helpful anyway and pretty careless to get caught, at work of all places.' Natalie shook her head. 'What a nightmare for her.'

'Don't feel sorry for her!' said Rachel. 'She threw herself at Rowan. It serves her right.'

Natalie looked a bit taken aback by the venom in Rachel's voice. 'That's a bit harsh, isn't it? She might have been a bit stupid but she's a mate of ours, and if they find out who it was they could have her up for unprofessional behaviour. That could be really serious for her.'

'What about me?' Rachel asked.

'What about you?'

'Well, it will hardly look good for me either. I invited Rowan,' said Rachel.

'Oh stop being so ridiculous,' said Natalie in her typically forthright way. 'They're not investigating Rowan; he doesn't even work for us. And they can hardly blame the person who invited him. That would be total nonsense. It might be a bit embarrassing for you, but no worse than that.'

Yup, never short of opinion, thought Rachel, annoyed by the fact that Natalie hadn't just agreed with her.

'I still think Shali should have known better and she is supposed to be my friend and I really don't need to be caught up in any more scandals. She's been texting him since, you know. I wouldn't put it past her to try to keep something going.'

'Do you think Rowan might want that?' Natalie asked.

'No, he told me he definitely didn't. He wants to work things out with Laura,' said Rachel.

'Well, I really wouldn't worry then, Rach. They just got carried away and it will all blow over pretty quickly.'

'God, I hope so. I still think Shali should have known that I'd be upset and backed off,' said Rachel, not ready to let it go.

'I doubt she was thinking that laterally at the time,'

said Natalie. 'I really wouldn't take it so personally. And anyway, what about Rowan – surely he's equally to blame?'

'Yes, yes, I know, you're right. I had a go at Rowan too, told him what an idiot he'd been.'

'Look, Rachel, I know it's not great and I can see how upset you are. But I really don't think that you should fall out with Shali over it. She's probably going to need our support, not another bollocking.'

Rachel knew that Natalie was probably right and it was much worse for them than for her, but somehow that didn't make her feel better or any less cross with Shali.

CHAPTER 11

Rachel was on the way home to help look after Naomi while Rowan took Laura away for the weekend. She'd spent most of the last couple of days worrying, lurching from decision to decision on what she should do about the 'cash for anonymity' situation at Beau Street and about Rowan and Shali. She'd heard from Natalie that the partners had decided to investigate the venue's complaint about the summer party and had asked anyone with information to come and talk to them, which of course she hadn't. Harry had even noticed how uptight she was and had kept asking what was wrong. She'd debated whether he really wanted to know or whether he just wanted her to cheer up as it was spoiling his social life. Somehow she feared it was the latter.

Rachel was glad to be getting away, even if it was a weekend of report writing and changing nappies. She'd have plenty of time to think.

She'd arranged with her mum to be home before Rowan and Laura got there so they could get organised. Rowan and Laura were driving down to Bath, dropping off Naomi and then heading on to a country house hotel about forty miles away.

When Rachel arrived at the station she jumped in a cab. Her dad was playing golf and her mum didn't like driving in the Friday evening traffic.

Her mum was in quite a state when she arrived. 'Oh darling, I'm so glad you're here to help me!' she announced the minute Rachel walked in the door. 'I'm so worried about getting everything right; you know how fussy Laura is.'

'Don't worry, Mum, we'll be fine.' Rachel gave her mum a hug. 'I'm sure we'll get plenty of instructions and it's only for a couple of days.'

'Don't get me wrong, I'm thrilled to have Naomi and I hope this will be the first of many little holiday trips here for her. I just want things to go well,' said Rachel's mum.

'We'll be a great team,' said Rachel. 'Now what do we need to do first?'

'We need to assemble a cot. Laura was worried that Naomi doesn't settle well in a travel cot, so your dad popped out and got a proper one. He didn't have time to put it together before he went to golf. Well actually, he probably did, but he was rather grumpy about having to buy a cot at all. I did tell him that it would get plenty of use, but he wasn't convinced.'

'Oh, I see,' said Rachel.

She hadn't quite expected to be assembling flat-packed furniture. It took them several tries, with quite a bit of swearing and laughing in equal measures, but eventually they got it up.

Rachel's mum stood back and admired their handiwork. 'How cute!' she said. 'You never know, maybe one day your own children will sleep in this cot. And just for the record, I would like loads of grandchildren.' She giggled and clapped her hands at the thought.

'Oh shut up, Mum,' said Rachel.

'Oh I'm sorry, darling, I'm just teasing. It's just so lovely to have you home.'

Rachel looked at the cot and tried to imagine Harry as a father. What a thought! He could barely look after his own house keys, never mind a baby. Rachel had thought a few times that they might get married eventually, but even that seemed a long way away right now. Might she have children in that cot one day? She guessed so, but she had no idea when or who the father would be. Maybe she should have more of a plan by now.

The loud ring of the doorbell broke Rachel's thoughts.

'That will be them,' said her mum, rushing down the stairs to the front door.

Laura came in holding Naomi, who was wrapped in a pristine, white blanket and wearing a pink stripy babygrow. Rowan followed, laden with bags and baby clutter. He dropped what he was carrying in the hall.

'Don't shut the door,' he said to his mum. 'There's more stuff still to come in from the car.'

How much stuff could they have? Rachel watched in amazement as the pile in the hall grew. There was a cool box, a suitcase, some sort of carry bag, a bouncy chair, a huge bag of toys, a steamer type thing that Rachel thought might be for bottles and a complicated looking strappy thing that looked like it could be quite a good bondage accessory but was probably a baby carrier. And even then Rowan hadn't quite finished.

Rachel went down and hugged Laura. 'Hi, Laura, you look well.'

She meant it. Laura really looked like she'd made an effort. Her neat bob looked newly cut and she was wearing a pretty floral top over jeans and red wedge sandals. The touch of shimmer on the inner corner of her eyes said party make-up rather than tired mummy make-up. Great start, thought Rachel hopefully.

'Rachel, thanks so much for offering to help. We're really grateful. I couldn't believe it when Rowan suggested this weekend away idea. I think he's a bit more of a romantic than I give him credit for,' said Laura.

She smiled happily at Rowan, who shrugged and looked understandably slightly embarrassed at the praise. 'Well, you know, it was about time,' he said, looking lost for anything more specific to say.

Rachel's mum took Naomi from Laura. 'Now, why don't I go and sit down with Naomi while you go through everything with Rachel. She's going to be in charge of remembering everything important.'

I am? thought Rachel. Since when?

'Oh, that's great. Well done, clever Rachel,' said Laura in a way that just about managed not to be patronising.

She opened her bag and took out several pages of

neatly written notes. It took a full twenty minutes for Laura to brief Rachel. By the end, Rachel's head was spinning. She had a full timetable of sleep, feed and play times, instructions for dealing with wind, nappy changes and food preparation, and contact telephone numbers set out in order of priority, like a disaster recovery plan. God, it looked exhausting!

'You have got all that, haven't you?' Laura asked, looking slightly concerned by Rachel's shell-shocked expression.

'Oh yes, totally, no problem at all. No more complicated than one of my deal timetables,' Rachel said.

'Okay, good. Let me just talk you through the food in the cool box, which needs to all go in the freezer. Now, as I was showing you on the timetable, Naomi's now eating solid food — all homemade, of course. Everything you need is in here.' She opened the cool box. 'Each pot is labelled and I've added colour coding to the labels so you can see which meal each pot is for — green for breakfast, yellow for lunch and red for tea,' said Laura.

Rachel peered into the blue and white cool box at the perfect rows of neatly labelled tiny pots of food. It looked impressive.

'There are defrosting instructions here,' Laura continued, pulling out yet another sheet of paper from the cool box. 'Ideally get what you need out of the freezer a few hours before she's having it. You can use a microwave if you forget, but just be really careful and stir everything well afterwards, as microwaving can leave hot spots.'

'Okay, right, got it,' said Rachel. So many potential hazards — what a nightmare!

Eventually Laura and Rowan were ready to go. Laura was close to tears as they said goodbye. 'Please take care of her,' she said, kissing Naomi for about the tenth time. 'Bye, sweetheart. Have fun with Grandma and Aunty Rachel. We'll be back soon.'

Aunty Rachel. She didn't like the sound of that at all. But she was quite moved by how upset Laura was. Rachel could see how hard she was finding it to leave and couldn't help thinking that she'd never felt that strongly about leaving someone. This whole baby thing; she had so much to learn.

'Of course we will, silly,' said Rachel, hugging Laura. 'I'll text you regular updates, let you know how she is.'

'Oh would you? Thank you. That would be fantastic,' said Laura.

'Come on, let's go,' said Rowan, taking Laura's arm and gently pulling her towards the door.

'Have a great time and see you on Sunday,' said Rachel's mum.

Rachel waved through the front window as they got into the car and could see that before they'd even pulled out of the drive Laura was in floods of tears.

'I hope they manage to enjoy themselves,' she said to her mum.

'Oh, I'm sure they will.'

'Look, can we sit down and work out a plan for the weekend? I've got quite a lot of work to do and I just need to know when I'm on call, so to speak.'

'Not very much at all. I'm going to be looking after

Naomi most of the time. I just wanted you to go through everything with Laura as I know she thinks you're a bit more organised than me.'

'Oh Mum, she doesn't think that at all,' Rachel lied.

'I just have a few hours' work at the shop tomorrow morning. Do you think you could look after Naomi then? The rest of the time you can just help me out here and there when you're not working.'

'No problem at all,' said Rachel, feeling very relieved that her whole weekend wasn't going to be spent knee deep in baby stuff.

Not long after Rowan and Laura left, Rachel's mum gave Naomi her last bottle of the day and put her to bed in the brand new cot.

'She went out like a light, bless her,' she said. 'Ah, here's your father back from golf.'

Her dad strode into the room with his light blue v-neck jumper slightly stretching to fit over his expanding middle.

'Hello, darling, how was your trip? Was your train on time?'

'Hi, Dad. Nope, twelve minutes late,' said Rachel, smiling to herself.

Her dad shook his head.

'I got a cab at the station fine, though; it was really quick,' said Rachel in a vague attempt to placate his train line annoyance.

'You made her get a cab?' Her dad looked reproachfully at his wife.

'You know I don't like driving on a Friday evening. Far too crazy with everyone rushing to get home from work,' said her mum. 'And I had loads to do here, getting ready for Naomi to arrive.'

Hmm, not including putting the cot together, thought Rachel, rubbing her wrist that was still sore from putting in what seemed like a hundred screws with a cheap screwdriver.

'So where is my lovely granddaughter?' said her dad, looking around.

'In bed.'

'Already? Blast it!'

'Dad, she's only seven months old — what did you expect? She's hardly going to be joining us for a sherry, is she?' said Rachel.

'Sherry, did someone say sherry? Super idea, Rachel,' said her dad, heading over to the drinks cabinet.

Rachel didn't have the energy to ask for a gin and tonic.

'Gosh, it's almost empty,' said her dad, holding up the sherry bottle as if someone else had been drinking it. 'Rachel, there's a new one in the cupboard in the utility room; be a love and pop and get it, will you?'

Rachel went through to the utility room, marginally irritated by her dad sending her off on errands like she still lived there. There was a large larder cupboard in the utility room next to the washing machine, tumble dryer and spare fridge-freezer. Her parents kept the cupboard so well stocked that she reckoned they could probably survive for a year without shopping if they had to. 'You never know', as her dad would say. Never know what? She had no idea, but preparing for the worst was just in his blood.

As she turned on the light to the utility room, the light bulb blew with a sharp crack, making her jump. She clicked the other light switch to the under cupboard lights, which didn't come on either. Damn, the fuse must have tripped! There was just enough evening light coming through the window for her to see what she was doing, so she opened the cupboard and hunted for the sherry. Her dad could deal with the bulb tomorrow; she'd had quite enough DIY for one day. Next to the sherry she spotted a bottle of vodka, so she grabbed that as well, 'just in case', and headed back to the sitting room.

The next morning, Rachel stayed in bed trying to ignore the baby noises coming from downstairs. She wasn't in charge until after breakfast and she intended to make the most of it. She'd done a good couple of hours' work after supper last night and deserved a lie in.

When she finally came down in her dressing gown her mum was humming to herself happily as Naomi lay in her bouncy chair on the floor gurgling. Babies do make some very odd noises, thought Rachel.

Her dad was reading the paper and as usual was talking out loud to no one in particular about the story he was reading. 'Honestly, it's a disgrace, these parents. They have no idea how to control their children. They should be the ones in court, not these kids.'

Rachel and her mum exchanged smiles.

'Coffee?'

'Ooh, yes please,' said Rachel. 'Morning, Dad, what are you up to today, apart from prosecuting parents, that is?'

'Busy day, busy day,' said her dad. 'Mike and I are finishing those shelves in the church this morning and then I've got a committee meeting at the golf club. We're looking at the plans to extend the ladies' changing rooms. It'll be a stormy one!'

Rachel had heard all about the plans to extend the ladies' changing rooms at the golf club many times. There had been an uproar when the plans were first put forward, as the changing room extension meant that the practice putting green would have to be moved about thirty feet to the right.

'I have no idea why they need any more room to change anyway,' her dad had said over and over again. 'They should just get rid of all those unnecessary mirrors and hairdryers, put in some more benches. Then there would be plenty of room.'

Rachel knew better than to engage in this debate. Her dad would never see that accommodating the increasing population of lady golfers at his club was more important than the position of the putting green.

'And I'm off to the shop, back about two,' said her mum. 'Grace and I are redoing the window display this morning. We got such a lovely dress in this week, yards of green chiffon. We just have to show it off. It's amazing what people will give away, you know. Must have cost a fortune new.'

'Has Naomi had breakfast?' Rachel asked.

'Oh yes, dear, ages ago. She had fruit baby porridge that Laura put in the fridge to defrost last night when she put all the rest of the food in the freezer.'

Rachel finished her coffee, went for a shower and then eventually got rid of her parents.

'Right then, tiny person, it's just you and me now,' she said to Naomi, crouching down by her chair. 'So, shall we have a look at what's on our fun-packed schedule for the morning?'

She examined the notes. They had wriggle time on a play mat (nappy off to get some air to important bits) followed by story time (books listed) followed by a walk in the pushchair and then lunch. That doesn't sound too hard, she thought.

The notes also said 'normally has a short nap in her bouncy chair at about nine a.m. for thirty to forty minutes'. Good, thought Rachel, off you go then. She looked at Naomi, who smiled back, not looking at all sleepy. Maybe she just needed some quiet. She carried the bouncy chair into the sitting room and put it between the sofa and a large armchair where it seemed a bit darker and calmer than in the bright kitchen. She put a blanket over Naomi and went back into the kitchen to make another cup of coffee.

After a few minutes she peeped into the sitting room and Naomi was asleep. How easy was that! Feeling very pleased with herself, Rachel looked at the notes again to see what was for lunch. Organic chicken casserole. That sounded quite good; she could do with something like that for lunch too. She headed to the utility room to get the chicken casserole out of the freezer. 'No microwave hot spots on my watch,' she whispered to the sleeping Naomi as she went past the sitting room.

She went into the utility room and opened the freezer door. As she did water ran out onto her shoes. 'What on the earth?' she said, stepping back from the freezer. She opened the first drawer of the freezer. Everything in it was defrosted. Melted ice cream was dripping onto packets of soft peas.

She looked around the room. No lights were illuminated on any of the appliances. Shit! The bulb blowing must have tripped the fuse for the utility room. The freezer had been off all night. She grabbed the drawer with Naomi's food in it. The neatly labelled pots were all dripping with condensation. Every single one had defrosted.

Rachel put her hand over her mouth. Holy fuck! She'd forgotten to tell her dad about the bulb blowing. It was totally her fault and now all Naomi's food was ruined.

She ran to the fuse board in the front hall, where the offending switch was flicked to off. She turned it back on and went back to the utility room. The under cupboard lights were on and the fridge-freezer was humming away.

She mopped up the water, shut the freezer door and changed the bulb in the main light. Then she sat at the kitchen table in shock. Now what was she going to do? She had twenty minutes maximum until Naomi woke up and about three hours until lunch. There was no other option. She would just have to make all the food again.

Rachel went into panic-driven overdrive. She ran into the utility room and wrote down all the meals written neatly on the pots: sweet potato and broccoli baby rice, apple and pear puree, fruity porridge – the list seemed endless. She then booted up her parents' computer and started searching for baby food recipes. As she found each one, she saved it as a favourite page so she could get it again quickly later and wrote down a shopping list. How could baby food have so many ingredients in it? Christ, organic chicken casserole needed homemade chicken stock!

She'd just about finished when Naomi woke up.

'Hi there, baby girl! So, bit of a change of plan this morning. We're having a walk in the pushchair now followed by cooking with Aunty Rachel. How does that sound?'

Naomi just smiled at her. You're very cute, thought Rachel.

She put Naomi in the pushchair, congratulated herself on remembering the nappy change bag even in this moment of crisis and headed off to the supermarket. As she arrived, she was confronted with a new dilemma. What do you do with a pushchair and a supermarket trolley? She was just about to attempt to push both when she saw a mother with a baby seat attached to the front of her trolley walk past. Hah! That was it. She found the mother and baby trolley section and switched Naomi into the trolley baby chair, leaving the pushchair in the 'designated pushchair parking area'. Good system, she thought; they do think of everything, these supermarkets.

Once inside, Rachel started at the fruit and vegetable section. She quickly collected the things on her list.

There seemed so much. How could one tiny person need this much stuff? After a few minutes practically running up and down the aisles, she'd got most things – just baby rice to find. She went to the baby section and started looking for baby rice. As she did, she noticed a jar of baby food labelled 'Organic chicken casserole'. Next to it was another labelled 'Vegetables with rice'. Rachel stared at the jars in amazement. There was everything she needed, or if not exactly the same, very similar. Why hadn't she thought of that before? Could she really get them instead? God, it would be easier.

Rachel hesitated – she was sure that Laura would never give Naomi food from jars.

She looked at Naomi.

'Can you eat food from jars?'

She looked furtively up and down the aisle, as if Laura might walk round the corner any second, and then picked up one of the jars.

'Of course you can, what am I saying? They can hardly sell baby food that will poison you, can they? Look, it says here, made from one hundred per cent organic ingredients with no artificial colours or flavours. Sounds like just the ticket to me.'

She hurriedly emptied her trolley of all the recipe ingredients and replaced them with jars of baby food. All she needed to do was refill the pots with food from the jars and no one would be any the wiser. Genius!

She was back at home in less than an hour and while Naomi kicked about on her play mat she washed and refilled each of the pots. The consistency was a bit different but her mum wouldn't know that and it would all be gone by the time Laura got back. She sent Laura a text: *Naomi had great night, now kicking about on play mat, about to have chicken casserole, all good, R.*

She soon had a reply: *That sounds fab! Just off for a long walk, lovely hotel, say hi to everyone, big kiss for Naomi, love Laura xxx.*

Rachel found a small pan and tipped the jar of organic chicken casserole into it and religiously stirred it as it heated up. She tasted it to check it wasn't too hot so many times that she felt that she'd practically eaten half the jar. She battled for a few minutes with the highchair tray, eventually managing to work out how it came off, and strapped Naomi in.

'Right,' she said, sitting down in front of the highchair, feeling rather exhausted, 'food time, missy. Hmm, yum yum, chicken casserole just like Mummy makes. Here comes the train, choo choo!'

Naomi looked slightly startled by the loud train noise and refused to open her mouth.

'Oh God, please eat it, there's a good girl. Look, it's delicious!'

She pretended to eat some and then put the spoon more slowly towards Naomi, who this time decided to play ball. Rachel held her breath waiting for her to spit it out, but Naomi swallowed it and quickly opened her mouth for more.

'Ooh, you do like it, hurrah!'

Naomi loved it. In fact, she couldn't get it down quickly enough, pretty much eating everything in the bowl.

'Well, look at that,' said Rachel, showing Naomi the empty bowl. 'Who says home cooking is best, eh? This is probably your equivalent of a takeaway, and we know how everyone loves a takeaway, don't we? Result. What a good girl you are.'

She then gave Naomi a jar of peach and pear puree, which was equally as popular.

After lunch she carefully put Naomi down for her afternoon nap.

God, that had been a stressful morning! Rachel decided she could also do with a lie down and collapsed in a heap on the sofa, falling asleep until the noise of her mum opening the front door woke her up.

'Hi, darling, I'm home,' shouted her mum from the hall. 'How was it?'

'Yes, all fine, no problems at all. We had a nice play and a walk and then Naomi ate a huge lunch. She's asleep now. I sent Laura a text too, and she seemed happy. They were just off for a long walk.'

'Oh well done, darling. I knew you'd be brilliant.'

Rachel smiled. Yes, quite brilliant, particularly in a crisis.

CHAPTER 12

After her mum took over babysitting duties, Rachel decided she needed to focus on her work. Sitting back at the desk in her bedroom felt weird. It had been the scene for hours of homework and just sitting there made her feel like she should be doing something. She sat with her elbows on the desk, her fingers locked together in an arch supporting her chin, and stared out of the window. She thought about Rowan and wondered how it was going with Laura. She was sure it was best not to tell her about Shali. If Rowan really wanted to work things out with his wife, then what would telling her achieve? Sometimes saying nothing was kinder. She certainly wouldn't be 'fessing up to Laura about giving Naomi shop-bought baby food and that's for sure.

Maybe that was what she should do about Beau Street too. Maybe saying nothing could be the right option. Rachel got up from the desk and lay down on her bed, staring up at the ceiling. If she did say anything to Carl Stephens about what she'd found, how would she explain how she'd got the black book? Sneaking into client offices would hardly go down as impressive behaviour. And was it really her job to act like a private investigator? She was meant to be reviewing the financial performance of the business. It was true that the business had been impacted, but all positively. Lloyd Cassidy's sales numbers were great and he made plenty of profit by charging well above list prices. Maybe it was pretty standard practice, and even if it wasn't, she wasn't totally sure it was her issue to resolve. She also really wanted her director promotion and she was sure that making a huge fuss on an important project wasn't going to help.

Rachel mulled over the arguments in her head over and over again. Her gut feeling was telling her that something wasn't right, but her head was telling her to ignore it. She took a deep breath and then said to herself out loud, 'Come on, girl, get a grip. Make a decision; it's not that hard.'

But it was and Rachel began to feel slightly panicked. After a few minutes of deep breathing and generally trying hard to calm down, her self-preservation instinct kicked in. Doing nothing was definitely her best option.

She got up, opened her laptop and started typing.

Recommendations for improvement

During the course of our review, we noted a few minor issues with the accurate recording of procedure details on sales records. We do not consider these to be a cause for concern, but recommend that management implement an additional review process, to ensure improvements are made in this area in due course.

As soon as she'd written it, Rachel felt better. Good thing she hadn't discussed it with anyone. She'd raised it as a minor issue, like Carl said, and that would do. No need to look into it any further; she could get on with the rest of the report.

She spent the next few hours drafting hard. By sherry time, her part of the report was just about finished and she was feeling pretty good about it. The week ahead suddenly seemed far less complicated and she almost started feeling sorry for Shali, but not quite.

Rachel had a lie in on Sunday and then spent the rest of the morning helping her mum look after Naomi. She was surprised to find that she was actually quite enjoying herself. Maybe babies could be fun, but she would still be glad to get back to London.

Rowan and Laura arrived back mid afternoon. Laura ran in from the car, picked up Naomi and hugged her so tightly that Rachel actually thought she might crush her. Only her absolute confidence that Laura knew what she was doing prevented her from shouting 'Careful!' out loud.

'Oh, I've missed you so much!' Laura looked up at Rachel and her mum and smiled. 'How was she?'

'She was perfect,' said Rachel's mum. 'No trouble at all. And what an appetite! She ate practically everything we put in front of her.'

'Really?' Laura sounded surprised. 'You did do well! It takes me ages to feed her and then I can only normally get her to eat half of the pot, maybe sometimes a bit more.'

'Oh no, she ate most of each pot every meal. Like a

little starling she was, mouth open, loving every spoonful,' said Rachel's mum.

'Wow, what got into you?' Laura said to Naomi.

Rachel winced. Clearly the takeaways were more popular than Mummy's home cooking. 'It might be just the air here. You know, building up her appetite a bit. Anyway, what about you two? Did you have a good time?' Rachel asked, keen to change the subject.

'We had a really lovely time, didn't we, Rowan?' Laura beamed at Rowan.

'Yes, we did. The hotel was very smart and our room was great; spectacular views. We had a great meal in the restaurant on Saturday night as well. We went for the tasting menu – you know, where you get loads of small courses. Bit pricy but it was worth it, just delicious,' said Rowan.

Rowan caught Rachel's eye, raised one eyebrow and nodded slightly. The weekend had been good then.

Rachel hugged them both. 'I'll call *you* in the week,' she said to Rowan. She needed a full debrief.

They spent the next twenty minutes or so packing the car up and saying endless thank yous until Laura and Rowan finally left, Rowan driving and Laura sitting in the back next to Naomi.

'Now, mind those road works on the M4 at junction fifteen.' Rachel's dad was still shouting journey instructions through the car window as they drove away.

Rachel got back to her flat early evening and rang Harry.

'Hi, I'm back. Did you survive without me?' she asked.

'Only just, it was a close call. Looking forward to Jimmy Macks tonight, though. What time shall I pick you up?'

'Oh do we have to? Sure I can't persuade you to come over for a film and a bottle of wine?' Rachel asked. She was knackered and couldn't really face the prospect of a big night out.

'Absolutely not, you promised we would go — that was the deal,' said Harry.

'Alright, alright, yes, I guess did. Pick me up at eight o'clock then.'

'Oh cool, I'll book a cab now.' Harry sounded like an excited child.

Rachel ran a bath and made herself a strong gin and tonic. After a long soak and a refill while she got ready, she felt her energy levels rising back up to normal. She dressed in a pair of skinny black jeans and a funky print t-shirt emblazoned with 'Ready for bed' across the front.

'Great t-shirt,' grinned Harry as he picked her up.

Rachel gave him a long kiss. 'I missed you,' she said.

'Of course you did, I'm irresistible,' said Harry.

'Shut up, show off.'

They sat close together in the cab and Rachel laid her head on Harry's shoulder. He stroked her arm and they didn't say much else until the taxi dropped them outside Jimmy Macks.

As they went in they were hit by the odour of stale beer and cigarettes.

'Nice,' said Rachel.

'All part of the atmosphere,' said Harry.

They approached the bar and waited while a generously proportioned barmaid finished chatting to a couple of guys on bar stools. Eventually she wandered over to them. She wore heavy black eyeliner, black lipstick and a nose stud, offset by a worn looking grey vest and chainmail belt.

'Yeah?'

'Two pints of lager, please,' said Harry without checking with Rachel. It was clearly a pint of lager pub.

As Harry handed over the money for the drinks the barmaid dropped a couple of coins on the floor. She glared at Harry and turned round to pick them up, revealing a tattoo of a dove and a twisted bright orange g-string sitting well above the top of her low-cut jeans.

Harry looked at Rachel and pulled a face. Rachel stifled a laugh.

'That was one arse I really didn't need to see,' said Harry as they sat down close to the small stage at the back of the pub.

'Most of the regulars probably love it. In fact they probably charge extra for glimpses of hairy arses in this pub,' said Rachel.

Harry laughed. 'Look the band is setting up.'

Three guys in black t-shirts were on the small stage fiddling with various bits of equipment and doing 'one, two, one, two' type sound checks.

'What type of music is it?' Rachel asked.

'They're a kind of garage rock revival band,' said Harry.

'Oh right.'

Rachel had no idea what that meant, but it sounded

loud. As they started to play, Harry stood up and started bouncing about in front of the stage along with a few other scruffy but trendy looking people.

'Come on, Rachel, dance,' shouted Harry.

'Is that what you call it?' Rachel shouted back, laughing.

Harry grabbed her hands and pulled her up. 'You and me, babe, c'mon, let's dance.'

An hour and a half later, her ears were ringing with the sound of guitar riffs and her head was spinning from several pints of strong lager.

'They were pretty good actually,' said Rachel as she dropped back into her chair.

Harry sat down next to her, the front of his hair dripping with sweat. He ran his hands through it, pushing his hair back flat onto his head.

'Look at you, Mr Sexy-wet-look,' said Rachel.

'Just my natural boyish good looks,' he replied and put his arm around her.

They sat for a while watching the band pack up.

'You seem better — far more chipper than you were on Friday. Did you get your work done?' Harry asked.

Rachel was surprised and touched that he'd asked her about work.

'Yes, most of it,' she said. 'I was worrying about it quite a bit last week, but I think I've worked out how to deal with it now. I thought you weren't interested in my work?'

'I am if it's bothering you. What matters to you, matters to me,' said Harry.

'Bollocks,' said Rachel.

'Oh right, thanks. Here I am being a concerned boyfriend and all I get is abuse,' said Harry.

Rachel got up and sat on Harry's lap.

'Very sorry and thank you for your concern, kind sir.' She touched the front of an imaginary bonnet.

'I should think so too. Now come here, young wench,' said Harry, smiling.

They kissed for a few minutes until Rachel thought that people were starting to look at them. She sat back down on her chair.

'Did you tell all about the mystery celebrity night visits?' Harry asked.

'Sort of. I raised a recommendation about them improving their record keeping,' said Rachel.

'Was that it? No big scandal then?'

'Well, not really. I don't actually know for definite that there's anything wrong with the odd late night appointment and I only had a couple of copied sheets with celebrity names on. Hardly a tonne of evidence.'

'What copied sheets?' Harry asked.

Rachel had forgotten that she hadn't told Harry about the black book. 'Oh, er, I copied a few pages out of a private appointments book that had a few well-known names in it — actresses, TV stars, daughters of the rich and famous, that sort of thing.'

'Really? Who?'

'I can't tell you that otherwise I'd have to kill you afterwards,' Rachel said solemnly.

'You can tell me. After all, you already told me about Francesca Hart. Won't say a word.' Harry winked and tapped the side of his nose.

God, he's sexy, thought Rachel through her lager haze.

'Well, I can't tell you any more names, but I can tell you a bit of a scandal. Celebrities are paying one of the doctors extra to book in under false names so that they can be guaranteed total anonymity. The false names means that there are no records that they were ever there.'

Harry sat up. 'Are you sure?'

'Yes, the appointments book that I copied had two names for each person: the real name and then the name that all the records are in.'

'Wow,' said Harry. He sat for a moment. 'And you haven't put the names in your report?'

'Well, no, not exactly.' Rachel knew that she'd probably said too much, even though it was only Harry. 'Anyway, that's quite enough work talk. They just called last orders.'

Rachel walked unsteadily to the bar and ordered two more pints of lager with whisky chasers. 'To hell with tomorrow, let's party,' she said to Harry when she got back to the table.

'I'll drink to that,' he replied and downed his whisky in one go.

Rachel grinned and did the same.

'Christ you are lovely,' he said slowly. 'Let's go home.'

Rachel looked at Harry and nodded. They left two full pints of lager on the table and jumped in the first cab they could find back to Rachel's flat.

The next morning she dragged herself out of bed

and down to the local cafe for the traditional hangover cure of a cooked breakfast.

'Do you want fried or scrambled eggs?'

'Fried.'

'Brown or white toast?'

'Definitely white.'

A large lady with a whiskery chin wearing a grubby-looking apron scribbled some illegible symbols on a small pad and handed it to the man cooking at the back of the transport cafe. 'One full breakfast, fried, white,' she shouted as confirmation. The man grunted.

Rachel took her large mug of dark tea and sat down on a moulded red plastic chair that was attached to the table. Around her various tradesmen were tucking into combinations of breakfasts, mostly with chips, and either reading the sports pages of tabloid newspapers or talking about them. They eyed her suspiciously as she lifted her sunglasses onto the top of her head so that she could read her emails on her phone.

The bearded lady shuffled out from behind the counter and dropped a huge plate of cooked breakfast in front of Rachel. 'There you go, love,' she said, grinning and showing off a mouthful of uneven stained teeth.

'Thank you very much,' said Rachel, suddenly very conscious of how loud and proper her voice had sounded.

Kill or cure, she thought as she looked at the plate of food shimmering greasily under the strip lighting. She felt shocking. God knows what time she and Harry had got to bed. The sound of the alarm going off had sent her bolting out of bed. For a couple of minutes she'd thought she didn't feel too bad, but then the full force of her hangover had kicked in. She'd rung the office and told them she'd be at Beau Street for the morning and then emailed AJ and Rosa to say that she'd be in the office. That was the good thing about being on a project: far easier to get lost for a few hours. There was no chance of Harry moving until at least lunchtime, so Rachel had left him snoring away and jumped in a cab in search of a restoring fry-up.

Half an hour later she pushed her empty plate away from her, not sure whether she felt better or not. She definitely felt less shaky but still felt quite sick; probably now, though, due to being too full. She looked at her watch. It was nearly eleven o'clock: time to get going. She paid the bill, buying a bottle of bright orange energy drink at the same time, and headed over to the Beau Street offices.

AJ was on his own in their project room when she arrived.

'Morning, how was the office?' he asked as Rachel sat down.

'Oh, you know, large square building, lots of windows, that sort of thing,' said Rachel.

AJ grinned. 'Tom popped round to see you earlier.'

'Did he? What did he want?'

'Not sure, he didn't say. I told him you were briefing Carl in the office.'

'Oh well done, good covering,' said Rachel.

AJ looked confused. 'That's where your email said you were.'

'Oh I was,' said Rachel quickly. 'Just good that you made it clear to Tom, that's all.'

She spent a few minutes organising herself and then headed off to Tom's office. On the way she passed Lloyd Cassidy and Audrey Fox sitting on one of the occasional corridor sofas, deep in conversation. What was it with those two?

She stuck her head round Tom's door. 'Were you looking for me?'

'Rachel, hi, yes, come in, come in. How's it going? Are you going to be ready for the presentation to the buyers?'

'Yes, pretty much on track. A few loose ends to tie up, but that's it. We should be able to give a pretty clear report to the Equinox team when they arrive,' said Rachel, ignoring the slight flutter in her stomach.

'Excellent, excellent. I'm very pleased with how things have been run here, Rachel, and I shall be reporting that back to Carl.'

'Thank you, that would be very kind,' said Rachel.

'There's just one more area that we'd like your help with. Equinox are keen to have a joint marketing plan ready for when we hopefully do this deal. They've asked us to start briefing our PR company to work with us on it. I've spoken to them and they're keen to get a few facts and stats on the business so they can think about the sort of messages we should lead with. My team are totally snowed under and you've had most of the information as part of your work. I was hoping that you'd help brief them?'

'Of course,' said Rachel. 'It would be an extension

to our work, though, and therefore cost extra. Is that going to be okay?'

'Yes, that's fine. It shouldn't be a big job, though, so don't get carried away,' said Tom. 'Now, the person you need to speak to is Clive Steele from Cavanaugh PR. Here's his number. Could you give him a ring today? They're keen to get going.'

Clive Steele? Rachel recognised that name. Maybe they'd worked together on another deal.

'Yes, will do.'

Rachel left Tom's office feeling quite elated. Not only was he happy with their work but he'd given them some extra to do. Carl would be pleased with the fee increase.

'Your phone rang while you were gone,' said AJ when she got back to the room.

She looked at her phone. She had a missed call from her mum. Agh, she really didn't have the energy to chat, but maybe it was important. Rachel rang her back.

'Oh, darling, thank you for ringing back.' Her mum sounded like she'd genuinely expected her not to. 'You left your white fleece here at the weekend and I was just wondering if you wanted me to post it?'

Right, not important at all then.

'No, that's okay. I've got plenty of others. It can wait until I'm down next,' said Rachel.

'Well, if you're sure? It's no trouble to send it. I'm going to the post office anyway. We're getting some new posters done for the shop and I need to send our ideas to the designers. Can you imagine – Grace and I working with proper designers!'

Rachel couldn't and she wasn't sure that a poster for good-as-new clothes really required much design input. Still, it kept them happy.

'Yes, I'm sure, thanks.' Rachel changed the subject. 'How's Dad?'

'Grumpy, as usual,' said her mum cheerily. 'The freezer has broken — can you believe it? We found everything in it had defrosted and then frozen again. Very strange. Your father spent hours fiddling with it this morning trying to work out what happened. He thinks it must have been a power surge, so he's changed all the plugs and it seems to be working again now. We had to throw everything away and you know what he's like about wasting food. He's gone to the golf club to calm down. Still, look on the bright side. I've got a whole freezer full of new and exciting food. Good thing it didn't happen while Naomi was here.'

'Yes, very lucky, and how odd,' said Rachel.

Lucky too that buying a new freezer full of food counted as excitement in her mum's world.

CHAPTER 13

Rachel's telephone started ringing in her handbag as she walked wearily towards the tube, lugging a large briefcase full of Beau Street files. Her arms and head were aching and she needed a drink. She scrabbled around in her cavernous brown leather handbag for her phone, then dropped to the floor so that she could use both hands. 'Fuck, where is it?' A lady walking past nearly jumped out of her skin and gave her a very disapproving look, like she was some sort of hoodie abusing local residents. Rachel emptied her umbrella, book, hairbrush, diary, keys and several dog-eared letters onto the pavement until she could see the flashing screen of her phone tucked away in one corner.

'Yes?' she yelled into the phone when she finally managed to answer it.

There was a yelp at the other end. 'Wow, no need to shout! I've got my car headset on. You nearly blew my eardrum!' It was Rowan.

'Sorry, shit day, really busy, raging hangover and

then I couldn't find my phone. The bloody thing never stays in its little pocket. I just emptied half my bag onto the street so I could find it. Think I need a new bag.' She knew she was ranting.

'Well, hello to you too, and that's the most pathetic excuse for buying a new handbag that I've ever heard. If you want a new bag, just buy one; don't blame it on your mobile phone.'

Rachel laughed, picked up the contents of her bag and the briefcase and went to sit down on a nearby bench. 'Sorry, right, all calm now. So tell me, tell me, how are you, how was the weekend?'

'Yes, very good, really very good actually. Laura was pretty stressed about going, well, as you saw when we left. But fair play to her, she went through with it and as she said herself she managed to forget she was a mother for at least a few minutes!'

'I could see how upset it made her leaving. Surprised me actually. I had no idea how tough it would be,' said Rachel. 'Does she suspect anything?'

'No, I'm pretty sure she doesn't. She's definitely noticed that I've been paying more attention, though. Sometimes I think I'm trying too hard – you know, trying to make amends – and it's all too much. I think I just need to be normal with her but somehow I've forgotten what normal should be like.'

'Did you talk to her about the fact that she seems to be only interested in Naomi?' Rachel asked.

'Not in so many words, but we did talk about the fact that we need to spend more time together on our own. Laura suggested we could maybe have a "date night" each week, where we have a proper night out somewhere together,' said Rowan.

'Oh my God, that sounds like a hideous American idea,' said Rachel without really thinking, and then quickly added, 'Sorry, that was a bit harsh. It might help, I guess, if you're both keen.'

'To be honest, Rach, I'll stand on one leg in the middle of Trafalgar Square dressed as a chicken if it helps.'

'I somehow don't think that will be necessary,' said Rachel, laughing at the idea. 'I'm glad things are moving in the right direction for you both. You were a bloody idiot but at least you're trying to make it right.' Rachel felt a rush of protectiveness towards her brother. He was a genuinely nice guy.

'Yes, I am,' said Rowan, sounding very resolute. 'Look, I think you should also know that I'm meeting Shali for a drink this week.'

Rachel's jaw dropped and all her feelings of protectiveness vanished in an instant. 'What?! I don't believe it. Why on earth would you do that?'

Rachel was livid. What was the point of putting all that effort into a romantic weekend and then proceeding to fuck it all up again?

'It's not what you think,' said Rowan.

'Really? What is it then?'

'I need to close things off with her, you know. I'm not the sort of bloke who has one night stands and then never speaks to the girl again. I want to explain face to face that I'm working things out with Laura and that we won't be seeing each other again.'

'Oh right, so you're all concerned about treating people properly all of a sudden. I didn't notice you caring much about that at the summer party,' said Rachel.

'That doesn't mean I can't try to do the right thing now. A message from you and a few texts doesn't seem right. Shali at least deserves an explanation.'

'Does she?'

'Yes she does, and you should know that.'

Rachel paused and felt a bit guilty. She really didn't want them meeting up again but she couldn't manage Rowan's life for him. She sighed loudly — it was his lookout.

'Well, you do what you think,' said Rachel. 'Just be careful, that's all.'

'Yes, yes, I will. Have you spoken to her recently, by the way? You really shouldn't let this come between you.'

'Not since I gave her your message, but I haven't been in the office very much recently,' said Rachel, knowing that was just an excuse. Maybe she should speak to Shali before she met Rowan — warn her to leave him alone. She shook her head. It was none of her business. She would just have to let them get on with it.

'Look, Rowan, I'd better go. I'm just on my way home.'

Rachel fumed all the way home on the tube until she got bored with worrying about it. She had better things to think about, like the tonne of work she had to do that evening. Shit! She suddenly realised she'd forgotten to phone the PR guy, Clive Steele, and made a mental note to do it first thing.

Harry had texted her earlier to see if he could come round, no doubt hopeful of a repeat performance of the night before. Rachel rang him when she got in.

'You're late back,' said Harry, sounding put out that she hadn't rung him earlier.

'Big week, lots of meetings, presentation to prepare for. I'm shattered actually,' said Rachel.

'How about a glass of wine and a massage?' Harry asked hopefully.

'I need to work tonight and tomorrow night too probably,' said Rachel. 'I've had to lug a whole load of files home so that I can finish everything off on this job. It's going to take me quite a while and I'm not going keep breaking my arms carrying all this about.'

'Maybe I could come and help you with your filing, check everything is in the right place?' Harry wasn't giving in.

'Harry, I really need to work, okay? It's just for a couple of days. I need to go through all my notes and paperwork one last time, check I've covered everything. I don't need any distractions.'

'Oh, okay, I see.' Harry sounded like he'd finally got it. 'What time will you be home tomorrow?'

'Probably late again; after eight, I expect. But I need to work tomorrow too,' said Rachel.

'Yeah, yeah, I heard you. I just wanted to know what time to ring you, check you're okay — not drowning in paperwork or anything.'

Sweet boy, thought Rachel.

'I'll ring you once I'm back,' she said.

'Alright, don't work too hard. I'm off to the pub,' said Harry.

Rachel wasn't surprised.

The next day in the office, both AJ and Rosa were feeling pretty stressed.

'We've still got a lot do to be ready for the presentation,' said AJ, nervously tearing bits off his notebook. 'The report's not finished and we still need to write the slide pack.'

'We'll be fine,' said Rachel reassuringly. 'Look, Equinox are just expecting a progress report; we'll have some more time after the presentation to dot the i's and cross the t's. We just need a good draft of the report ready to give them and we'll probably only need twenty or so slides for the presentation. That won't take us long to put together. Carl is out tomorrow to do his final review and I'm sure he won't have too many comments. The report's in good shape already so we're pretty much there.'

'Shall I start the slide pack?' Rosa asked.

That was one of the things Rachel really liked about Rosa. She was so proactive.

'Great idea, Rosa. Look, why don't we all sit down and brainstorm what needs to be in the presentation and then Rosa can get on with putting an outline together.'

The three of them sat together for over an hour chatting through their findings and the main messages that they needed to give Equinox.

'We definitely need to show them how quickly

some of the newer procedures have been growing,' said AJ. 'I know that's a key part of the strategy going forward − focusing on the hot trends.'

'We also need to show that the core business has been growing too, though,' said Rachel. 'It's not just about the new procedures.'

'That's true,' said Rosa. 'Why don't we put the sales numbers for both on the same slide, like this.'

Rosa sketched out a couple of pie charts side by side on a slide, one showing sales for the top five most popular procedures and one for the hot trends.

'Yup, like it. Let's go with that,' said Rachel.

'Do you think we should include something on the nature of the customer base?' AJ asked.

'Yes, definitely,' said Rachel. 'Where's that customer summary file?'

'You took it home,' said AJ.

'Oh shit, yes I did, plus a load of others. I didn't bring them back today as I was going to work on them again tonight.'

'That's going to make things a bit tight,' said Rosa. 'We can't afford to miss a whole day.'

Rachel thought for a bit. 'I'll go and get them and then stay late here tonight. I'll grab some lunch for us on the way back − that will save a bit of time.'

'You don't mind?' Rosa asked.

'No, my fault for being lazy. I should have brought them back this morning. Right, won't be long.'

She left Beau Street and flagged down a cab. She couldn't face getting the tube. As she approached her flat she could see that the front window was open. That was funny; she was sure she'd left it shut. She got out of the cab and made her way to her front door. As she turned the lock, the door opened after half a turn. The double lock wasn't on. She'd definitely double locked the door when she left.

Her heart started to pound. Was there someone in her flat? She gingerly opened the front door a few inches and listened carefully. She couldn't hear anything. Surely if there were burglars inside then she would hear them ransacking the place? And besides, there was no damage to the front door. She must be imagining things.

She opened the door wider and walked quietly inside, looking over her shoulder in case someone followed her in. Stop being ridiculous; there's no one here! she said to herself sternly. But at the same time she took her umbrella out of her handbag and held it out in front of her.

As she opened the sitting room door a loud cough made her scream in fright.

Harry leapt to his feet in alarm. 'Christ Almighty, Rachel!'

'Harry! You scared the living daylights out of me. I thought someone had broken in. What are you doing here?'

Harry didn't say anything. He put his hands in his pockets and looked at the floor. Rachel looked around the sitting room. Her Beau Street files were strewn all over the sofa and the floor. It didn't make sense.

'What the fuck have you been doing?'

She walked towards the sofa. On the coffee table

was a notebook covered with Harry's childish handwriting. Several of the files were open on the sofa where he'd been reading them.

'Harry?' She looked at him in disbelief. 'Why have you been going through my stuff?'

Harry sat down on the arm of the sofa and rubbed his forehead. 'I wanted some information,' he mumbled.

'What? I don't understand. What sort of information?'

Harry took a deep breath, stood up and looked at her. 'Look, the thing is, Rachel, I spoke to a friend of mine in the business. He works with the tabloids, knows them inside out. I told him about your little scandal — you know, celebs paying over the odds for boob jobs and using false names and all that. Well, he said it would be a massive story, worth a fortune if we could show it was true. So I was looking for those pages you told me about, the ones with both the real and the false names on. They need proof that the story is true; it protects them against libel if they know they have something to back it up.'

Rachel stared at him, aghast. She couldn't believe what she was hearing. 'They're not here; they're with the rest of my papers out at Beau Street. You were going to take my work and sell it to the papers?'

'It's a chance of a lifetime for us — can't you see that? There are so many names, the story would just run and run. I spoke to one of the tabloids — you know, just to get an idea of what they might pay. They said if I could prove it, we'd be talking huge sums — hundreds of thousands maybe,' said Harry.

'You've spoken to the papers about it?'

Rachel felt sick and her legs started to go wobbly. She needed to sit down.

'Just one,' said Harry.

'Oh my God, Harry, how could you!' Rachel was close to tears. 'What about me? What about my job? I could be fired on the spot, struck off for professional misconduct, God knows what else. Have you any idea?'

'Well, that's the clever thing,' said Harry. 'You wouldn't have anything to do with it. I'd handle everything. That's why I was going to get the proof without telling you. I didn't think you'd be back for ages. The papers would never know where the information came from and journalists never reveal their sources. You just need to give me a copy of those pages.'

'You aren't seriously expecting me to give them to you?' Rachel was incredulous.

Harry came over and took both her hands. He looked at her, wide eyed, almost desperate. She could feel he was shaking too.

'Rachel, I love you. I want to do this for both of us. If we make enough money you wouldn't need to work so hard, maybe not at all, then we could spend more time together.'

Rachel shook his hands off in anger. He was so full of it. 'Love me! You love me, do you?' Tears were flooding down her cheeks. 'You selfish bastard! This has nothing to do with me. I have a job, a career ahead of me. But what does that matter to you? Nothing, nothing at all. You just do what you want and bugger the consequences for me.'

'It's not like that.' Harry steadied himself and tried again. 'Look, if we end up getting married and maybe have kids, you'd stop work then anyway. This would just mean you could stop a bit sooner. So you see, it wouldn't really make that much difference.'

Rachel couldn't believe what she was hearing. It was going from bad to worse. Harry had never mentioned marriage before, let alone children. And now he'd raised them both, but in the worst possible circumstances.

'Why would I stop work?' She couldn't quite believe she was actually going to engage with him in this farcical debate, but she needed to know the answer.

'Everyone knows that children need their mothers at home and we'd be no different,' said Harry.

'Do they now?' Rachel's eyes flashed with anger. 'So let me get this right: you thought you'd sell this story to papers, using evidence from my project, and get a load of cash that would never be traced to me. Then we get married, have kids, I give up work to stay at home to look after them and we live happily ever after?'

'I wouldn't put it exactly like that,' said Harry. 'I just wanted to explain why it would work for both of us, set us up for the future.'

'You're off your fucking rocker!' Rachel shouted so loudly she made Harry jump.

'Alright, calm down,' he said.

'I will not bloody well calm down!'

'We wouldn't be doing anything illegal, you know. Provided the story is true, there's nothing to stop the papers paying for it.'

'It would be against the rules for me, you idiot! I don't seem to remember my ethical rules saying that it was okay to sell confidential client information to the papers.' Rachel looked terrified. 'Have you told anyone the company name?'

'No,' said Harry.

'Are you sure?'

'Yes, I'm sure. I needed proof before I could start giving them any details. I just gave them a general idea of the story.'

'To both your mate and the paper you spoke to?'

'Yes, both.'

'Well, I guess that's something.'

Rachel paused.

'Now get the fuck out of my flat.'

Harry looked at her in shock. 'What?'

'You heard, get out of my flat.' She walked towards him, her face streaked with make-up, struggling to contain her emotions. 'And I mean now,' she added in a low croaky whisper.

'Shall I call you?' Harry asked.

'Get out!'

Rachel didn't stop screaming until Harry had run out of the flat and shut the door behind him. Then she fell to her knees on the floor with her head in her hands, struggling to catch her breath between sobs.

How could he have done that to her?

CHAPTER 14

Rachel sat on the sofa in her flat feeling totally numb. Her face was red and blotchy and her head was pounding. She looked at the files around her and shook her head in disbelief for the hundredth time. What had he been thinking? She slowly got to her feet and started packing away the files as if she was on autopilot. AJ and Rosa would be expecting her back at Beau Street by now. She placed the briefcase by the front door and then went into the bathroom to attempt to repair her make-up. God, she looked a mess. She washed her face and gently reapplied her eye make-up, trying to disguise as much of the puffy redness as she could.

I must stay calm, she kept saying to herself as she fought back the tears. She also felt light-headed and shaky, like she might faint. Maybe she should eat something. She opened the fridge and stared blankly into it, not able to face any of its contents. In the end she opted for a slice of bread and butter, the childlike comfort of it making her feel slightly steadier.

She left the flat with the sole purpose of getting

through the next few hours until she could get back home again. That was as far forward as she could think. She walked slowly round to the local corner shop and picked up sandwiches and snacks for lunch, just about mustering a half smile for the lady behind the counter, and then headed back to Beau Street.

She could tell that AJ and Rosa knew something wasn't right as soon she came into the room. She saw them exchange glances and AJ nodded at Rosa as if to indicate that she should be the one to say something, somehow sensing that it might be 'girl talk'.

'Coffees all round?' AJ asked and escaped from the room, giving Rosa time alone with Rachel.

'Are you okay, Rachel?' Rosa asked after a few moments. 'You look a bit peaky.'

'Oh yes, fine, thanks. Just got a bit of a headache, that's all. Think maybe it's the humid weather.'

Rachel stared hard at the papers in front of her as she spoke. The concern in Rosa's voice had automatically made her close to tears and the tremble in her voice soon gave away that it was more than that.

'Look, you've been rushing about quite enough today. Why don't you go home on time? AJ and I can stay and burn the midnight oil, break the back of the presentation.'

Rosa's kind gesture was just about too much for Rachel. A few tears leaked out onto the desk underneath her. Rosa put her hand on Rachel's arm.

'That's okay, I'll be okay. I just need a minute.' Rachel fanned her face with her hand and took a deep breath. She looked up and composed herself enough to manage a smile. 'I'm fine, honestly.'

AJ returned with the coffee. He looked at Rosa quizzically, but she just shrugged her shoulders and shook her head very slightly.

It took Rachel every ounce of energy to keep her composure for the rest of the afternoon. Her computer screen kept swimming in front of her as the tears kept threatening to return. She managed to draft a few slides but mostly she just shuffled paper.

'Maybe I will call it a day now, get an early night, try to kick this headache,' Rachel said eventually. She really needed to go home.

'I'm sure that's a good idea,' said Rosa straight away. 'We can cope, can't we, AJ?'

'Er, yeah, sure,' said AJ.

'Thanks, guys. I'll come in early tomorrow, make sure we don't get behind.' Rachel tried not to let the relief show on her face.

As she was on her way out she bumped into Fred the security guard, who was carrying some boxes across reception.

'Hello, Ms Altman. Have you had a good day?'

Rachel looked at his cheery, wrinkled face, felt a rush of warmth towards him and immediately felt like crying again. God, she was totally vulnerable to decent, honest people being kind to her.

'Clinging to the wreckage, Fred.' Rachel tried to smile in an ironic 'only joking' sort of way.

'Oh dear! Well, there are no storms forecast in this area, so you should be home and dry tomorrow,' Fred replied, enjoying the nautical word play.

'Thanks, Fred, let's hope so.'

Back at home, Rachel opened the fridge and looked at the bottle of white wine sitting in the door. She couldn't decide whether it was a good idea to drink it or not. She needed to get her emotional tumble dryer of a head under control and somehow work out what she should do next. Maybe tea with sugar would be better.

The list of things she needed to do kept whizzing through her head at such speed that somehow she couldn't catch anything for long enough to actually deal with it. She was exhausted.

She was sitting motionless on the sofa holding a rapidly cooling cup of tea when the doorbell rang, making her jump out of her skin and nearly throw the whole cup over herself.

'Shit!'

She put the cup on the coffee table and started towards the door. Then she froze. What if it was Harry? She wasn't sure she had the strength to withstand the inevitable emotional onslaught. She looked nervously through the security peephole. It wasn't Harry outside. It was Shali.

She jumped back from the door in surprise. Shali heard her.

'Rachel, it's me, Shali. Please let me in. I know you're cross with me but I really think we should talk. Rachel? Please?'

Rachel stood for a moment, totally unable to decide what to do, and then opened the door.

Shali looked very relieved. 'Oh, Rachel, I just had to come round. I can't bear it that you're so upset with me. I'm so sorry. I never really thought you'd be so hurt. Well, to be honest, I never really thought at all. It was all so spur of the moment. I want to make things right but I'm not sure how.'

Rachel couldn't say anything. She reached out both arms towards Shali and as she did so tears began rushing down her face. Shali ran towards her and held her tightly as huge sobs racked Rachel's chest.

'Shit, I had no idea you felt this bad,' said Shali, totally overcome by Rachel's reaction.

Rachel shook her head. 'It's… it's… not… that,' she said, the words coming out one at a time between jerky, tearful breaths.

Shali looked at Rachel's broken face. 'Oh my God, what's happened?'

'It's… Harry,' Rachel said through the tears, still not really able to talk properly.

'What, is he hurt, has there been an accident?'

Rachel shook her head.

'Look, come on, let's go and sit down so you can catch your breath,' said Shali.

They went into the sitting room and sat down on the sofa. Shali got Rachel a glass of water and, after a few minutes, Rachel had composed herself enough to talk.

'I came home unexpectedly at lunchtime today to get some Beau Street files that I'd left behind. When I got here I found Harry going through my things, my work things.'

'What? Harry? Why on the earth would he do that? He doesn't give a stuff about your work,' said Shali, and then quickly added, 'Sorry, didn't mean to be quite so blunt.'

Rachel hesitated. She hadn't meant to tell anyone about what she'd found but it was becoming clear to her that it had been a pretty stupid decision. She'd told Harry already, which was why she was in this mess, and she needed help.

'While I was working on the Beau Street job I found out that one of the doctors has been charging celebrities way over the odds for cosmetic surgery and booking them in under false names so they can totally hide the fact that they've had anything done.'

It sounded pretty bad when she said it like that.

Shali clearly thought so too. 'Really? Wow, that's well dodgy.'

'Well, the thing is, I mentioned it to Harry and he seemed really interested, so I told him a bit more about it. I was so pleased that he wanted to talk to me about my work – normally he's so standoffish about it – and I didn't think for a minute it would matter. God, I was such an idiot!'

Rachel began to cry again. Shali handed her a tissue.

'Well then, and you won't believe this, Harry decided that he could sell the story to the papers and make a load of cash out of it.'

'What? No!' Shali looked shell-shocked.

Rachel nodded. 'He'd wanted to come round last night but I told him I had to work and mentioned that I had all my files here. So he came round today when he thought I'd be out and went through them, looking for proof of the story.'

'Oh my God, Rachel, that's awful! I can't believe he would do that.'

'And then he tried to get me to go along with it by saying the money would set us up for the future. He even mentioned getting married and having kids. I'm sure that was just a ploy to try to win me over, the slimy bastard. And even if he meant it, what a totally fucked up way of bringing it up!'

Rachel became furious all over again as she recalled Harry's assumption that she would automatically give up work. She had the better job! If anyone was going to be giving up it should be him. Rachel sighed heavily. It was hardly a debate that they were now likely to be having.

'Did he find any proof? Shit, is he off trying to sell the story right now?' Shali looked alarmed and sat forward in her chair like she was about to sprint out the door and chase Harry down.

'No, thank God. The bits of paper he needed weren't here. They're locked in my desk. All that was here were the normal sales records and of course they don't mention any of the real names,' Rachel explained.

'How did you find out then?' Shali asked.

Rachel told Shali about seeing Lloyd Cassidy and Audrey Fox having a late night meeting with Francesca Hart and the black appointments book that she'd copied pages from.

Shali sat open-mouthed and spellbound as Rachel spoke, trying not to enjoy the drama and scandal too much. She'd never heard a story like it.

'Blimey, Carl Stephens must be doing his nut! Will it kill the deal?' Shali asked.

'I haven't told him about it,' Rachel said quietly and suddenly felt very ashamed. How could she have thought that saying nothing was the right option? She knew deep down that she'd taken the easy way out. What a coward.

'I don't understand,' said Shali. 'Why not?'

Rachel put her head in her hands. What a bloody mess.

'Carl's having an affair with someone who's involved – Audrey Fox, the nurse I saw.'

'You're kidding me! Are you sure? Fuck, I need a drink.'

Shali went to the kitchen and hunted out the bottle of white wine in the fridge. She then took two more bottles off the wine rack and put them in the freezer. It was going to be a long evening.

As they drank, Rachel told Shali about seeing Carl meet Audrey at the hotel and how he'd brushed her off when she raised her initial concerns with him.

'So you see, if I raise it with him, I'll have to ask him if he's having an affair. If he is then he needs to step down off the project,' said Rachel. 'Then we'll need to tell the buyers and, quite frankly, all hell will break loose. And on top of that, I'll have to explain that I was creeping around in client offices breaking into locked drawers. Hardly great for my promotion prospects.'

'Doesn't sound the best,' Shali agreed. 'But I don't think you have any choice. You can't let the deal go ahead without telling the buyers what you know, however hard it is to deal with. That's the whole point of your review. The Americans will sue the arses off us if they buy the business and then find out afterwards.'

Rachel knew Shali was right but she was already an emotional car crash. The thought of opening such a massive can of worms was just a crisis too far right now.

'I can't cope with it all, Shali, not on top of breaking up with Harry.' Rachel was shaking so badly she could hardly hold her wine glass.

'Is that what you're doing?' Shali asked.

'Well, I told him to get the fuck out of my flat.'

'Did you? Good girl.' Shali grinned at Rachel, who managed a smile for the first time that evening.

'Yeah, I did. And I'm pretty sure there's no way back from this. I'm sure he'll beg and plead and try every trick in the book to make me take him back, but what he's done is despicable, a total betrayal,' said Rachel.

'Harry's always been a bit wide but I never thought he'd stoop that low.'

Rachel winced at Harry being referred to as wide. Why was it that your friends only ever told you what they really thought about your boyfriends once you split up?

'I really don't think he saw it as such a big deal. You know, that's his business as a sports journalist – getting a good story and then selling it. As he said, it's not illegal or anything providing the story is true – well, not for him anyway. He just didn't think about the consequences for me. When I told him I could be struck off for breaching client confidentiality he looked genuinely surprised. What I can't bear was that he was going to try to do it without telling me. Imagine what would have happened if I hadn't come back?'

'I don't think I dare,' said Shali. 'Scandal about your client splashed across the front pages right in the middle of the deal? What a total nightmare. There would've been a huge witch hunt for whoever'd leaked the information. Even if they couldn't trace it to you, imagine how stressed you would have been!'

'I guess that Harry's plan must have been to tell me about it at some point, otherwise that story he gave me about doing it to plan for our future together was total bollocks.'

Rachel could tell from the look on Shali's face which she thought was more likely.

'Well, never mind all that. He didn't get anything, and as he's now the fuck out of your flat you can focus on how to deal with this unholy mess on your project,' said Shali.

'I don't know where to start,' said Rachel, feeling utterly exhausted.

'Well, we need a plan, and a damn good one. For that we need more wine and definitely some chips. I'm starving.'

Rachel lay back on the sofa and shut her eyes for ten minutes while Shali ran out to the fish and chip shop for two large bags of chips smothered with salt and vinegar. The smell of them as she came back into the flat made Rachel realise how hungry she was too. She was practically dribbling by the time Shali had set them out on the coffee table with a second bottle of very cold wine and a pad of paper.

'Right, let's make a list of who you need to talk to and in what order. Then we can go through your diary for this week and work out when you do what.'

Rachel felt that Shali was rather enjoying her crisis manager role, but she didn't mind. In fact, she really needed her help, more than Shali probably realised.

'Do I need to add "talk to Shali about Rowan" to this list?' Shali asked, trying to look serious.

'No, I think that can wait until next week,' said Rachel, grinning.

It took them about an hour to write the list and work out Rachel's diary for the rest of the week.

'Shit, that is officially the week from hell,' said Rachel as they sat and looked at it. 'Well, I'd better not drink any more if I'm really going to see Carl first thing. What the hell am I going to say to him?'

'How about, "Are you having an affair with Audrey Fox from Beau Street?" That would wake him up,' said Shali.

'I can't just pile in with that! I need to explain to him what I've found first,' said Rachel.

'Right, good point,' said Shali, smiling. 'I'll make some notes, then you can go through them again on the tube tomorrow, prepare yourself a bit. What are you going to say about the pages you copied out of the black appointments book? Could you maybe say it was left out somewhere? That might be a bit better than saying you broke into his desk.'

'No, I'm going to tell him the truth, however bad it is,' said Rachel, resigned to the fact that it was going to be pretty awful. 'I should have said something straight away, dealt with it properly, you know. Then maybe I wouldn't be in this mess.'

'Okay, the total truth it is then,' said Shali, taking a deep breath and picking up a pen.

When they'd finished, Rachel read over the notes, nodding her head as she read.

'Enough?' Shali asked.

'Yes, enough.' Rachel looked up at Shali. 'Thank you. I couldn't do this without you.'

'No problem. We'll work it out, you know. It will be fine in the end,' said Shali, trying not to sound hesitant.

'I'm not quite sure how, but let's see,' said Rachel. 'I think I need to go to bed.'

The two friends hugged as Shali left.

'Call me tomorrow, as soon as you can,' said Shali.

Rachel nodded and shut the door wearily. She slowly tidied up and climbed into bed, dreading the next morning but at the same time desperate for the sleep that would take her there. Fortunately the combination of hours of crying and several glasses of wine meant that it didn't take long for that sleep to come.

CHAPTER 15

For a few moments when Rachel first woke up, she felt quite happy. She wriggled around, enjoying the warmth and familiarity of her bed, and looked at the alarm clock. Time to get up.

Then, as the realisation of what the day ahead would be like came into focus, Rachel felt quite sick. Butterflies leapt around in her stomach like they'd suddenly grown kangaroo legs. She looked at the space next to her in the large double bed and her mind immediately turned to Harry. She buried her face in her pillow. God, she missed him already.

After a few minutes her tears turned to irritation at the impact he was able to have on her, and Rachel forced herself to get up and get ready for work.

On the way to the office she texted Rosa to say that she had an urgent meeting with Carl, she would be in mid-morning and could they get on with the presentation. Rachel knew they'd be somewhat alarmed by her having an urgent meeting they knew nothing about, but there was nothing she could do about it. In her week from hell diary, Carl had to be first. She would tell Rosa and AJ later.

Rachel sat staring at the neatly written notes Shali had written to help her prepare for the meeting. Just below 'Tell him the total truth', Shali had written 'Good luck, mate' and drawn a smiley face next to it. Rachel smiled to herself and then felt a bit ashamed of how she'd been treating Shali, blaming her for the whole Rowan incident. Maybe she had overreacted. Shali had been a total star last night.

As soon as she arrived in the office, she went to see Carl's secretary.

'I need to see him urgently this morning, as soon as possible. Can you sort something out?' she asked as Carl's PA peered unhopefully at her computer.

'He has appointments until lunchtime so the earliest you can see him would be about one o' clock,' replied the PA rather haughtily.

Rachel peered over her shoulder and looked at the entries in his diary.

'He's doing an appraisal first thing — can't you move that? This is very important; it's about the Beau Street project. Please, Margaret.'

'Stop looking at his diary; it's private,' said Margaret, and then seemed to notice Rachel's pale and worried expression. 'Look, I'll see what I can do. Give me ten minutes.'

Margaret rang Rachel a few minutes later.

'He'll see you now, and by the way, he wasn't best pleased, just so you know.'

Great, annoyed before we start, thought Rachel.

She headed to Carl's office, knocked on the door and went in.

'Right, yes, what is it, Rachel? Margaret said you needed to see me urgently. I thought everything was going fine on Beau Street?'

Rachel looked at his furrowed brow as he glared at her and almost lost her nerve. Her voice shook slightly as she spoke. 'There's an issue at Beau Street that I need to discuss with you,' she said.

'What sort of issue?' Carl asked. 'I thought our work was pretty much done.'

'Well, do you remember when I came to see you to give you an update a couple of weeks back and said that we'd found a few issues with sales records not having the right information on them?'

'Yes, something to do with the new computer systems. And I thought we'd agreed to write that up as a minor recommendation for improvement?' said Carl.

'Yes, we did. But since then I've found out that it's a bit more than that. One of the doctors, Lloyd Cassidy, has been charging his patients well above the list prices in return for being booked in under false names, so that no one can ever find out that they've had cosmetic surgery. Mostly it seems to have been offered to celebrities or other people who are in the public eye.'

Carl looked genuinely shocked. 'When did you find this out?'

'Well, about a week ago.'

'A week ago! So why am I only hearing about this now? For God's sake, we're presenting to Equinox on Monday.'

'I know. I'm so sorry, Carl. It's totally my fault. You see, the thing is, the way I found out wasn't exactly straightforward, and I couldn't decide what I should do about it. So in the end I did nothing, until now, anyway.'

'What do you mean not exactly straightforward?' Carl asked.

'I stayed late one evening and saw an actress I recognised arriving after the offices were shut. So I hid and watched where she went. I saw her meet Lloyd Cassidy and his nurse Audrey Fox.'

Rachel immediately noticed a reaction in Carl's face at the mention of Audrey's name.

'I saw them writing in a manual black appointments book, which Lloyd locked in his desk. After the meeting finished, I went into his office, got the key from its hiding place and got the book. It was a record of the real names of the patients and then the false name they were going to be booked in under, plus how much they were going to pay. I photocopied a couple of pages and checked the names against the proper records. Only the false names appear in the records and the payments were all made in cash so they couldn't be traced back to the real patients.'

'I can't believe you crept around clients' offices after hours breaking into locked desks! What were you thinking?' Carl looked furious.

'I know, really stupid. It was just a spur of the moment thing as I knew something wasn't right. Then I was really worried about the impact it might have on the deal if I told anyone, and that I'd probably be in trouble too. So I decided to say nothing and leave it as it was, noted in our report as a minor issue with record keeping,' said Rachel.

Carl stood up and paced around his office, thinking. After a few minutes, he asked, 'How do you know that there's only one doctor involved?'

'Well, I don't for definite. But all of the invoices we found that didn't show any details of the procedure that had been performed, the ones that just said "other", were ones raised by Lloyd Cassidy. They were also paid in cash, which is unusual. I guess there could be more but we didn't find any.'

'Would the celebrities not be recognised when they came in?'

'I think that they've been seeing them in the evenings, when everyone has gone, including when they do the surgery, which is why Lloyd needs his nurse in on it,' said Rachel, waiting for Carl to react again to the mention of Audrey.

He looked at her sceptically, then said, 'They'd need an anaesthetist in on it too, if that's the case.'

Rachel thought for a moment. 'Yes, you're right. I guess they must do.'

'And they presumably don't have proper medical histories for these patients either if everything is under false names.'

'No, probably not,' said Rachel. 'I hadn't thought of that.'

'Seems like there have been quite a few things you didn't think of,' said Carl sharply.

Rachel looked at the floor, not quite sure how to respond.

Carl sat back down and opened his drawer, taking out a large notebook. 'Right, let's start again. Right at the beginning. Tell me everything that happened, what documents you have, who you saw, on what dates — everything.'

Rachel felt like she was in a police interview for the next half an hour as Carl fired question after question at her and wrote copious notes in his book. She couldn't decide whether that was a good or a bad thing.

When they had finished, Carl sat upright in his chair. 'Right, I think I have the full picture,' he said.

'What are we going to do now?' Rachel asked.

'We're going to have to sit down and take Tom Duffy through everything' said Carl.

'Are we going to put this in our report for Equinox too?' Rachel asked.

'No, not at the moment. I want to talk to Tom about it and agree how we handle it. You'd better brief AJ and Rosa and get as much information as you can to support what we know.'

'I think we'll probably need to talk to Lloyd Cassidy and Audrey Fox again to do that. Perhaps we could do that together?'

'Well, let's see, shall we,' said Carl. He didn't seem keen on that idea. Funny that.

She had to ask him directly about Audrey. She took a deep breath.

'A week or so ago, I was meeting my brother for lunch at The Brook Hotel and I saw you there with Audrey Fox. You seemed — well, how can I put it —

somewhat friendly. Are you having a relationship with her?'

There, she'd said it.

Carl looked shocked, sat back in his chair and ran his fingers through his hair.

'That's none of your business,' he said.

'It is when she works for our client. You're meant to declare any client relationships,' said Rachel.

'So you're now the expert on client ethics, are you? Maybe you should have remembered a few more of the rules before you started sneaking about client offices,' Carl retorted.

'You haven't answered the question,' said Rachel, ignoring his dig at her.

'Audrey and I have known each other for years. I met her through Tom Duffy. We're old friends, no more. Now you need to watch your step, young lady. Running round accusing people of unethical behaviour really isn't a very good idea. Don't forget I'm on your promotion panel in a couple of months.'

'Is that a threat?' Rachel asked, somewhat incredulous.

'No, it's just a reminder,' said Carl. 'I want you to do well at the panels, Rachel. You're ready to be a director. You just need to show that you've calmed down a bit. This sort of knee-jerk reaction to things doesn't help.'

Shit, thought Rachel, this isn't exactly going as planned.

'Sorry, I just got a bit worried when I saw you, that's all,' said Rachel.

'Well, I think we have enough to worry about already, so let's focus on that. Can you make sure that we can see Tom Duffy first thing in the morning?'

'Okay, I'll call you later to confirm he can see us,' said Rachel.

'As you're here, there's something else I'd like to raise with you,' said Carl. 'As you probably know, we had a complaint from the venue where we held the summer party about some inappropriate behaviour by some of the guests and I'm leading the investigation into it.'

Rachel nodded, not sure what was coming next.

'Well, I've received the descriptions given by staff who saw the people concerned. Apparently they opened the door to a small conference room from an adjacent room to get some extra chairs and saw a couple having sex on a table.'

Oh my God, Shali and Rowan had been seen! Rachel couldn't believe it. She was sure they didn't know that anyone had come in. Shali would be mortified.

'They gave a description of an Asian woman in a silver dress and a tall dark-haired man in a dinner suit. The man is a bit hard to identify, could be anyone. But doesn't the woman sound a bit like someone you might know? Sounds rather like Shali, don't you think? She had a silver dress on. And didn't she bring your brother as a guest, the stumbling drunk I seem to remember? He was tall with dark hair.'

Carl leaned forward across the desk.

'Do you think I'm getting close?'

'Er, I don't know, really, no, I don't think so,' Rachel mumbled.

'Now the thing is, I need to tell the rest of the partner group whether I have enough details to work out who it was.' Carl waved a piece of paper across the desk at her. 'It would be much better for those concerned if they came forward and owned up to knowing who was involved.'

Rachel didn't say anything. She wasn't going to admit anything without talking to Shali first.

'Well, you have a bit of a think about that, why don't you,' said Carl. 'I'll see you tomorrow.'

Rachel left Carl's office feeling even more worried than before she'd gone in. Had she wrongly accused him of having an affair with his client? She was sure she'd been on the right track about Audrey. And what a nightmare about the summer party. Carl wanted her to own up that she knew who it was. She texted Shali: *Went v badly, urgently need to meet u. Lunch?*

When Rachel arrived out at Beau Street she made an appointment to see Tom Duffy the next morning, then sat down to brief AJ and Rosa. They both sat very quietly as Rachel told them about Lloyd Cassidy.

'Why didn't you tell us before?' AJ asked.

'I wanted to talk to Carl first, agree how we should handle it,' said Rachel. 'It wasn't the greatest decision of mine to get the black book out of his desk. It was a bit of a, well, knee-jerk reaction. But anyway, we know now, and provided we're right then it won't be too bad. However, not one for you guys to follow, okay?'

They both nodded, looking rather excited by this unexpected turn of events.

'So, we need to gather as much information as we can on this before my meeting with Tom Duffy tomorrow morning. Rosa, why don't you help me for a bit? And AJ, you finish the presentation. It's nearly done, isn't it?'

AJ nodded.

Rachel got out the two photocopied black book pages that she had carefully hidden inside her notebook. She also took out a copy of the June Mayfield/Lisa Albrecht invoice that she'd found earlier. She sat down next to Rosa and talked her through what was recorded in the black book.

'This shows the link between the real name and the false name, you see? And then this is the invoice under the false name where it shows it being paid in cash.'

Rosa looked at the invoice. 'The invoice amount isn't the same as the amount in the black book.'

'Isn't it?' Rachel looked at the two documents. The black book said six thousand eight hundred and fifty pounds, but the invoice was for *five* thousand eight hundred and fifty.

'God, I hadn't noticed that,' said Rachel.

'What's happened to the difference?' Rosa asked.

Rachel and Rosa looked at each other. Rachel was pretty sure they both knew what the answer was: it was in Lloyd Cassidy's pocket. If so, that was far more serious. The fact that he was using false names was one thing, but this was fraud: stealing from his fellow partners.

'Right, we need to trace each of the invoices for these two pages as quickly as we can,' said Rachel.

Rachel and Rosa worked furiously for the next hour, looking up each of the false names listed and then finding the invoiced amount. Rachel did the searches and Rosa recorded the findings on her laptop. There were twenty-eight entries on the two pages covering a period of a couple of months.

'Right, the total amount charged per the black book is a hundred and ninety-four thousand six hundred pounds, but the total amount actually invoiced is a hundred and fifty two thousand two hundred. That's forty-two thousand four hundred pounds short, assuming that the clients actually paid the amount in the book,' said Rosa.

'Wow, in two months? That's not good,' said Rachel.

'How do we know what cash the clients actually paid him? This handwritten book doesn't prove anything,' Rosa asked.

Rachel sat and thought for a few moments.

'To be honest, I don't think we do – not without asking the clients to confirm it, and they're hardly likely to do that seeing as they chose to pay extra to make sure there were no records with their name on. We'll just have to report what we know.'

Rachel felt quite sick. The size of the fraud could be huge and she'd nearly missed it. How could she have convinced herself that it wasn't that important? God, what a wakeup call this project was turning out to be.

CHAPTER 16

Rachel couldn't decide how best to break the news to Shali that she and Rowan had been seen, so in the end she just blurted it right out. As she'd suspected, Shali was horrified.

'You saw Carl this morning and he said someone came in and saw us, actually, well, at it? Is that what he said?'

Rachel nodded.

'Oh my God, how embarrassing! Do you think they watched?' Shali asked.

That hadn't even occurred to Rachel. Probably.

'No, no, I shouldn't think so,' she said to Shali. 'The way Carl described it, they just looked in and then left again.'

'Oh no!' Shali covered her face with her hands. 'What a total disaster. I'm meeting Rowan tonight.' Shali looked up anxiously at Rachel. 'He said that he'd told you?'

'Yes, he did. He said he wants to explain things to you face to face,' said Rachel.

'I know. He's such a nice guy. I said it wasn't

'necessary but he insisted.' Shali stared slightly dreamily out of the window.

'He's working things out with Laura, you know,' said Rachel, slightly unnerved.

'Yes, I know. Will you call him first? Tell him that we were seen. I can't bear to.'

'Yes, okay, if you want. Also, Carl made it pretty clear he wants the people who know who it was to own up. I don't think he's exactly expecting Rowan to drop in and see him, so that means you and me,' said Rachel.

'And if we don't?' Shali asked.

'He can work it out anyway. He probably just needs to talk to more people to show that he can confirm the descriptions,' said Rachel.

'So damned if we do and damned if we don't. Great,' said Shali.

They sat in silence for a few minutes, sipping their drinks and staring at the other people happily enjoying their lunches, oblivious to their crisis.

'I guess I'll have to go and see Carl. That will probably be better than him asking loads of questions. Do you think it will get out?' Shali asked.

'It shouldn't do,' said Rachel. 'This sort of thing is meant to be confidential.' But hardly ever is, she thought.

'God, I bet I get a right bollocking,' said Shali.

'I'm sure you can explain that it was just a one-off and that you don't usually do that sort of thing.'

They both knew that wasn't quite true.

'Anyway, Carl is hardly one to talk – Mr Hotel

Room himself,' said Shali. 'Maybe I should do a deal with him: we won't tell if he doesn't.'

'Well, he's denied he's seeing Audrey and I didn't actually see them do anything, so we can't prove it,' said Rachel. 'Anyway, that would be madness, far too risky. He'd probably shop us for trying to blackmail him.'

'Alright, stupid plan. I'll have to tell him I was with Rowan,' said Shali, now resigned to the fact that she had no choice but to own up.

'I'm sure he'll talk to me about that too,' said Rachel. 'I'll get some big lecture about my choice of guests at important functions.'

'Better than being fired.'

'They won't fire you!' said Rachel. 'It's not that bad.'

'Are you sure? I bet they could if they wanted to,' said Shali.

'Well, they won't want to. You're too highly rated. They'll probably just send you on a training course or something,' said Rachel.

'What, a course on how to keep your knickers on? That would be a new one for Payne Stanley,' said Shali.

They both giggled loudly at the thought.

Rachel looked at her watch. 'I'd better get back. Got a major "shit hitting the fan" meeting to prepare for.'

'God, what a pair we are!' said Shali.

As Rachel walked back to work, her phone beeped in her bag. She had a text from Harry: *Have been total fool. Can we talk? I need you, babe. H.*

She stared at it sadly. 'Well, I don't need you,' she

said out loud to herself, and texted back the first words that jumped into her head: *Leave me alone. It's over.* Before she could change her mind, she pressed send and saw her words flash on the screen. Is that what she really meant to send? Was that really true? Too late now.

Rachel rang Carl as soon as she got back to the office after lunch. She confirmed their appointment with Tom Duffy first thing in the morning and then went on to tell him about the invoiced amounts being less than the amounts noted in the black book.

'He's still charged them over the odds,' Rachel explained. 'But we think that he's kept some of the cash for himself and only put the lower amounts through the books.'

Rachel couldn't help herself and added, 'And Audrey does all Lloyd's paperwork for him, so we think she must be in on it too.'

'You've just noticed this?' Carl asked.

'Yes, when we sat down this morning to get the supporting information you wanted. We've looked up every invoice that we have names for. They're all less than the amount in the black book.'

'Maybe the black book isn't the right amount?' Carl suggested.

'Well, why would they bother to write it down then? When I saw Francesca Hart come in she was there when Lloyd wrote in the book. She gave them cash at the time and I'm sure what they wrote is what she agreed to pay.'

'Okay, well get down everything you have and let's

talk to Tom tomorrow. This really isn't great,' said Carl.

'I know,' said Rachel. For anyone, she thought.

Rachel was determined to show that she was organised and in control for when Carl came out in the morning. As she ran though her to-do list, she realised in horror that she hadn't rung Clive Steele from the PR company as Tom had asked her to. He was bound to ask her about it in the morning. She quickly picked up her phone. Clive Steele wasn't in, so she was put through to one of his team.

'Tim Archer, can I help you?'

'Oh yes, good afternoon, this is Rachel Altman from the corporate finance team at Payne Stanley. We're working with the Beau Street Group at the moment and Tom Duffy asked if I could give Clive Steele a call to see if we could help provide you with some information for their new marketing plan. I understand that Clive isn't in at the moment.'

'Yes, that's right, but it's me that you probably want to speak to anyway as I'll be leading the work from our side. Clive runs the place,' said Tim.

Rachel had thought she recognised Clive's name but she was pretty sure she didn't know anyone who was the head of a PR company. It must be someone else.

'Oh, I see,' said Rachel. 'When would you like to meet? Early next week works for me.'

It would be good to get the Equinox presentation out of the way first.

'That's too late for our deadline, I'm afraid. I was

hoping that we could meet as soon as possible. Tomorrow would be ideal,' said Tim.

Tomorrow! That didn't give her much time to prepare, but at least she could report progress to Tom when they met. Plus, she'd forgotten to phone them and she could do without getting the blame for them missing their deadline. She would just have to fit them in.

'I'm busy first thing, so it would have to be after that. Maybe around lunchtime?'

'Midday would work for me,' said Tim.

'Fine, let's do that,' said Rachel, looking wearily at her packed diary. At least they were getting paid extra for helping this PR company out.

That evening, Rachel lay exhausted on the sofa in her flat talking to Rowan on the phone. She'd got hold of him on his way to meet Shali and he was equally mortified that they'd been seen.

'Shit, Rachel, that's awful!'

'I know, I'm sorry, but I thought it was only fair that you knew,' said Rachel.

'God, I wonder which side of the room the adjoining door was?' said Rowan.

'Does it matter?' Rachel asked.

'Well, yes, it does. Did they see our heads, or well, how can I put it, not our heads. Oh what a nightmare, it doesn't bear thinking about.'

All sorts of images flashed through Rachel's head that she quickly tried to get rid of.

'I guess you'll never know,' said Rachel. 'The thing is that work knows it was Shali. One of the staff gave enough of a description that they could work it out.'

Rachel told Rowan all about her meeting with Carl Stephens and accusing him of seeing Audrey Fox.

'He is so seeing her, the lying bastard.'

'Did you actually see anything?' Rachel asked.

'I saw them holding hands. Well, he had his hand on her arm, anyway,' said Rowan.

'That's not quite the same as holding hands. Maybe that was just in an old friends sort of way,' said Rachel.

'I'm sure his wife wouldn't have thought so if she'd seen them,' said Rowan.

'Maybe, but I guess we can't be sure. Anyway, I'm afraid Shali is going to have to own up to Carl that it was her. Otherwise she'll just get in more trouble. So I thought I'd better warn you. Just so you know. If it does get round then people will probably work out that Shali was with you,' said Rachel.

'It's bound to get round,' said Rowan. 'I know what your place is like − no one can keep anything quiet. But I guess there's not much I can do about it now. Will Shali be in big trouble?'

'Hard to say for sure. She might get away with a warning, but it will still be on her files and that's not great,' said Rachel. 'She'll just need to behave herself for a while, let it all die down.'

'Shit, I feel even worse now,' said Rowan. 'Good thing you caught me before I meet her. It gives me a bit more time to work out what to say to her.'

'Where does Laura think you are?' Rachel asked.

'Out with a mate from university. More lies.'

'That should be it after today, though,' said Rachel, waiting for Rowan to agree with her.

He didn't. 'Well, you can tell that boyfriend of yours that it's the last time I play drinking games with him for a while. Far too dangerous.'

Rachel felt a lump in the back of her throat and tears pricked at her eyes. 'He's not my boyfriend anymore. We've split up,' she said slowly.

'What! Why?' Rowan asked.

'It's complicated.'

'It generally is,' said Rowan.

Rachel told Rowan what had happened.

'So my life is now total shit,' said Rachel. 'Everything is going wrong.'

'Have you seen Harry since?' Rowan asked.

'No, he's texted me saying how sorry he is. Bit late for that,' said Rachel.

'Maybe you should give Harry a chance, Rachel. Listen to what he has to say. You know, sometimes us blokes do really stupid things, even to people we love. I should know.'

'Rowan, he was going to steal from me and sell the story to the papers!'

'So you could have a better future together,' said Rowan.

'You don't believe that load of old crap, do you? I'd have thought that you of all people would see through that.'

'I think that it's possible that he believed it, which is what matters. He probably just didn't think it through properly. You know how impetuous he is,' said Rowan.

'That's no excuse,' said Rachel. 'Anyway, we're not

having this conversation. Stop defending him. It's over and that's that.'

'Alright, alright,' said Rowan. 'Just trying to put the other point of view across. Sometimes things aren't as black and white as they seem. At least you and Shali are talking again.'

'She's been great, to be honest. Totally behind me,' said Rachel.

'Of course she is,' said Rowan.

'Say hi and tell her I'll call her tomorrow when you see her, will you?' Rachel asked.

'I'll give her a kiss from you too, if you like,' said Rowan, adding quickly, 'only joking.'

'That's not funny, Rowan,' said Rachel.

'No, sorry. Look, I'd better go. Are you sure you'll be okay?'

'I'll be fine,' said Rachel.

Would she really be fine? Rachel wasn't sure. And the prospect of meeting Tom Duffy in the morning to break the bad news didn't exactly make her feel any better.

She got up and was on her way to run a bath when the phone rang.

'Please don't hang up,' said Harry as soon as she answered.

'What do you want?' she asked. Her legs felt a bit wobbly so she sat down on the stairs.

'To see you. To say sorry.'

'I think it's a bit late for sorry. The damage has been done,' said Rachel.

'Can we at least meet? Just give me a chance to

explain. Half an hour — that can't hurt, can it? Look, I'll be in the pub on the corner in an hour. I'll wait there,' said Harry.

'I don't know, Harry, is there any point?'

'Please, think about it. I'll wait anyway, until closing time.'

'Harry, I…'

But he rang off before Rachel could say anything else.

As she lay in the bath she looked at the bathroom clock. Harry would be in the pub soon, ordering himself a pint, playing the fruit machine. She couldn't decide whether to meet him or not. Would her anger at him be enough to hold back the inevitable charm offensive? And if she wasn't having him back, what would it achieve? But on the other hand, she did want to hear him say sorry. Maybe that would make her feel better, make it easier to move on.

Although she'd thought she'd still not made a decision, Rachel soon found herself standing in front of her wardrobe choosing something to wear. What sort of outfit would best portray terribly hurt but in control? She hated the fact that she was shallow enough to care what she wore, but the truth was she did. She carefully picked out a pair of tight-fitting black trousers, a black vest and long chunky-knit cream cardigan. The comforting softness of the cardigan seemed like the right balance against the sharp black outline underneath. Then she spent several minutes doing her make-up to ensure it looked like she wasn't wearing any, and then left for the pub. Half an hour, that was all she would give him.

As Rachel approached the pub, she started to feel really nervous and wrapped her cardigan tightly round herself. She saw Harry straight away, sitting at a table near the bar. The red patterned carpet and dark brown wooden tables seemed to make the atmosphere in the pub even more dingy than usual.

Harry stood up. 'Hi. I'm so glad you came. What would you like to drink?'

Rachel could tell he was nervous too. 'Diet coke, please,' she said, not really trusting herself to drink anything stronger.

'You've got half an hour,' she said as Harry sat back down.

'I've really missed you,' said Harry and put his hand on Rachel's arm.

She pulled it away. 'Why should I even listen to you?' she asked.

'I'm really sorry, Rachel. I acted like a complete idiot and you have every right to be furious with me. But I didn't know that I could have caused you so much trouble,' said Harry.

'It would have been obvious if you'd taken two seconds to think about it,' said Rachel.

'Well, that's it, you see. I've been thinking about this and I honestly don't know if it would.' Harry sat forward excitedly, keen to make his point. 'You see, I don't really listen that much when you talk about your work and so I didn't understand what sort of responsibilities you have. So it wasn't so much that I didn't think about you, I just didn't actually know that it would matter so much.'

He sat back, looking quite pleased with his argument, which he felt got him, at least partially, out of jail.

'Why didn't you listen to me?' said Rachel, somewhat taken aback by Harry's reasoning.

'Well, it wasn't, er, very interesting. All those facts and figures, you know, not really my thing,' said Harry.

Rachel looked at him. 'You don't find me interesting?'

'Of course I find you interesting! In fact, I think you're amazing. But that's not the same as being interested in your work,' said Harry.

He's like a child, thought Rachel. How could he possibly think that telling me he doesn't listen to me will make things better!

'You can't separate the two, Harry. What I do comes as part of me. It's a package. You can't just pick off the bits you like and ignore the rest. You think I'm interested in your endless sports stories? I listen to them because they're about you and that's what makes them interesting, not the subject itself.'

Harry looked deflated. 'Look, I'll try much harder from now on. We can talk whenever you like about your day, what you've been doing, and I promise I'll pay attention,' he said.

'Harry, this is a relationship we're talking about, not a study course,' said Rachel.

'What do you want me to do then?' Harry asked. 'Just say and I'll do it.'

Rachel sighed and shrugged her shoulders. 'I don't have all the answers. All I know is that this isn't working.'

'Well, I want to make it work,' said Harry. 'I want us to be back to normal, spending time together, out having a good time.'

'That's what you really want, isn't it? A good time girl who isn't too complicated. Someone who'll settle down, look after the kids and cook you dinner every night. Not someone with a career, a life of her own, that disrupts your social life,' said Rachel.

'That's not true,' said Harry. 'I want you and everything that comes with it. And I don't want someone cooking me dinner every night. Three nights a week is plenty.' He grinned at her.

'This isn't a joke, Harry,' said Rachel.

'No, no, of course it isn't,' said Harry, trying not to smile. 'Look, can't we at least try? Give it another chance, see if I can do better?' he asked.

'Is this really what you want, Harry? Us together, you know, long term. Because there's no point us going through all of this for some temporary fix,' said Rachel.

'It is what I want,' said Harry. 'Definitely.'

'And what about my career, what if I keep working no matter what happens?' She couldn't bring herself to mention children.

'I'm totally fine with that,' said Harry.

But Rachel knew that Harry would say pretty much anything if he thought it would convince her to have him back.

'I need some time to think,' she said, not feeling able to just say no to him there and then.

'Okay, I'll go to the bar and get us another drink,' said Harry.

'Harry, I need days not minutes!'

'Oh, alright then,' said Harry and he sat back down. 'Will you call me?' he asked.

Rachel nodded.

'When?'

'In a few days, next week maybe. I'm not sure exactly,' said Rachel.

'Is there anything I can do in the meantime?'

'No,' said Rachel and she got up to leave.

'I love you and I want you back,' said Harry.

'I know,' said Rachel.

She turned around and walked away.

CHAPTER 17

Harry's words were still resounding in Rachel's head as she got ready for work the next morning. Was she really that dull? She'd never thought so. Her life certainly didn't feel dull right now. Maybe she did talk about her work quite a lot, but didn't everyone? After all, it's where you spend most of your day. It made her furious to think of the hours and hours she'd spent listening to Harry showing off and telling people his 'oh so funny' journalist stories. She threw her dressing gown down onto the floor as she dressed. 'Selfish bastard!'

Her anger only subsided when she left the house and started focusing on the day ahead, as it was quickly replaced with fear at the thought of meeting Tom Duffy. How was he going to react? Clearly it wasn't their fault Lloyd Cassidy was on the take, but it was down to her that they now had so little time until the presentation to the buyers next week. What were they going to tell Equinox?

Rachel sat down on the tube, neatly tucking her

legs under her navy skirt suit. She sat forward slightly in her chair so the back of her jacket didn't crease and tried to relax. The silk scarf she'd tucked inside her shirt like a cravat was too warm for the tube and was making her feel a bit faint. She let out a loud sigh and the man opposite her, who was wearing a rather theatrical looking three-piece suit, smiled and nodded knowingly. The buttons on his waistcoat strained to hold his stomach in as he leaned forward slightly.

'Damn rat race,' he said. 'I know how you feel.'

Rachel forced a half smile and immediately wished that she had a paper to hide behind. She really hoped he wasn't going to try to engage her in conversation as she really didn't have the energy. She opened her bag, took out her phone and pretended to study her emails. It seemed to do the trick and the man didn't say anything else.

At the next stop a heavily pregnant woman got on as the carriage completely filled up from both ends. The three-piece suit man leapt out of his seat and waved his hand towards it with a deep bow.

'My dear, please have my seat,' he said to the woman, who took it gratefully.

What a gentleman, thought Rachel, and then felt a bit guilty about trying so hard to ignore him earlier. Maybe she should be a bit nicer to people.

As she arrived at Beau Street, she exchanged the usual weather pleasantries with Fred and then said a very pointed 'Good morning' to the receptionist as she walked past. The receptionist looked up slightly, startled by the unexpected show of friendliness. Her over-suntanned face creased slightly at the edges as she smiled but her forehead didn't move at all. 'Oh, er, yes, good morning,' she said and then quickly turned back to the gossip magazine she was reading.

AJ was already in the project room when Rachel arrived. He handed her some files and then paced up and down behind her as she looked at them.

'It's all in there,' he said. 'Draft of the report, all the paperwork we have on Lloyd Cassidy, a draft of the presentation and an agenda for the meeting. Rosa and I stayed late to get it finished,' said AJ.

'Wow, thank you, this is brilliant,' said Rachel. 'Please sit down, though. You're making me nervous.'

'Sorry, not really had anything like this happen on one of my projects before, that's all,' said AJ.

'Nor me,' said Rachel.

'Really? I would have thought someone with your experience would have dealt with this loads of times.'

Rachel wasn't feeling very experienced at that moment. In fact, she felt bloody terrified. She sat flicking through the files as the door burst open and Rosa came rushing in.

'So sorry I'm late,' she said. 'Some idiot fell under my train.'

'You're not late,' said Rachel, 'and that's a bit harsh on some poor squashed person.'

'Sorry, I just really wanted to be in early so I could help you get ready,' said Rosa.

'That's okay,' said Rachel, smiling at Rosa's bright-eyed enthusiasm. 'I think we're in good shape.'

'How long until Carl gets here?' AJ asked.

Rachel looked at her watch. 'Twenty minutes. Plenty of time for a coffee.'

The three of them went down to the canteen, grabbed a coffee each and sat down.

'I just want to say that this has been a really great project,' said Rosa. 'Hard work, but great. I've really enjoyed working for you as well.'

'Me too,' said AJ.

'Ah, thanks, guys,' said Rachel, touched. 'By the way, do you talk to your friends about your work much?'

'No, no, not at all. I'm very careful about client confidentiality,' said Rosa quickly, looking slightly worried by the direction of the question.

AJ nodded in agreement.

Rachel laughed. 'I'm sure you are, but that's not what I meant. I meant, do you talk generally about what we do, and do your friends or other halves or whoever find it interesting?'

'My girlfriend always says I don't talk to her enough,' said AJ. 'She'd listen to me talk about work all day if I let her.' He then looked slightly embarrassed, as if he hadn't meant to disclose such a personal fact.

'My friends think what I do is cool. Sometimes it takes a bit of explaining, you know, that we work on businesses being bought and sold. But mostly they get it,' said Rosa.

'Why?' AJ asked.

'Oh nothing. I just worry sometimes that people might find it a bit boring, that's all.'

'Bollocks,' said AJ. 'There's nothing boring about

working out how much a business might be worth.'

'I agree. A company's numbers are the windows to its soul,' said Rosa wistfully. 'They tell us everything. We're like the tarot readers of the financial world.'

'Very poetic,' said Rachel, grinning.

'And anyway, it's not the job that makes things boring,' said Rosa. 'It's the people that do it. It's only dull if they are.'

Rachel's heart sank. She knew that Rosa was right. It was her that didn't interest Harry enough to listen, not what she did.

'Shit, look who it is,' hissed AJ.

Lloyd Cassidy was standing at the counter ordering some breakfast.

'Look at him,' said Rachel. 'Standing there without a care in the world, no idea about the bombshell we're about to drop.'

They watched as he chatted to the canteen lady behind the till. She giggled like a young girl as he paid, clearly enjoying whatever joke he'd just made.

'He's coming this way,' said Rosa and they all sat up and tried to act normally.

'Good morning,' he said cheerily as he walked past their table.

Rachel nearly choked on her coffee. 'Morning,' she spluttered.

AJ and Rosa smiled politely at him.

'Bet he won't be quite so friendly the next time he sees us,' said Rachel once he was safely out of earshot.

'Let's get out of here,' said AJ.

Carl arrived moments after they got back to the

project room. There was a quiet resolution to his mood that quickly took over the room. Rachel was relieved that he was so calm. She needed that steady influence. They talked through the meeting plan in low voices for a few minutes and then Rachel and Carl got up to go.

'Good luck,' said Rosa, and Rachel saw the slightly terrified but excited glances that she and AJ exchanged with each other.

Tom Duffy was in a cheerful mood as they went into his office.

'Carl, good to see you. I must say that your team have been doing a great job, very ably led by Rachel here,' said Tom. 'Come on, sit down, sit down.'

They sat round the meeting table in Tom's office and he poured them each a glass of water.

'Now, you called this meeting, is that right?' Tom asked.

'Yes, that's right. We have a few matters that we need to talk to you about,' said Carl.

Rachel's heart started pounding so loudly that she thought Tom might hear it.

'Oh yes?' Tom looked concerned.

'We believe that we've uncovered a fraud,' said Carl very slowly and calmly.

'What?! You're joking?' Tom blinked several times in what seemed to be some sort of involuntary reaction.

'I'm afraid not,' said Carl. 'Rachel, would you mind getting out the relevant paperwork.'

Rachel jumped at the mention of her name and hastily opened the files. She tried to stop her hands from shaking as she took out the photocopied pages of the black book and the paperwork that they had on each entry.

Carl carefully took Tom through it.

'So you see, in addition to the breaches in proper record keeping, we think that Lloyd Cassidy has been taking money out of the business.'

Tom looked like he couldn't believe what he was hearing. 'How long have you known?'

Rachel held her breath. Too long.

'We only worked out the final piece of the puzzle yesterday,' said Carl.

Wow. Carl had protected her. She owed him big time.

'Do you know how much money he's taken?' Tom asked.

'No, we'll need Lloyd to give us his manual records in their entirety for us to work that out,' said Carl.

'The amount of the shortfall for the two months of records we do have was just over forty thousand pounds,' said Rachel.

'Jesus Christ!' Tom banged the table with his fist, making both Carl and Rachel jump. 'He's worked here for years. He was one of the first partners in the business with Charles. Could you be wrong?'

'We don't think so,' said Carl.

'I saw him take a large envelope of cash from an actress on the evening that I, er, found this book,' said Rachel.

Tom shook his head in disgust. 'Is it just him?' said Tom. 'Are others involved?'

Carl hesitated.

'His nurse, Audrey Fox, was with him when I saw him,' said Rachel, stepping in to answer. 'She does all his paperwork for him, so we think she must know. We don't know if she has taken any money as well, though.'

'I bet she has. Those two are as thick as bloody thieves. I've been convinced that they're having an affair for ages,' said Tom.

Rachel felt Carl shift uncomfortably beside her.

'Well, we won't know for certain who's involved until we look into it further,' said Carl. His voice sounded tight, as if he was forcing himself to speak calmly.

Tom got up from the desk and paced around the office. 'This is a total disaster. I need to tell Charles straight away. He'll be devastated. He and Lloyd have been friends for years. This business is his life, you know. Christ knows what we tell Equinox. They'll probably run for the hills when they hear.'

Tom looked like he could see the money he was going to make on the deal evaporating in front of his eyes.

'If we get enough information, we can probably restate the company's results without Lloyd's figures in. Maybe we could present those to Equinox, show them that the rest of the business has been doing really well?' Rachel suggested.

'Yes, good point, we could do with that as I can tell you that Lloyd will be out on his bloody ear if this all turns out to be true. He won't get a penny from the sale − if there is any sale, that is,' said Tom.

'Perhaps we should agree what to do next?' said Carl.

Tom sat back down at the table with a thump. He put his head in his hands and stared miserably at the floor.

'Tom?' said Carl, peering up under his arched arms. 'Are you okay?'

Tom sat up. 'Not really. But I guess we'd better get on with it. I'll call Charles as soon as we're done. Then we'd better meet Lloyd – see what he's got to say about all this.'

'Do you want us there?' Carl asked.

'Absolutely,' said Tom. He opened the door of his office. 'Linda, could you get Charles on the phone, quick as you can, and then can you arrange for Lloyd Cassidy and Audrey Fox to come and see me? We'll need a meeting room as Carl and Rachel will be joining me. Thanks.'

Carl would be coming face to face with Audrey! And if he was having an affair with her then it was going to be a nightmare for him. Even if they were just friends, Rachel was sure that Carl still wouldn't want to see her in trouble. And Tom clearly thought that she was having an affair with Lloyd. Maybe she was seeing them both? Either way, it was going to be an interesting meeting.

'Right, anything else we need to organise?' Tom asked.

'We need to agree what we'll tell Equinox and when,' said Carl.

'It's probably best that we speak to their advisers, Clinton Wahlberg, first. Let them brief their client. But we've got to look into it a bit more first, make sure we have all the facts right,' said Tom. 'I'll call them in the first instance but then I'm sure they'll want to speak to you and agree how to approach the presentation on Monday.'

'Oh, by the way, Tom, I've been in contact with Cavanaugh PR and I'm meeting them at lunchtime today, so we can get them the information they need,' said Rachel.

'Oh right, good,' said Tom. 'Not that we necessarily need a new marketing plan now. Bloody Cassidy.'

Linda popped her head round the door. 'I've got Charles on the phone and the meeting with Lloyd and Audrey is set up for three o'clock this afternoon, upstairs in meeting room four.'

Rachel and Carl made their way back to their project room.

'How did it go?' AJ asked as soon as they came in the room.

'As well as can be expected,' said Carl. 'Tom was pretty livid. It's a real blow for them.' Carl turned to Rachel. 'You did a good job, nice and calm, well done.'

Rachel wanted to thank him for not saying anything about her delay in speaking up, but she didn't want to raise it in front of Rosa and AJ.

'I've got a few calls to make and then a partners' lunch, so I'll head off now and come back later, in time for three o'clock,' said Carl.

'Okay, no problem,' said Rachel, quite relieved that he wasn't going to sit with them.

After Carl left, Rachel sat and recounted their meeting to AJ and Rosa, who both sat wide-eyed, listening avidly.

'So then I suggested we redo the analysis without any of Lloyd's sales figures, show what the business looks like without him. Tom seemed to like that idea,' said Rachel.

'Gosh, did you? Well done,' said Rosa.

'But that will take us ages,' said AJ, more concerned about their workload than keeping Tom Duffy happy.

'Well, let's see what happens this afternoon. I've got a meeting with the PR guys first. At least that should be pretty straightforward,' said Rachel.

As they were talking there was a knock on the door.

'Come in,' said Rachel.

It was Alex Fisher from the lawyers. It seemed that they'd also found a few things not quite right with Lloyd Cassidy's records. Alex explained that they had evidence of a potential negligence claim against Lloyd by a celebrity who'd paid inflated rates for her procedures.

'… and I was wondering if you'd come across any evidence of that?' Alex asked.

Yes, and some, thought Rachel. She spent a few minutes sharing what they'd found with Alex. It would be important when they presented to Equinox that all the advisers were on the same page.

After she'd finished with Alex, Rachel left the project room and headed for the ladies' toilets. As she walked down the corridor she saw Audrey Fox stepping into the lift with her coat on, talking on her mobile phone. Where was she going? It suddenly occurred to Rachel that Carl had just left too. Was she going to meet him? Surely not. But it was certainly possible. Carl had at least an hour before his lunch appointment. Maybe he wanted to tip her off, warn her about what was happening. Should she follow the nurse? But what if she was wrong? She didn't want another knee-jerk reaction to get her into trouble.

As Rachel stood frozen, unable to decide what to do, she watched as the lift doors shut and Audrey disappeared from view. Shit! She ran over to the lifts and pressed the down button. After what seemed like an age, the lift arrived back up. She stepped in and pressed the button for reception, and once there walked briskly across the foyer, resisting the urge to break into a run, and went out onto the street. She looked up and down the street but there was no sign of Audrey. Damn!

She went back inside and stuck her head around the door of Fred's small security room. He was sitting in a battered, red leather armchair with gold studs around the arms, listening to the shipping forecast. He jumped as Rachel came in.

'Gosh, Ms Altman, you didn't half give me a fright. I was miles away, I was. Southeast seven or eight in Wight tonight, you know,' said Fred, looking concerned.

'Really? Oh dear.' Rachel had no clue what he was talking about.

'Fred, I was wondering whether you'd seen Audrey Fox go out a moment ago?' Rachel asked.

'No, sorry, love. Been in here for the last ten minutes. Would you like me to give her a message for you when she comes back?'

'No, that's okay, thanks,' said Rachel. 'I'm seeing her later anyway.'

Rachel went back upstairs, annoyed with herself that she hadn't acted faster. She would just have to wait until the meeting later on, see how Carl handled it.

As she got out of the lift, Charles Sutton hurried past her in the direction of Tom Duffy's office. His face looked tense with worry. Rachel had only met him a couple of times, but he'd come across as a genuinely nice guy — a bit old fashioned maybe, but really passionate about the business. Rachel shook her head. There was nothing worse than being let down so badly by someone you trusted.

And she should know.

CHAPTER 18

Rachel waited impatiently in an airless, windowless meeting room in the basement at Beau Street, kicking herself for not being better prepared. It had been the only room she could get at short notice and she'd also been too late to book any lunch or coffee, which was not a great start. She had sent AJ out for a selection of sandwiches from the local deli instead, which had come back on paper plates. Bits of brightly coloured roasted vegetables mixed with slices of ham or feta cheese had been laid randomly across chunky bread cut into triangles. A few pieces of damp rocket had been laid around the plates in an attempt to perk up an otherwise uninspiring spread. She'd at least managed to get some bottles of water, but they'd have to get coffee from the crappy machine at the end of the hall. Plastic cups and paper plates, very professional. These PR guys were probably used to something a bit flashier, but there was nothing Rachel could do now.

She looked at her watch. Tim Archer was already ten minutes late. She grabbed the opportunity to try to prepare by flicking though their files and reminding herself of the information they had that might be useful.

Ten minutes later, Tim rushed into the room looking like a mad scientist who'd just blown himself up. His short brown hair was sticking up in all different directions, his tie was crooked, as were his glasses, and he was sweating profusely. He was wearing a badly fitting brown suit and a pair of very battered black shoes with incredibly thick soles that formed a ridge round the outer edges like an inflatable dingy. As a result, he bounced up and down as he walked.

Rachel stared at him. He couldn't have been less like the sort of person she'd been expecting to meet. He made the deli sandwiches look almost posh in comparison. How could Beau Street have hired him to help with their image-driven marketing campaign? It was almost comical. Rachel concluded he couldn't possibly have been at the pitch meeting.

'Hello, you must be Rachel Altman,' said Tim, proffering a large, sweaty hand that Rachel shook with as little contact as she could get away with. 'So sorry I'm late. Traffic was rubbish, but I'd left the office too late anyway. Clive Steele has decided he's going to join us. Sent me into a bit of a flat spin, actually, as he didn't tell me until last night. You know what it's like when the boss suddenly says he's turning up. Makes you check your work a few more times, eh!'

Rachel couldn't help smiling at his honesty.

'That's okay, don't worry. Is he on his way?' Rachel asked.

'He'll be here in about ten minutes. Said we should

start as he can't join us for the whole meeting – he's having lunch with someone from here afterwards, I forget who.' Tim stared absently into space, trying to remember.

'Maybe Tom Duffy,' Rachel suggested. 'They know each other quite well I think.'

'No, it's a woman. I heard him on the phone in the office last night. Alice, Annie someone? Anyway, it doesn't matter,' said Tim.

'Not Audrey Fox?' Rachel asked in surprise. The nurse was turning up all over the place! Why would she be meeting Clive Steele?

'Yes, that was it. Audrey Fox. Anyway, shall we get started?'

Tim sat down and started taking papers out of his briefcase.

Much to Rachel's relief she found the meeting pretty easy. Most of the information Tim wanted they already had, and those bits they didn't have wouldn't take long to prepare.

'You see, we just need some killer stats to make these headlines pack a punch. A top quality joint marketing plan is a really big part of making this deal work,' said Tim. 'The information you have as part of your report will really help with that.'

'What like fifty per cent of women have bunions?' Rachel asked, recalling Charles Sutton's comments about the growth in toe reshaping.

'I was thinking of something more like "We performed more than two thousand breast augmentations procedures last year, so when it comes to finding someone you can trust, we think size matters",' said Tim.

'Very good,' said Rachel, laughing. Maybe he was better than he looked. 'We have all the details on the numbers of the procedures they've performed each year, so that's easy,' she said.

They were mid discussion on what else Tim needed when there was a knock on the door.

'That will be Clive,' said Tim, jumping up to let him in.

Clive Steele was short and stocky, with curly black hair and a moustache. He was wearing a navy blazer with gold buttons and a pair of beige trousers that were rather faded and stretched at the waist. The handkerchief in his breast pocket said smart, but it didn't look like the rest of his clothes had been listening. His jacket had dandruff on the shoulders and the elbows were shiny with wear. His brown, slip-on loafers, once quite formal, were in need of a polish and showing their age. Rachel looked at him in amazement. What a pair he and Tim were. How on earth they'd landed this job she didn't know. However he did look familiar. She thought she recognised his name, but she couldn't work out how. She racked her brains.

'Ah, Rachel Altman, how are you?' said Clive, holding out a chubby hand.

He clearly knew who she was.

'Gosh, I'm sorry, have we met? I did think your name seemed familiar but I'm afraid I couldn't place it,' said Rachel, rubbing her nose.

'Oh, don't worry, it was quite a few years ago and I

guess you've probably tried very hard since to forget about me,' said Clive, winking at her.

Rachel frowned. He was a bit creepy. What could he be talking about?

'Corporate finance at Payne Stanley now, eh? Very impressive. I take it you're not into climbing clock towers any more then?' Clive asked, grinning at her slightly sleazily.

Rachel took a sharp intake of breath. How did he know about the clock tower? She'd been at university then.

'How do you know about that? You seem, er, well…'

'… older than you,' Clive finished. 'Yes, I am, much. I wasn't a student; I was on the board of governors.'

Clive Steele from the board of governors at university. Holy fuck! Rachel's memories came flooding back.

It had been a cold evening in November during her last year at university and Rachel and a group of friends had been out on a pub crawl. Rachel had a tutorial at ten o'clock the next morning and if past form was anything to go by she was likely to be late. She wasn't that great at mornings, particularly after a big night out.

Rachel was also sleeping with her economics tutor. Adam Radford was twelve years older than Rachel, but still young for a university lecturer. Rachel had fallen in love with him the moment she saw him. He had collar-length blonde hair, green eyes and shoulders like a lumberjack. Instead of the usual corduroy trousers and jumpers with elbow patches, Adam was often to be seen in a tight-fitting t-shirt and black jeans, which caused Rachel to spend hours dreaming about taking them off. After a few weeks of following him around and generally swooning in his direction, she'd unashamedly thrown herself at him. It had worked.

They were soon spending most nights together, regularly making Rachel late for her classes. Adam was much more disciplined about getting up. In the centre of the university buildings was an ornate Victorian building with a small octagonal clock tower offset to one side. The clock chimed loudly on the hour, and as Rachel rushed late and sweating into Adam's tutorials, he would often say, 'The clock tower has chimed already, Rachel. We all heard it. Do please try to be on time.' Rachel would look very serious and apologise, later catching his eye and giving him a long, smouldering look. Before long, the expression 'making the clock chime' took on a whole new meaning for them.

On the night of the pub crawl, Rachel had been drinking heavily. Each stop had involved at least one pint of lager or glass of wine, mostly followed by some hideous tasting liqueur chaser. As last orders were being called, Rachel had heard the clock tower chime and smiled to herself. As she played out the usual scene at Adam's tutorial the next morning in her mind, she had a totally crazy idea. She should climb up the clock tower and change the time! That would be hilarious – she could turn up late for Adam's tutorial the next morning and the clock wouldn't have chimed. It would be her and Adam's little secret, as only they would know what it meant.

She finished off her compulsory glass of sickly aniseed flavour green liqueur and wandered out of the pub into the cold evening air. She surveyed the climb in front of her. It didn't look too hard. There was a large fire escape at one side of the tower that would take her onto an adjoining roof. She could scramble across the roof and then onto a wide ledge just below the clock. The hands of the clock would be easy to reach from there.

Apart from being quite steep, the fire escape was easy. Rachel got to the top and peered over the edge at the sixty or so foot drop below her. The top of the fire escape was attached to the wall just below the roof line and she had to stretch pretty high to get a good grip on the guttering and pull herself up on the roof. The roof tiles were much more slippery than she'd envisaged, and for the first time she started to feel a little scared. The cold was also starting to have a sobering effect and her short skirt and high heels weren't ideal roof climbing attire.

She wriggled slowly commando style across the roof and over to the ledge by the clock tower. Swinging her legs over the edge of the roof, she managed to climb backwards onto the ledge and then slowly stand up. She'd made it! She reached up to the big hand on the clock face and tried to push it back. It wouldn't move. She tried again, pushing as hard as she dare given her precarious position, but it still didn't budge. Bugger! You must need to be inside the clock tower to move the hands.

She turned round and started to climb back. She

reached up towards the gutter and pulled, but as she did, it started to come away from the wall. She slipped slightly on the ledge, letting out a sharp scream, and just managed to grab a drainpipe to steady herself. She waited a few moments until the panic had subsided a bit and then tried again, but the gutter just wasn't strong enough to hold her.

As she hung on to the drainpipe, terrified and freezing cold, she heard a group of students laughing and joking below her and decided to shout for help. It took the students quite a few moments to work out where she was, and at first they thought it was quite funny. However, they soon realised that it really wasn't and called the fire brigade. Rachel's fingers were just starting to go numb as she heard the sirens of the fire engine approaching and, as a handsome young fireman helped her onto the rescue platform at the top of a very long ladder, she couldn't decide whether to laugh or cry.

News of the 'clock tower incident' spread like wildfire and for a short while she was almost a celebrity. Adam, however, hadn't seen the funny side. After a long talk and lots of tears and pleading on Rachel's side, he'd ended their relationship, citing 'age differences'. And just as her heart was breaking, she was called in front of the university's board of governors, including one very slimy Clive Steele, to explain her actions.

In a final act of kindness towards her, Adam had written a very supportive letter to the board, citing somewhat falsely what a talented student she was. In front of the board, Rachel had grovelled, begged and pleaded to be given another chance. In the end, they'd given her a written warning and a fine. Rachel then had to finish off her year being taught by a distant and very grown-up Adam. The whole experience had been totally humiliating.

And Rachel certainly didn't need it being brought up now. She had quite enough on her plate and she didn't think that Payne Stanley would see the funny side.

'Yes, well, as you say, that was many years ago,' said Rachel to Clive Steele in a brisk voice.

'This all sounds very intriguing,' said Tim. 'Come on, fill me in. What's the story here?'

'It's nothing,' said Rachel. 'Clive was a governor at my university, that's all.'

Rachel looked pointedly at Clive.

'Yes, I guess that's all, for now,' said Clive, raising one eyebrow. 'How nice that we know each other, though. I'm sure that means we'll be able to work very well together.'

Rachel didn't like the implication in his voice or the leering look on his face. He clearly thought that he had something on her and it looked like he intended to make the most of it. Well, two could play at that game.

'I understand that you know Audrey Fox,' said Rachel. 'Tim mentioned that you're having lunch with her after this.'

Clive looked surprised and frowned at Tim, who shrugged back at him.

'Yes, that's right,' said Clive. 'Do you know her too?'

'Only through this project. Is that how you got this assignment?' Rachel asked, trying to look innocent. She couldn't see how this pair of misfits had ended up working for Beau Street otherwise. There must be hundreds of other PR firms they could have chosen.

Clive shifted uncomfortably. 'No, we were awarded the project after a competitive proposal. But Audrey is an old friend and she was very supportive of us during the process,' said Clive.

Gave them the inside track more like, thought Rachel.

'Yes, I understand Audrey is very good to her old friends,' said Rachel.

She found it hard to believe that Audrey's relationship with the distinctly dumpy Clive could be anything more than friendship. He was hardly in the same league as Carl, or Lloyd Cassidy for that matter.

Clive eyed Rachel sharply and changed the subject. 'Perhaps we should get on,' he said, sitting down next to Tim.

Rachel was sure she was onto something. And if she wanted to make sure that Clive didn't start telling people about the clock tower story, she needed to get to the bottom of it.

CHAPTER 19

Carl came back to the project room at Beau Street about ten minutes before the three o'clock meeting with Lloyd Cassidy and Audrey Fox was due to start. Rachel studied him carefully for outward signs that he'd met Audrey while he'd been gone. There were none. He was as calm and composed as when he'd left.

'Did you get your calls done?' Rachel asked.

'Yes, thanks,' Carl replied.

He wasn't giving much away.

'How was the partners' lunch? Did you eat somewhere nice?' Rachel asked.

'Yes, fine, thanks. We ate near the office,' said Carl.

That's a bit vague, thought Rachel, but she daren't ask any more questions. Instead, she briefed him on her meeting with Clive and Tim, minus the university link with Clive obviously, and also told him about the lawyers coming to see her.

'That doesn't sound good. Tom could do without some messy legal issue to deal with as well. Still, that's for the lawyers to sort out,' said Carl. 'Right, we'd better go. Now, calm and professional at all times, no matter what happens, okay?' said Carl.

'Got it,' said Rachel.

What was he expecting might happen? Maybe he knew something she didn't.

Carl and Rachel arrived at the meeting room before anyone else and sat down at one end of the table. Tom Duffy and Charles Sutton followed shortly afterwards.

Carl got up and went to greet Charles. 'Charles, I'm so sorry to be the bearer of bad news,' he said.

Charles shook his head. 'Let's hear what he has to say first.' He was clearly hoping that Lloyd might have some miracle explanation.

'Of course,' said Carl.

'Unfortunately, we've also heard from the lawyers about a possible negligence claim against Lloyd relating to one of the patients who booked in under a false name,' said Tom, shaking his head. 'Not sure how we're going to handle that one. No proper medical records, patient consent forms in the wrong name – it's a minefield. Anyway, one thing at a time. We'd better sit down; I think they're on their way up.'

Carl nodded at Tom supportively. 'Yes, I heard about that. Very difficult,' he said and went to sit down.

Rachel held her breath as she heard more footsteps coming down the corridor. Lloyd Cassidy and Audrey arrived together. Lloyd was impeccably dressed as ever in a navy double-breasted suit and shiny purple shirt that seemed to show off his tanned looks even more than normal. Rachel noticed that his cufflinks were a pair of expensive looking gold dice. How apt. Audrey, on the other hand, looked slightly frazzled. Her normally neat blonde hair was rather out of place and her cheeks were flushed. She nervously smoothed down the front of her dress and sat down. Lloyd sat next to her.

Charles shut the meeting room door and then sat down directly opposite Lloyd. For a few moments, no one spoke.

'Now, would someone mind telling me what this is all about?' Lloyd asked, smiling broadly at the assembled room.

'As you are aware, Lloyd, we're in the middle of a possible sale process and as part of that we have commissioned a series of reports on our business for the potential buyers,' said Charles, looking at Lloyd over the top of his black-rimmed glasses.

Lloyd nodded.

'Well, Payne Stanley here has been looking at the financial side of things.' Charles gestured towards Rachel and Carl. 'And, well, they have drawn to my attention the fact that they've found some irregular transactions involving your clients.'

'Really?' said Lloyd, looking surprised, but not unduly concerned. 'What sort of irregular transactions?'

'The sort where you book clients in under false names and where some of the cash they pay goes in your pocket,' said Charles. 'Does that ring any bells?'

'What? No, not at all. I have no idea what you're talking about,' said Lloyd, raising his voice slightly above normal as if to emphasise the point.

'Perhaps we can jog your memory,' said Charles.

Rachel thought he sounded rather like a detective in an old movie.

Tom looked at Carl and Rachel. 'Could we have your files, please?'

Rachel got up and walked round to where Tom was sitting. She opened the files and quietly showed him where the copied pages from the black book were. Tom took them out of the file and gave them to Charles. He pushed them across the table towards Lloyd.

'Would you mind explaining what this is?' Charles asked.

Lloyd looked at them and for the first time seemed very uncomfortable.

'Where did you get these?'

'From your office,' said Tom. 'Or rather, Rachel did.'

Rachel waited for the inevitable rebuke from Lloyd, but none came. He just stared at the pages in front of him and said nothing. Eventually he looked up.

'This has nothing to do with Audrey,' said Lloyd.

'What doesn't?' asked Charles, surprised at his unexpected response.

'All of this.' Lloyd waved his hands over the papers. 'She shouldn't be here.'

Audrey sat impassively beside him as he spoke. Other than still looking slightly flushed, she didn't show any reaction to Lloyd's comments.

Rachel couldn't believe what she was hearing. She looked at Carl but his face was emotionless too.

'Perhaps if you explain to us what's been going on, then we can decide who should or shouldn't be here,' said Tom.

Lloyd glared at him angrily. 'I'm telling you that she knows nothing. I haven't involved her. Please let her leave.'

'Is this right, Audrey?' asked Charles.

Audrey looked slightly pained, as if she thought the answer should be obvious. 'I'm afraid I have no idea what you're all talking about. I simply do Lloyd's paperwork for him as he instructs me. No more.'

'Do you recognise those records?' asked Tom, pointing at the pages in front of Lloyd.

Audrey looked at them. 'No, I've never seen them before.'

Rachel's jaw dropped. What an outright lie! She had been in the room when Lloyd had taken the book out. But she probably couldn't prove that Audrey knew what was in it, as it would be her word against Audrey's.

Charles and Tom looked at each other.

'We will discuss this matter with Lloyd in the first instance then,' said Charles. 'But if we find any evidence of your involvement…'

'You won't,' said Audrey before he could finish his sentence.

How could she be so sure? Rachel was astounded. And why was Lloyd so intent on protecting her? Maybe they were having an affair as Tom had suspected.

Audrey got up and left. After she'd gone, Rachel noticed Carl seem to visibly relax. Had he warned her what was coming?

Charles leant forward across the table towards Lloyd. 'So, let's start again, shall we? Have you been taking money out the business or not?' he asked.

Lloyd's face started to go red and he suddenly leapt out of his seat, making everybody jump. 'Only what was rightfully mine in the first place, you miserable old bastard!'

Even Carl looked shocked at his outburst.

'I beg your pardon?' said Charles.

'I always wanted this business to take on more celebrities — you know, maximise our reputation, raise our profile. But you've always been dead against it.' Lloyd paced up and down the room, only stopping now and then to point an accusing finger at Charles. 'You and your old-fashioned views have left the business stumbling about in the dark ages. Thanks to me we've had far more clients than we ever would have done if we'd listened to you! You really don't have any idea what you're doing. Our strategy is pathetic.'

'Our strategy has been agreed by all the doctors here,' said Charles. 'It is *our* plan, not mine.'

'Rubbish!' shouted Lloyd. A few drops of spit flew out of his mouth as he spoke and his grey hair flopped down onto his forehead where it stuck to the beads of sweat that had started to appear. 'You've got them all in your back pocket! None of them are brave enough to stand up to you, that's all.'

Rachel looked at Charles. His kindly, round face and slightly forgetful manner hardly made him the most frightening person she'd ever met.

'Lloyd, please stop shouting and sit down,' said Tom.

'I bloody well will not,' said Lloyd, glaring at Tom again. He clearly didn't like him. 'You people, you have no idea,' ranted Lloyd to no one in particular. 'It's my reputation that keeps the clients coming in. Yes, I have charged them more than the list prices. But why? Because they wanted me. Not Beau Street, but me, Lloyd Cassidy.'

He looked at Charles. 'You would never let us promote ourselves, never spend any money on advertising in the right places. So I built the business myself, never mind what you thought,' said Lloyd. He tossed his head angrily.

Rachel sat very still in her chair. God, Lloyd was really losing it.

'Our clients want a discrete service. They don't want some practice that has been splashed over the tabloids and gossip magazines,' said Charles. 'You don't understand the difference between reputation and fame, and that's always been your problem.'

'Well, you don't understand how to make money and that's always been your problem!' Lloyd shouted back.

'You were one of the first partners in this business with me, Lloyd. I have trusted you every step of the way and this is how you repay me. You've driven a coach and horses through our professional practices, put the business massively at risk and stolen from your fellow partners. You are a disgrace!' Charles was livid.

'*I* am the best doctor here,' said Lloyd, jutting out his chin. 'It's the rest of the business that's a disgrace.'

Charles stood up and banged the table hard. 'Right, I've had enough.'

Rachel felt slightly panicked. It was getting nasty. Should she do something? Calm and professional at all times, that was what Carl had said. She looked at Carl and he shook his head slightly to indicate they should both stay quiet.

Charles picked up the phone. 'Linda, can you ask Fred to come in, please.'

Fred? What did they want with Fred? It was hardly the time for a weather forecast.

A few seconds later the door opened and a very stern looking Fred came in followed by a much younger and burlier security guard that Rachel didn't recognise. They must have been waiting outside.

'Lloyd, you are suspended pending a full investigation into your actions. Fred, could you escort Dr Cassidy to his office so he can clear his desk and then off the premises. Please make sure he does not remove anything except personal items,' said Charles.

'Of course, Dr Sutton,' said Fred. 'This way, sir,' he said to Lloyd.

Lloyd stepped backwards away from Fred, his eyes flashing with rage.

'Don't make me call the police,' said Charles. 'It's bad enough for you as it is; please don't make it worse.'

'Let me tell you, Charles, you will be hearing from my lawyers,' said Lloyd.

'And you will be hearing from ours. This investigation is not over yet,' said Charles resolutely. 'Now please leave.'

'Fine, if that's the way you want to play it, then on your head be it,' said Lloyd.

And with that he marched out of the room, quickly followed by the two security guards.

There was a stunned silence after he left.

Charles got up and stared out of the window, occasionally shaking his head. He sighed deeply and turned round. 'I'm very sorry that you had to see that,' he said to Rachel and Carl. 'Lloyd has always wanted to push the boundaries in search of the glamour clients. But I never thought he would go this far.'

'Neither did I,' said Tom. 'What a mess.'

'I'm also very grateful to you that you found out,' continued Charles. 'Although I have no idea what it means for our sale process. Tom, will you let Equinox know? I guess you need to do that through Clinton Wahlberg?'

Tom nodded.

'Well, can you ask them to let Lawson Green know that I'll ring him over the weekend? Hopefully I can reassure him that the rest of our business is not made up of cheats and liars.'

Lawson Green was the CEO of the Equinox Practise. Rachel was meant to be presenting to him next week. If they were going to be able to show them the numbers for the business without Lloyd, they needed the black book.

'Would it be possible for us to take Lloyd's manual record book from his office now? Then we could try to work out how much money he's been taking,' said Rachel to Tom.

She also wanted to look for some link that would prove that Audrey was involved. There was no way that she should get off scot-free.

'Yes, of course. Shall we look for it now?' Tom asked.

Rachel looked at Carl, who nodded.

Tom and Rachel headed off towards Lloyd's office. Rachel was pretty worried they might bump into him, but by the time they got there, the office was empty.

'Where do you think this book is then?' Tom asked.

'In the left-hand desk drawer,' said Rachel.

Tom tried the drawer; it was locked.

'I wonder where he keeps the key,' said Tom.

'It was hidden under a vase,' said Rachel.

Tom raised his eyebrows at her.

'I saw them one evening when I was working late,' said Rachel.

She looked at the mantelpiece. The small square vase was gone and there was no key to be seen. They both searched the office for a few minutes but found nothing.

'We'll have to break the lock,' said Tom.

He rang down to Fred. 'Fred, could you come up to Lloyd Cassidy's office and bring some tools? We need to open a desk drawer that's locked.'

After a few minutes Fred arrived.

'Has Dr Cassidy left the building?' Tom asked.

'Yes he has, Mr Duffy. We made sure of that, and we've taken his pass away. Terrible business.' Fred shook his head gravely, but Rachel had no doubt that he was secretly relishing all the excitement.

He took out a small piece of wire and fiddled for a few moments with the lock. After a few goes he turned the lock and the drawer opened.

'Wow, Fred, where did you learn how to do that?' Tom asked.

'Misspent youth, Mr Duffy,' said Fred, grinning, and he winked at Rachel.

Rachel looked in the drawer and, to her huge relief, the black leather book was there. She took it out and flicked through the pages.

'These records only go back about three years. That's fine for our presentation as we're only focusing on the last few years, but it won't give us the full extent of the money that he may have taken. Shall I have a hunt for some more?'

'Yes, thank you, that would be helpful,' said Tom. 'We'll need to catalogue everything that's here as part of our investigation, so don't take anything away, will you.'

'No, of course not,' said Rachel.

'I'll be in my office if you need me,' said Tom.

Rachel felt very odd going through Lloyd Cassidy's desk, even though this time she had permission to do so. She quickly searched the other drawers to see if she could find any other record books, but there were none − just medical journals, research papers, patient notes, that sort of thing. She really wanted to find something that showed Audrey had known what was going on, but she didn't really know what she was looking for, which didn't help.

She opened the filing cabinets and started working her way through the hanging folders, all neatly labelled by Audrey. At the back of the second drawer she found a file marked 'miscellaneous'. Inside was a confidential memo to Lloyd Cassidy from Charles Sutton on the possible tie up with Equinox and copies of three different proposal documents from PR companies, including one from Cavanaugh PR. On the front covers were scribbled notes in Audrey's handwriting, comparing the fees from each one. On the cover of the Cavanaugh document Audrey had written 'needs to drop £5k'. So slimy Clive had been given a helping hand! Rachel bet that Audrey had told him exactly what was in the other proposals and what he needed to do to win the work. She wasn't sure exactly why Audrey would want to help Clive, but she bet that it wasn't simply because they were old friends.

She took the file down to the photocopier and took copies of all of the notes. They would be good insurance in case Clive started getting a bit too chatty about his days as a university governor.

Rachel finished going through the rest of the files but could find nothing else that grabbed her attention. Unless she found records going back further they wouldn't be able to tell how long Lloyd had been taking cash bookings or how much he'd skimmed off over the years. And she also couldn't find anything that showed that Audrey had known about it. Damn it!

She sat down and rubbed her forehead. She was sure that Audrey was up to her neck in it. They just had to prove it. She bent down to pick up her bag and noticed that her phone was flashing. Yet another text message from Harry. *Thought you were going to ring me?* He had then typed sorry so many times that Rachel got tired of scrolling down to read them.

She didn't reply and she had neither the time nor the energy to call him. She needed time to think, time when she wasn't flat out lurching from one work crisis to another, if that was possible on this project.

CHAPTER 20

Rachel left Lloyd's office and walked wearily back to the project room. As she entered the room, Carl stood up to leave. She looked across at AJ and Rosa, who both looked a bit tense.

'I have to go,' said Carl. 'Do you have what you need to redo the presentation for Monday?'

'Yes,' said Rachel and waved the black book at Carl. 'That was all pretty unpleasant, wasn't it?'

'Yes, very,' said Carl.

Much to Rachel's frustration, he seemed reluctant to discuss it further. She had so many questions. Should they try to find the link to Audrey?

'There are a few things I could do with talking through with you, if you have a minute,' said Rachel.

'Sorry, I can't stop now. I have another meeting to go to. Perhaps you could call me later?'

'Oh, okay, no problem,' said Rachel as Carl walked out past her.

Rachel shut the door.

'Has Carl told you what happened?' Rachel asked AJ and Rosa.

'No, he's hardly said a word. He seemed really stressed when he came back and just paced up and down. He just said that Lloyd had been suspended and we needed to get on and prepare for Monday,' said AJ.

'We didn't dare ask him any questions; he seemed too cross,' said Rosa.

Rachel looked at her watch. It was just gone four p.m. She was sure when she'd spoken to Carl's PA to arrange the meeting she'd said that Carl was free all afternoon. So where was he going? Could he be meeting Audrey? Should she follow him?

When she'd seen Audrey leaving earlier she'd been too slow to react and she was determined not to make the same mistake again.

'I think I'll just grab some fresh air − bit of a headache coming on. Won't be long,' said Rachel, and she walked quickly out of the project room after Carl.

She caught up with him as he waited for the lift and they got in together.

'Just popping out for some fresh air,' said Rachel.

Carl just nodded.

'It was a real shock to see Lloyd Cassidy shouting and swearing like that, didn't you think? I thought Charles handled him pretty well,' said Rachel.

'Yes, he was very calm considering,' said Carl, shifting slightly uncomfortably. Rachel got the impression that he really didn't want to talk about the meeting anymore.

As they left the front of the offices, Rachel said

goodbye and walked away in the direction of the nearby park. She looked back over her shoulder to see Carl walk off in the other direction. If he was going back to the office he would have got in a cab. She turned around to follow him.

As she darted in and out of doorways and peered into shop windows trying to look inconspicuous, she decided she would make a rubbish private detective. Fortunately, Carl was marching ahead with hardly a backward glance, making him pretty easy to follow. They walked for about ten minutes until Rachel realised they were getting close to The Brook Hotel. She hung back a little further and watched as Carl crossed the road and headed into the hotel. A minute or so later, Rachel followed.

As she entered the foyer she quickly checked the reception desk. A tired looking business man and a Japanese tourist stood waiting patiently in the queue for the next available receptionist. Carl wasn't in the queue or at either desk. Rachel looked towards the sofa area and she couldn't see him there either. She walked tentatively across the foyer towards the bar, conscious of the fact that if she wasn't careful she'd probably walk straight into him. She looked into the bar and there he was, sitting with Audrey Fox. Damn him. She'd been right!

She went over to the sofas and chose a seat where she could see into the bar and sat down. She picked up a magazine and pretended to read it while watching Carl and Audrey.

They were sitting face to face at a small table covered by a white tablecloth. At Audrey's side was a bottle of wine in a silver wine cooler. The waiter poured Carl a glass of wine as Audrey put her hand across the table towards him. He took it and they sat for a few moments holding hands and talking. Carl then leaned across the table and kissed her. Not for long, but long enough for Rachel to know for certain that they were definitely not just old friends.

Rachel felt furious. Carl had lied to her and made her feel terrible for questioning him. What a shit! And no wonder he'd found that meeting so difficult.

She put her magazine down and openly sat watching them together. She didn't care now if Carl saw her. If he did, she would give him a piece of her mind. However, they were far too engrossed in each other to notice her sitting out in the foyer and the conversation seemed to be getting heated. Audrey was sitting back with her arms folded and was shaking her head, looking really quite unfriendly all of a sudden. Carl, on the other hand, was leaning forward with his hands outstretched towards her, almost like he was pleading with her. What was going on?

Rachel sat forward, intrigued. It was clear that they were arguing. Then suddenly Audrey got up, grabbed her handbag from beside her and stormed out of the bar. Her knee-length, black boots clicked loudly on the marble floor as she marched across the foyer and she flicked her scarf around her neck, throwing her head back at the same time, as if she deliberately wanted to complete her dramatic exit in style.

Rachel looked back at Carl. He was sitting at the table with his head in his hands. Eventually he sat up and looked around and waved to the waiter. Rachel expected him to get the bill but instead the waiter got out his pad and a few minutes later brought Carl what looked like a large whiskey. He sat nursing it between his hands, staring straight ahead.

It was no good. Rachel had to sort this out once and for all. She took a deep breath, got up and walked into the bar.

'Hello, Carl.'

Carl turned round in shock. 'Rachel, what are you doing here?'

'I followed you,' said Rachel.

She sat down in Audrey's seat. The waiter hurried over, trying not to show any reaction to the change of woman at the table.

'Can I get you a drink, madam?'

Rachel looked at Carl's drink. 'I'll have one of those, please.' She smiled politely at the waiter and then at Carl, who was still sitting open-mouthed at the shock of seeing her.

'I've been sitting in the foyer watching you for the past twenty minutes, so please don't insult my intelligence again and give me all that crap about you and Audrey being just good friends,' said Rachel. 'How long has it been going on?'

Carl looked down and shook his head miserably. 'Nearly two years,' he said eventually.

'Two years! Carl, you should never have taken on this project. You know that we can't have relationships with our clients.'

'The thing is, I kept telling myself that I would

finish it, but somehow I never quite did,' said Carl. He looked visibly upset and took a large swig of his whiskey.

'It looked like you were arguing just now,' said Rachel.

'Oh Christ, I've been such a fool.' Carl rolled his eyes upwards and put both hands over his mouth. 'I've been giving her money and lots of it.'

'What for?' Rachel asked.

'Nothing in particular. She told me that she was really in debt, finding it hard to make ends meet on a nurse's income. So I gave her money, for clothes, holidays, that sort of thing. I even bought her a car,' said Carl.

'Wow, lucky her,' said Rachel.

'Well, when you told me about this scam Lloyd had running, at first I couldn't believe that she'd be involved. But the more I heard, the more I was sure she must be. Anyway, I confronted her about it.'

'Did you tip her off that we'd told Tom Duffy?'

Carl nodded.

'Carl, no!'

'I thought I was doing the right thing, trying to protect her. But as it turns out, I didn't need to. She had Lloyd Cassidy to do that for her. It was a total shock when Tom Duffy mentioned that he thought they were having an affair, and I didn't think for a minute that it would be true. But when I warned her about the meeting, she went all mysterious and just told me not to worry and that she'd sort it out. And then, in that meeting, when the first thing he did was to get her out the frame, well then I knew.'

'Knew what?' Rachel asked.

'That Lloyd is sleeping with her too. Did you see how flushed she was? I bet that was down to her using her usual charms to get Lloyd to do what she wanted.'

Carl had clearly been on the receiving end of Audrey's persuasive manner at some point too.

'So I asked her just now, straight out, whether she's been seeing him too. And well, her response was pretty clear. She couldn't begin to understand why I might have thought we were in an exclusive relationship. She also said that I shouldn't forget that I'm the one who's married whereas she's a free agent, perfectly entitled to see who see likes, when she likes.'

'Well, I guess that the definition of an exclusive relationship when one person is already married is a bit of a grey area,' said Rachel, and then quickly realised that probably wasn't helpful.

To her horror, Carl looked quite close to tears. 'She's probably been seeing him the whole time, for all I know,' said Carl. 'And to think, I nearly left my wife for her.' His chin trembled slightly as he spoke.

'Shit, Carl.' Rachel couldn't help feeling sorry for him. He looked like a broken man.

She waved at the waiter. 'Two more whiskies, please.'

'Do you think Lloyd also gave her money?' Rachel asked.

'I'm sure he bloody well did. I know what she's like. If there was money floating about, she'd make sure she got some.'

Rachel was sure that was true. She'd always thought that Audrey Fox looked like trouble. It suddenly occurred to her that Clive Steele probably had money too, despite his less than polished appearance. He did own a PR business, after all.

'Does Lloyd know about you and Audrey, do you think?' Rachel asked.

'I doubt it. She's been enjoying herself far too much, taking both of us old fools for a total ride.' Carl grabbed Rachel's wrists across the table. 'We need to get her, Rachel. Prove that she's involved, make sure she gets what she deserves,' said Carl. His bulging eyes and desperate expression made him look slightly demented.

'Carl, you should really stand down from the project,' said Rachel.

'But it's over now, Rachel, really and truly over this time, so there's no relationship to report. I'm hardly going to try to protect her now.'

'Gunning for her so you can get even doesn't make you independent either!'

'Do you think she's involved?' Carl asked.

'You know I do,' said Rachel. 'I've said so from the beginning.'

'Well, then,' said Carl. 'And you'll be there to make sure we play it straight.'

'I don't know,' said Rachel.

'Please, Rachel. Let's just finish the project properly. That's all I'm asking. I know that if we try hard enough, we'll be able to show she's involved. And that's our job: to investigate things thoroughly. You wouldn't be doing anything wrong.'

He was right. She had been determined to look into it anyway. And despite the fact that he had cheated on his wife and lied to her, for some reason she wanted to help him. He needed her help. Rachel thought for a few moments and then it suddenly dawned on her – maybe she should get him to help her too, well, Shali anyway!

'Only if you agree to go easy on Shali with this whole summer party investigation thing. She really doesn't deserve to have the book thrown at her. It wasn't that bad, you know. It's not like she was sleeping with a client or anything,' said Rachel. Ooh, that was good.

'Alright, alright, point made,' said Carl. He thought for a moment. 'What if I make sure that she only gets a minor warning, no more, okay? I can't really do better than that. The other partners know too much already.'

'And keep it confidential? She doesn't need the whole office talking about it,' said Rachel.

'I'll do my very best,' Carl said.

That was a pretty good result – the best they could hope for.

'Okay, let's get on with it. For now anyway.'

'Thank you, thank you,' said Carl. He let out a huge sigh and slumped down in his chair. He looked relieved but exhausted.

'I'd better get back. AJ and Rosa will be wondering where on the earth I've got to.'

'Start with the invoices,' said Carl. 'We need to show she knew they weren't for the right amount.'

'Okay,' said Rachel. 'We'll try.'

But she didn't feel that confident that they would succeed.

Rachel walked back to the Beau Street offices feeling rather light-headed. Two whiskies on an empty stomach weren't really ideal preparation for working late. She dived into a small metro style supermarket and grabbed a triple-pack BLT sandwich and a family-sized pack of pretentiously named crisps that were really just plain old salt and vinegar.

AJ and Rosa were desperate to hear all about the Lloyd Cassidy showdown meeting, as they were now calling it. Between stuffing sandwich and crisps in her mouth, Rachel told them what had happened. She didn't mention Carl and Audrey. She was working on a need-to-know basis, and they didn't need to know.

'So they threw him out of the building?' Rosa was astonished.

'Pretty much,' said Rachel. 'He got to clear his desk first but that was it.'

'Will they involve the police?' AJ asked.

'I don't know. Beau Street are going to do their own full investigation into what he's been up to. I guess after that they'll decide whether they should bring the police in or not.'

'Wow, heavy stuff,' said AJ.

'So, here's the good news. We have Lloyd's manual records for the last three years so we can work out how much he's been taking out. The bad news is, we need the presentation for Monday redone to show the business without Lloyd and that will probably mean we need to work the weekend.'

'Don't worry, we'd already figured that much out,' said Rosa.

'I also want a large sample of these records looked at. Maybe fifty or so. We need to check whether there's any evidence that Audrey knew what was going on. She claims she was just doing what Lloyd told her to do. The manual books are all written by him, so we can't prove for definite at the moment she knew what was going on just because she's his nurse.'

'Fifty! That will take hours,' said AJ.

'Well, you'd better get on with it then, hadn't you?' said Rachel, smiling. 'Rosa, you start on the black book. Work out the total amount charged each year per the book and then work out the total actually invoiced. The difference is then our missing cash. I'll start reworking the presentation.'

As Rachel flicked through the pages of their presentation she started to feel incredibly nervous about Monday. She didn't feel at all ready. The whole team would be there, but she'd be the one doing most of the talking. She needed to practice.

She went out into the corridor and rang Natalie — she was good at this sort of thing.

'There's a serious chance that I'll be totally crap unless you save me,' said Rachel. 'Could you come round tomorrow evening and help me rehearse?'

'There's nothing I'd like more than to spend my Friday night listening to you droning on about face lifts and boob jobs,' said Natalie.

'I promise to provide food and wine,' said Rachel.

'I should think so! Can Shali come too? Help me out. Hell, we might as well at least try to enjoy ourselves while we're at it,' said Natalie.

'I'll ring her too and let you know,' said Rachel.

When Rachel rang Shali, she also told her about doing a deal with Carl over the summer party.

Shali was amazed. 'Are you sure he meant it?' she asked.

'Yes, I'm pretty sure he did, but I guess we'll have to wait and see to be certain,' said Rachel.

'God, let's hope so. Wow, I owe you, and I mean more than just helping you with your presentation, but I'll do that as well,' said Shali.

'Thanks, you're a star. Natalie's coming round at eight. By the way, how was your drink with Rowan?'

'Yeah, fine. It was bit awkward to begin with, but once we got talking for a bit it was okay. He's such a gentleman, you know. He really wanted me to know that he's not some playboy who does this sort of thing all the time and then never calls.'

'Did he talk about Laura?' Rachel asked.

Shali laughed. 'Yes, about every other minute. He was really trying to stress the point that he still cares about her,' said Shali.

'Well he does,' said Rachel.

'That much I gathered,' said Shali.

'Do you feel bad about it?' Rachel asked.

'Not really. If circumstances were different then maybe we would be quite a good match. But they're not, so that's that.'

Rachel felt relieved. It did sound like that was the end of the matter. At least that was one less thing to worry about. 'I'm sure there will be another hot man just round the next corner,' she said.

'Yup, I'm sure there will be too. See you tomorrow,' said Shali.

CHAPTER 21

Shali and Natalie were both in high spirits when they arrived at Rachel's flat. Rachel, on the other hand, was feeling totally knackered. Both the stress of her crisis-ridden week and Harry's continual texting, saying how sorry he was and how much he needed her, had left her emotionally drained. As a result, her promise of food consisted of a series of takeaway menus. She'd at least been to the off licence and bought wine.

Luckily the off licence had a decent selection of wine ready chilled, as Rachel hadn't been home early enough to chill it herself. She and Rosa had spent the day frantically working through their presentation, changing all the analysis so they could show the results of the business both with and without Lloyd Cassidy, while AJ had patiently worked his way through a huge sample of Lloyd's false name clients. Much to Rachel's frustration, though, he hadn't found any evidence so far that Audrey had known what was going on. They'd had a final debrief at about seven o'clock and then they'd all left for the day as they were back in on

Sunday making final preparations for the Equinox presentation on Monday.

Natalie jumped onto Rachel's sofa and clapped her hands. 'Right, come on both of you, let's get this show on the road,' she said. 'Where's your presentation, Rachel?'

'In my briefcase,' shouted Rachel from the kitchen as she opened what she was sure would be the first of many bottles of wine.

Natalie rummaged about in Rachel's briefcase and pulled out the presentation. She put it on the coffee table in front of Shali and herself and started flicking through the pages.

'Looks pretty smart,' said Shali as Rachel came in carrying the wine glasses.

'Thanks. I've got Rosa Castelli working with me and she's brilliant on this sort of document. She made it look really professional. It's just me that's going to be crap.'

'If you start off thinking like that then you probably will be crap,' said Natalie. 'Being good at presenting is all about confidence and positive thinking.'

Natalie was naturally confident and also a total training junkie. She'd done pretty much every course Payne Stanley offered and was always reading self-help books called things like *How to Be Better Than Your Boss* or *Negotiate Your Way to Success*.

'Easier said than done,' said Rachel.

'Rubbish,' said Natalie in her typically outspoken way. 'You just need to practice a few times, let us grill you for a bit and you'll soon feel differently about it. So c'mon, up you get.' She signalled with her hand for Rachel to stand up.

'God, do I have to stand?' Rachel asked. 'I'm knackered.'

'Will you be standing on Monday?' Shali asked.

'Yes, probably.'

'Then yes, you do,' said Natalie.

Rachel got wearily to her feet, now slightly regretting that she'd called in the cavalry to help her rehearse.

Shali and Natalie sat up expectantly on the sofa.

'Good morning, ladies and gentleman,' said Rachel. 'I…' She didn't get any further.

'Stop,' said Natalie, holding up her hand. 'Are you opening the meeting? Won't Carl do that?'

'Well, yes, he will,' said Rachel.

'First rule of presenting: start strongly. So you need to practice exactly what you'll be saying on Monday. Start again.'

Shali laughed and topped up both her and Natalie's glasses. 'Slave driver,' she said to Natalie.

'If we're going to do this, we might as well do it properly,' said Natalie.

'Thank you, Carl. Good morning, everyone. As Carl mentioned, my name is Rachel Altman and I have been leading our work here at Beau Street.'

'Better,' said Natalie.

Rachel carried on, working her way through the first few pages of the presentation. She then turned over to the page with the two pie charts that Rosa had put together, showing the top five most popular procedures on one and the fasting growing new procedures on the other.

'That slide looks like a pair of tits,' said Shali, making Natalie laugh hysterically.

'It does not,' said Rachel. But the more she looked at it, the more it did. Her mouth twitched as she tried not to smile.

'See, you think it does too,' said Shali.

'Alright, maybe a bit. You bloody kids. Can I carry on now?' Rachel asked.

'Please do,' said Shali.

Shali and Natalie grinned at each other, then set their faces back to serious, ready to listen.

'Stop it! You're making me laugh,' said Rachel.

'What? We aren't doing anything,' said Natalie.

'Stop pulling those faces,' said Rachel.

'What faces?' Shali asked, pulling in her cheeks like she was sucking something very sour. Natalie followed suit, screwing her nose up like a pig. They then both collapsed on the sofa in fits of giggles.

Rachel grinned at them. 'Guys, please, get a grip. I've only just started!'

'Sorry,' said Natalie, gathering her composure. She pulled Shali upright on the sofa and they both sat very still as Rachel continued.

It took well over two hours and a mountain of Chinese takeaway for Rachel to get to a point where Natalie felt that she could stop. She'd been through the whole presentation three or four times with Shali and Natalie firing questions at her.

'And so, Miss Altman, just to conclude, what are your views on penis enlargement?' Natalie asked.

'I'm definitely all for it, particularly after a few

glasses of wine,' said Rachel, picking up the glass of wine in front of her.

'I'll drink to that,' said Shali, raising her glass.

The three of them clinked glasses and then burst out laughing.

'Well, there's no doubt that you know your stuff,' said Natalie, catching her breath.

'You think?' Rachel asked, still needing plenty of reassurance.

'Absolutely,' said Shali.

Rachel knew that Shali and Natalie were hardly a knowledgeable audience, with what little they did know about cosmetic surgery having been gleaned from magazines or TV shows – unlike the Equinox Practise, who were leading experts in their field. Still, it was better than nothing and she certainly felt more ready than she had done earlier.

'Right, now Miss Whiplash has finished with you, on to the important stuff,' said Shali. 'What are you going to wear?'

'God, I've not even thought about that. I'm not sure it really matters that much,' said Rachel.

'Of course it matters! People only listen to about half of what you say – the rest is all based on appearance. Or something like that anyway,' said Shali.

'I think what you mean is that only about twenty per cent of the impression you make is what you say, the rest is all non-verbal. And Shali's right, appearance is a huge part of that,' said Natalie.

'The bedroom it is then!' Shali declared and stood up, grabbing her glass and the rest of the open bottle.

They went through into Rachel's bedroom where Natalie and Shali took up positions sitting on the bed while Rachel dipped in and out of her immaculately organised wardrobe.

'How about this?' she asked, holding up a black trouser suit.

'Too dull,' said Shali. 'You need something with more personality than that.'

Natalie nodded in agreement.

Rachel flicked through the hangers and pulled out a navy trouser suit with a dusky pink pinstripe.

'Better, but still a bit safe,' said Shali.

'How about a dress?' suggested Natalie.

'With boots,' added Shali.

Rachel thought of Audrey Fox flouncing across the foyer of The Brook Hotel in her dress and boots. She had certainly made an impression. She took out a damson checked shift dress with cap sleeves and a pair of black knee-length, suede boots. She raised her eyebrows enquiringly at Shali and Natalie.

'Perfect — professional with attitude,' said Shali.

'Yup, that will do the trick,' said Natalie.

As Rachel put away her clothes, Shali and Natalie sat chatting on the bed. Natalie idly picked up a CD of Harry's that was still on the bedside table.

'Bit trendy for you this, isn't it?'

'It's Harry's. He's well into them.' Rachel paused. 'Or he was, anyway.'

'Sorry,' said Natalie, putting the CD down. 'I shouldn't fiddle.'

'That's okay. I was probably going to throw it away

soon anyway,' said Rachel. She looked at the floor, didn't move for a few moments and then burst into tears.

Natalie leapt up off the bed and put her arm round Rachel. 'Sorry, Rachel,' she said, 'that was really thoughtless of me.'

'It's alright, it's not your fault,' said Rachel. 'I'm just really tired, that's all. Bloody Harry. I don't know what to do. He's desperate for me to forgive him.'

She blew her nose, sat down and recounted to Shali and Natalie their pub encounter earlier in the week.

'He really is an arse,' said Natalie. 'You're way more interesting than him; he's just too arrogant to see it.'

'No, Natalie, tell us what you really think,' said Shali.

Natalie grinned. 'Sorry, again. Mouth engaging before brain, as usual.'

'I've said I'll ring him to let him know my final decision in the next few days,' said Rachel.

'Final decision on what?' Natalie asked, somewhat incredulously.

'On whether I'll give him another chance,' said Rachel.

Natalie raised her eyebrows and opened her mouth to speak. But Shali glared at her and she shut it again.

'Only you can decide whether to do that,' said Shali. 'Look, let's go back into the sitting room and I'll raid the cupboards for chocolate.'

She came into the sitting room a minute later holding various packets of biscuits. 'Chocolate chip cookies, Viennese shortbread or some oat baked crumbly things?'

'Chocolate chip cookies,' said Natalie and Rachel in unison.

As they sat on the sofa chatting and eating cookies, Rachel suddenly felt an overwhelming desire to go to bed. Her head was starting to ache and she was totally worn out.

'Guys, I'm really sorry but I think I need to crash,' said Rachel.

'No problem, we'll shoot,' said Shali.

'Thank you both, for everything,' said Rachel.

'No problem. And don't worry — you're going to be great on Monday,' said Natalie.

'And go with your gut feeling on Harry. In my experience it's nearly always right,' said Shali.

Shali was probably right. The problem was that Rachel's emotions were in such a whirl that she couldn't work out what her gut was telling her. The only message she was getting from her body right now was that it needed sleep, and plenty of it.

By Sunday morning, Rachel was feeling much more energetic. She'd spent an easy Saturday pottering round the shops, followed by some serious pampering at her favourite beauty salon. She'd been scrubbed, buffed and oiled to within an inch of her life and had drunk gallons of herbal tea. It had made her feel so relaxed that she'd been in bed just after nine o' clock and had slept for ten straight hours.

She got up slowly, dressing casually in jeans, silver trainers and a plain white t-shirt. She tied her hair back into a ponytail and sat down on the sofa with a huge mug of tea. She rubbed her neck, which was still feeling slightly sore from her tension-relieving massage. She'd agreed to meet AJ and Rosa at Beau Street at ten, so she didn't need to leave for another half an hour or so.

She picked up the presentation that had been sitting on the coffee table since Friday night. Shali was right: it did look pretty smart. She put the presentation back in her briefcase and checked her phone. She had three text messages, all from Harry, each one increasingly incoherent. She checked the sent times. The first was sent about midnight with the other two being sent quite close together at around three a.m. No early night for him then. Still, at least he was thinking about her. The fact there was no chance he'd be up and that she had no idea what to say to him stopped Rachel from calling him back.

As she sipped her tea, she tried to work out what her gut feeling was telling her. She didn't feel so angry with him any more, but she also didn't know if he was really the right guy for her. She had to look long term. The image of the cot she'd assembled at her parents' house jumped into her head, but however hard she tried, Rachel simply couldn't imagine a scene there that included Harry in it. He just didn't fit.

She sighed and stretched her arms out. Time to make a move.

Rachel was first to arrive at Beau Street. She was greeted by the young, burly security guard who'd helped Fred escort Lloyd Cassidy off the premises. He greeted her very politely, checked her off against his list and then waved her through.

'Lovely morning, don't you think?' Rachel asked.

He looked at her in surprise and then out of the window, as if he needed to check. 'Er, yes, I guess so.'

Rachel smiled to herself. He wasn't a patch on Fred.

Rosa joined her a few minutes later carrying a tray of coffees for the three of them.

'Ooh, thanks, Rosa, proper coffee — just what the doctor ordered,' said Rachel, grabbing hers.

'AJ not here yet?' Rosa asked.

'No, not yet,' said Rachel.

AJ arrived over half an hour late, by which time his coffee had gone cold. He was clearly hugely hungover.

'You look like shit,' said Rachel.

'I feel like shit,' said AJ. He sat down and took several large gulps of his cold coffee.

'That's really not very helpful, AJ. You know we've got a load to do,' said Rachel.

Rachel felt a bit guilty about having a go at AJ. How many times had she rocked up to work with a bad hangover? Thanks to Harry, more times than she cared to remember. But she was in charge and they had a big deadline looming.

'Sorry,' said AJ. 'I got a bit led astray by a load of my old university mates. I'll be alright in a bit. I don't suppose you have any headache tablets?'

Being master of the work hangover, Rachel had a bagful. She grabbed AJ a couple of painkillers that had probably been supplied by Marco from her local pizza place. She also gave him some indigestion tablets and Rosa went to get several glasses of water from the water fountain.

'Right, let's go through the presentation from the

start. I'll be leading it but you two should chip in, particularly when I'm talking about the areas you covered. You need to be ready to support me with the detail,' said Rachel.

She got up and went through her presentation. Her Friday night rehearsal session had really helped. She felt far more confident. But as she got to the slide with the two pie charts, she started laughing.

'What's funny?' AJ asked, staring at the slide. 'Have we done it wrong?'

'No, the slide is fine. It's just that I was practising on Friday night and my judging panel thought that this slide looked like a giant pair of breasts,' said Rachel, giggling. 'Sorry, I know that's very childish.'

'Very apt,' said AJ, grinning.

'Don't say things like that!' said Rosa. 'I'll start laughing tomorrow if you're not careful. I'm a hopeless giggler, especially when I'm nervous.'

'I'm sure that none of us will feel like laughing with a mass of serious looking Americans in the room. Not to mention Carl, Tom Duffy and Charles Sutton,' said Rachel.

'That's true. I feel terrified already just thinking about it,' said Rosa, shuddering.

Once they'd finished practising, Rachel turned her attention to AJ's sample testing on a load of the black book entries.

'Right, talk me through what you've done, step by step,' said Rachel. There must be a link to Audrey somewhere, she thought.

AJ opened his files. 'I've been through each entry

from the beginning. The paperwork trail starts with the false name being entered onto the system. We don't have access to medical records, but I would guess that even if we did, none of these would have any, as they're not using the right names. Audrey has done all the paperwork. You can see her name against these records as the person that input them. I've then checked all the way through to the paper invoices. They all have some missing procedure details, as they were all just coded to "other", and they were paid in cash, but we already knew that. It doesn't show that Audrey knew the real names or knew that the clients agreed to pay more than went through the books.'

'Can you show me some invoices?' said Rachel.

AJ handed Rachel a handful from his pile. Rachel sat and flicked through them, shaking her head. There must be something.

'They're all very neat, those invoices,' said Rosa, looking up. 'Most of the others have been quite dog-eared.'

'What do you mean?' Rachel asked.

Rosa got a file from her desk. 'These ones aren't Lloyd's clients, mind you. I got these for another part of the analysis I was doing,' said Rosa.

The invoices in Rosa's file all had a small strip at the top of the page where the front page had been torn off. The strip was generally quite ragged from where the invoices had been pushed in and out of filing cabinet drawers. Many of the strips were loose or sticking upwards.

Rachel clapped her hands in delight. 'Rosa, you're a genius.'

'Am I?' said Rosa, looking confused.

'Look at these invoices!' said Rachel, excitedly waving the pile AJ had given her. 'They're all produced in triplicate. Back one for deep filing, middle one for the office and the top one is for…?'

Rachel paused, waiting for AJ and Rosa to finish her sentence.

'The client,' said AJ.

'Exactly,' said Rachel. 'For the client. But these aren't torn off. Audrey hasn't sent these ones, has she? And why not, I wonder? Perhaps it's because she knew that the client names aren't real! If she was "just doing the paperwork as Lloyd asked", then surely she would have sent the front copy to the client just like all these others.'

Rachel sat back in glee. That was it: they had her!

'Wow, of course she would. Who'd have thought it would be so simple? If she'd just torn the front page off and thrown it away we would probably be none the wiser,' said Rosa.

'We'll need to talk to her about it first, surely,' said AJ. 'Make sure there's not some other reason we haven't thought of?'

'Yes, yes, you're right, we should. We can do that as soon as we've got the presentation out of the way tomorrow. But I'd like to see her get out of this one,' said Rachel, trying not to sound too jubilant.

CHAPTER 22

Rachel whacked the toilet seat with her rolled-up newspaper and shouted 'I can do this!' at the blank wall behind the cistern. A small bead of sweat started to appear on her forehead, which she dabbed with a piece of toilet paper. She closed her eyes for a few seconds, took a couple of deep breaths and then repeated the whacking and shouting process. After a couple of minutes her arm started to ache, so she put the newspaper down on the toilet seat and began jogging up and down, touching her right hand to her left knee and vice versa, while sucking air loudly in and out, like she was a boxer in training.

A sharp rap on the toilet door made her jump.

'Hey, are you alright in there?' asked a voice that to Rachel's horror had an American accent.

'Er, yes, fine, thanks. Just, umm, warming up a bit.'

Rachel stood frozen still in the cubicle until she heard the footsteps leave. She opened the door and peered out. Shit, who had that been? Could it have been someone from the Equinox team? Rachel prayed that it wasn't. She hadn't heard anyone come in. Maybe she'd been shouting too loudly to hear the door go. It was Natalie who'd persuaded her to do warm-up exercises before she presented when she'd rung to wish her good luck last night.

'You need to get the adrenaline pumping,' Natalie had said. 'Get your energy levels up. That way when you get in the room you'll already be on fire.'

She'd also told Rachel that doing exercises that connected one side of the body to the other helped make the two sides of the brain work together. This meant that her brain would be alert and ready to problem solve should she get any difficult questions. Natalie had read about it in some book or other. It had all sounded pretty convincing at the time. But rather than feeling on fire, Rachel now felt like a prize idiot. She was hot and sweaty and red with embarrassment. Great!

She left the toilets and went back to the project room where Carl, AJ and Rosa were all waiting. AJ looked slightly pale and Rosa was fidgety with nerves, hopping from one foot to the other. As usual Carl appeared calm and composed. Rachel had briefed him earlier on the link to Audrey that they thought they'd found. Although he didn't say as much, Rachel could tell from the glint in his eyes that he was delighted.

'Shall we go up?' Rachel asked, hoping that no one had noticed her flushed face.

Carl nodded and they left the project room and made their way up to the Beau Street boardroom. The vast room was empty when they arrived to give them time to set up and organise where they would each sit. After a few minutes of fiddling with technology and rearranging chairs, they were ready. As they waited, Rachel realised she was feeling pretty good about her presentation. In fact, she was almost looking forward to it. Maybe Natalie's exercises had worked after all.

However, as more and more people began filing into the room, Rachel's confidence began to ebb away. The bankers arrived first. Meredith Romaine swept into the room, followed by her colleague, the rather tired looking Alfred King. It looked like he'd really been burning the midnight oil. Rachel bet that Meredith was a right slave driver.

Meredith came over to greet them. Her shoulder-length, curly, dark hair had been pinned into a high quiff at the front that made her look even taller and more intimidating than usual.

'My client is very much looking forward to today,' said Meredith. 'As you know they were pretty unhappy to hear about the whole fraud business. But they're carrying on with the sale process, for the moment at least. Let's hope you guys can show them some good news.'

For some reason, even though she was smiling broadly at them, she sounded ever so slightly threatening.

'We can only do as well as the company has,' said Carl.

Quite right, thought Rachel. We're not miracle workers.

Charles Sutton and Tom Duffy arrived next.

'The Equinox team are on their way up,' said Charles. 'I will suggest they sit here opposite Carl. There are three of them: Lawson Green, their CEO, Brenda Martinez, their in-house legal counsel, and Ryan Miller, their commercial director. Ryan has been the one leading most of the negotiations from their side so far.'

Everyone sat down, leaving three places free opposite Rachel and Carl. Rachel's palms began to feel a bit sweaty and she rubbed them on the lap of her checked dress. It was rather warm to be wearing knee-length boots but Rachel hadn't had the time or the energy to pick out another outfit.

After a few minutes the Equinox team arrived. Lawson Green was in his late fifties and looked rather like a giant bowling ball. He was dressed in beige, chino trousers with a huge waistband and a blue, short-sleeved shirt with a white collar. His hair was combed to the side with a military-straight parting and was very thick right down to his ears. Rachel couldn't help wondering if it might be a wig. Brenda Martinez was about the same age and was dressed in a pillar-box-red suit with big shoulder pads that matched her big hair. She looked tough as old boots. Ryan Miller was probably in his late thirties, sporty looking, suntanned and, Rachel thought, actually rather good looking.

Rachel, Carl, AJ and Rosa all stood up as they came into the room, being the only ones who hadn't met them before. They then played rather a long game of musical handshakes, as each of them introduced themselves.

'Really pleased to meet you all,' drawled Lawson Green, vigorously pumping each hand up and down like he was jacking up a car. Brenda Martinez, on the other hand, was much more reserved, holding out a rather cold and stiff hand with a thin-lipped smile. Rachel was terrified that she'd been the American voice that had talked to her in the ladies', but Brenda didn't seem to show any reaction when they shook hands. Ryan Miller was quite charming, smiling and laughing as he walked round. Rachel thought he was acting more like he was at a baseball game than a crucial business meeting.

It didn't take long for the meeting to get into full swing. After the usual introductory pleasantries, Carl stood up and spent about five minutes giving an outline of the work they'd been doing, which was greeted by lots of enthusiastic nods from the American contingent. Carl was a very proficient speaker, with a low and methodical tone that was almost mesmerising. Rachel found herself so engrossed listening to him that she almost forgot she was up next.

'So, I think that it's best that I sit down and let those who really know what they're talking about take you through our findings,' said Carl. He turned to look at Rachel.

'Oh, yes, right, thank you,' said Rachel, jumping up. God, she was glad that she'd been practising. Strong start – that was what she needed. 'Thank you, Carl. Good morning, everyone. As Carl mentioned my name is Rachel Altman and I've been leading our work here at Beau Street.'

Rachel talked through the slides slowly and carefully,

making sure she kept regular eye contact with Lawson Green as she did so. 'Know who the most important person in the room is and make sure they feel like you're talking to them personally,' Natalie had said.

'So, Lawson, as you can see the core business has been growing steadily with sales growth each year of between seven and eight per cent. Now, I believe you're all aware of the fact that Dr Lloyd Cassidy has been suspended, pending an investigation into some irregular transactions?'

There was a series of disappointed nods from the Equinox team across the table.

'Well, we have adjusted these figures so you can see them both with and without his sales figures. This lowers the growth rates a little, to between five and six per cent,' said Rachel.

'That's not so great,' said Ryan. 'Our offer was based on the higher numbers.'

'But if we look at some of the faster growth areas − the newer procedure types − then the impact is much less apparent, as Lloyd Cassidy didn't undertake many of these new procedures. You can see that the growth rates are largely unchanged when you exclude his sales figures,' said Rachel.

'And our newer procedures are some of the areas that you're most interested in,' said Charles enthusiastically to Lawson Green. 'Our toe-reshaping business is going like a train, helped by the fact that these super high heels are all the fashion at the moment. More than fifty per cent of women have bunions, you know, and just as many hate their toes in open sandals.'

Rachel couldn't quite believe that this sort of image madness was such big business. She had visions of some goliath of a woman with huge, fat, hairy legs coming in to have her feet reshaped to the size of a pixie.

'Thank you, Rachel, for explaining that. Very helpful,' Charles added.

Rachel nodded modestly at Charles, secretly delighted with the public praise, and turned to the next slide, which was the one with the two pie charts. The sides of Rachel's mouth twitched as soon as she saw it and she felt the urge to giggle well up in her chest. She took a deep breath and started to talk.

'Now, these two pie charts…'

But she quickly had to stop as a small laugh escaped from her mouth that she tried to disguise as a sort of high-pitched cough. She looked at the floor and desperately tried to compose herself. She tried to replace the image of a huge pair of tits with the thought of her parents dying in agony in some terrible car crash or of small children starving in Africa. But it wasn't working.

Rachel could tell that the assembled audience was starting to become uncomfortable with her silence. AJ was sitting looking into his lap with his hand over his mouth. His shoulders were shaking. That was the last straw. Rachel's face began to crack and she was just about to start laughing when AJ leapt about ten feet in the air with a shout. Everyone turned round to look at him.

'Oh my goodness! I'm so sorry,' said Rosa, getting up too. 'I've knocked my glass of water everywhere. Are there any napkins?'

Tom Duffy jumped up and grabbed a large handful of napkins from the coffee tray on the sideboard. He handed them to AJ, who dabbed at the large wet patch in his lap. AJ looked at Rosa in bewilderment, who just gave him a small knowing look and began mopping up the puddle of water on the table. Carl looked at them both furiously.

'Perhaps we should take a quick break,' said Charles. 'Let's reconvene in a few minutes.'

Rachel almost sprinted out of the room in relief and headed straight for the ladies'. She leant over the sink and gently splashed some cold water onto her cheeks. Shit, she'd very nearly blown it.

A few moments later Rosa followed her.

'God, I'm so sorry, Rachel, but I couldn't think what else to do. You looked like you were about to lose it, so I just panicked and threw my glass of water into AJ's lap.' Rosa was white and shaking.

Rachel grabbed her and hugged her tightly. 'Oh my God, Rosa, you totally saved me. I can't believe that just happened! I've spent weeks discussing every type of body part imaginable without laughing and then I completely lose it over a fucking slide with two pie charts on. Can you believe it?'

'It was probably just the pressure,' said Rosa. 'Are you feeling okay now? We should probably go back in a minute. Carl looked cross enough as it is.'

'I'll handle Carl, I promise. Don't worry; he'll be fine. And thank you, Rosa, I really mean it. I don't normally need my team to save me by chucking water over each other.'

Rosa grinned.

'Hey, no laughing,' said Rachel, grinning too.

When they got back in the room, Carl was still apologising profusely to Charles and Tom.

'Absolutely no problem,' said Charles. 'It's just one of those things. We'll be back on track in a few minutes.'

Rachel managed to finish her presentation without laughing and sat down feeling incredibly relieved that it was over. The trauma of nearly fucking up so badly meant that she'd been a bit shaky and had stumbled over her words a few times – nothing too disastrous, but her performance certainly hadn't been the triumph she'd been hoping for. She'd really wanted to impress Carl, show she was ready to be a director, but somehow she didn't think she'd succeeded.

She had also found it hard to read the team from Equinox. Were they still interested? She couldn't tell. Ryan had asked lots of questions about what the business looked like without Lloyd Cassidy, probably so they could re-cut their offer. Alfred King had furiously scribbled down all the answers as it was undoubtedly his job to work out a new valuation for the business, probably by the next morning or some other equally ridiculous deadline, the poor guy.

As the meeting broke up Brenda Martinez came over to chat.

'Thank you for your presentation, very informative,' said Brenda. She leant towards Rachel and dropped her voice to a low whisper. 'And by the way, your little toilet psyching-up session seemed to do the trick. I thought you did very well.'

Rachel's face dropped. Oh no! How embarrassing. She would definitely have to kill Natalie later.

'Er, thank you,' said Rachel, totally lost for anything else to say.

'I used to find that sort of thing really useful too when I was training,' said Brenda wistfully.

Training! Rachel was hardly a trainee. Patronising old cow.

'Actually, I qualified several…'

But before Rachel could finish, Brenda had turned away and started talking to Lawson Green.

Rachel shook her head. Fuck it. More humiliation.

As she headed out of the room she almost walked straight into the team of lawyers who were waiting to go in for their meeting with Equinox and Beau Street. She remembered Alex Fisher from their previous meetings.

'How did it go?' Alex asked.

'So, so,' Rachel replied. 'Good luck in there. There's a cast of thousands.'

Rachel, AJ and Rosa headed back towards their project room. Carl managed a cursory 'well done' before disappearing for the lifts to head straight back to the office. Rachel's heart sank as he left. If he'd been impressed with her then he'd kept it well hidden.

'I think that went okay, don't you think?' said Rosa when they were back in their project room.

'What, apart from you throwing water over me! I'm bloody soaking,' said AJ.

Rosa and Rachel looked at the wet patch on his crotch and couldn't help giggling.

'AJ, I'm so sorry, it was totally my fault. Rosa was just trying to save me from making a complete arse of myself and I think she was actually pretty inspired. Look, why don't you go home and change, take a few hours off,' said Rachel.

'Oh that's okay, it'll dry.' AJ stared down at his damp trousers. 'And besides, I want to come and see the Fox woman with you. I don't want to miss out on my chance of some action. I'll go and stand under the hand dryer in the gents' for a bit.'

'God, don't burn anything, will you,' said Rachel. 'Although I guess we're in the right place if you do!'

AJ grinned and wandered off towards the gents' with a slow wide-legged walk.

Rachel had temporarily forgotten that they'd arranged to meet Audrey Fox. It wasn't going to be easy and she'd decided to bring AJ for moral support. She hoped that Audrey might react better if there was a man in the room.

'Now make sure you use your charm on her,' said Rachel to AJ when he returned. 'We really don't need her to go nuts at us, like Lloyd did with Charles.'

AJ was fiddling with his groin as she spoke.

'Everything alright down there?' Rachel asked, nodding towards his crotch.

'Yeah, yeah. It's just that my boxers are made of this stretchy material that doesn't seem to dry very quickly. You'd have thought that it'd be the sort of thing that they'd design to do exactly the opposite.'

Rachel held up her hand and looked away. 'Yeah, too much detail, thanks. And you can't start doing that when we meet Audrey. She'd have a fit. Actually, she'd probably leap across the table to give you a hand, knowing her. But either way, it wouldn't be good,' said Rachel.

'Alright, noted. Do you want me to flirt with her?' AJ asked.

'No! Just be polite, charming, make her think we don't really suspect her.'

AJ was walking pretty much normally by the time they were outside Audrey's office.

'Ready?' Rachel asked.

AJ nodded.

They knocked on the door and waited. Audrey opened the door wearing a pair of linen wide-legged trousers and a tightly fitted, navy, satin blouse. As she turned around, Rachel could see the hint of some very high cut knickers though the linen material. She saw AJ look too and then quickly avert his gaze.

'Thank you very much for seeing us,' said Rachel in her politest voice. 'We know that you're very busy, so we won't take long.'

Audrey sat down behind her desk and looked at them impassively.

'What is it you want?'

'In the light of the recent, um, issues with Dr Cassidy, we've been performing some additional tests so we can try to assess the scale of the problem. And we need a little bit of help from you, if that's okay,' said AJ, beaming at Audrey like some sort of demented spaniel.

Rachel hoped Audrey couldn't see the remainder of the small damp patch on his trousers.

'Oh yes? How's that then?' Audrey asked.

AJ pulled his chair forward towards the desk and handed a small pile of invoices across to Audrey. As she leant forward to take them, she gave them both a good flash of her ample cleavage. Her gold leaf necklace flapped forwards and backwards and came to a halt, nestled neatly where it had started.

'We think you raised these invoices; is that right?' Rachel asked, resisting the temptation to lean across and shut AJ's open mouth next to her.

Audrey looked at them. 'Yes, that's right.'

'Well, we were just wondering why they still have the front sheet on,' said AJ, cocking his head sideways, trying to look innocent. 'We thought that was the copy that was sent out to the clients.'

Audrey looked down sharply at the invoices. 'Gosh, I can't remember that. I raise hundreds of invoices. Perhaps the client asked us not to send it or something.' She sounded quite irritated.

'Yes, I'm sorry, I'm sure it is difficult to remember. But there are quite a lot of them. We've found at least fifty so far. It seems like it happens quite often,' said AJ.

'Well, I don't know why, I'm afraid,' said Audrey, folding her arms.

'What happens if you don't send this copy?' Rachel asked.

'Nothing. The client doesn't have a copy, that's all,' said Audrey.

'How do they know what to pay then?' AJ asked.

Yes, good point, thought Rachel.

'Well, er, they probably had already agreed it with their doctor,' said Audrey.

'Surely they'd still want a receipt, though. It does seem very odd that so many haven't been sent,' said Rachel.

'What are you implying?' Audrey asked.

'We're not implying anything. We just need to understand why it might have happened.'

'Well, I don't have an explanation, other than it must have been an oversight,' said Audrey.

'And you're sure that you can't think of any other reasons?' AJ asked.

'No,' said Audrey, holding AJ's gaze as she sat back in her chair, uncrossed her legs and crossed them back the other way.

This is getting ridiculous, thought Rachel.

'Well, we think there's another reason,' said Rachel.

AJ looked at Rachel in surprise.

'These invoices are all for people who were booked in under false names and the amounts aren't what they'd agreed to pay. We think that's why you didn't send them out: because you knew they weren't real,' said Rachel.

Audrey glared at her. 'Do you now! Well, an interesting theory but total rubbish,' said Audrey.

Rachel began to get angry. Audrey was lying through her teeth, again. 'I don't think it's a good idea for you to lie to us.'

AJ took a sharp intake of breath and looked at his shoes.

'I saw you with Lloyd when you met Francesca Hart. You were there when she gave Lloyd cash and you saw him write down her record in his black book – you know, the one that you denied ever having seen before,' said Rachel.

Audrey opened her mouth to speak, then shut it again.

'Did Lloyd also give you some of the cash he took?' Rachel asked.

'How dare you!' said Audrey.

'Oh we dare, because we know it's true,' said Rachel, feeling increasingly bold: Audrey had nowhere to go.

'And what does Carl say about all this?' Audrey asked.

Rachel heard the warning note in her voice.

'He's fully briefed and totally supportive of our position,' said Rachel.

Audrey threw back her head and laughed. 'Fully briefed! That makes a change for Carl. He looks so much nicer without.'

AJ gasped and Rachel looked at Audrey in shock.

'Oh, didn't you know? Oh yes, I have to say, Carl is *an expert* in customer service.' Audrey raised her eyebrows suggestively and leaned forward towards them. 'And let me tell you, there are plenty more shocks where that one came from. You want me to tell your place all about what Carl has been up to, do you?'

Rachel looked at Audrey in horror.

'Oh, but then he'd be in terrible trouble, wouldn't he? What a shame that would be. And what would his wife say?' Audrey held up her hands in mock horror.

'You wouldn't do that,' said Rachel.

Audrey smiled at Rachel. 'Wouldn't I? Are you sure?'

Rachel looked at Audrey's smug face, her eyes glinting with pleasure. No, she wasn't sure. Shit! Rachel couldn't bring herself to say that, so she said nothing. AJ also seemed speechless with fright.

'Well, I suggest if you don't want that then you take your half-baked theories, put them neatly back in your little boxes and kindly leave my office.'

Neither of them moved.

'I said this discussion is finished. Off you run,' said Audrey, waving them away.

Eventually Rachel got up and marched out of the room and AJ scurried after her.

'Oh my God, do you think she was telling the truth?' AJ asked when they were out of earshot.

Rachel sighed. 'I know she was. She's been seeing Carl for nearly two years.'

AJ stopped dead. 'What?! And you knew already? How come?'

'Long story but it's over between them and I told Carl I wouldn't say anything. And you mustn't either.'

'Oh my God, I can't believe it,' said AJ, his eyes wide with a mixture of shock and excitement. 'Can I tell Rosa?'

Rachel hesitated. It was probably best that they both knew.

'Yes, alright, but absolutely no one else, okay? Not a word until I've worked out what to do next,' said Rachel.

But Rachel didn't even know where to begin. Audrey had them cornered.

CHAPTER 23

Rachel, AJ and Rosa were all sitting slumped in their chairs, drinking yet more coffee.

'I'm totally worn out,' said AJ. 'What a day! I still can't quite believe it.'

'Nor me,' said Rosa. 'Carl and Audrey Fox! Who'd have thought it.'

'Never mind that she was also seeing Lloyd Cassidy. What a woman!' AJ almost sounded impressed.

Rosa shook her head in disapproval. 'What a way to behave.'

Rachel felt more than worn out. She felt totally emotionally drained. The endless injections of caffeine seemed to be having less and less impact and the out of control whirring in her brain was giving her a headache.

'I had hoped that we'd all be on a bit of high now — you know, with the presentation done and our report nearly final,' said Rachel. 'Instead I feel crap. My presentation was all over the place, and unless we dump Carl right in it, it looks like Audrey, the bitch woman, will get away with it.'

Rachel didn't say it, but the fact that she'd split up with Harry wasn't exactly helping her mood either.

'We should go for a drink, cheer ourselves up,' said AJ.

Rosa and Rachel both looked at him wearily.

'Come on, liven up you two. We deserve it,' said AJ.

He was right, thought Rachel. They did deserve a break.

'Yes, alright, why not,' said Rachel. 'There's a good pub I know not far away. It's quiz night on a Monday. Quite fun and lively. Why don't we go there for a couple?'

It was a pub that she and Harry used to go to quite often. It was always a great night. They would drink copious beers, fight over who knew the most quiz answers and then mostly end up in bed. As she thought about it, Rachel felt a rush of affection for Harry. Christ, he'd been fun, even if he was a total shit. Rachel forced herself to smile at the others, trying to ignore the emotional tug of war going on in her stomach, and decided that she really must call Harry later. She couldn't carry on in limbo like this for much longer.

The Drum and Bass was a modern gastro pub that had changed its name as often as it had decor. It now had a large open plan seating area and waiter service, a far cry from when it had been called The Red Lion and had prided itself on its collection of real ales. The darts board had been replaced with a neatly scribed blackboard showing the specials of the day and small cardboard triangles promoting a pretty decent wine list perched on each table.

Rachel, Rosa and AJ sat at a table in one corner and Rosa picked up the wine menu.

'What shall we have?'

'Champagne all round, I think,' said Rachel. 'Perk us all up.'

'I'd rather have a pint actually, if that's okay,' said AJ.

'Of course it's okay, all the more for me and Rosa,' said Rachel, putting her arm round Rosa and giving her a friendly hug.

Rachel ordered their drinks, putting her credit card behind the bar to start a tab, just in case they needed another round. She watched the barman, dressed in what appeared to be compulsory black trousers and shirt, carefully open their bottle of pink fizz and perch it in a bucket half full of ice.

'Quiz sheet to go with that?' he asked.

'Yes, why not,' said Rachel.

She took the drinks over to the others and sat down.

'Quiz time,' she said, waving the sheet. 'We just need a team name.'

'What sort of name?' Rosa asked.

'God, have you never done a quiz before? Some sort of silly team name that says something about us, like the Beau Street Babes or something like that, but much better,' said Rachel.

'How about Beer Today, Gone Tomorrow, or Gin'll Fix It,' said AJ, grinning and downing half his pint to make the point.

'Oh right, I get it,' said Rosa, thinking. After a minute she said, 'What about the Wrinkle-free Wizards or Natural Born Quizzers?'

'Ooh, get you, very good!' said Rachel, impressed, and then screwed up her face in thought. She was hopelessly competitive and wasn't going to be outdone on some pub quiz name game. 'Hah, got it,' she said finally, triumphantly. 'How about Salmon Fish Face and the Trout Pouts, or Wonky Willy and the Plastic Factory.'

They all roared with laughter and spent a happy ten minutes suggesting even cruder and cruder team names that they knew they'd never use. In the end they opted for 'Universally Challenged', which they all agreed was both clever and witty.

'Just like us,' said Rachel, already well down her third glass of champagne.

As they sat chatting, a large group of people came bounding noisily into the pub.

'Hurry up, you lot. The quiz starts in five minutes,' shouted the guy at the front of the pack.

Rachel looked up. She knew that voice. It was Jonny Strauss, a workmate of Harry's. Walking a couple of paces behind him, dressed in a black leather jacket and jeans, was Harry. Rachel's heart jumped. She watched him walk across the bar, laughing and chatting to his friends. Damn he looked good.

The group sat down at a large, round table and started shouting their orders at Jonny, who was already at the bar. Rachel knew Jonny fairly well — he was a regular in Harry's party crew — and she vaguely recognised two of the other guys, but she didn't know the rest at all.

'Rachel, did you hear me?' Rosa was talking to her.

'Sorry, Rosa what were you saying?' Rachel forced herself to look away from Harry.

'I was just saying that we need to put our form in, before they start without us,' said Rosa.

Rachel didn't want to get up. She hadn't decided if she wanted Harry to see her or not. He was sitting with his back to her, oblivious to the blind panic he'd created in the corner.

'I'll do it,' said AJ.

'Great, thanks. Ladies' room calls,' said Rachel to Rosa and rushed to the safety of the toilets that were on her side of the pub. She went into the cubicle and sat down on the toilet seat. Now what should she do? She tried hard to remember how cross she was with Harry, but the anger didn't come. Instead she felt breathless and slightly excited, like she was on a first date. Maybe it was the champagne or the fact that she hadn't seen him for a while. But whichever it was, Rachel suddenly felt an overwhelming urge to give him another chance. Go with your gut feeling, Shali had said. So that's what she would do.

Rachel carefully reapplied her make-up and brushed her hair. Although she'd been a bit hot, she was very happy she'd stuck with her dress and boots combination – a mixture of sexy and school mistress. Harry would love it.

When she got back to the table, AJ was back with the quiz sheets and they were busy studying the first round of questions.

'It's science and nature. Doesn't look too bad,' said AJ.

Rachel refilled her glass and by the time they'd worked their way through the questions, it had disappeared. She needed a bit of Dutch courage.

'So is a newt an amphibian or a reptile, which are we going for?' AJ asked.

'I'm sure it's an amphibian, like a frog,' said Rosa.

'But don't they have scales, which would make it a reptile?' said Rachel, glancing over at Harry who seemed equally engrossed in the debate on his table.

'Buggered if I know,' said AJ.

'No, a newt has smooth skin. I'm sure it's an amphibian,' said Rosa.

'Let's go with that then. I've never been that close to a newt, only as pissed as one,' said Rachel, laughing. This was fun. Good old Harry pub, good old quiz.

She got up.

'Just going to say hi to someone I know over there,' she said to AJ and Rosa and began to walk slowly towards Harry, mulling over how long she would wait until she put him out of his misery and let him know that she was giving him another chance.

As she approached, Harry sat up from peering over the quiz questions and stretched his arms out behind his back. But instead of putting both his arms back down, he put one of them round the girl sitting next to him, who responded by sliding closer to him and nuzzling his neck.

Rachel froze in her tracks. Who the fuck was that? Even from behind, she could see that the girl was young, really quite young actually. She felt breathless and dizzy, like she'd been punched hard in the stomach, and stared at them, unable to tear her eyes away. Harry stroked the girl's arm and then pushed his fingers into her hair, massaging the back of her neck. The affection of it made Rachel feel sick and the anger that she'd searched for in the toilets earlier suddenly arrived, and it arrived with a bang.

She marched over to the table and tapped Harry on the shoulder. He turned round, still laughing from some joke they were all sharing. But the joke didn't last long. Harry's face dropped almost as quickly as his arm and he bolted out of his seat.

'Rachel, what are you doing here?'

'Who is that?' Rachel asked, pointing at the offending girl. The girl turned round and looked up at them. Her smoky eye make-up was slightly smudged and her lips were pink and sticky with lip gloss. Her cropped hair was tussled and messy, completing the just-got-out-of-bed look to perfection.

'Hi, I'm Zoe,' she said, smiling lazily at them both.

Harry grabbed Rachel's arm and pulled her away towards the bar. Rachel flicked his arm off hers and stood in front of him, blocking his way.

'I asked you a question.'

'Rachel, let's sit down,' said Harry. He looked around anxiously. 'Over there,' he said, pointing to a small table for two in the corner.

Rachel hesitated but then, conscious that people were starting to look at them, she reluctantly followed Harry over to the table. She sat down bolt upright with her arms folded and raised her eyebrows quizzically at Harry.

'Well?'

'She's a student trainee working with one of Jonny's mates.'

'She looks about six,' said Rachel, scowling.

'She's nineteen actually,' said Harry.

'How long have you…' Rachel couldn't bear to finish the sentence. She felt the tears welling up in her eyes, but she fought them back.

'I've only just met her,' said Harry.

'What about us? I thought you wanted another chance, or was that just another pack of lies?' Her chin trembled with a mixture of rage and indignation.

'No, of course it wasn't. I meant everything I said. But I've hardly heard from you and you did tell me it was over, remember?'

Harry reached into his pocket and took out his phone. He found the text she'd sent him that said *Leave me alone. It's over* and pushed his phone towards her with the message open, like it was his 'get out of jail free' card.

'You were pretty clear,' he said. 'I couldn't wait forever.'

'Harry, it's been less than a week! And besides, we have met since that text and I told you I would think about it.'

'Yes and you were frosty as hell. It was pretty clear to me that we had no chance. You said you'd ring me and you haven't.' Harry sat back sulkily in his chair.

'You know I've been totally flat out at work. I've hardly had a moment to breathe, let alone think about us. We only finished presenting our findings this morning,' said Rachel.

'So work comes first, does it? Right, I see,' said Harry.

'No, of course it doesn't. It's just the way things worked out.'

'Seems like work is all you care about to me,' said Harry.

'That's not fair, and besides, if you really wanted us to get back together, you would have waited a couple of weeks,' said Rachel.

'I had no one to go out with and it was boring as hell. Zoe was just someone to play with. She doesn't mean any more to me than that,' said Harry.

Fuck, he was shallow.

'Oh, that's nice for her, a plaything for your amusement.'

'I didn't mean it like that. I was just trying to say that it's not serious,' said Harry.

'How could it be serious? You've only known her five minutes.' Rachel glared at him.

Harry looked confused. 'Sorry, did I miss something? Are you saying that you want us to get back together, that you want me back?'

The directness of the question gave Rachel a lump in her throat. She said yes and no several times in her head, before she dared speak.

'I at least expected you to wait for me while I thought about it, rather than jumping straight into bed with someone else because you were bored!'

'That's not what I asked,' said Harry.

'No, I do not want you back,' said Rachel. How could she say anything else given all he'd done?

'Well, I can see who I like then. You can't have it both ways,' said Harry, sitting back and folding his arms.

Rachel wanted to cry with frustration. 'If you really loved me then you wouldn't need someone else.'

'That's female emotional bullshit,' said Harry. 'It doesn't work like that in the real world.'

Rachel stared at him, stung by the criticism. 'Clearly not in your world, anyway,' she said.

They sat glaring at each other when Jonny suddenly appeared at the side of the table.

'Mate, sports round. Sorry to interrupt,' said Jonny, smiling apologetically at Rachel. 'Which golf course was the first Open Golf Championship played on?'

'Prestwick in Scotland,' said Harry without even hesitating.

'Genius, I told them you would know. Thanks, mate.'

Jonny darted back to the table, totally unaware of the sensitivity of the conversation he'd just interrupted. He announced the answer to the table, making Zoe turn round and look at Rachel and Harry, her brow furrowed slightly with confusion. She smiled shyly at Harry, shrugged her shoulders and turned back to the quiz.

'I think your playmate wants you,' said Rachel. Her voice sounded shrill and bitter.

'Well, at least someone does,' said Harry and he got up and walked away.

It took all Rachel's willpower to stop herself shouting 'So do I!' and throwing herself after him. Harry didn't love her and he didn't deserve her. Her head knew that, but why did her heart feel like it had been smashed into tiny pieces?

Rachel walked slowly back to her table where a rather bemused AJ and Rosa were sitting.

'Wasn't that your boyfriend?' Rosa asked. 'The one you took to the summer party?'

Rachel nodded, biting her lip.

'Are you okay?' AJ asked.

Rachel shook her head. 'No, not okay, not okay at all, actually,' she said and the tears began to flow down her cheeks, splashing onto the table in small, neat puddles. Rachel's chest began to heave up and down as she tried to hold back the sobs.

'Shit! We'd better go,' said AJ. He turned to Rosa. 'I'll settle up; you take Rachel outside.' And he sprinted over to the bar, glaring at Harry as he did.

Rosa took Rachel's arm and guided her out of the pub. By the time they got outside, Rachel was a sobbing wreck, her face streaked with make-up.

Rosa hugged her tightly and stroked her head. 'Shush, shush, come on now, it will be okay.'

AJ appeared next to them and stood awkwardly with his hands in his pockets, not quite sure what he should do next.

After a few minutes, Rachel tried to gather herself. 'Sorry, so sorry. I just had a bit of a shock, that's all.' She rummaged round in her handbag for a pack of tissues and began trying to mop up the damp mess on her face.

'Here,' said Rosa, gently taking the tissue from Rachel's hand and wiping away the streaked make-up as best she could.

'Well, he's bound to be in the wrong, that's all I can say,' said AJ, trying to be helpful. 'Us blokes always are.'

Rosa glared at him.

'What? It's true. When was the last time you had a row where you were in the wrong?' AJ asked Rosa.

'Shut up, AJ,' said Rosa.

AJ shrugged and raised his hands as if to say, don't shoot the messenger.

'I'm sure it will blow over,' said Rosa, still with her arm protectively around Rachel.

'Not this time,' said Rachel, sniffing and dabbing her eyes.

Harry had somehow managed to make her feel that it was all her fault. She should have been clearer with him. She shouldn't have put her work first. Never mind that he had totally betrayed her trust and then cheated on her – well, okay, maybe not strictly cheated on her, but as near as, damn it. Fuck, why couldn't he have just waited for her? Harry had shown his true colours this time. He needed attention more than he needed her. There was no going back now. It was over and that was that.

'Look, why don't we all start a bit later tomorrow?' suggested Rosa. 'A bit of a lie in would do us good, don't you think? Recharge our batteries a bit.'

'Yes, good idea. Let's come in for lunchtime,' said Rachel.

AJ hailed Rachel a cab and, after lots of reassuring them that she would be fine, she headed home on her own. She lay in bed staring into the dark, replaying the events of the evening in her head. Should she have done something differently? Might Harry have waited if she'd phoned him sooner? Had she really been too busy to decide what to do? It didn't matter now anyway. Harry wasn't the right guy for her and she was better off without him. She fell asleep telling herself that over and over again, in the hope that when she woke up in the morning it would turn out to be true.

CHAPTER 24

The sunny freshness of the park did little to help Rachel's mood as she sat on a bench sipping her extra large takeaway coffee. Although she'd slept for nearly ten hours, she still felt exhausted. The haze caused by the previous night's champagne still hovered around in her head and her stomach was knotted so tightly she was finding it hard to eat anything. The shock of seeing Harry with someone else had morphed overnight into a dull acceptance that it was over between them.

Rachel watched as the plethora of runners and dog walkers wound their various routes around the park. Just watching them made her feel tired. Where did they get their energy from? Rachel wasn't sure she could run upstairs at the moment, let alone run round the park.

As she contemplated the day ahead, Rachel knew she had to see Carl to let him know about Audrey's threat to tell all. But rather than being worried about it, she felt numb. Whatever happens, happens, she told herself. It didn't seem so important any more. Maybe she'd been taking work too seriously.

She also knew that her chances of promotion to director were probably fading fast. She'd nearly missed a major fraud and her presentation to Equinox had been a bit of a fuck up. Then on top of that, just as she was trying to turn around her reputation as an unreliable party girl, her university past might come back to haunt her. Being disciplined for climbing historic buildings while being drunk and disorderly was hardly something that she'd put on her CV when she had applied to Payne Stanley. They probably wouldn't have hired her if they'd known.

An elderly lady walking a particularly ugly pug dog smiled at Rachel as she walked past. 'Lovely morning,' she said. 'Makes you feel happy to be alive, don't you think?' Her bright eyes shone out from a wrinkled face that looked remarkably like her dog's, and she seemed full of energy in spite of her curved back and walking stick.

Rachel looked around. It really was a lovely morning. The sun was glinting gently through the trees, dappling the grass with green and yellow stripes. The park's flowerbeds were bursting with colour and for once the sound of birds chirping and children shouting was louder than the traffic noise.

'Yes, it is a lovely morning actually,' said Rachel, smiling.

The pug dog growled at her and then farted loudly, somewhat spoiling the moment. Rachel tried hard not to giggle.

'Cornelius, stop that!' said the lady, tapping the dog on the head with the end of the lead. She grinned cheekily at Rachel and then shuffled away, dragging a reluctant Cornelius behind her.

Rachel watched her walk away and then stood up, feeling slightly ashamed. She was young, fit and healthy, on a good day really pretty attractive and not exactly stupid. She had a great job, her own flat and no farting pets. In fact, when she thought about it, she had plenty to be happy about. She just needed to get a grip and deal with what was in front of her, one step at a time.

'Come on, snap out of it. Let's get this show on the road,' she said out loud.

She went back to her flat and made herself two rounds of cheese on toast, which she ate in front of the TV with a large glass of orange juice. She then had a long shower, rubbing herself all over with an exfoliating shower cream until her skin was glowing and pink. She washed and straightened her hair, applied a little more make-up than she normally would for work and dressed in a navy skirt suit with canary yellow shirt underneath.

When she arrived at Beau Street she stopped to have her customary chat with Fred.

'You look nice today, Ms Altman, very sunny,' said Fred, his eyes twinkling at her.

'Thanks, Fred. To be honest, I was in need of a bit of sun today. Been working a bit too hard. You know how it is,' said Rachel.

Fred nodded knowingly at her. 'I do, I do. This job is long hours too, you know. I was here before seven this morning. Still, it means I got to see the sun come up this morning. You can't beat a good sunrise, you know. You can tell a lot about the weather from different colours of the sunrise.'

'Really? What's the weather forecast today?' Rachel asked generously.

'Mainly sunny with some light cloud cover this afternoon,' said Fred.

Rachel smiled. She was going to miss Fred.

'We're probably finishing today or tomorrow, you know, Fred. We're pretty much done here,' she said.

'What a shame! Well, it's been a pleasure to meet you, Ms Altman. Do pop in and say hello every now and again, won't you?'

'Yes, I will, and good luck with the alternative career plans,' said Rachel, nodding knowingly at Fred.

'Ah well, I have some news there actually,' said Fred.

'Really?' Rachel was amazed. He hadn't actually got a new job, had he?

'My sister-in-law has asked me to help out with newspapers for the blind. She's a volunteer reader for them and they need some more help. And guess what? I'm going to be reading the weather! It's only a few hours a week, mind, but I'm really excited about it.' Fred looked over the moon.

'That's fantastic, Fred! I'm delighted for you, and what a good cause too. Well done,' said Rachel, squeezing his arm.

'Oh, I doubt anything much will come of it,' said Fred. 'I'll probably still be here in ten years' time.'

Rachel was touched by Fred's confidence that he'd still be working ten years from now.

'And if you are, they'd be lucky to have you,' said Rachel.

Fred beamed at her. 'Well, yes, maybe they would,' he said.

AJ was sitting eating a sandwich when Rachel got to the project room.

'How are you feeling?' AJ asked.

'Not bad, thanks. Better for the slow start,' said Rachel.

'He's a bloody idiot if you ask me,' said AJ, and then looked a bit concerned that he'd said the wrong thing again.

Rachel grinned at him. 'Thanks. I think I'm just working that out.'

'What's the plan for today?' AJ asked.

'I'm going to go and see Tom shortly, see how the deal is progressing with Equinox, and then I need to pop back to the office and see Carl, talk to him about what we do about Audrey,' said Rachel.

'Can I come?' AJ asked hopefully.

'No, sorry, I think it will be better if I see him on my own,' said Rachel.

'You get all the good jobs,' said AJ.

'Awkward jobs more like. Anyway, if you and Rosa can try to clear all the square brackets we have in the report and then start handing all the files back.' She looked around at the piles of paper and coffee cups scattered around their project room. 'We also need to clear this room out before we go. I've never seen so many coffee cups.'

'Ooh, did someone say coffee? White with one sugar, please,' said AJ.

Rachel smiled. 'Alright, I'll get coffee. You start sorting out those files.'

She walked down to the coffee machine and as she got there she saw Clive Steele kneeling down, fiddling with the cup dispenser.

'Problems?' Rachel asked.

Clive looked up at her. 'Hello, Rachel, how nice to see you. Yes, can't seem to get a cup to come out.'

'You need to flick the little arm across,' said Rachel. 'It gets stuck sometimes.'

'Where?' Clive asked.

'Just inside the cup dispenser on the left,' said Rachel.

'Can you show me?' Clive asked, peering into the hole.

Rachel knelt down beside him, reached in and flicked the small arm inside the cup dispenser, making a cup drop down into the dispenser. 'There,' she said, standing up.

Clive stayed on his knees to survey her legs.

'Very nice. And I bet they look even nicer higher up,' said Clive, tilting his head so he could look up her skirt.

Rachel stepped away from him in horror. 'I beg your pardon!'

Clive stood up and laughed. 'Just a bit of banter, you know. I'm sure a fun girl like you likes a bit of flattery every now and again.' He leant over and patted Rachel gently on the bottom. 'And now that we're going to be working together, I'm sure we can be very good friends,' said Clive.

'Would you kindly keep your hands to yourself!' said Rachel, pushing his arm away.

'Oh don't be like that. Otherwise I might have to tell a few people about your little clock climbing escapade. Tom would love to hear about it, I'm sure. He loves a good story.'

Rachel couldn't believe what she was hearing. What a disgusting little man!

'Don't you dare threaten me,' said Rachel. 'And besides, I know all about you and Audrey Fox, so you'd better be careful.'

'What about me and Audrey Fox? I don't know what you're talking about,' said Clive.

Rachel wasn't sure she knew the full story but decided to gamble. 'I know that you were sleeping with her, that she gave you the inside track to make sure you won this project and that in return you gave her money.'

Rachel held her breath. That was quite an accusation.

Clive stared at her. 'What a load of crap,' he said.

Rachel steeled herself. 'Did you bid five grand less than the other companies to win this job by any chance? I've seen Audrey's notes on the pitch documents. I could always check with Tom if you like?'

Clive went a bit pale and rubbed his forehead. Rachel could tell she was on the right track.

'Er, no need to do that. I'm just being friendly as we do need to work together, after all. Tom has made that quite clear,' said Clive.

'Well, I'll make sure that you have all the information

you need. One of my team will do that. But just to be clear, I won't be working *with you* at all, friends or no friends,' said Rachel.

'Well, you'd better hope your reputation stays intact in the meantime,' said Clive.

'So had you,' said Rachel, trying to look braver than she felt.

'What happened to the coffee?' AJ asked when Rachel came back into the room empty-handed.

'It looked even more disgusting than usual. I'll go out to the Italian on the corner instead. Look, I bumped into one of the guys from the PR company just now. They still need a few bits of information from us. Would you mind dealing with it from now on? I've got quite a lot to do already,' said Rachel.

'Sure, no problem,' said AJ.

She wrote Tim Archer's contact details down for AJ and sent Tim an email explaining that AJ would be his point of contact from now on.

Rachel stood in the queue at the coffee shop still feeling a bit shaken by her encounter with Clive. Would it really matter if he said anything? It was so long ago. Rachel wasn't so bothered about her reputation, which if she was honest probably wasn't that great anyway. She was more concerned that she hadn't told Payne Stanley when she had applied to them, even though she wasn't sure whether she was required to or not. Somehow she just didn't feel it would be helpful to her promotion prospects if it came out now. But Rachel felt tired of worrying. She probably wasn't getting promoted this time round anyway, so she might as well go ahead and tell Carl before someone else did. That would take the wind out of Clive's sails.

AJ rang to say that Rosa had arrived just in time for Rachel to add a third coffee to the order.

'Plus three of those round chocolate pastry things,' she said to the amply proportioned lady serving behind the counter.

'Good choice, they're quite delicious,' she said. 'We bake 'em fresh every day. Anything else?'

'No, that's it, thanks,' said Rachel. She could have bought the whole shop, it all looked so good.

AJ, Rosa and Rachel sat in the project room happily sipping coffee and scoffing their chocolate pastries.

'Very good call,' said Rosa. 'These are yummy.'

'Have I got it round my mouth?' Rachel asked. 'I'm seeing Tom in a minute.'

'No, you're fine,' said Rosa.

Rachel knocked on the door of Tom Duffy's office.

'Hi, Tom. How are you? I thought we should probably have a quick catch up as we're nearly done here. Did you get any feedback from Equinox on our presentation?' Rachel wasn't sure she wanted to hear, but she knew Carl would ask.

'Ah, Rachel, yes, we did. Good timing actually. They have a couple of follow up questions and I was about to ring Ryan Miller. Could you stay and we can do it together?'

Rachel hadn't been expecting another grilling. 'Can I just pop and get my files?'

'Sure,' said Tom.

She dashed back to the project room.

'Shit, Tom wants me to do a call with Equinox,' she said to AJ and Rosa as she rushed into the room and started madly grabbing bits of paper.

'What about?' Rosa asked.

'No bloody idea, just some "follow up questions". That's all Tom said. God, I hope I can answer them.'

'Here, take my pack,' said Rosa. 'It's all labelled and in order, so you should be able to find anything you need.'

Rachel flicked through Rosa's immaculately organised file.

'Thank you, life saver. Again,' said Rachel, smiling at Rosa gratefully and rushed back to Tom's office.

Tom had already called Ryan when she got back to his office.

'Ryan, Rachel is just joining us now,' said Tom.

'Hey there, Rachel, thanks for joining us,' said Ryan. 'We found your presentation very useful by the way. You guys had certainly been thorough, which is very comforting.'

'Thank you,' said Rachel, inwardly cringing at the prospect of what might have happened had she kept quiet and Equinox had found out about Lloyd after they'd bought the business. Thorough would not have been the word they'd have used then!

'Look, we're wondering what data you have on the performance of other doctors? Before we move forward, we need to be sure this wasn't a one-man show and that the business can survive without Cassidy.'

'Yes, we have plenty of data on that, Ryan. We looked at it when we stripped Lloyd Cassidy's sales out of the numbers we showed you.' Rachel turned to the relevant pages in Rosa's pack and moved slightly so Tom could see them too. 'There are several other doctors with sales levels very similar to Dr Cassidy's and plenty of others with very positive growth rates. Take Stella Webb, for example,' said Rachel, running her finger across the table of figures. 'Her client base has grown by more than fifteen per cent over the last two years. I can send you the information we have, if it's okay with Tom?'

'Yes, please do, this looks very helpful,' said Tom, nodding at Rosa's carefully presented analysis. 'And don't forget, Ryan, we're also working on those new income streams we talked about to replace Lloyd.'

'Yeah, I know, but if you could email that data it'd be real useful too,' said Ryan.

'Of course,' said Rachel. She didn't know what new income streams they were talking about, but decided it probably wasn't anything to do with her. That was for Tom and Ryan to sort out.

Ryan ran through a few more questions, all of which Rachel found she could answer easily. Maybe she did know what she was talking about after all.

'Thank you, that was great, very helpful,' said Tom when the call had ended. 'I think we're finally getting there. Equinox were naturally quite concerned about the whole Lloyd Cassidy débâcle at the outset, but when you showed them what the business looked like without him, they were much more relaxed. They were very happy with your full report too, very detailed,' said Tom.

'Oh that's good,' said Rachel, pleasantly surprised.

'And they commented on the efforts you've all been to. Brenda Martinez in particular said she could tell how well prepared you were.'

Rachel went red with embarrassment. 'Oh right, that's good. Have they firmed up on their offer?' she asked, quickly changing the subject.

'At the moment they want to reduce their original offer to take account of our lower sales figures without Lloyd. But we're trying to find some alternatives to plug the gap, and luckily Charles has managed to do a deal with Lloyd. We won't involve the police provided he agrees to leave with immediate effect and doesn't take any money from the sale of the business. So with a bit of luck, we might end up with an offer that doesn't change that much,' said Tom.

'That's really good news. I'm surprised Charles and Lloyd are even speaking, though,' said Rachel.

'I don't think it was a very pleasant conversation, but in the end it made sense for both of them. We're pretty sure that the money he's giving up from his share of the sale is much more than he could have skimmed off over the years.'

'I'm not sure you'll ever know unless you find some more records. I didn't find any when I looked. Are you close to agreeing a deal with Equinox then, do you think?' Rachel asked.

'Yes, quite close,' said Tom. 'Equinox have still got their legal investigations to finish, which aren't proving exactly straightforward, and everything has to be approved by the board, so there's still a way to go before it's a done deal. Plus, we've got to work out how the businesses would operate together – who'll do what jobs, all that sort of thing. That's Stella's job. But at least we've got the main valuation points agreed.'

'I'm seeing Carl in a bit so I'll tell him. I'm sure he'll want to ring you himself. The team are just finishing up now. I think we'll probably be done today or tomorrow, so we'll be back at our own offices after that,' said Rachel. 'Once we've finished off a few square brackets in the report, we'll send it round as final.'

'Thank you for all your hard work,' said Tom, smiling. 'I know it hasn't exactly been straightforward.'

No, it certainly hasn't, thought Rachel.

In the taxi on the way to the office, Rachel reflected on the fact that Lloyd had done a deal with Charles. What would happen if they told them Audrey was involved too? Presumably they'd just quietly get rid of her too. But Rachel wasn't sure whether they'd be telling Tom and Charles about Audrey or not. That would have to be Carl's call, and it wasn't going to be an easy one.

Carl was on the phone when Rachel arrived at his office. He waved her into the room and gestured that she should sit down. It sounded like he was talking to someone about a new project.

'Yes, that's no problem. I'm confident we could meet those deadlines. It sounds like a very interesting business. I can see why you would want it. How about I come to see you early next week, say Tuesday?' Carl clicked away at his on-screen diary. 'Eleven o'clock? Perfect, Ian, see you then.' He put the phone down.

'Sorry about that,' he said. 'Call from a good contact of mine thinking of buying out a smaller competitor.'

'Interesting business as you said?' Rachel asked.

'No, not at all, makes radiators, but that's interesting to Ian — he's in the same business.'

Rachel grinned. 'I look forward to that one.'

'So what's the latest on basket case Beau Street then? Found any more frauds today?' Carl asked.

He was clearly in a good mood.

'No, but I'm afraid there is more bad news,' said Rachel.

Carl's face fell. 'What now?'

'Well, we went to see Audrey about the invoices that hadn't had the front copy sent out. She was pretty unhelpful, as you might expect. She just said it must be an oversight and she had no idea why they hadn't been sent.'

'Well, she was bound to say something like that,' said Carl. 'We should just hand the invoices over to Tom, tell him what we think and let them investigate it.'

'It's not that straightforward, I'm afraid,' said Rachel.

'Why not?' said Carl.

'I told her that we thought she knew exactly what was going on and she didn't send the invoices out as the people they were addressed to didn't exist. I also asked her if Lloyd had given her a cut of the money he took,' said Rachel.

'That was a bit direct! What did she say to that?' Carl asked.

'She got a bit nasty. She said that if we continued to push down this route then she'd, um, tell Payne Stanley about you and her. She knows that would get you into trouble.' Rachel looked anxiously at Carl.

Carl stood up. 'The conniving, two-faced…' He restrained himself from finishing the sentence.

'What do you want to do?' Rachel asked.

Carl thought for a while. 'We'll play her at her own game. I'll talk to her, tell her that if she says anything about us I'll also tell Lloyd Cassidy. I bet Lloyd won't be so keen to protect her if he finds out what she's been up to.'

Rachel suddenly realised Lloyd wouldn't know about Clive Steele either. But neither did Carl and she would have to tell him if they wanted to use that with Audrey too.

'I think Audrey has been playing the same games with someone else too, someone Lloyd probably won't know about either,' said Rachel.

'Really, who?' Carl looked astounded.

'Clive Steele. He's head of Cavanaugh PR, the company working with Beau Street on a new joint marketing plan for when the Equinox deal happens. We got some extra work from Tom to help them out, remember?'

'What has that got to do with Audrey?'

Rachel explained about finding the pitch documents in Lloyd's office.

'I thought they'd seemed a bit of an unlikely choice for the work. Lloyd was getting copies of all the deal documents as he was part of the senior management team. Audrey used them to help give Cavanaugh the inside track,' said Rachel.

'I still don't see how you know for definite that they were, well, er, in a relationship.'

Rachel looked at the floor. 'Carl, I need to tell you about something that happened when I was at university.'

Carl looked totally bemused. 'What the hell has your time at university got to do with anything?'

Rachel explained the whole story to Carl, who sat and listened in silence.

'So, you see, Clive wanted us to be, well, friendly, and said that if I wasn't he would tell people about me being disciplined for climbing the clock tower,' said Rachel. 'And the thing is, I didn't say anything about it when I applied to work here.'

Rachel looked at Carl, her brow furrowed with worry.

Carl threw his head back and laughed loudly. 'Christ, Rachel, if we didn't employ people just because they had a good time at university, we wouldn't have any employees left at all! I don't think that there's a partner here who doesn't have some minor misdemeanour or other lurking in the closet,' said Carl.

'Really, are you sure? I don't need to tell HR or anything, you know, just in case it comes out later on?' Rachel asked.

'No, definitely not. It was a matter for the university and they dealt with it. End of subject. Really, you don't need to worry. Let the lecherous old bastard do his worst. I think it's a bloody great story! I can just see you dangling off some clock tower, waiting to be rescued by the fire brigade. Hilarious!' Carl chuckled to himself.

Rachel felt hugely relieved. She needn't worry now if Clive did say anything.

'I'd still rather the whole world didn't know. I'm trying really hard to get this director promotion and it won't exactly enhance my reputation, will it?' said Rachel.

'I don't think it will matter, it was so long ago. But we don't need that sort of thing happening now, though,' said Carl.

'No, of course not,' said Rachel, mindful of her recent spate of Harry-induced hangovers. At least there was one up side to breaking up with him.

'And while we're on the subject, I wanted to talk to you about the director promotions,' said Carl.

'Oh yes?' said Rachel, concerned.

'Yes, I want you to know that I'll be supporting your case for promotion. You've done really well on this project. I know it hasn't been easy. You perhaps didn't get every decision quite right but that's not unusual. We all learn as we go.' Carl smiled at her ruefully.

'Really? Carl, that's great news, thank you!'

'I'll put something in your development plan about remembering to consult more on key issues, but that's quite normal at your level. And just to be clear, I'm not doing this just because you helped me. You genuinely deserve a good review for this job.'

Rachel smiled warmly at Carl. 'Thanks. And it's certainly been an experience I won't forget, that's for sure!'

'Good. So look, I'll call Audrey and nicely explain to her that if she mentions anything about us to Beau

Street, Payne Stanley or anyone else for that matter, I'll tell Lloyd about her relationship with me and with this Clive Steele guy,' said Carl.

'We can only show at the moment that she probably knew that the paperwork wasn't right,' said Rachel. 'It doesn't prove that she took any money. Only Lloyd knows that. And if he finds out she's been seeing other men, he could easily drop her right in it.'

'Yup, he certainly could,' said Carl.

'Oh, I forgot to say, I saw Tom earlier. He told me that Charles Sutton has done a deal with Lloyd. They won't involve the police in return for Lloyd leaving immediately and giving up his money from the sale of the business,' said Rachel.

'Audrey will probably be out of a job too then, once we tell Tom,' said Carl.

Rachel nodded. 'Shall I tell him then?'

Carl stared out of the window. Rachel could see it was a hard decision for him.

'Yes, I'll let you know once I've spoken to her,' Carl said eventually.

CHAPTER 25

Rachel, Natalie and Shali were sitting in an Italian bistro tucking into huge plates of pasta. Rachel needed comfort food and this seemed to be doing the trick.

'So you're pretty much done with the fantastic plastic project then?' Natalie asked, twirling a large mouthful of rich and creamy spaghetti flecked with basil round a fork.

'Yes, pretty much, but with two people being sacked for fraud, fantastic isn't exactly the first word that springs to mind,' said Rachel.

Carl had rung Rachel earlier to recount his conversation with Audrey. At first she'd shouted, ranted and threatened, but then eventually she'd shut up and listened.

'So it was pretty clear that Lloyd knew nothing about me or this Clive Steele bloke,' Carl had explained. 'And she needs him. He's her only source of income. Apparently he's thinking of going back to South America to work there and wants her to go too. She was waiting to see how things worked out at

Beau Street before she decided, but I think we just helped her make up her mind. Anyway, she definitely won't be saying anything about us now and that's for sure.'

'Oh, Carl, that's good news. I'll talk to Tom then. And by the way, I'm really sorry about you and Audrey, the whole situation. No one's really winning here, are they?' Rachel had said. She'd expected to feel pleased that Audrey was getting her comeuppance, but instead for some reason she'd just felt rather sad.

'No, I guess they're not,' Carl had said.

Tom Duffy had listened in steely silence as Rachel explained why they were certain that Audrey had known at least something about Lloyd Cassidy's cash for anonymity scam. And later on, AJ had burst into the project room to say that he'd been returning some files and had seen Fred helping a tearful Audrey pack up her desk.

'Amazing really,' said Shali.

'Totally,' agreed Natalie. 'My projects are never this interesting.'

Rachel had decided not to tell any of the other partners about Carl's relationship with Audrey. He'd protected her when she'd taken too long to speak up about Lloyd and she knew for certain that it was over between him and Audrey. There seemed little point now. He'd been a bit of idiot, but then so had she! AJ and Rosa had also promised not to say anything and she was pretty sure that she could trust them. Plus, it was hardly in their interests to upset her. With a bit of luck she'd be a director soon.

'Carl was pretty pleased with how it went, though, in the end,' said Rachel.

'I went to see him yesterday about the summer party investigation,' said Shali.

'Oh my God, did you! How did it go?' Rachel asked.

'Well, apart from being the most embarrassing twenty minutes of my life, not too bad all things considered,' said Shali. 'I think he knew that he couldn't give me too much of a big lecture. But even so, being asked not to shag guests at work events was still pretty awful. I just mumbled a load of stuff about it being out of character and that it wouldn't happen again and he seemed to believe me.'

Natalie and Rachel exchanged amused glances.

'What! It won't,' said Shali.

'No, no, of course not,' said Natalie, shaking her head and winking at Rachel.

'Not until the next time, anyway,' said Rachel.

Shali laughed. 'Shut up, you two! Anyway, I've got a written warning for "inappropriate behaviour" that will go on my HR file. But Carl says that should be the end of it, provided I keep my head down.'

'Oh I'm sure you'll be very good at that,' said Rachel, giving Natalie a knowing look.

Natalie snorted with laughter and spat her mouthful of wine across the table.

The three of them giggled hysterically as Natalie mopped up the wine.

'Anyway, enough about me,' said Shali, catching her breath. 'We're meant to be cheering Rachel up. How's it going without Harry?'

'Pretty crap actually,' said Rachel. 'Still, no point moaning on about it. I'm better off without him.'

'And we don't want to listen to you moaning about it either,' said Natalie.

'Here, here,' said Shali.

The three of them clinked their oversized glasses of red wine together.

'He was very good looking, though,' said Shali.

Natalie glared at her. 'Not helpful.'

'I was just saying!'

'Well don't. Rachel doesn't need our opinions on him. She's made her own mind up,' said Natalie.

'Yup. I've decided he's a shallow, immature prick,' said Rachel.

'Yes, I'm afraid he is,' said Natalie, nodding.

'Listen to you! I thought Rachel didn't need our opinions, you hypocrite,' said Shali, laughing.

'I was just agreeing with her. That's not the same thing,' said Natalie.

'Yes it is,' said Shali.

'Look, it's okay, guys,' said Rachel. 'The world is still turning. It's not that big a deal. I'll get a bit of a break now that Beau Street is pretty much done. Bit of a rest and I'll be fine.'

'Ooh, I've got a good idea,' said Natalie. 'Sue Martin is organising the office sailing race this weekend. She asked me if I wanted to go as a couple of people couldn't make it due to jobs over-running, but I've got a wedding this weekend so had to say no. You should go instead! It sounded brilliant fun.'

'I don't know the first thing about sailing,' said Rachel.

'That doesn't matter. Beginners are welcome. There are about six boats in the race, I think. They race round the Solent somewhere for the afternoon and then there's a big barbecue and disco in the evening. It would be good for you – you know, get out of London, meet a few new people,' said Natalie.

'I don't know, sounds a bit energetic to me. I thought I might go shopping on Saturday,' said Rachel.

'Well, think about it,' said Natalie. 'I'll forward you her email. I'm sure they still need a couple more people.'

'What are you doing Saturday night?' Rachel asked Shali, thinking that some post shopping company might be good.

'My sister is up, I'm afraid, and we're having dinner with Mum and Dad,' said Shali.

'Oh, okay, no problem,' said Rachel. Maybe she would just go home too. After all, she could do with the rest.

'Look, it's the department's quarterly drinks next month. Why don't we all go to that? Make a bit of a night of it, you know, maybe go to a club after or something. It's been ages since we have had a really good girls' night out,' said Natalie.

'I'd be up for that,' said Rachel.

'Me too,' said Shali. 'In the meantime, I think we need another bottle. This one seems to have mysteriously evaporated.'

The next day, Rachel was sitting in the office rather regretting the previous night's red-wine-athon. She hadn't actually got home that late, but the combination of the heavy food and forgetting, as usual, to drink enough water had left her feeling jaded and sluggish. As she sat staring at her blurry computer screen trying to decide what work to pretend to do next, she spotted Sue Martin on the other side of the office. Sue was one of those people who bounded about all day as if they'd been injected with caffeine but were, in fact, just annoyingly fit and healthy. She was girl-next-door pretty, with a super practical short bob that she often had tied up into a mini ponytail and, unlike most people, she didn't end up with bits of hair falling out of it or fuzzy short bits sticking out round her face. Her hair was far too healthy for that. Her skin looked fresh and glowing, and she was wearing hardly any make-up. That morning she made Rachel feel rather bedraggled and slovenly in comparison.

Rachel clicked open the forwarded email from Natalie about the sailing weekend. Maybe Shali and Natalie were right; she did need a bit of break. 'A weekend of exciting competition, fun and fresh air' it promised. Rachel took out her compact mirror, attempted to dab away the alcohol shine on her face and then walked over to where Sue was standing chatting with a couple of other people.

'Hi, Sue, not interrupting, am I?' Rachel asked.

'Hi, Rachel. Not at all, we were just gossiping. How are you? I haven't seen you in the office for a bit,' said Sue, smiling widely at Rachel.

'Fine, thanks. I've been working out of the office most of the time for the last few weeks. Anyway look, Natalie mentioned to me that you might need a couple more people to make up the numbers for the sailing race this weekend,' said Rachel.

'Yes we do. Why, can you come? That would be brilliant!'

'I'm a total beginner, though. I can't even row, let alone sail,' said Rachel.

'That's okay, loads of people are beginners. Each of the boats is being skippered by someone from the sailing company that we've chartered the boats from. You just need to be able to pull a rope, that's all,' said Sue.

'I think I can just about manage that,' said Rachel, grinning.

'Fantastic. I'll email you all the details — where you need to be, what you need to bring, all that sort of thing. We're meeting at ten o'clock on Saturday morning at the marina. The directions will be in the email. Is that okay?' Sue asked.

'Great, I'll be there,' said Rachel.

She felt quite excited when she got back to her desk. Sue's enthusiasm was infectious. It did sound fun and she felt better now that she had some concrete plans for the weekend and no time to wallow about feeling sorry for herself.

Rachel spent the next hour going through a rather long backlog of emails, including several from IT reminding her that she needed to bring her computer down to the third floor for an urgent security upgrade. Time for a coffee anyway. She would take her computer down and then head out for a coffee afterwards.

It didn't take long for Rachel to find where she was

meant to go on the third floor. Large signs directing her to the IT helpdesk were posted on every available wall space and when she arrived there were at least ten people in front of her. Rachel stood impatiently in the queue. How long could it take to hand a computer in? But as she watched, Rachel realised that the update was being installed while you waited. In front of her two other employees, one guy and one girl, computers in hand, were chatting.

'So what time do we need to be there again?' asked the girl.

'Ten o'clock at the marina,' said the guy.

Rachel studied them a bit more closely. They must be going on the sailing weekend too. They were both pretty sporty looking types, a bit younger than her but not much. Both had low intensity golden suntans that Rachel assumed came from living an outdoor lifestyle.

'Don't forget to bring flares, will you,' said the guy, nodding seriously at his female companion.

'No, don't worry. I've already packed them,' she replied.

'Good, I did the grab bags last night. I think they should fit quite easily in the starboard lockers,' said the guy.

'Oh I'm sure they will. What's the weather forecast, do you know?'

'Five gusting six, I think. That should keep us on our toes.'

Flares, grab bags, starboard locker? What were they talking about? It was all very confusing. Rachel hoped that her instructions were at least going to be written in a language she understood. But before she got any more clues, the pair changed the subject and starting discussing a TV programme on sharks that one of them had seen the previous night. Rachel shuffled slowly down with the queue, mulling it over. She knew what flares were. That was easy. She'd seen those white naval uniforms with the flared trousers loads of times on the TV. Starboard she was pretty sure meant either left or right, but she wasn't sure which. She would have to look it up, along with the other things they'd been talking about. At least then she could try to look like she had a vague idea what was going on.

Once her computer had been injected with a suitable amount of safety software, instead of going out for a coffee Rachel headed back up to her desk. She opened up her instructions and looked at the list of things to bring. No mention of flares, just 'suitable sailing clothing'. She wondered why the list wasn't more specific. That guy in the queue had made it pretty clear how important it was to wear flares. Maybe it was part of sailing etiquette, one of the things you were just expected to know.

Next she went online and looked up the definition of a grab bag. It read 'a bag or holdall that can be grabbed quickly in case of a sailing emergency'. That sounded pretty straightforward. And starboard was right, port was left. Rachel was pretty sure she would remember that. Her dad had always insisted that the bottle of port they had after Christmas lunch was passed to the left.

Feeling pleased with her research, Rachel shut down

her computer and headed out for a coffee. As she sat cradling her drink in the coffee shop, thinking about the weekend ahead, she realised that she only had one pair of flares and they were jeans. She was pretty sure that people didn't sail in jeans. Rachel looked at her watch. She was having lunch with Rowan at one o'clock. If she popped to the shops now, she could just go straight on to meet him afterwards.

Ten minutes later, Rachel was in a cab heading for Oxford Street. There were plenty of white trousers about in the shops to choose from and Rachel soon found a pair. They were made of heavy cotton and had a flat panelled front with four navy buttons doing up the vents at each side. They were perfect! Rachel also found a navy striped, off-the-shoulder, bat-wing t-shirt. It was maybe a bit low-cut for sailing, but it went so perfectly with the trousers she decided she just had to have it. She also managed to pick up a new dress and a pair of shoes that would be perfect for the girls' night out.

Rowan was already at the restaurant when Rachel arrived laden with bags. They'd opted for a low key brasserie style restaurant down a small back street off Baker Street with small chrome tables set quite close together.

'Been busy then?' Rowan asked, watching with amusement as Rachel tried to stuff her bags into the tiny space between her chair and the wall.

'Oh, you know how it is, just a quick power shop before lunch. Anyway, how are you?'

'Yeah, good thanks. Working a bit too hard, but otherwise fine,' said Rowan.

'Makes a change,' said Rachel, surveying the long list of complicated looking salads on the menu.

'Wine?' Rowan asked.

'No, I think I'll have a beer actually. Bit too much wine last night,' said Rachel, grinning.

'Maybe you should have water then,' said Rowan.

'Good idea, with my beer,' said Rachel.

Rowan laughed at her. 'God, what are you like,' he said.

'Thirsty,' said Rachel. 'How's Laura? Things going okay?'

Rowan smiled. 'I've got some news actually,' he said.

'What sort of news?' said Rachel, looking slightly alarmed.

'Laura's pregnant again,' said Rowan.

'What? Oh my God, that's fantastic.' Rachel hesitated. 'It is, isn't it?'

'Yes, it is. We're both over the moon. You mustn't say anything, though. It's still very early days. We only found out this weekend,' said Rowan.

'No, of course not,' said Rachel. 'Wow, that was quick work. Naomi's not even one yet!'

'I know. Two children under two – we must be mad,' said Rowan, laughing.

Rachel could tell that Rowan was genuinely thrilled.

'It must have been all that extra attention you've been paying,' said Rachel, raising her eyebrows in amusement.

'Something like that,' said Rowan. 'At least it made me wake up and realise how lucky I am. Laura has been on much better form and I've even been looking after Naomi on my own. Getting it all wrong still, no doubt, but having far more fun with her than I expected.'

'She is really very cute,' said Rachel, remembering her defrosted food horror day with Naomi with real affection.

'Yes, she is. I've got a few recent photos on my phone. Do you want to see them?' Rowan asked.

Rachel grinned. It was funny to see Rowan playing the proud dad. 'Go on then,' she said.

Rachel made appropriately admiring noises at the pictures of Naomi that were in fact a bit dark and nothing very special.

'Have you told Mum and Dad yet?' Rachel asked.

'No, not yet. We thought we would wait a bit. You're the first person we've told actually,'

'Wow, I'm touched. But as you know, I'm very good at keeping secrets,' said Rachel, tapping the side of her nose.

'Yes, you are,' said Rowan. 'And thank goodness for that!'

Rachel smiled at her brother. A new baby, how exciting! It seemed like things were finally getting back on track for him and Laura.

CHAPTER 26

By Friday evening, Rachel was really excited about the sailing trip. She'd dug out a white skirted mac that went brilliantly with her new white trousers and had spent ages going through her wardrobe choosing something to change into for the disco. She'd also packed herself a grab bag, carefully choosing a brightly striped canvas beach bag that zipped at the top. In it she'd packed everything she could think she would need in an emergency: phone, money, her iPod (in case it took a while to get rescued), two handy-sized packs of tissues, some headache tablets, a packet of biscuits, a big bag of sweets (to keep spirits up), a bottle of water, some hairbands and a small towel. Rachel looked at her neatly packed bag and smiled. Her father would be proud of her − nothing better than being prepared, 'just in case'. Once she'd finished packing the rest of her things, she had a long bath and went to bed early.

The next morning Rachel stepped out of her car at the marina and looked around. Rows and rows of boat masts bobbed gently in the wind, making a low jangling noise, like a giant wind-chime. The marina was surrounded by newly built white and grey apartments with large glass fronts, many with balconies overlooking the water. She checked her reflection in the car window, belting her mac tightly around her waist and pushing her sunglasses up onto her head to complete her casual, but brilliantly nautical outfit.

As she walked towards the boats she could see a large group of people congregating next to several identical sailing boats. It didn't take long to spot Sue Martin. She was standing on the steps down to the pontoon holding a clipboard and shouting instructions at people on one of the boats. Rachel looked at her in surprise. She seemed to be wearing a pair of very unflattering dungarees with a long-sleeved top underneath. As she got closer she could see that they were in fact waterproof dungarees. Rachel looked around and, to her horror, all she could see was a mass of people in various different combinations of brightly coloured waterproof clothing, busying themselves with boat preparations. There wasn't a single pair of white flares in sight.

'Rachel, hi, over here, come and register,' shouted Sue from her makeshift office on the steps.

Rachel walked over to Sue, feeling completely ridiculous in her boating get up. She was totally overdressed. She looked down at Sue's welly-like sailing shoes and then at her own navy ballet pumps and cringed. What a fuck up.

Sue looked at her. 'Did you bring some clothes to change into?'

'Only for the disco later,' said Rachel. God, this was embarrassing.

'Don't worry,' said Sue breezily. 'I'm sure there will be some things you can borrow. You're on boat number three, over there with Luke.'

Sue pointed towards a boat that was moored out in the water against two other boats.

'How do I, er, get out to it?' Rachel asked.

Sue grinned at her. 'You climb across the other two boats.'

'Ah right, thanks,' said Rachel.

She started clambering across the first of the boats, smiling and nodding to the crews already on board, trying to look nonchalant. She climbed down into the cockpit area of the first boat with her rucksack and grab bag swinging precariously from side to side as she went. As she climbed back out the other side towards the second boat she knelt on a neatly coiled wet rope that left brown whiplash stains across the front of her pristine white trousers and her navy pumps slipped about like someone had covered the soles with baby oil.

'Fuck it,' said Rachel in frustration as she slipped onto her knees for about the tenth time.

'Here, let me help you,' said a voice from above her. 'I'm Luke, by the way, your skipper for today.'

Rachel looked up at the outstretched arm. Luke had short cropped hair and a very square jaw that was lightly covered with day old stubble. He was wearing a pair of red waterproof trousers and a tightly fitted red and navy striped top.

'Thanks, I'm Rachel,' she said, slipping again as he pulled her onto the boat. 'Sorry, not exactly got the right shoes.'

'Or anything else for that matter,' said Luke, looking her up and down and laughing. 'You're going to be bloody freezing.'

Rachel stared at Luke indignantly. There was no need to laugh at her quite so quickly. 'I thought the forecast was for sun?'

'It is, but it's going to be windy too. The wind chill can make it feel much colder,' said Luke.

'Oh I'm sure I'll be fine,' said Rachel, trying to look relaxed as she manoeuvred herself onto a seat.

'Do you know the others?' said Luke, nodding at the three other people already onboard.

'No, I'm afraid I don't, but we are quite a big company,' said Rachel.

'Let me introduce you then,' said Luke.

Luke introduced Rachel to James, Will and Sonya, all of whom looked to Rachel like proper sailing types. They certainly had all the gear anyway, although Will claimed to be a 'virtual beginner'.

'Oh look, here's the safety team coming to give us a briefing,' said Luke, as two people jumped nimbly on board. Rachel recognised them as the couple she'd heard chatting in the IT helpdesk queue in the week. She stared at them. She would have thought that at least the woman would have been in flares. She'd definitely heard her say that she'd already packed them. It was so unfair.

Rachel sat and listened carefully to the safety

briefing, trying to ignore the amused glances at her flapping white mac and now grubby white flares. Always wear your life jacket and listen to the skipper in case of an emergency seemed to be the long and short of it.

'Right, anyone got any questions before we get going?' Luke asked once the safety team had moved on to the next boat.

'Where shall I put my grab bag?' Rachel asked.

Luke looked at her and then around on the floor. 'I thought the grab bags were already on board,' he said. 'The safety team put one on earlier.' He lifted up one of the seats in the cockpit and opened a large locker underneath. 'Yeah, it's in here. I thought so.'

'I also packed one myself,' said Rachel, keen to show that despite her impractical dress she had at least done something sensible.

'Did you?' Luke looked surprised. 'Where is it?'

Rachel held up her canvas beach bag. Luke raised his eyebrows and grinned at her. Sonya stifled a laugh.

'It looks a bit small,' said Luke. 'And besides, we can only take one grab bag in an emergency. Ours has things in it like a VHF radio, an anchor for the life raft, distress flares, a GPS signalman, water and rations for the crew, fishing equipment, torches, blankets, that sort of thing.' He looked enquiringly at Rachel's less than bulging shoulder bag. 'And yours?'

Distress flares! Rachel began dying quietly inside. How was she to know that she'd been listening to the safety team?

'Oh, well, er, mine is, umm, more personal than

that. You know, just a few things that I like to have with me. Obviously it's not for actual emergencies, more for if we, well, just need to, you know, get on and off quickly,' Rachel stammered, trying not to go red.

'Oh right, great,' said Luke, smiling at her in amusement. 'Why don't you put it here, next to the helm. That way you can get to it any time you need to. Right, shall we get going? I just need two of you to help me cast off. James and Sonya, can you do the side ropes for me and bring the fenders in.'

Rachel sat down miserably and watched Luke start the engine and steer the boat out of the marina. This trip was meant to be making her feel better, helping her recharge her batteries, but instead she just felt out of place and humiliated. And these know-it-all sporty types were starting to get on her nerves.

'It'll take us about twenty minutes to motor out to the race course,' said Luke. 'Not much to do until then, so why don't you all just sit down and relax for a bit. There are some beers in the fridge if anyone would like one.'

Beer! Now that sounded better, thought Rachel.

'I'll get them,' said Rachel, practically leaping down to the fridge in one jump.

She handed round beers to everyone except Luke, who didn't want one. She began to relax as she sat sipping her beer. The sun was warm on her back and the boat was quietly lapping its way through the water. As they passed the headland and went out into the open waters of the Solent, the wind picked up and the size of the waves increased markedly.

'Right, time to put the sails up,' said Luke.

He spent a few minutes talking each person through what he wanted them to do. Rachel just had one rope to pull up out of its clasp, which Luke told her was known as a cleat, whenever he shouted 'Ready about'. Will would pull the rope in on the other side of the boat at the same time and that would swing one of the front sails round when they changed direction. It didn't seem too hard.

As soon as the sails went up the total demeanour of the boat changed. It seemed to crash far more against the swell of the waves and started tipping heavily to one side, which Rachel didn't like at all. And, just as Luke had said she would, she started to feel cold. She could see the other boats sailing up and down nearby, their crews leaping around the boats like brightly coloured grasshoppers, getting ready for the start of the race, but she had no idea which way they were supposed to be heading.

A loud bang made Rachel jump.

'Five minute gun,' shouted Luke. 'Let's head for the start line. Ready about!'

Rachel yanked her rope out of the cleat and was about to let it loose when Luke shouted, 'Not yet, Rachel. Wait until the nose is round.'

Rachel clung on to her rope, twisting it round her hands and leaning backwards until Luke nodded at her to let it go. The sail flapped round and then went taut on the other side of the boat. The next few minutes were so hectic that Rachel didn't have time to think. Luke turned the boat round over and over again, trying to get the perfect start position. There was lots of shouting of 'water' and 'starboard', as the boats all got quite close to each other. Rachel had no idea what was going on but she found the drama and excitement of the start totally exhilarating.

'Well done, Luke, great start,' shouted Sonya as all of the boats eventually started heading in the same direction. As the boat powered along towards the first race marker, leaning hard over in the strong winds, the water began splashing over the sides. It splashed onto Rachel's face, streaking her mascara, and ran over the edge where she was sitting, soaking her trousers. After a few minutes she began to shiver.

'James, can you take the helm a minute? Just steer towards the mark; we don't need to tack again,' said Luke and he came and sat down next to Rachel. 'Your lips have gone blue,' he said. 'Is that mac waterproof?'

Rachel felt the water seeping in through the seams of the mac and shook her head.

Luke looked down at her wet trousers. 'Jeez, you're soaking already. You can borrow my spares. They'll be a bit big, but at least you'll be dry. There's a grey duffle bag below deck. In it are some tracksuit bottoms, a sweatshirt and some waterproof trousers. You should put some socks on too. They're a bit knackered, I'm afraid, but at least they're clean.'

'Won't you need them?' Rachel asked.

'I'm not planning on falling in today,' said Luke, grinning. 'And besides, if we really need more dry clothes, the rescue boat will have some.'

Rachel went down below deck and found the bag.

She took out Luke's clothes, hurriedly stuffing back in the boxer shorts that fell out at the same time. She took off her wet trousers and put on Luke's tracksuit bottoms. They were much too big, so Rachel took the belt off her white mac and put it round the top of the trousers, folding the waistband over the top. They looked ridiculous but at least they stayed up. She then put on the sweatshirt and the waterproof trousers with dungaree style straps, rolling up the sleeves of the sweatshirt and the legs of the trousers several times so she could get her hands and feet out. Finally she put on Luke's light brown socks and squeezed her feet back into her navy pumps, completing perfectly her clown-like appearance. But there was little point being embarrassed now; she'd made a total fool of herself so many times already it couldn't get much worse.

Rachel took another beer out of the fridge, went back up on deck and put her hand on hips.

'How do I look?' she said, grinning at the others.

'Very cute,' said Luke.

'And warm,' said James.

'Your make-up is a bit smudged,' said Sonya quietly.

'Thanks,' said Rachel.

She got her canvas beach bag from the locker next to the helm where Luke was steering, took out her emergency pack of tissues and wiped her eyes. She then took out her bag of sweets and offered them round. 'I always find it helpful to have sweets in a wet clothing emergency,' she said to Luke.

'Absolutely,' said Luke, grinning at her. 'Me too.'

Rachel went back to her position by the side rope

and sat down, marvelling at the new warmth and comfort she was feeling. She was ready for anything now. Bring it on!

'Right, get ready to go round the mark,' shouted Luke after a few minutes. They raced towards the red buoy at breakneck speed and ended up round the mark in first place.

'Yee hah!' Rachel shouted as their boat turned away from the others. Her hair was stiff with sea water, her make-up was ruined, she was dressed in somebody else's oversized clothes, but she felt great. She put her face into the spray and closed her eyes. This was fun.

'Wind's picking up,' said Luke, looking at one of the dials below the steering wheel. And before long, the sun disappeared behind some ominous grey clouds and it really started to blow. The boat crashed up and down over the waves and Rachel suddenly started to feel sick. The combination of beer and sweets wasn't ideal preparation for some rough weather.

'Are you okay?' Will asked, seeing her go a bit pale.

'I feel a bit queasy,' said Rachel.

'Keep your eye on the horizon,' said Sonya.

Rachel tried to watch the horizon but the rise and fall of the boat was getting in the way. Before she could stand up and get a better look, the nausea won out and she was sick over the side of the boat. The side rush of the wind blew bits of sick across the side of her face and into her hair. She grabbed her hair, held it back into a makeshift ponytail and leant over the edge, balancing on one hand. Luke suddenly appeared next to her, gently took hold of her ponytail and put her other hand firmly back on the side of the boat. She retched violently over the edge, coughing and spluttering on the bits of chewed sweets that flew out into the foamy water below. Once the contents of her stomach were safely overboard, Luke handed her a tissue and a bottle of water.

'God, I'm so sorry,' said Rachel, wiping her face with the tissue.

'That's okay, but I could do without you falling overboard,' said Luke. 'Feeling better now?'

Rachel nodded.

'Apart from being a sicky disgusting mess, that is,' she said.

'Come and steer for a bit,' said Luke. 'That makes you look forwards and should help stop you feeling sick.'

'Steer? Are you sure? I don't have the first clue what I'm doing,' said Rachel.

'Really? You surprise me,' said Luke, looking at Rachel's comedy clothes, sick-filled hair and streaky face. 'And there I was thinking that you were the experienced sea-faring type.'

'Ha, ha, very funny,' said Rachel, feeling that if she didn't laugh, she might cry, and that would be a humiliation step too far.

Rachel steered the boat for the next ten minutes or so, following Luke's instructions to the letter. And Luke turned out to be right again: concentrating on where the boat was going made her feel much less sick. The rest of the race went in a bit of a blur. The high winds and choppy seas meant that the boats were throwing themselves round the course at some speed. Rachel pulled her rope in and out of its cleat so many times she lost track — she was too busy enjoying herself. And in the end, after much shouting and rope pulling, their boat came in a close second.

'Cheats!' Rachel shouted in good humour at the winning boat as its crew leapt about hugging each other and punching the air.

Rachel gingerly hugged her own crew members too.

'Sorry I smell a bit sicky,' she said, laughing.

'No you don't,' said Will, pulling her into a hug with one arm and shaking hands with Luke at the same time.

Rachel turned to hug Luke, who grabbed her towards him, sniffing at her hair.

'Yes you do, very sicky in fact,' said Luke.

Rachel felt her stomach leap as Luke pulled her up against him. Unlike her, he smelt of aftershave and sweat, a much more attractive combination.

'Thanks for the clothes. I'll take them home and wash them,' said Rachel, looking up at Luke and suddenly feeling slightly shy.

'God, don't worry. They're only old spares. Just chuck them back in the bag,' said Luke, stepping away from her.

'I've got the clothes that I brought for the barbecue. I'll change into those and give you these ones back,' said Rachel, starting to go below deck to change.

'I'm coming to your barbecue actually. Your company invited all the skippers. So why don't you have a shower in the clubhouse and give me the clothes then,' said Luke.

'Oh right, okay, good idea,' said Rachel, pleasantly surprised by the fact that she would be seeing more of Luke later.

'Oh, don't forget your, um, grab bag,' said Luke, trying not to smile. He reached down and took her beach bag out of the locker by the helm.

'Thanks. Hopefully I'll look a bit less of mess when you see me next,' said Rachel, pushing her matted hair away from her face.

'Well, you certainly couldn't look much worse,' said Luke, laughing.

'Thanks!'

That was at least the fourth time Luke had laughed at her that day. But for some reason that she couldn't really explain, Rachel didn't actually mind.

CHAPTER 27

Rachel was sitting on her sofa staring at her phone on the coffee table, waiting for it to ring. It didn't. 'Ring, damn you!' she shouted at the phone and looked at her watch for about the hundredth time.

Luke had said he would ring her at 'about eight' and it was now gone twenty past. Rachel tried to stay calm: it didn't mean that he wasn't going to call. To a lot of people 'about eight' could mean any time really. They'd got on so well at the barbecue and she was sure Luke wasn't the unreliable type — quite the opposite, in fact. She paced round her flat trying to recall every detail of the evening. Had she done anything to put him off? She didn't think so. He'd definitely been impressed with her transformation from sick-splattered sailing crew member to disco diva.

When her phone finally rang, Rachel was in the kitchen making a cup of tea. She sprinted into the sitting room and then stood by the phone, forcing herself to let it ring a couple more times. No point looking too keen.

'Hello?'

'Hi, is that Rachel?'

'Yes it is,' said Rachel, composing herself.

'Oh hi, it's Luke from Events Sailing,' said Luke. He sounded very relaxed.

'Luke, hi, how are you?'

'Yes, good, thanks. Another hard day on the water. But at least none of my crew were sick or needed to wear my clothes, so that was a plus,' said Luke.

Rachel laughed. 'That was lucky.'

'Look, I was wondering if maybe we could meet up one night this week, maybe grab something to eat, if you're free that is?'

Oh yes, she was free, more free than he knew.

'That would be great. How about tomorrow night?' Rachel asked.

'I've got running club tomorrow night but I could do Wednesday?' said Luke.

Running club! That was a bit healthy.

'Yes, Wednesday is fine too,' said Rachel a bit too quickly. Damn! Now she sounded like she had no social life of her own.

'Wednesday it is then. Where shall we go?'

'Maybe you could come here and we could just wander down to one of the local restaurants?' Rachel suggested.

'Sounds great,' said Luke.

After the call, Rachel bounced around her flat in excitement and then rang Shali.

'Well, I think he sounds fab!' said Shali after listening to Rachel recount every last detail of the sailing trip and ensuing phone call. 'If he was still interested after seeing you make such a complete prat of yourself then he must be good news.'

'I think he might be a bit of a health nut, though. He looks really fit and he said he was going to a running club tomorrow night,' said Rachel.

'Well, you'd better hurry up and check out his stamina then, hadn't you?' said Shali, laughing.

'Shali! I only met him on Saturday,' said Rachel. 'I hardly know him.'

'You know he's a great boat skipper, what more do you need?' Shali asked.

'Actually he's the technical director of the sailing company, which means he's responsible for running and maintaining the boats. He skippers as well just because he loves being on the water. He's got an engineering degree, you know, and has done loads of different events stuff — rally cars, motor boats, that sort of thing. He said that he's usually in charge of running the equipment because of his engineering background.' Rachel knew it sounded like she was showing off but she couldn't help it.

'He sounds like a right action man,' said Shali.

'Well, I'll find out when I see him,' said Rachel.

On Wednesday evening Rachel sat in the Chinese restaurant round the corner from her flat feeling overdressed, again. Luke had arrived dressed very casually in jeans and a navy fleece. She'd nearly worn jeans too but in the end had opted for a knee-length black velvet skirt and a long-sleeved red top, which now seemed like the wrong choice. She gulped at her wine nervously.

'How was running club?' Rachel asked.

'Yeah, good, thanks,' said Luke. 'It was fitness training night, so lots of sprints and shuttle running, that sort of thing.'

'Sounds hideous. Do you do a lot of running?' Rachel asked.

'A fair bit. It helps me stay fit and I just find I feel better afterwards,' said Luke.

Rachel had to agree that he looked pretty good.

'I don't do anything, well, fitness wise that is. Obviously I do something, I mean, I have a job, of course,' said Rachel, conscious of the fact that she was rambling.

'Well, you look alright to me,' said Luke.

Rachel smiled at him. 'Thanks, but to be honest I think I'm living on borrowed time. I work too hard and drink too much and will probably wake up one day soon looking like a wrinkled old hag with a huge beer belly.'

'I doubt it,' said Luke.

'Well, I definitely need a bit of a break. That's why I signed up for the sailing weekend. The last few weeks have been totally manic.'

'Really? Why?' Luke asked.

Rachel hesitated. For some reason she suddenly had an overwhelming urge to tell him everything.

'It's a long story,' she said.

'Well, I'm in no hurry,' said Luke, sitting back in his chair.

Rachel and Luke talked nonstop for the next two hours and by the end of it Rachel felt both emotionally drained and a bit drunk.

'So, as you can see, I'm a total basket case,' said Rachel.

'It sounds like you dealt with things pretty well to me,' said Luke.

'Well, maybe in the end,' said Rachel, not very convinced.

'So is this cosmetic surgery job finished now then?' Luke asked.

'Our bit is. But they've still got the legal side to sort out, stuff like that, before it's a done deal.'

'Do you know what you're onto next?'

'No, not yet, but my boss did mention something about a business that makes radiators,' said Rachel, wrinkling up her nose.

'That sounds a bit more, well, down to earth than – what did you refer to it as? – the tits and arse job?'

Rachel laughed. 'That's the technical term, obviously.'

'Obviously,' said Luke.

'Maybe down to earth is what I need. After all, a change is a good as a rest,' said Rachel.

And that doesn't just apply to my next project, thought Rachel, looking at Luke.

'Look, I've got an idea. If you need a bit of a change, you know a fresh challenge, I'm running a ten-k race with the running club in six weeks' time. It's open to anyone. Why don't you have a go? I could help you train,' said Luke.

Rachel's jaw dropped. 'Run? Me? No, I don't think I could. That's not my thing at all,' she said, shaking her head.

'Of course you could,' said Luke. 'It would just be a matter of starting slowly. Honestly, I'm sure you would feel much better. It would give you a real energy boost, a goal to aim at — you know, something a bit different going on.'

'Oh, I don't know,' said Rachel. She'd been feeling pretty knackered but she wasn't sure that running about all over the place was the answer. Six weeks wasn't that long either. It sounded like a pretty tall order.

Luke seemed to read her mind. 'Why don't we just give it a try? It would be fun,' he said.

'It might be for you. I'd just end up as a sweaty blob,' said Rachel.

'You ended up as a sicky blob when we were sailing, but you still loved it,' Luke reminded her.

It was true: she had loved it, and the buzz it had given her afterwards. Maybe it would be worth a try, and in any case, it would mean she could see lots of Luke.

'Well, maybe we could give it a try. I'm not promising I'll do the race, mind you. We'll have to see how it goes.'

As they walked home from the restaurant Rachel put her arm tentatively through Luke's. He responded by smiling and ruffling her hair. They walked back to Rachel's flat without saying much, just enjoying the stillness of the evening air and the closeness of each other. When they got to Rachel's front door, she couldn't decide whether to invite Luke in or not. In the end, he made the decision for her.

'I'd better go. Thanks for a great evening,' he said.

He leant forward to kiss Rachel on the cheek, but

she turned her head and brushed her lips onto his instead. Luke shivered slightly and pulled her towards him. They stood holding each other tightly for a few moments and then Luke slowly leaned down and kissed her, properly this time, causing Rachel's back to arch involuntarily and her legs to go rather wobbly.

'I think I can still smell sick,' said Luke, snuffling gently round her neck.

'Liar,' said Rachel, smiling.

Luke stepped back and took both her hands.

'So, when shall we start training then?'

'I don't mind,' said Rachel. 'Whenever suits you.'

'How about tomorrow then? Call me when you get back from work and I'll pop over.'

'Okay, although I can't quite believe I've agreed to this,' said Rachel. 'I must be mad.'

'I like mad,' said Luke, kissing her again. 'In fact, I like mad a lot.'

A couple of days later, Rachel met Shali for a catch-up.

Shali stared at Rachel across the coffee shop table. 'You're doing what?'

'Training for a ten-k,' said Rachel.

'Wow, you must really like this guy,' said Shali.

'It's not that. It's good for me, that's all,' said Rachel.

'Yeah, right!' Shali looked like she didn't believe a word of it. 'So have you started training yet?'

'Yes, we've just done a few gentle jogs so far. I think Luke is trying to work out exactly how unfit I am! Anyway, it wasn't as bad as I thought it would be. I was a bit stiff the next day but nothing more than that and I slept really well.'

Shali eyed Rachel suspiciously. 'And you didn't dive into any bushes for some cheeky outdoor sex?'

'No we did not! Not yet anyway. We're, you know, taking things slowly,' said Rachel, grinning.

'Oh right, that's nice,' said Shali, faking a yawn.

'Yes, it is actually,' said Rachel.

'When are you seeing him next?' Shali asked.

'Tomorrow morning, early. We're going to start running before work a couple of days a week. I think it will be a bit easier than when I'm knackered after work,' said Rachel.

'How early?' Shali looked alarmed.

'Six o'clock,' said Rachel, grimacing.

'I can't believe that some bloke is getting Rachel Altman out of bed at six o'clock in the morning to go running. It's a bloody miracle,' said Shali.

'Leave me alone,' said Rachel, punching Shali gently on the arm.

'No seriously, I'm pleased for you, Rach, really I am,' said Shali, giving Rachel a hug.

'I'm pleased for me too,' said Rachel, grinning.

Three weeks later, Rachel, Shali and Natalie were standing chatting in Bar Q at the department's quarterly drinks. On the small, high-topped table next to them sat a bottle of champagne in an ice bucket. Stood next to it was a large bottle of water.

'So how long left to go until the race?' Natalie asked.

'Just over a fortnight,' said Rachel.

'Are you going to be ready?' asked Shali.

'I hope so. I've been training really hard and Luke thinks I will. I'm not trying to get a brilliant time or anything. If I do it in less than an hour, I'll be happy,' said Rachel.

'Well, I have to say, you look fantastic. Whatever you're getting up to with Luke seems to be working,' said Shali, adding quickly, 'not that you didn't look fantastic before, by the way.'

'Thanks. I can't tell you what a difference it's made,' said Rachel. 'I've got so much more energy and I'm loads more focused at work. Having a few nights of not drinking and running instead has just transformed me. Carl doesn't quite know what's hit him!'

'How is the radiators job, by the way?' Natalie asked.

'Radiating, thanks,' said Rachel, laughing. 'Actually going very well. Carl is really pleased. It's a much more complicated business than you might think. There are so many different types of radiators and the distribution system is really very fragmented and…'

But before she could finish, Shali put her head on Natalie's shoulder and they both closed their eyes and started to snore.

Rachel started laughing. 'Yes, alright, very funny guys.'

'Sorry, did you say something?' said Natalie, pretending to wake up.

'I was just saying that it was going fine, thanks,' said Rachel.

'Oh, right, good,' said Natalie.

'And are things going fine with the lovely Luke too, apart from the running, that is?' Shali asked.

Rachel couldn't help grinning. 'Yes, very promising.'

'That sounds like a school report that actually means "could do better",' said Shali.

'Well, I don't. I mean very promising,' said Rachel. 'What's surprised me is how much fun we can have doing nothing. Last Sunday we took a picnic to Primrose Hill and just sat there reading the papers, watching the world go by and chatting. Nothing very exciting, but I loved every minute of it. Harry would never have done that in a million years, not when there were perfectly good cafes selling fry-ups or pubs showing football matches available anyway.'

Shali and Natalie smiled at Rachel.

'Well, here's to the next chapter,' said Natalie, picking up her champagne glass.

'Hold on, the fitness queen needs some more water,' said Shali, topping up Rachel's glass.

'And there was me thinking we'd agreed to have a big night out,' sighed Natalie.

'Sorry. I'm running at six o'clock. I haven't given up completely but I just can't do it the night before an early run, otherwise I feel like shit,' said Rachel. 'Anyway, I'm still capable of being interesting and funny without drinking half a bottle of champagne.'

'Are you? Oh I'm not sure,' said Natalie, shaking her head and looking at Shali. 'What do you think?'

'I very much doubt it,' said Shali. 'If that radiator story is anything to go by, we're in for a really dull evening.'

'Fuck off the pair of you,' said Rachel.

And the three of them laughed until Rachel had tears in her eyes and Natalie needed the loo.

'Back in a mo,' said Natalie and she headed off to the ladies'. Rachel and Shali carried on chatting and laughing for a few minutes until Shali stopped and looked at Rachel seriously.

'Look, while we're on our own, I've got something to tell you,' said Shali.

'What?' Rachel asked, concerned by the expression on Shali's face.

'It's a bit of a confession really. I've been meaning to ring you but then I thought it would be better if I told you face to face,' said Shali.

'Told me what?' Rachel asked, frowning. This didn't sound good at all.

'I've been, umm, seeing someone,' said Shali, shifting uncomfortably.

Rachel's hand flew up to her mouth. Oh my God, she was seeing Rowan again!

'Shali, no! How could you? I thought it was all over between you. Hasn't Rowan told you that Laura's pregnant again?'

'It's not Rowan,' said Shali.

'Who then?' Rachel looked confused.

'Harry,' said Shali.

Rachel looked at Shali in amazement. 'You've been seeing Harry?'

Shali nodded.

'Since when?'

'Only since last week. I bumped into him at Jimmy Macks and we sort of hit it off,' said Shali. 'I thought with you seeing Luke and everything that you'd be okay with it.'

Shali closed her eyes and screwed up her face like she was preparing herself for the worst, but instead Rachel burst out laughing.

'You're not cross then,' said Shali, tentatively opening one eye.

'No,' said Rachel, just so relieved that it wasn't Rowan. 'Not cross at all. In fact, now I come to think of it, you two are probably perfect for each other.'

Shali frowned at Rachel. 'I'm not sure that's a compliment.'

'No, neither am I, but hey, who cares as long as you're having fun,' said Rachel, laughing.

'I am,' said Shali, laughing too.

'Well, you of all people should know what he's like, so good luck to you!' said Rachel.

'It's just a bit of fun,' said Shali. 'I don't expect it to last.'

'Good, low expectations from the start. That's definitely the right approach with Harry,' said Rachel. 'Good for you.'

'So you definitely don't mind?' Shali asked.

'No, I don't,' said Rachel. She really didn't and was very happy with the thought that maybe Harry had finally met his match.

Rachel spent the evening chatting with Natalie and Shali as well as others in her department, broken only by the occasional shimmy on the tiny dance floor in the corner of Bar Q.

As Rachel went to the bar to get another bottle of water Carl appeared by her side.

'Having a good evening?' he asked.

'Yes, very good, thanks,' Rachel replied.

Carl leant towards her and lowered his voice. 'Look, I'll talk to you properly in the office but I wanted you to know that I'm stepping down from looking after Beau Street. We've won a major new client that the other partners want me to handle but it's a big time commitment. So I've had to trim down my client base and, well, given where we are, Beau Street was a logical choice to be on the list to go.'

'Oh I see. Good news on the new client, but Tom will be disappointed, I'm sure,' said Rachel.

'Actually I've spoken to him already and he's fine with it. Particularly when I told him you would be taking over.'

'Me?'

'Yes you, with some support from another partner, of course. But with a much bigger role than you have now — you know, their main contact, running everything day to day, that sort of thing. You're the obvious choice.'

Rachel was stunned. 'Wow, thank you.'

'And I have no doubt that you can do it,' said Carl. 'Let's talk next week.'

'Carl, I'm so grateful. Thank you! That's brilliant…'

But Carl wasn't listening. He had already wandered off in the direction of the dance floor.

Rachel went back to join the others, hugging herself with delight. Her own client! Well, nearly anyway. What a turn up for the books.

'Hey you two, have you seen old Pauline Rowe?' said Natalie as Rachel returned from the bar.

'No, why?' Rachel asked.

'Look at her — she's off her face,' said Natalie. 'She's stumbling all over the place.'

The three of them watched as Pauline swayed from side to side as she stood at the bar, talking loudly to one of the other staff managers. She was dressed in a less than flattering pair of black trousers that were a couple of inches too short and a shiny cream shirt tucked into a wide pink neon belt at the waist. Her ample bottom stuck out at the back and her stomach hung over the belt at the front. It wasn't a great look.

'She'd better not put a scarf on with that belt, otherwise she'll turn into sausages,' said Natalie, causing Rachel and Shali to giggle hysterically.

'It's not like her to be drunk. She's usually so prim and proper,' said Shali.

'Maybe it's a special occasion. How funny. Anyway, I'd better go,' said Rachel reluctantly. 'It's getting late.'

She said goodbye to Shali and Natalie and headed out of Bar Q to look for a cab. It was a bit weird leaving a work do stone cold sober, but at least it meant she wouldn't be getting woken up by the taxi driver. She'd been standing waiting for a couple of minutes when she heard laughing behind her. It was Pauline Rowe and the other staff manager, who Rachel vaguely recognised from one of the other departments. They were stumbling along, holding on to each other, both equally drunk.

'We'd better get ourselves into a cab,' said Pauline, looking around.

Her friend dropped her arm and wandered towards the road. 'I'll look for it. You sit yourself down,' she said, waving vaguely towards a raised flowerbed with a small wall round it.

Pauline sat down clumsily on the wall. As Rachel watched, she swayed backwards and forwards a few times and then completely tipped over backwards straight into the flowerbed. Rachel ran over to help her, trying hard not to laugh.

'Pauline, are you okay?' Rachel peered over her sticking up legs. Her trouser legs had slipped up towards her knees, revealing a pair of rather laddered, light brown pop socks. Pauline was wriggling hard, trying to get her head out of the shrub that she'd fallen into. Rachel jumped into the flowerbed and helped Pauline up, carefully unpicking her cream shirt from the thorny branches.

'Er, thank you,' said Pauline, brushing herself down and picking bits out of her hair.

'No problem,' said Rachel.

Pauline's friend eventually noticed what was going on and appeared by Rachel's side.

'No bloody cab yet. Just saw one and I tried to jump in front of it, but he didn't stop,' she said.

I'm not surprised, thought Rachel.

'I'll flag you one,' said Rachel. 'Why don't you both sit down again, carefully this time.'

It didn't take Rachel long to flag down a taxi, although the driver didn't look best pleased when he saw Pauline and her new best mate stumbling out of the shadows towards his cab.

'Please try not to be sick,' Rachel whispered quietly to Pauline as she helped her into the cab. Pauline glared at her and slammed the door.

Rachel grinned smugly to herself as they drove away. That had felt good.

Rachel could see the finish line in the distance. Her lungs were burning and she couldn't feel her legs, but she forced herself to speed up. All around her, red-faced runners were pushing themselves equally hard towards the finish. She looked at her watch. It read fifty-four minutes, eighteen seconds. If she really sprinted, she might just break fifty-five minutes. That would be even better than she'd hoped for.

'Come on, Rachel, you can do it, keep going,' yelled Luke from the side of the course. Rachel clenched her fists and sprinted as hard as she could, head down, legs pounding on the well-worn grass track. She crossed the line in fifty-four minutes and forty-eight seconds and then promptly collapsed onto a grass bank a few metres past the finish already well splattered with gasping runners.

'Stand up, stand up,' shouted Luke as he sprinted towards her. He pulled Rachel up onto her feet and gently bent her head over. 'Otherwise you might be sick. Put your hands on your knees and take big slow breaths.'

Rachel breathed slowly in and out until the burning eventually subsided. She stood up and paced up and down, catching her breath. Luke just stood quietly and watched her.

'Okay?' Luke asked after a few minutes.

'Yeah, just about,' said Rachel, her face still beetroot red.

'Well, now you can talk, did you see your time? It was fantastic!'

Rachel nodded, grinning.

'Well done,' said Luke, picking her up and swinging her round. 'I'm so proud of you.'

Rachel felt a rush of pride too. She'd done it! Her heart was pumping with adrenaline and she felt tingly all over. It was a great feeling.

She took Luke's hand and squeezed it hard. 'Thank you for everything,' she said, tears pricking her eyes.

'You're welcome, you mad, crazy thing,' said Luke, kissing the top of her head.

'Come on, let's go. I'm starving and I need a beer,' said Rachel.

'Rachel! It's ten o'clock in the morning,' said Luke.

'I know, I'm only joking,' she said, cuddling under Luke's arm. 'And besides, you're the only vice I need right now.'

ACKNOWLEDGEMENTS

From us both

We would like to say a massive thank you to everyone who has helped us on this wildly exciting journey from city slickers to authors.

To Midas PR - for believing in us right from the start and backing us all the way. Tony, Fiona and Tory, we couldn't have done this without you!

To Matador - for seeing the potential in the series, making the publishing process so user friendly and for putting up with our endless questions.

To afishinsea - for turning our outline ideas into genius, style icon covers and for the rest of our brand imagery. Your service is outstanding.

To Charlie Wilson - for your editorial support, patience and attention to detail. Our books were transformed from amateur scripts to real proper books under your watchful eye. Thank you!

To the Millennium Ten – for fun, friendship and providing us with endless material!

From Penny

I would like to thank all those that kept the world turning while I was locked away in my office for months on end. Lisa, Kate, Carolyn, Sofie and Graham – you are the best team anyone could hope for. I am so grateful to all of you and sorry if I forget to say so! These books are as much for you as anyone.

To my friends and family, for putting up with me droning on for hours about the books. At least now you can see them for yourselves, rather than just listen to me trying to describe them!

From Joanna

Thanks to Gemma, Faye and Kerry without whom the books would have taken twice as long. Thank you for everything you do and thanks for letting me bounce ideas off you!

To all my friends and family, especially the Wednesday morning coffee gang and the school run mums, who provide daily support and laughter. Also to Kath, Lucy and the Animals (you know who you are!) for keeping me in touch with the Legal world.